DEAD
WATCH

DEAD
WATCH

JOHN
SANDFORD

THORNDIKE
WINDSOR
PARAGON

This Large Print edition is published by Thorndike Press®, Waterville, Maine USA and by BBC Audiobooks Ltd, Bath, England.

Published in 2006 in the U.S. by arrangement with G. P. Putnam's Sons, a division of Penguin Group (USA) Inc.

Published in 2006 in the U.K. by arrangement with Simon & Schuster UK Ltd.

U.S. Hardcover	0-7862-8624-5	(Basic)
U.K. Hardcover 10:	1 4056 1484 6	(Windsor Large Print)
U.K. Hardcover 13:	978 1 405 61484 9	
U.K. Softcover 10:	1 4056 1485 4	(Paragon Large Print)
U.K. Softcover 13:	978 1 405 61485 6	

The text of this Large Print edition is unabridged.
Other aspects of the book may vary from the original edition.

Set in 16 pt. Plantin.

Printed in the United States on permanent paper.

British Library Cataloguing-in-Publication Data available

Library of Congress Cataloging-in-Publication Data

Sandford, John, 1944 Feb. 23–
    Dead watch / by John Sandford.
      p. cm.
    "Thorndike Press large print basic" — T.p. verso.
    ISBN 0-7862-8624-5 lg. print : hc : alk. paper)
    1. Legislators — Fiction. 2. Large type books. 3. Political fiction. I. Title.
PS3569.A516D43 2006b
  813'.54—dc22
                                        2006009492

DEAD
WATCH

1

Despite the mist, she spent an hour working Chica, and working herself, and she smelled of it, mare-sweat and woman-sweat, with a tingle of Chanel No. 5. They'd turned down the trail from the south forty, easing along, and she could feel the mare's heart beating through her knees and thighs.

The mist hadn't felt cold while they were jumping, but now they were cooling off, and her cheeks and forehead were pink, and her knuckles were raw. A shower, she thought, would be nice, along with a hot sandwich and a cup of soup.

They'd just crossed the fence. She turned in the saddle to watch the gate relatch behind them, and saw the face in the tree line. There was no question that it was a face — and in a blink, it was gone, dissolving in the trees.

She turned away from it, casually, tried to capture an afterimage in her mind. A pale oval, truncated at top and bottom, with a dark trapezoid beneath the oval. The face of a man who'd been watching her through binoculars, she realized. The dark shape, the trapezoid, had been arms, joined at the binoculars, in a camouflage jacket.

A thrill of fear ran up her spine. They might be coming for her.

She suppressed the urge to run the mare, but not the urge to push her into a trot. They came down the fence line and she took the remote from her pocket, pointed it at the inside gate, and it swung open in front of them. They went through, and she turned and closed the gate, her eyes searching the tree line as she turned. Nothing. They went on to the barn, Chica in a hurry now, anticipating the feed bag.

When she came off the horse she was feeling loose and athletic and was beginning to question what she'd seen. Was she losing it? Was the pressure pushing her over the edge? There'd been nothing but a flash of white.

Lon, the barn man, came over as she led the horse inside to the smell of horseshit and hay and feed, the odors of a comfortable life. She brushed a fly away from Chica's eye as she handed the reins over. "I worked her hard, Lon. She's pretty warm."

Then over the groom's shoulder, in the lighted square of the open barn door, she saw the housekeeper jogging across the barnyard, a folded newspaper over her hair to deflect the rain. Lon, an older, hook-nosed man whose skin was grooved like the bark on an oak tree, turned to look and said, "She's in a hurry."

She met Sandi, the housekeeper, at the barn door. "Sandi?"

"Two men are here."

"Two men?"

"Watchmen," Sandi said.

She looked up at the house: "Did you let them in?"

"Um, it's raining . . ." Sandi was suddenly afraid that she'd done wrong. "I left them in the front hall."

"That's okay. That's fine." She nodded. "Tell them that I'll be a moment."

Sandi fled back across the barnyard into the house. She and Lon talked about the horse for another thirty seconds, then, as she turned toward the house, Lon said, "Be careful, Maddy."

She took her time, cleaning her boots on the boot-brush outside the door, and on the mat inside, peeling off her rain suit and helmet, shaking out her hair, hanging the gear on the wall-pegs in the mud room. Still wearing the knee-high boots, she clumped across the kitchen and up the back stairs to the bedroom. From the closet, she got the bedroom gun, a blue-steel .380. She jacked a shell into the chamber and disengaged the safety, stuffed it in her jacket pocket.

She was afraid of the Watchmen, but more than that: she was also interested in what they'd say and excited by the prospect of conflict. She wasn't exactly a thrill-seeker, but she enjoyed a test, and the more severe, the better. She'd been a rock climber, she drove fast cars. And always the horses: the horses might someday kill her, she thought. Riding was as dangerous as a knife fight.

She took the back stairs down to the kitchen, walked out through the living room to the front entry. Two men waited there, both in leather bomber jackets, blue shirts, and khaki slacks. They'd put on their uniforms for the visit.

She knew one of them: Bob Sheenan, who worked behind the parts counter at Canelo's Farm & Garden. He was about fourth or fifth in the local Watchmen ranks. She knew the other man's face, but not his name.

"Been out riding?" Sheenan asked when

she walked into the entry.

She didn't answer. No pleasantries for the Watchmen: "What do you want, Bob?"

"Well, now . . ." Sheenan was a big man, with a bar-brawler's face: pale blue berserker's eyes, one damaged eyelid half-shading his left eye, scar tissue under both of them, a crooked banana nose, large yellow teeth. He smelled of pizza and beer, though it was not yet ten o'clock. "You're telling people that the Watchmen had something to do with your husband."

"You did," she said flatly. "I want to know where he is. If you're not here to tell me, then get out."

He jabbed a finger at her, and stepped closer. "We had nothing to do with your husband. If you keep talking that way, we will take you to court."

She squared off to him. "Or beat me up?"

"We don't do that."

"Bullshit. What about that Mexican kid two weeks ago? You broke his cheek-bones."

"He was attempting to escape," the second man said.

"You're not the police!" she snapped. "You're supposed to be Boy Scouts. What were you doing capturing him, huh?"

Sheenan and the second man looked at each other for a second, confused, then Sheenan pulled himself back. "I don't care about the Mexican. That's got nothing to do with this."

She bared her teeth: "Is this coming from Goodman? Or is this just some moronic crap you made up on your own?"

"This is not crap, missus." His eyes widened and his shoulders tensed, as if he were about to strike at her. "You are tearing down our good name. I don't know what your husband is up to, or where he's gone, but we will find out. In the meantime, you shut your fuckin' mouth."

"I'm not going to shut my mouth," she said. "I'll tell you something, Bob: you better be here on Goodman's orders, because you're going to need as much backup as you can get. If you came here on your own hook, I'll have your balls by midnight. Now: Are you going to get out, or do I call the sheriff?"

Sheenan shuffled a half step forward, looming, not worried at the threat. The security cameras were on. All this was on tape. She refused to move back, but slipped her right hand into the pocket of the jean jacket, touched the cold steel of the .380.

"Something's going on here," Sheenan hissed, jabbing the finger again, but not touching her. "We're going to find out what it is. In the meantime, you stick close to the house, missus. We don't want something to happen to you, too."

Then he laughed, and turned, and walked out. The other man held the door, and before pulling it closed behind him, said, "We're watching."

She exhaled, walked into the library, out of range of the security cameras, took the pistol out of her pocket with a shaking hand, and engaged the safety. Her biggest fear was that they would do something stupid — that they would stage an accident, a mishap, a mystery killing, a disappearance. Even if they were eventually caught, that wouldn't do her any good.

She could hear the local news anchor: ". . . and then she vanished, into the same darkness that took her husband." She'd worked as a reporter for a television station in Richmond, and used to write that stuff; that's how she'd do it.

She'd been planning to run for two weeks. Sheenan had pulled the trigger. She put the gun back in her pocket, headed for the stairs, and shouted, "Sandi?" Sandi came out of the kitchen, wiping her hands on a dish towel. "Yes?"

"I'm going into town. Did you pick up the dry cleaning?"

"Yes, I did. I've still got them in the kitchen."

"I'll need the red blouse and the gray slacks. Bring them up, and put them on the bed. I'll be in the shower."

"What about the schnitzel? Will you be back for lunch?"

"I'll get a bite in town. You and Lon and Carl could have sandwiches . . . and leave one for me in the refrigerator. I'll eat it cold, this afternoon."

"Yes, ma'am."

She took the pickup into Lexington, driving too fast, enjoying the feel of the back end kicking out in the turns, grabbing the gravel and throwing it. She was moving fast enough that anyone trailing her would be obvious. If anyone was there, she didn't see him. The face across the fence haunted her: Had it been real? Was it imaginary?

In town, she stopped at the bank, took out five thousand in cash, returned two books to the library, filled the truck's gas tank, went to the feed store and picked up four bags of supplement for the horses. At the post office, she turned off the mail and had it forwarded to Washington. The window clerk was a Watchman, but he was whistling as he put together the temporary change of address, and smiled at her when she said good-bye.

With the chores done, she stopped at Pat's Tea House for a scone and a cup of tea. Pat was a friend, a fellow horsewoman, and came over to chat, as she always did: "How's everything?"

"Delicious," she said. "Listen, can I borrow your phone to call Washington? I left my cell at home."

"Absolutely. Stop in the office when you're done."

She made the call, thinking all the time that she was being paranoid. They wouldn't be watching the phones. Would they?

She was back at Oak Walk at one o'clock, sent Sandi to get Lon and Carl. When the three were assembled in the kitchen, she told them that she was going to Washington and didn't know when she'd be back.

"With the controversy about Lincoln and with the Watchmen visiting this morning, I think I'd better move into town

15

for a while. So you three will be running this place. Deborah Benson will deliver your paychecks on Fridays. If you need to buy anything big, call me, we'll talk, and I'll have Deborah issue a check. I'm going to leave three thousand in cash with Lon. If you need to buy small stuff, use that, and put the receipts in the Ball jar on the kitchen counter. I'll leave the keys for the truck and the car with Lon."

They had questions, but they'd done this before.

"Any idea when you'll be back?" Lon asked.

"I'll check back every once in a while, just to ride, if nothing else. But it could be a while before I'm back full-time — probably not until we find Linc," she said.

When she was satisfied that the farm would be handled, she ate the cold schnitzel sandwich, opened the safe and removed and packed her jewelry, packed a small suitcase with clothes she wanted to take to the city, went to the security room, took the tape out of the security cameras, and put in a new one.

She spent another hour on Rochambeau — Rocky — an aging gelding that had always been one of her favorites, then cleaned up, put on her traveling clothes,

16

and wandered around the house at loose ends, until four o'clock, when she heard the gate-buzzer chirp. She looked out the front window down the lawn where the driveway snaked up from the road. Two cars were coming up the hill, a gunmetal gray Mercedes-Benz sedan and a black Lincoln Town Car.

She went out on the porch when the cars stopped in the driveway circle. A chauffeur got out of the Benz and waited. Another chauffeur got out of the Town Car and held the back door. A young woman got out, followed by a slightly older man, both carrying briefcases. Madison met them at the top of the porch stairs.

"Hello," the woman said. "I'm Janice Rogers, this is Lane Parks, Johnnie said to say hello for him. He will see you tonight."

"Two cars?" she asked.

"Johnnie thought a convoy would be better," Rogers said. "If you're really worried . . . it would make it more complicated for anyone to interfere with us."

"Good. Let me get my things," she said.

The trip into D.C. took a little more than three hours. Her attorney, Johnson Black, was waiting on the porch when the Benz pulled up to the town house, alerted by the two junior attorneys in the Town

Car. Black was dressed like his name, in shades of black, under a black raincoat, but with a brilliant jungle-birds necktie.

She got out, the chauffeur popped the trunk to get her luggage, and she walked up the sidewalk and Black kissed her on the cheek and said, "Quite an adventure."

"The kind I don't need."

"Randall James is coming over tonight, if you don't mind. He wants to talk about those tapes — he wants you on his show tomorrow."

She was fumbling for the keys to the front door, found them. "You think that'd be the thing to do?"

"Well, I'll have to look at the tapes, but so far, the press is acting like we're just bullshitting about Linc and Goodman. This could change things. Depends on the tapes . . ."

Randall James had a noon gig as the Washington Insider on the local ABC outlet. The show got to the right demographic.

James showed up at nine o'clock, an unctuous man with careful black hair, a sharp nose, and a dimple on his chin. He would, she thought, lie for the pure pleasure of it; but he had the demographics.

He sat in the chair, watching the tapes, checking her profile from time to time. When they were done, he said, "I'll put you on right at the top, at noon. Live. This is great shit, Mrs. Bowe." He picked up a remote and ran back to the point where Sheenan had shuffled toward her. The threat seemed more explicit on the tape than it had in person. James froze the scene, said, "Look at the face on that fucker . . ."

Her name was Madison Bowe. Her husband was an ex–U.S. senator from Virginia, who, two weeks earlier, had vanished after a speech in Charlottesville. Vanished like a wisp of smoke.

Next day.

The governor of the Commonwealth of Virginia stood in the living room of the private quarters on the second floor of the governor's mansion, watching the television. He was flushed, angry, but silent.

His brother was not. His brother screamed at the television: "Look at the bitch, Arlo. *Look at that bitch.* She's ruinin' you, and she knows it. Goddamn her eyes . . ."

"She's good at it," Arlo Goodman said after a moment, a small smile on his face.

19

"That silly ass Randall James is wearing a toupee, huh? He looks like a circumcised cock being attacked by a rat."

Darrell Goodman wasn't amused. He sat on the couch behind the governor, wearing a tan raincoat, his hands in the pockets, a tennis hat shading his eyes, making them invisible in the already dimly lit room. His body was canted toward the TV, trembling with tension. "You want me to . . ."

The governor turned and pointed a finger at him: "Nothing. Nobody goes near her, not for any reason. I'll make a statement, sweetness and light, apologize, kick the Watchman's ass. What's his name? Sheenan. We kick his ass. But if anything happened to her, I'd be cooked. Done. Finished. Stay the fuck away from her."

"What about Sheenan? Maybe he's working with her. Maybe it was a setup."

The governor grunted: "If that was a setup, he oughta get the Oscar. But it wasn't a setup, Darrell. That was a real, honest-to-God barefaced threat. He thought he was doing the right thing."

"Dumb fuck, getting on tape."

"Let it go. I'll have Patricia deal with him. But I'll tell you what, this is no way to get to be president."

Darrell Goodman studied his brother,

his calm face, the smile as he watched the televised assassination. Sooner or later, the governor would realize that they were in a war. Then he'd do more than rave. Then he'd get angry, then he'd move. Darrell looked forward to the day.

The hunter knew Madison Bowe's name. He'd seen her picture, had never met her, had no idea where she lived, had no thought that she might be in his future. As she spoke to a half million people on Randall James's show, he knelt on a rubber tarp, not forty miles from her farm, waiting. Above him, the sun was a dull nickel hidden in the clouds.

The rain had come every night for the past three, courtesy of a low-pressure system stalled over the Appalachians. The night before, the rain began just after 3 a.m. He'd woken in his guest room, upstairs in the cabin, snug under the slanting tin roof. He'd listened for a few moments, the water whispering down a drainpipe, the cotton smell of the quilt around him, and then he'd rolled over and slept soundly until four-thirty.

He woke at four-thirty every morning. When he opened his eyes, he lay quietly for a moment, surfacing, then looked at the bedside clock, stretched, and got out of bed. He did fifty push-ups and fifty sit-ups on the colonial-style hooked rug from China, then a series of stretches, working hard on his bad leg. As he was finishing his routine, he heard an alarm go off down the hall.

He grabbed his jeans and a pair of fresh underpants from his bag, and padded barefoot down the hall to the bathroom. Better first than at the end of the line . . .

He brushed his teeth, skipped shaving, showered quickly. Out of the shower, he dried himself with his designated towel, pulled on the shorts and jeans, and opened the door. Peyson Carter was leaning against the opposite wall, green eyes, sleepy, wrapped in a bathrobe, holding a hair dryer.

"Morning, Jake," she said, not looking at his bare chest. His name was Jake Winter. "Billy's just getting up."

"Yeah, let me get out of your way."

He slid past her in the hallway, careful not to brush against her. Peyson was his best friend's wife. Since Billy Carter first brought her around, fifteen years ago in college, he'd been a little in love with her. Some of the feeling, he suspected, was returned. They were always careful not to touch, because there might be a question of exactly when the touching would stop. And she loved Billy . . .

The guys downstairs were slower getting up, but by the time he'd gotten dressed and into his boots, and gathered his coveralls and gear, they were moving around. He could hear the downstairs shower going, and the plop-gurgle of the coffeemaker, the smell of hot coffee on a cool, rainy morning.

As he left the room, Peyson came out of the bathroom, steamy and pink, wrapped in the robe, and he said, "Scrambled?" and she said, "Yes," and shouted, "Billy, get up," and he followed her down the hall, watching her ass, and God help him, if Billy his best friend ever died in a car wreck, he would be knocking on this woman's door the next week.

Peyson went on to the other bedroom and he turned down the stairs.

In the kitchen, he started breaking eggs into a bowl, got some muffin-premix poured into pan-molds, fired up the oven, took a package of bacon out of the refrigerator. Bob Wilson came out of the down stairs bathroom, hair wet from the shower, and said, "Rain."

"Mist."

"Gonna make the woods quiet, anyway. Hope the birds don't hunker down."

Sam Barger walked sleepy-eyed from the bedroom and asked Wilson, "You all done in the shower?"

"Yeah, go ahead."

"Rainin'," Barger said. "TV says it should be outa here by noon."

They took a little time over breakfast: the smell of muffins rising in the oven, bacon and eggs, coffee, the pine-wood walls of the cabin. Peyson Carter across from him, curly blond hair, catching his eyes. Did all attractive women keep a spare tire?

They hunted together every spring and fall, looking for Virginia wild turkeys, four men, one man's wife. They had the routine down. Everybody knew what to bring — bows, boots, camo, pasta, booze, garbage bags, toilet paper, target faces — and everybody knew about where he or she would set up. They were all bow hunters. Between the five of them, they averaged two turkeys per season. Turkeys were tough.

All that brought him to the rubber tarp, where he knelt in the gloom, waiting for his bird to move. A little hungry now, trying to ignore it. The four-foot-square mat made it possible to shift his weight silently; he had to shift frequently because of his lame leg. The tangle of brush around him made it possible to draw the bow without the motion being seen.

He had a Semiweiss Lighting compound bow, the draw weight adjusted down to provide for a very long hold. He was shooting carbon-fiber arrows, one-inch broadheads with stoppers. A good-sized tom hung out in the oaks behind him. And the tom would be coming out to this cornfield, and with luck, following a track along a shallow ravine below him. He knew the bird sometimes did that, because he'd seen the scat and the tracks on scouting trips.

Whether the tom would do it this day, he didn't know.

He waited, listening, straining to see in through the brush, the problems of the bureaucracy falling away from him. He'd hunted most of his life, since his grandfather had first taken him out when he was six years old. He hunted deer and turkeys in Virginia, elk and antelope out west. When he was hunting, he stepped into a Zen-space and became part of the landscape. Time didn't pass, nor did it stop; it simply wasn't. He faded away from himself and his day-to-day problems.

He'd been in place since dawn. The sun came up, rose higher, broke briefly out of the clouds, disappeared again. A breeze sprang up, played with the oak leaves, died again; squirrels ran across the ground, noisy beasts; a chickadee stopped on a branch a foot from his nose.

He saw it all, but didn't look at it. He was waiting . . .

When the cell phone went off.

"Ahhhh . . . Jesus!"

The sound was stunning, like being hit in the face by a snowball. He rushed back to the present, out of the Zen-space to the here-and-now. He unzipped a panel on his camo, pushed his hand through to a shirt pocket underneath, and took the phone out.

"Yes." The only people who had the number for that phone were people he needed to talk with.

A woman's voice, quiet, cultivated: "Jake, this is Gina Press. I'm sorry to bother you, I understand you're on vacation. The guy needs to see you."

"When?"

"Today. Where are you?"

"Down in the valley. It'll be a while."

"It's pretty urgent. Can I put you on the log for four forty-five?"

He looked at his watch: One o'clock. "Okay — but give me a hint."

"Madison Bowe."

"I'll be there."

The killer could feel the pull of the .45 in his pocket, pulling down on his shoulders, and maybe his soul.

He was moving Lincoln Bowe. Bowe was pale, naked, unconscious, a sack of meat, for all practical purposes. The killer had him slung in a blue plastic tarp, purchased at a Wal-Mart, and wrestled him down the narrow stairs, under the single bare basement bulb.

He was a big man, straining with the load, trying for a kind of tenderness while moving two hundred pounds of inert human being. He wore blue coveralls from Wal-Mart, purchased for the murder, and a hooded sweatshirt, with the hood pulled over his head, and plastic gloves. He knew all about DNA, and it worried him. A hair, a little spit, and he could wind up strapped to the death gurney, a needle in the arm . . .

He got the load down, puffing and heaving all the way, then looked back up the stairs: two minutes and he'd have to take the body back up. But he couldn't do the killing upstairs, the neighborhood was too tight, somebody might hear the shot.

He moved Bowe under the light, spread the tarp, exposed him. He was lying on his back, soft and helpless. His body was dead white, touched here and there with blemishes, pimples, the rashes and scrapes of an out-of-shape man in his fifth decade. He looked at Bowe for a few seconds, then said aloud, "Here we are. Christ Almighty."

No response. Bowe had taken an overdose of Rinolat.

The killer took the .45 out of his pocket, an old, worn gun, made in the first half of the twentieth century, bought at a weekend sale, inaccurate at any distance farther than arm's length. Which was enough for the task.

He cocked it with a gloved hand, then thought: "The phone book. Damnit." He ran up the short flight of stairs, got the phone book off the kitchen table, and went back down, closing the door behind him. The phone book already had two bullet holes in it: tests he'd done out in the Virginia countryside. He placed it on the naked man's chest.

He slipped the safety and said, "Linc . . ." and thought: *Ears . . . damnit.*

He put the safety back on, ran back up the stairs, and got the earplugs. They were two bullet-sized bits of compressible yellow foam, made for target shooters. He twisted each one, fitted them into his ears, waited for them to reexpand. If he'd fired the gun in the confines of the basement, without the ear protection, he wouldn't have been able to hear for a week.

He slipped the safety again, teared up, wiped the tears away, pointed the pistol at the point where the phone book covered the naked man's heart, said, "Lincoln," and pulled the trigger.

Without the earplugs, the blast would have been shattering; it was bad enough as it was. The naked man bucked upward, his eyes opening in reflex, the pupils milky with sleep. He stared at the killer for a second, then two, then dropped back flat on the floor.

"Holy mother," the killer said, appalled. He stood staring for a second, shocked by the milky eyes, by a possible gleam of intelligence, the hair rising on the back of his neck. Then, after a moment, he stooped and picked up the phone book. The slug had gone through, and blood bubbled from a purple hole in the naked man's chest. The hole was directly over his heart.

He engaged the safety on the .45, slipped the gun back in his pocket, and squatted.

The naked man wasn't breathing. His eyes, when the lids were withdrawn, had rolled up, showing only the whites. He pressed a plastic-covered finger against the naked man's neck, waiting for any sign of a pulse. Didn't find one. Lincoln Bowe was dead.

He rolled Bowe up, enough to look at his back. No exit wound. The phone book had worked like a charm: the slug was buried inside the dead man.

The killer was silent, kneeling, looking at the face of the man on the floor. So many years. Who would have thought it'd come to this? Then he sighed, stood up, pulled the magazine on the pistol, jacked the shell out of the chamber, replaced it in the magazine. Looked at the stairs.

This would be the dangerous part, moving the body. If the cops stopped him for anything, he was done.

But they'd made their plans, and he was running with them. He had a lot to do. He stood, still looking at the dead man's face, then said, "Let's move, Linc. Let's go."

2

Jake stopped at home and changed into a suit and tie, and then caught a taxi to the White House. He checked through the west working entrance, walking first past the outer gate, where a guard examined his ID, then through the inner gate with the X-ray machines.

The X-ray tech, a new guy, spent five minutes looking at his cane, until an older guy came by, glanced at it, and said, "It's okay. Mr. Winter's a regular."

Once through security, he was slotted into a waiting room that offered coffee, newspapers, and high-speed Internet. The room had recently been redecorated — the walls painted blue, the First Lady's favorite color, and hung with portraits of former First Ladies.

One of the formers, Hillary Clinton, smiled down on the bald spot of John Powers, a Georgetown professor and some-time advisor to the Department of Defense. Powers was sitting in an easy chair reading the *Wall Street Journal.* He and Jake knew each other as consultants, and as denizens of Georgetown.

"I'm much more important than you are," Powers said to Jake, folding the paper as Jake limped in. He was an urbane man, who looked like he might have run an art gallery. His over-the-calf socks were dark blue with ladybug-sized smiling suns on them. "I publish in *Foreign Policy.*"

"That may be true, but my neckties are from Hermès," Jake said, dropping into a chair across from him. "Wait'll the faculty senate hears that you were reading the *Journal.*"

"They all read it, in secret, greedy little buggers," Powers said. He probed: "Are you over for the boat review?"

Jake shook his head and lied. "Nope. I don't know why I'm over. Probably the convention. History stuff, working it into the program, successor to John F. Kennedy, Lyndon B. Johnson, William Jefferson Clinton, great Americans all, blah-blah-blah."

"The convention." Powers smiled, showing a set of glittering teeth. Campus rumor said that he'd had them veneered for television. "I'm here for the boats. Vice President Landers is leading the charge."

"Good luck with that." Jake opened his case and took out his laptop, balanced it on his knees, turned it on.

"You don't mean that," Powers said, tilting his head. Few people at Georgetown would have.

"I do," Jake said. "I hope they build them all."

Powers brightened, remembering. "Ah. That's right. You were in the military."

"For a while." The boats were five atomic-powered attack carriers that would cost twelve billion dollars each. "With the budget as it is, and the old people loading up behind Social Security, I don't think you've got a chance in hell."

Powers frowned, said, "The Chinese and Indians . . ." A tall man in shirtsleeves stuck his head into the room and nodded at Powers. "Whoops, here I go. See you at school." Powers took a step away, then said, "Really? Hermès?"

"Yup."

"What do they cost now? Two-fifty?"

"Yup."

When Powers was gone, Jake plugged into the Net, did a search for Madison and Lincoln Bowe. He got sixty thousand hits, filtered them to the last three days, and caught a reference to a Madison Bowe interview on Channel 7's *Washington Insider* with Randall James.

He called it up from the station's news cache and watched Madison Bowe do her thing: "They've got him, I know it." The camera made love to her face. "They've got Lincoln. If they don't, why are they so worried about me? They did everything they could to shut me up. I'll be honest, I'm very worried. I'm worried that they'll kill him when they're done with him . . ."

She had tapes of a big shambling man threatening her in her own house. The tapes were made more effective by their security-camera, cinéma-vérité quality. "This is how they work," she said after the tape ran out. She was appealing, with a nervous lip-nibble that made a male hormone jump up and shout, *I'll take care of you.*

"This is what they're doing to our America," she said, speaking directly to the camera.

They, Jake mused, were *us.*

He was moving fast now, scanning the Net news, learning as much as he could about her, and about Lincoln Bowe, and the circumstances around Lincoln Bowe's disappearance; and about their friends, their political allies. Lincoln Bowe had been a conservative Republican, faithful to the party and to the conservative cause, and an aristocrat. Madison Bowe was a lawyer's daughter, smart, media-wise, good-looking, the perfect mate for a rising Republican star.

Then the star had fallen, brought down by Arlo Goodman.

The fight had started with Goodman's run for the governorship, through the rise of the Watchmen, and then into Bowe's re-election campaign. Bowe had been the big stud in Virginia politics, Goodman coming up in the other party, a threat to Bowe's eminence. A fight that started out as political quickly became personal.

Bowe: *Have you seen him with his Watchmen? Just like Munich in the 1930s, a tin-pot dictator with his political thugs, a little Hitler without the mustache . . .*

Goodman: *Did you ever see that picture of him during Iraq I? The baby-faced bigshot lawyer with his aristocratic chums, with his friends from Skull and Bones, playing poker and smoking Cuban cigars. Let the poor boys die; but none of our precious little richies with their snowy white sweaters with the big blue Y on the chest . . .*

Bowe must have rued the day he'd worn

that Yale sweater, let himself be shot in the sweater and shorts, sockless with tasseled loafers, a big cigar and playing cards on the table, the unruly hair falling over his forehead — a harmless, attractive photograph at twenty-four that would be shoved up his ass at forty-six . . .

Goodman had won the gubernatorial race. Two years later, with a lot of help from the White House, and a nationwide money-raising campaign, he'd spearheaded the campaign against Bowe. Bowe had lost his Senate seat to a Goodman crony.

Bowe had lost, but he hadn't shut up. He had the money and the family to re-create himself as the administration's most prominent critic, able to say what sitting members of Congress, too worried about maintaining their share of the pork, could not. Some thought he might run for his old Senate seat again. Some thought if the Republicans came back in, he might be in line for an ambassadorship, the Court of St. James's, or Paris.

Then he'd vanished. Stepped into a car, and was gone, moments after making a vicious attack on the administration's Syrian policy, and, domestically, on special-interest groups who supported the president.

The media had gone crazy. And the longer Bowe was gone, the crazier it had gotten.

ABC had compared his disappearance to Judge Crater's and Jimmy Hoffa's, with hints of organized crime. CNN had done a special that spoke darkly of Nazi, Middle Eastern, and South American politics. They'd intercut the film with shots of the Watchmen, in bomber jackets and khaki slacks, meeting in a football stadium in Emporia, with Goodman on a stage in front of a huge American flag; the implication was clear.

Fox had won the ratings war with a show on even crazier theories, including alien abduction and spontaneous combustion.

Jake had been waiting for forty minutes, and was still paging through media commentaries, when his cell phone rang. Gina. "You're on the log. Come on up."

Jacob Winter was thirty-three years old, six feet two inches tall, rangy, bony, with knife-edge cheekbones, a long nose, black hair worn unfashionably long, arty-long, and pale green eyes. His ex-wife referred to him as Ichabod-in-a-suit, after Ichabod Crane. He did wear suits: a saleswoman at

Saks had once taken two hours of her life to coordinate neckties and shirts and suits with his eyes, and to explain how he could do it himself.

"Your eyes are the thing," she'd said. "The right tie brings them out. Frankly, you would not normally be considered a great-looking guy, too many bones in your face, but your eyes make you *very* attractive. Your eyes and shoulders . . ."

Yes. The kind of guy who attracts saleswomen from Saks. Not a bad thing; her comment had cheered him for a week. *A man of style . . .*

Jake had been born in Montana and raised on a ranch. His mother was an engineer, his father a rancher's son and a lawyer and eventually a congressman. Jake came late in their lives. Since his parents were both Catholic and pro-life, and politics were involved, the pregnancy was tolerated, but they weren't much interested in raising another kid — Jake's siblings were fifteen years older than he.

When he was two, his parents, moving between Billings and Washington, began leaving him for longer and longer periods with his grandparents. By the time he was five, they were out of his life. His grandmother died when he was nine; his grandfather followed when he was fifteen. His parents didn't want him. After a year of prep school, he went to college at the University of Virginia, a lonely sixteen-year-old with a history book under his arm.

He graduated at nineteen and could afford to do as he wished — when his grandfather died, his will specified that the ranch be sold, and that the money go to *Jake,* rather than to his father . . .

Two weeks after graduation, he was in Army Officers Candidate School. He spent eight years with Army Intelligence. The first two years had been in training. The third, fourth, and fifth he'd spent in Afghanistan with a series of Army special forces teams.

At the beginning of the sixth year, he was standing too close to a roadside bomb when it went off on the outskirts of the town of Ghazni. A piece of shell the size of a softball cut through his hip. A medic had stuffed Stop-Flo padding into the hole in his leg and butt and on the medevac chopper, said, "Shit, man, you're lucky. If you'd been standing ninety degrees to the right, that would've been your balls."

The rest of the sixth year was spent at the Walter Reed Army Medical Center in

Bethesda, getting his leg to work again.

Then, still in therapy, he was posted to the Pentagon, where he discovered an uncanny ability to navigate the world of bureaucracy. While his military colleagues worked on assessments of Chinese special-forces training or the electronic characteristics of Indian shoulder-mounted missiles, Jake's work had been done inside the Pentagon, the various limbs of Congress, and the rat's nest of bureaus and departments that surrounded the intelligence agencies.

He found things out; became the Sam Spade of the circular file, the Philip Marlowe of the burn bag.

And though he could eventually run five eight-minute miles, in a hobbled, wind-milling way, the Army would never consider him fully rehabilitated. That career was gone — he could stay in, take staff jobs, and someday retire as one of the colonel-intellectuals who argued war theory. Not interested.

Instead, as he worked through rehab and then in the Pentagon, he'd gone to graduate school at Georgetown, with the idea that he might teach at the university level. He'd written his PhD thesis on twentieth-century modernist ideas as they'd bled into politics, and had then rewritten the thesis as a book, *Modernism & Politics: The Theories That Changed the World.*

He'd gotten solid reviews in the important journals, and followed the first book with *New Elites,* a study of professional bureaucracies. That had nailed down his status as a political intellectual. He didn't do television. Television, he thought, was sales. He was research and design.

He'd gotten married before he'd been wounded; the marriage hadn't survived rehab. Wouldn't have survived anyway, he thought. The woman was a crocodile. Although, he thought, if she'd known that he would wind up at the White House . . .

His most influential publication had never seen hard covers. At the urging of a military friend, he'd written *Winter's Guide to the Inside,* a map and guide to the military/intelligence complex. It had become the best-selling Pentagon samizdat.

The *Guide* had also gotten him a part-time job with the second most important man in the country.

Ten seconds after Gina called down, Jake met a Marine Corps captain on the indoor side of the waiting room, and followed him into an elevator, up, and then down the eggshell white halls to Danzig's office.

Going to see *the guy*. The guy was Bill Danzig, the president's chief of staff. Danzig had been a deputy secretary of Defense two administrations back, then a Pentagon consultant when the party was out of power. He'd been given a copy of *Winter's Guide*, and when he moved to the White House, Jake went on his consultants list.

Jake had done twenty jobs for him in three years, tracking down problems in the bureaucracy. As Danzig came to trust him, the problems became more difficult, the assignments more frequent.

Not quite a full-time job, but lucrative. The job also gave him access to some interesting government computers. Interesting, anyway, for a man who wanted to know what really happened.

A Secret Service agent was standing in the hall outside Danzig's office door, wearing the neat suit, crisp shirt, and a burgundy necktie, with ear-bug. He nodded at Jake and the jarhead, stepped into the middle of the hallway, blocking a farther walk down the hall, toward the president's office, and politely indicating the entrance to Danzig's office.

Jake nodded and took the turn. The Secret Service man said, "Nice to see you again, Mr. Winter."

"Nice to see *you,* Henry," Jake said. Jake remembered everybody's name; it was part of his talent.

Danzig's outer office was twenty-five feet wide and twenty feet deep, with a small room to one side for printers and copy machines. He had three secretaries. Two sat opposite each other against the side walls, at identical cherry-wood desks, peering at computers.

A third sat behind a broad table, an antique with curved, carved legs pressing into the deep-blue carpet, under a portrait of Theodore Roosevelt, beside the door to the inner office. The table was littered with paper, bound reports, a few family photographs, and a vase of cut cattleya orchids, large yellow blooms dappled with scarlet.

The third woman was Gina, the important one, the one who'd called him. She was in her forties, with a dry oval face and close-cropped hair, bright blue eyes, wrinkles in the skin of her neck. She nodded and smiled, as though she wouldn't cut his throat in an instant if her boss asked her to. She said, "Great tie," and touched a button on her desk. Danzig now knew Jake was waiting.

"Great halter," Jake said. "Is that new?"

Gina touched the ID halter at her neck, from which her White House ID dangled; turquoise cabochons set in Navajo silver. "I just got it — my husband bought it for our anniversary."

"Nice antique look," he said. "I like it."

ID cards separated Washington insiders from the tourists. The elite-insiders were now separating themselves from the clerk-insiders with gemstones: the sale of jeweled ID halters had been booming.

Gina glanced at her desktop, where a diode had gone green. She said, "Go on in. He's waiting."

Bill Danzig was tying his shoe. He looked up as Jake came through the door, grunted, and said, "Don't buy round shoelaces."

"I'll make a note," Jake said.

Danzig pointed at a chair and Jake sat down. "What's your schedule?" Danzig asked. "Do you have any time?"

Jake shrugged. "I can always make time. We're on Easter break this week, so I've got a week and a half clear."

"Excellent. Now. What do you know about Madison Bowe?" Danzig asked, settling back. He was a fat man, with shoulders slanting down from a thin neck. He had small black eyes and thinning, slicked-back, dandruff-spotted black hair. The odor of VO5 hung about him like the scent of an old apple.

"What I've seen on television and been reading in the papers," Jake said.

"Give me a one-minute version."

Jake shrugged: "Madison Bowe, thirty-four years old, married money in the shape of former U.S. Senator Lincoln Bowe, forty-six. Tells the networks that Lincoln Bowe gave a quote *moderately hot-tempered speech* to a group of Republican law students at the University of Virginia."

Danzig made a farting noise with his lips; Jake paused, then continued.

"Afterward, she said, he was seen getting into a car with three men in suits, and disappeared. Witnesses told her that the men seemed to be law-enforcement personnel, complete with short haircuts and ear-bugs. Mrs. Bowe says she was told by a highly placed source that the Watchmen picked him up. She fears for his life, since they would never be able to admit afterward that they actually did that."

"That's true," Danzig said.

"She also says that she was being watched on her farm near Lexington, and had been threatened by Watchmen. She has a videotape to prove it. The intimidation part. If the tape isn't a complete fake,

I'd say she had reason to be frightened. The guy, the Watchman, acted like he was in the SS or something . . . and that's about it. I mean, there are more details . . ."

"Fucking media," Danzig said. He picked up a yellow pencil and began drumming it on his desktop. "Fucking little right-wing Virginia Law assholes, fucking horse-farm owners. This is the biggest circus since Bill Clinton's blow job."

"Yes, sir."

"She's good-looking, too. Madison Bowe. Blond. Good tits, great ass. The media like that."

Jake said, "Yes, sir, I've seen her on TV."

"Lincoln Bowe did not give a quote *moderately hot-tempered speech,*" Danzig said. He paused, watching Jake's face from under his hooded eyes. "If you actually heard it, it was borderline nuts. He sounded like he might be drunk. He essentially said that the president and the Senate minority leader are criminals. It was completely out of control."

"Yes, sir."

Danzig flashed a thin-lipped fat-lizard's smile: "I should ask, Jake — have any questions occurred to you?"

"The obvious one. Did the Watchmen take him?"

Danzig spun in his leather chair, a complete turn, caught himself before going around a second time: "That's the question. And the answer is *We don't know.* It's possible, I suppose. God only knows what Goodman is cooking up down there."

"So what's our problem?" Jake asked.

"Embarrassment. Goodman is one of us, we can't deny it. We loved that whole Watchman idea, the idea of volunteering for America — it was like the Peace Corps, but for us. Like something John Kennedy might have thought of. Best of all, it didn't cost anything. Now people are starting to say that they're a bunch of Nazis. We wanted to get rid of Lincoln Bowe, we wanted to get him out of the Senate, and we gave Goodman everything he needed to do the job. Then Bowe disappears, and it all comes back to bite us in the ass."

Jake nodded. There wasn't much to say. The Democrats, with the president leading the way, had poured seventy million dollars into the Virginia election, had used Goodman as their point man.

"So. Find out what happened to Bowe," Danzig said. "Legal as you can. Use the FBI for the technicalities. But find him and give me updates through Gina."

Jake said, "What's the FBI doing? I'm

not sure I could help."

Danzig was irritated: "The FBI — they're doing a tap dance, is what they're doing. They know a dead skunk when they see one. They're out looking around, but I've been talking to the director, and I know goddamned well that they don't have their hearts in it. They're saying that there's no evidence of a kidnapping, no evidence of force, no evidence of anything. They just stand around and cluck."

"So, what do I do?"

"Kick some ass. Turn over some rocks. Go threaten somebody," Danzig said. "Do what you do. We need to get this thing out of the way. We can't carry this through the summer, into the election, for Christ's sake."

"How much time?"

Danzig shook his head. "No way to tell. It's already a mess. Right now, we're sitting tight, going back-door to all the media, talking about how it's a Virginia problem, not a White House problem. They've bought it so far. But you know how that works: one thing changes, and they'll turn on you like a pack of rats."

"What's my authority?" Jake asked. Sometimes Danzig didn't want anyone to know who was interested.

"I am," Danzig said. "You can use my name. Gina will back you up."

"Okay." Jake slapped his thighs. "I'll move on it."

As he got up and turned to go, Danzig asked, "Kill any turkeys?"

"Nope. Interrupted by a phone call."

"Life in the big city, son," Danzig grunted, already flipping through the paper in front of him. "Maybe you can squeeze a little blood out of this job."

Out of Danzig's office, Jake walked with an escort to the working door, then into the sunshine through the security fences to the street, where he caught a cab home. The magnolias were in full bloom, pink and white, beds of daffodils jumped up like yellow exclamation marks. Early April: the cherry trees would be gorgeous this week down at the Tidal Basin, if you could get to them through the tourists. He made a mental note to stroll by, if he found the time.

Several days of rain had washed the city clean. The Washington Monument needled into the sky, telling the world exactly who the studhorse was. The streets were lined with flowers, busy with bureaucrats with white ID tags strung around their necks, fat brown briefcases dangling from their hands. Good day in Washington when even the bureaucrats looked happy.

Jake lived in Burleith, north of Georgetown, in a brick-and-stone town house that might have been built in the early twentieth century, but was actually a careful replica only fifteen years old.

At the moment, his street was torn up. The owner of a town house three down from his, a stockbroker, had convinced the other residents to rip out the old concrete sidewalks and replace them with brick walkways. Bricks would enhance the value of the neighborhood, the broker said, and would increase the resale value of their houses by making the neighborhood more like Georgetown. Jake was indifferent to the idea, but went along because everybody else agreed to do it. Besides, the noisome little asshole was probably right.

Because of the street work, he had the cabbie drop him at the entrance to the alley at the back of the house, carded through the fence lock, and climbed the stoop to the back door.

He ran a bachelor house: a functional kitchen, a compact dining room, a living room with a wide-screen television, a den used as a library and office, and a half-bath; and on the second floor, a master bedroom suite, a guest bedroom, and a third bedroom where he hid all his junk — obsolete golf clubs, a never-used rowing machine, old computer terminals that were not good enough to use, but too good to throw away, three heavily used backpacks and two newer ones — he was a bag junkie. He also had a gun safe, a bow locker, and a pile of luggage.

The furnace, a washer and dryer, the telephone and electric service panels, and the master box for the alarm system were all tucked away in a small basement. A two-car garage had been added to the back of the house and occupied most of the backyard.

He kept the place neat with two hours of cleaning a week, usually done on Saturday morning. He wasn't a freak about it, simply logical. Two hours a week was better than two straight days once a quarter.

By the time he got home, the workday was over. He went online with the Virginia State website, found a name for the governor's chief of staff — Ralph Goines — and tracked him down through the FBI telephone database, then called him on his unlisted home phone. He identified himself and said, "I need to see Governor Goodman. Tomorrow if possible."

"Could I tell the governor why you want to talk to him?"

"It's about Lincoln Bowe. If you saw Randall James's show . . ."

"We did see it. Absolutely irresponsible," Goines said. "Mrs. Bowe has been carrying on a campaign of slander and innuendo."

"So which one was the big guy in the videotape, the one with the leather jacket?" Jake asked. "Slander? Or Innuendo?"

Bitch-slapping bureaucrats was one way to wake them up. Pause, five seconds of silence: "We are looking into that. It's possible that it was a setup."

"Right," Jake said. He let the skepticism show in his voice. "Maybe the governor could tell me about it."

Back and forth, and eventually an appointment: "One o'clock, then. Be prompt. The governor's a busy man."

Jake nodded at the phone, said, "Sure," and hung up, turned to his computer, and went back online.

Because of his work with Danzig, he had limited access to government reference files. He went into the FBI telephone database again. The Bowes had a place in

Georgetown, not far from him, and were also listed at a place in the Blue Ridge, and in New York. He found an unlisted cell-phone number for Madison Bowe and called it.

She answered on the third ring.

3

Madison Bowe lived in a four-story red-brick town house in Georgetown, up the hill from M Street. Jake paid the cabdriver, straightened his tie, climbed the front steps, and rang the bell. She met him at the door, barefoot, wearing black slacks and a hip-length green-silk Chinese dressing-gown. She didn't smile, but looked up and asked, "You're Jacob Winter?"

"Yes, I am." Jake had only seen her on television, where everyone was cropped to fit the screen and gorgeous blondes were a dime a dozen, and you paid no attention. But Madison Bowe was real, and the reality of the woman was a slap in the face. She was smaller than he'd expected, had short blond hair, a sculpted nose, direct green eyes, and a touch of pinkish lipstick. She spoke with a soft Virginia country accent, in a voice that carried some bourbon gravel.

She still didn't smile; looked up and down the block, then said, "I hate it when I have to trust a Democrat."

"I apologize," Jake said. "I'll go home and kill myself."

Small blondes were his personal head-turner. His ex-wife might have been air-mailed to him directly from hell — but she, too, had been a small blonde, and right up to the end, even at the settlement conference, the sight of her had turned him around. As did Madison Bowe. And Madison smelled good, like lilacs, or vanilla.

"You better come in," she said, ignoring the wisecrack. "We're in the parlor."

He limped after her. He noticed her noticing it.

The other half of the "we" was a lawyer named Johnson Black, who was sitting on a sofa facing a coffee table, a delicate china cup in his hand. Jake saw him a half-dozen times a year at different lobbyist dinners. He was balding, with merry, pink cheeks and half-moon glasses. In his late sixties, he was one of the classic Washington regulars who moved between private practice and federal appointments.

Black wore a dark suit, as always, but had taken off his brilliant tie, which was draped over a shoulder. He stood up, smiling, to shake hands: "Jake, goddamnit, I couldn't believe it when Maddy said *you* were coming over. I told her you were a good guy."

"I appreciate that," Jake said. "How've you been, Johnnie? How's the heart?"

"Ah, I'm eating nothing but bark and twigs. It's either that, or they do the Roto-Rooter on me."

Madison was watching Jake. "Johnnie says you're teaching at Georgetown," she said. "Why's a professor . . . ?"

"I'm not a professor. I teach a seminar. I work for the government as a consultant," Jake said. "I specialize in . . ." He paused, looked at Johnson Black, and said, "I don't know. What do I specialize in, Johnnie?"

"Hard to tell," Black said. "Maybe forensic bureaucracy?"

"That's it," Jake said, turning back to Madison. "Forensic bureaucracy. When something goes wrong, I try to find out what *really* happened."

Madison sat on the couch next to Black. She didn't smile back, hadn't smiled yet, and he really wanted to see her smile. Jake took an easy chair, facing them across the coffee table, put his case on the floor by his feet, leaned forward.

"The president has ordered me to find Senator Bowe. I'm going to start kicking bureaucrats, I'm going to raise hell over at Justice, with the FBI, with Homeland Security, and I'm going to talk to

Governor Goodman."

"In other words, you're going to make a big public relations show, because the president is feeling the heat," Madison said.

Jake shook his head: "No. No show. That's an explicit part of my deal — I don't do public stuff. But I will find your husband. There's a reason he's gone."

"Because he spoke out. Because he was critical of Arlo Goodman and his thugs, and was tying them to this administration," Madison said.

Jake held both hands up, palms toward Madison: "Mrs. Bowe: I heard you on television. I will keep that possibility in mind. But there are other possibilities, and I'm not going to let any of them go."

"What other possibilities?"

"That your husband disappeared for reasons of his own," Jake said.

"You can't believe that," she said, her back rigid. Her hands twisted in her lap, and he was happy that his neck wasn't between them.

"I don't believe anything in particular, Mrs. Bowe," Jake said. "But there's been speculation to that effect. That this is an effort to embarrass Arlo Goodman. That you're jerking him around. There are radio talk show people saying that your appearance on TV was part of that effort."

Her face was intent, earnest: "It was *not* . . ."

Jake overrode her: "I'm outlining the possibilities, as I see them. I didn't come over here to argue with you, or to comfort you. I need to ask some questions and to make a request."

She settled back on the couch and crossed her arms over her chest. "What do you want?"

"Your husband is too important a public figure to disappear on his own," Jake said. "If he disappeared of his own volition, then either you, or some close friend, knows where he is. I want you to call all of his close friends. Tell them that if they know anything about Lincoln Bowe, I want them to get in touch with me. We are now at the point where somebody's going to jail, to prison, for involvement with this disappearance. That if this started as a joke, nobody's laughing anymore."

Now Madison leaned forward, her eyes locked on his: "That's what I want! I want somebody to say that in public. The president. The attorney general. That we're talking about prison. Or the death penalty. Or something. Finally get some pressure on whoever's got him. They've just been out there playing around . . ."

"So you'll make the calls?"

"Yes — but that won't help," she said. "He did *not* disappear on his own. He is not with a friend. He would have told me. Even more . . ."

She hesitated, and Jake said, "What?"

"He spends most of his time at our New York apartment," she said. "He had two cats there. When he disappeared, probably that Friday afternoon, nobody realized that he was gone until Monday, when he missed appointments. When we called the apartment, the maid answered. She said he wasn't there, but not only that: nobody had fed the cats over the weekend. They had no food or water, they were drinking from a toilet. Linc would never have done that, let the cats go like that. Even if he was planning to disappear, he would have made up some excuse to see that they were taken care of."

Jake looked down at his lap and touched his forehead with his middle finger, unconsciously rubbing. In any hunt, any interrogation, there were key moments, when somebody said something that might seem obscure, that looked like a minor point but was, in fact, critical.

Madison misinterpreted his reaction: "What? You don't believe me?"

"No, no," Jake said, looking up again. "It's the single piece of information I've gotten so far that makes me think you're right. That he didn't go away voluntarily."

For the first time, her attitude softened. "I've been trying to tell everybody that. He'd never abandon the cats."

He watched her for a few seconds, then said, "You say he spent most of his time in New York. Did you spend that time with him?"

"No, I . . ." She stopped, looked at Black, and then said, "We're not exactly estranged. We're friendly. But we don't live together much anymore. He spends most of his time in New York, I spend most of mine at our farm. We mostly intersect here, in Washington . . . when we do."

Jake took that as a complex of evasions suggesting that they no longer were in bed together.

"Do you think . . . if you're only friendly, that he might have another friend? Somebody that he might have gone off with for a while?"

She was exasperated: "No, I do not. Frankly, if he was going to do that, he would have told me. And he would have fed the cats."

Okay. Enough of that.

Jake looked at Black, then Madison: "There's a concept, in the bureaucracy, called *The Rule.* Have you heard of it?"

Madison shook her head, but Black nodded. "From *Winter's Guide*: You ask, *Who benefits?*"

Jake said, "Exactly — though I didn't think of it. I just picked it up." He held Madison's eyes: "In any analysis of a confusing political problem, the rule is to ask, *'Who benefits?'* You will find the answer to *any* political or bureaucratic question, if you can answer that one correctly. Now, Senator Bowe vanishes under suspicious circumstances, and you ask, 'Who benefits?' "

"So?" she asked.

Jake shook his head: "It sure as hell isn't this administration. The biggest beneficiaries so far have been your husband's political allies. The biggest loser so far has been Arlo Goodman."

"But . . ."

"I know what you think about Governor Goodman, that you dislike him."

"He's an asshole," she said.

"So you see my problem. Your husband disappears, and almost nobody is hurt except Arlo Goodman. And, by extension, other Democrats. The election is in seven months . . ."

Madison looked at Black, and then back at Jake, anger again surfacing as a red flow up her neck and into her cheeks: "All right, let's work through it again — because you're wrong about who benefits. It's not just a few Republicans against Arlo Goodman — a lot of people are scared of him. The Watchmen are like the Klan, or the Mafia, or the Gestapo. They take their orders from Goodman. If Lincoln's never found, and nobody is ever caught, people become even more afraid of the Watchmen. That's what they want. They want the fear. They want control. Who benefits if we don't find Lincoln? The Watchmen do."

"That's a little overblown," Jake said. "They're a bunch of guys in leather jackets. Boy Scouts who got old."

Her voice rose, never became shrill, but he could feel the anger in it: "That's how they started. Most of them are still that way. Old Boy Scouts. But some of them . . . In Lexington, the Watchmen came to my house and tried to put me under house arrest. No warrant, no crime, just the Watchmen. Now they're starting up in other states. You don't know how dangerous Goodman is. He won't stop with the governorship. That's small potatoes.

He's aiming for the presidency."

"I'm seeing the governor tomorrow," Jake said. "I'll talk to him about it."

"For all the good that'll do," she snapped.

"Back to the point: we don't benefit. I'm not sure I buy the analysis on the Watchmen, but I'll keep it in mind. So: who else? Is there another party?"

She shook her head. "I don't know. If you start thinking it's Arab terrorists or the Masons or the Vatican or a thousand-year-old conspiracy, you'll probably kill him. The answer is closer than that."

Jake nodded and picked up his case. "Okay. Make those phone calls, please. I'll leave my private number for call-backs."

"You're going to find him."

He nodded. "Yes. I will. He was last seen getting into a car with two or three other men. That was not an innocent ride, because not a single person has come forward to explain. So that, I think, must be the moment he disappeared, or began disappearing. And *that* means there's a group of men who know where he is, what happened. I am going to hound everyone who can do anything to help us break that group. I *will* find him."

"Be careful where you look. Especially in Virginia."

"The Watchmen don't frighten me," Jake said.

"That bothers me," she said.

"Why?"

"Because that might mean that you're too stupid to find Lincoln."

They stared at each other for a moment, poised over the coffee table, and then Jake cracked a smile: he really liked her. "Okay."

When he left, she shook his hand. Her hands were harder and rougher than he'd expected, probably from riding, or working around the farm, he thought. He turned on the stoop and said, "I'll talk to the governor about you — get you back to your farm, make sure you're not harassed. If I need more information, can I come back?"

"Yes, you may, anytime," she said. "If we don't find Linc pretty soon, he's gone. We'll never find him."

Black, standing behind her, said, "And hey, take it easy, huh? Listen to what Maddy's saying about the Watchmen. From what I hear, you were always a little too quick to jump out of the airplane."

When Jake was gone, Madison said to Johnson Black, "The Virginia state police and the FBI are looking for Linc. They're not getting anywhere, so the president sends some bureaucrat to look for him? This is going to help? Am I going crazy?"

"He's not exactly a bureaucrat," Black said.

"That *forensic bureaucracy* thing was cute," she said, as they idled back into the living room. "But what does it mean?"

"Jake fixes things," Black said. "If there's some really screwed-up problem, that nobody can fix, and that *must* be fixed, Jake fixes it. He makes lists of people who need to be fired, who need to be promoted. He has ears all over the bureaucracy . . . he scares the heck out of those people. And that's what's got to be done if you want to find Linc."

"We need to scare bureaucrats?"

"That's right. People are looking for him, they're paying attention because of all the media coverage, but they're not *desperate* to find him. Jake can make people desperate. He can make them feel that their careers are on the line if they don't — and sometimes, they are."

"Hmmp." She settled back on the couch. "I suppose it's better than nothing."

"He used to be married to Nikki Lange, you know."

Her eyebrows went up: "You're kidding me. He's the guy?"

"He's the guy. Couldn't last, of course. Nikki's too deeply involved with herself."

"And her money," Madison said. "Did he get alimony?"

"No. He told the judge that all he was asking for was his life. The judge almost fell on the floor laughing — she knew Nikki, too. Besides, Jake's pretty well fixed. Inherited a Montana ranch. Sold to a movie star for big bucks."

"Maybe he rides," she said.

"I'm sure he does." Black smiled. "I was watching you two talk — you got sort of *engaged*."

She stuck her tongue out at him, then said, "He's not entirely unattractive."

Black snorted. "Just . . . take it easy. Jake is a little strong for most people. As I understand it, he pretty much held his own with Nikki."

"He jumps out of airplanes?"

"Jake was in Afghanistan for years. He killed people — that was his job. So. You can toy with him, but I wouldn't annoy him."

"Mmm," she said again. "Maybe he can do something. Maybe we need somebody who'll jump out of an airplane."

Jump out of an airplane.

He dreamed of jumping out of airplanes that night, jumping all mixed up with the face and figure of Madison Bowe; but mostly jumping. Other jumpers talked about their best moment; popping the chute, flying . . . but for Jake, it had always been that instant when he hit the wind, hit the slipstream, the slap and tickle, the moment of commitment.

He'd liked Afghanistan, the fighting, the comradeship, the countryside, the Afghanis. In Washington ex-military circles, the fashion called for a grudging, manly acknowledgment of having been there, of the toughness of it, but nobody was supposed to have actually *liked* it, to have loved the exhilaration of combat.

But he did. He'd liked the night runs, he'd liked the ambushes, he'd liked the assaults. He hadn't minded, too much, the occasional pain, right up until the time he took the bad one. He hadn't even minded that pain, though he hated the disability that came with it.

He didn't dream of the disability, though: he dreamed of the airplane door, of the helicopter rope, of the night-vision stalks through the rocky ravines . . .

He didn't wake up smiling, but he didn't wake up unhappy, either.

In the morning, after his usual four and a half hours of sleep, he cleaned up and went downstairs, ate toast and eggs, then spent an hour with online newspapers, catching up. When he'd finished with the papers, he went out on the government networks, going deeper on Lincoln Bowe and Arlo Goodman. By seven-thirty, he had their biographies down. He made a call to the FBI, then called a cab.

The day would be warm, he thought, as he locked the door. It must have rained sometime overnight, because the gardens and sidewalks were still wet, but now the skies were clearing again, and sun slanted down through the trees along the street. Because of the torn-up sidewalk, and construction equipment in the street, he walked out to the end of the block to wait for the taxi.

The driver was maybe twenty-one, silent, sullen even, wearing an old tweed coat over a T-shirt, and a flat tweed hat.

"Hard night?" Jake asked.

The driver's eyes went up to the mirror. "They're all hard, buddy."

Jake suppressed a smile: the cabbie was

living in a movie, delivering movie lines.

The FBI's J. Edgar Hoover Building was a bland outcrop of bureaucratic rock on Pennsylvania Avenue, halfway between the White House and the Capitol. Jake checked through security, got an elevator. He didn't need directions.

Mavis Sanders was the FBI's assistant deputy director for counterterrorism. She met him at the door to her inner office. "Another headache," she said. She was smiling, but her voice wasn't.

"How have you been, Mavis?" Jake asked. He kissed her on the cheek.

"My day wasn't too bad until seven-thirty a.m., when I got the note that said you were coming over," she said.

"C'mon, we're old chums."

"Yeah. Sit down, old chum." She was a slender fine-boned black woman who'd made her reputation tracking Iranian-based jihadists. She dropped into her chair, looked at a piece of paper, set it aside, knitted her fingers on top of her desk, and asked, "What's up?"

"The president and the chief of staff have decided that I should find Lincoln Bowe. I need access to your investigative files, and then I need you — somebody, but preferably you — to make this thing a priority and get it settled."

"It *is* a priority."

"Bull. Everybody's playing pass-the-hanky, hoping for the best," Jake said. "Your Richmond guys are doing liaison, you've got nobody really senior involved, except in PR."

"Jake, I really don't know anything about it."

"I'd like to get Novatny working on it."

"Why us?" she asked, with exasperation. "We don't do murders, and we've got a full plate."

"Because you can talk privately to the director and tell him that the president is serious about this and that he's pissed. Tell him that bureaucratic asses are going to be hanged, that careers are going to end. Okay?"

"Okay . . ."

"And because you're the smartest people I know over here. And because, even though you don't do murders, you do work counterterrorism, and this has got the flavor of a conspiracy. That's what we need to penetrate: the ring of guys who picked up Lincoln Bowe. And finally, you've got guys who might possibly keep their mouths shut. We don't want this to become a

70

bigger deal than it already is. We want it to end."

Her mouth turned down and she said, "It can't get much bigger. Did you see Madison Bowe on television?"

"Yes. I talked to her last night."

She looked at him for a moment, sighed, and said, "All right. I'll talk to the director."

"And he'll go along."

"Yeah. If you stand him in a half-mile-an-hour wind, he can tell you which way it's blowing."

"And we get Novatny."

"Something can be worked," she agreed.

"Terrific," Jake said. He pushed himself out of the chair. "I won't bother you any longer."

"You'll mention my name to the guy?"

"Absolutely," Jake said. "You'll be an ambassador in two weeks. What country do you want?"

"Fuck you."

"Thanks, Mavis. Who do I talk to about the files?"

She found an empty conference room for him, and a clerk brought him a short stack of paper, computer printouts. Too short, he thought, when he saw it. The federal investigation was being run out of the FBI's Richmond office, but the feds hadn't actually taken control of it. Most of the work was being done by the Virginia Bureau of Criminal Investigation, which was treating Bowe's disappearance as a missing-persons incident.

But not a routine one.

From paperwork copied from the state cops to the FBI, Jake understood that the cops thought they were on a murder hunt, or possibly some kind of fraud. The police had interviewed the last few friends who'd spoken to Bowe, the people who'd attended the speech he'd given at the law school, and had collected a half dozen interviews done by the NYPD, including the maid who'd found that the cats had gone hungry.

One comment had been repeated a couple of times: Bowe had been drunk in public on at least two occasions before he disappeared. Personal problems? Another woman he was hiding from Madison? But would that have him drinking during the day, on the way to public appearances? He'd have to be a far-gone alky to do that.

And a close friend of his, asked by the FBI if Bowe drank, said that he'd never seen Bowe take more than two drinks in an evening.

Maybe he'd just started? Something had just happened?

Besides, Jake thought, speculations on alcoholism were pointless. Whatever had happened to Bowe had happened in the presence of a number of short-haired men with ear-bugs. He hadn't gotten blind drunk and put the car in the river; he'd disappeared during the middle of the day.

Jake was still going through the paper when Chuck Novatny stuck his head in the door. He was trailed by his partner, George Parker.

"Man, you're gonna get us in trouble," Novatny said, without preamble.

"Ah, you enjoy your access to us elite guys," Jake said. He stood up and shook hands with Novatny, then reached past him to shake with Parker. "Look what it's done for your career."

"Yeah. Fifteen minutes ago, I was in the canteen eating a salmonella-infected chicken salad on a three-day-old hamburger bun," Parker said. "I can barely stand the eliteness."

Novatny was wiry, sandy haired, fifteen years into his FBI career, a maker of model airplanes that he flew with his sons. Parker was tall, thick, and dark, with a lantern jaw and fifteen-inch-long shoes; a golfer. They both wore blue suits, and Jake had a feeling that the suits reflected a shared sense of humor, rather than the FBI culture. They were competent, and even better than that.

"Lincoln Bowe," Novatny said.

"Yes. This is what you've got," Jake said, waving at the paper on the conference table. "Mostly secondhand crap from the Virginia cops."

"You need us to . . . ?"

"Kick ass. Take names. Threaten people. Push anybody who might know anything. Starting . . ." Jake looked up at the wall clock. "Now."

"We've got some things to clean up," Novatny said. "Send the paper down to us when you're through, we'll be on it in a couple of hours. We've been wondering when somebody would start to push."

"When Madison Bowe went on the noon news," Jake said.

"What a coincidence. That's when we started wondering," Novatny said.

They left, and Jake went back to the paper, typing notes into his laptop.

The witnesses who'd seen Lincoln Bowe get in the car with the men with ear-bugs said he hadn't seemed under duress. He'd seemed to expect the ride, and he had no other ride waiting. The men were described as large, white, with business haircuts, wearing suits. One witness said Bowe had been smiling when he got in the car.

The abandoned cats argued for duress. The smile argued for cooperation.

On the one hand, he had only Madison Bowe's word that he cared about the cats. On the other, if Bowe had been picked up by somebody who'd stuck a gun in his ribs and said, "Smile, or I'll blow your heart out," he might have smiled despite duress.

"Huh." No way to make a decision yet. He needed more information.

One thing was clear from the interviews by the Virginia cops: Bowe's speech to the law students had been wicked, and more than one person said that he seemed to be emotionally overwrought, and at the same time, physically loose. He'd been so angry that he seemed, at times, to be groping for words, and at other times, had used inappropriate words, words that simply didn't fit his sentences.

Again, one witness thought he might have been drunk.

Jake looked at his watch, gathered and stacked the paper, called the clerk, told her to send digital copies of everything to his secure e-mail address, and to take the paper to Novatny's office.

Time to see Arlo Goodman.

Jake grabbed a cab back home, made and ate a peanut-butter-and-jelly sandwich, then headed south in his own car, a two-year-old E-class Mercedes. Washington to Richmond was two hours, depending on traffic, south through the most haunted country in America, some of the bloodiest battlegrounds of the Civil War.

Jake had walked all of them, on the anniversaries of the battles. Civil War soldiers, he'd concluded, had been tough nuts.

As was Arlo Goodman.

Four years earlier, Goodman had been the popular commonwealth's attorney for Norfolk, a veteran of Iraq, and politically disgruntled.

His political unhappiness stretched in several directions — and he could do something about one of them. Norfolk was at the center of a series of military complexes; convinced that a terror attack was possible, he put together a team of five investigators, including his brother, a former special forces trooper. The team had set up an intelligence net in the port areas, extending to a couple of other independent cities; later, they recruited volunteer watchmen, all veterans.

Lightning struck.

A group of dissident Saudi students began planning some kind of attack, although exactly what kind was never determined. One of the watchmen picked up on it and talked to the investigators. The apartment of one of the Saudis was bugged, and Goodman got tapes of five students talking about weapons possibilities, and targets, including atomic submarines. The investigators followed them as they bought maps and took photographs.

At one point, three of the students went out to a state park and spent the afternoon throwing Molotov cocktails — gasoline and oil mixed in wine bottles — into a ravine, to see what would happen. The investigators filmed the explosions. They had the motive, the planning, the means. The Saudis were arrested in a flashy bust at their apartment, and the conviction was a slam dunk.

The next day, Goodman announced the formation of a veterans group called the Watchmen, to keep watch over the streets of Norfolk, in an effort to control street crime, prostitution, drugs, and to keep an eye out for "suspicious activities."

As a popular prosecutor, he had a base. With the Watchmen being replicated in other counties, he had a spreading influence.

Although he was technically a Democrat, he admitted that he had little time for either the Republican or Democratic parties. When the Democratic Party decided to back a liberal candidate for governor, he launched a maverick campaign for the nomination.

He was, he said, a social conservative — he'd never met a Commandment he didn't like — but an economic liberal. He wanted more help for the elderly, more for veterans, a higher minimum wage for beginning workers. He pushed for a state income tax that would apply only to the well-to-do, progressive license fees for automobiles that rose dramatically for cars that cost more than forty thousand dollars.

He took 45 percent of the Democratic vote in a three-way primary, and 59 percent of the vote in the final.

People who liked Goodman said that he was charming, down-to-earth, intelligent. People who disliked him said that he was a rabble-rouser and a demagogue, a Kingfish, a little Hitler — the last accusation pointed at the Watchmen.

Asked about the Hitler comparison, the governor said, "These same people, on both sides, have had this state mired in a political bog for fifty years. Now we're moving again. Now we're getting things done. So we create a volunteer force, to help keep an eye on possible terror targets, to help elderly people get their meals, to help mobilize in case of natural disaster, *and they call them Nazis.* Isn't that just typical? Isn't that just what you'd expect? I have two words for them: 'Fuck 'em.' "

He'd actually said "Fuck 'em," scandalizing the press corps, but nobody else, and his popularity moved up a half dozen points in the polls.

Two years earlier, with Goodman then only a year in the statehouse, Lincoln Bowe was running for a second term in the Senate. He was widely assumed to be an easy winner.

With encouragement from the White House, Goodman had supported a lightweight Democrat named Don Murray, and had been the local force behind the Murray campaign. The president had done a half dozen fund-raisers. The campaign went dirty, and Murray beat Bowe by four thousand votes, with an independent candidate trailing far behind. Goodman and the Watchmen had been either credited or blamed for Murray's win, depending on which party you were from.

The bitterness that flowed from the campaign had never stopped.

Jake made Richmond in two hours and fifteen minutes, including a frustrating six minutes behind a fifty-mile-per-hour, boat-towing SUV that precisely straddled the highway's center line; and an accident in which a blue Chevy had plowed into the rear of another blue Chevy. A highway patrolman was talking to the Chevy drivers, both women in suits, while ignoring the traffic jam they were creating.

By the time he got to Richmond, he was pissed, and Richmond was not the easiest place to get around, a knotted welter of old streets cut by expressways. Goodman's office was in the Patrick Henry Building on the southeast corner of the Capitol complex.

Jake found the building, and after ten minutes of looking, spotted an empty parking space four blocks away, parked, and plugged the meter. He got his cane and briefcase out of the backseat, walked over to Broad Street, across Broad past the old city hall, and left along a brick walkway.

The walkway and the capitol grounds

were separated by a green-painted wrought-iron fence; the fence was supported by posts decorated as fasces, which made Jake smile. As he approached the Patrick Henry Building, he saw two Watchmen sitting on a bench outside the door, taking in the sun. They were in the Watchman uniform of khaki slacks, blue oxford-cloth shirts, and bomber jackets.

When Jake came up with his cane, they stood, two tall, slender men, friendly, and one asked, "Do you have an appointment, sir?"

"Yes, I do, with the governor."

"And your name?"

"Jake Winter."

One of the men checked a clipboard, then smiled and nodded. "Go right ahead."

As Jake started past, the other man asked, "Were you in the military?"

Jake stopped. "Yes. The army."

"Iraq? Syria?"

"Afghanistan," Jake said.

"Ah, one of the snake eaters," the man said. "Have you thought about joining the Watchmen?"

"I don't live in Virginia," Jake said.

"Okay," the man said. "We'll be coming to your neighborhood soon. Think it over when we get there."

"You were in the army?" Jake asked.

"He was a fuckin' squid," the other man said. "Excuse the language."

Jake laughed and said, "See you," and went inside.

Inside he found an airport-style security check. Goines showed up, apparently alerted by the Watchmen, as Jake was processing through the X-ray and metal detectors.

"Mister Winter?" Jake nodded, and as he retrieved his briefcase and cane, Goines said, "This way."

Goines was annoyed. A small blond man with a dimpled chin, a ten-cent knockoff of his boss, he carried a petulant look. His eyes were like a chicken's, and like a chicken, he cocked his head to the side to look at Jake as they rode up a couple of floors in the elevator. He led the way to his office, past a secretary in an outer cubicle, and said, "This better be important," and pointed at a chair as he settled behind his desk.

"There are some indications that the Watchmen may be involved in the detention of Lincoln Bowe," Jake said, crossing his legs. "The president wants me to find Bowe. He wants me to find him now."

"What indications?"

"Rumors, mostly," Jake said. "The FBI investigation is picking up vibrations that the Watchmen are involved, or, at least, that a lot of people think so."

"That's a bunch of crap." Goines stood up again, walked over to his window, hands in his pants pockets, looked out his office window. He had a view of an aggressively blank-walled building on the other side of the street, part of a medical center. "People seem to be lining up to shoot at us. If it turns out that a Watchman is involved, he's on his own, he's an outlaw. We sure as hell don't condone it."

Jake said, "Just before he disappeared, Bowe called the governor a cocksucker."

Blood drained away from Goines's face, and a quick tic of fear passed across it. He shook his finger at Jake but said, casually enough, "That was unforgivable. Governor Goodman is a sophisticated gentleman, a successful lawyer before he entered public service. He understands the likes of Lincoln Bowe. He would never go after Bowe, but you can't blame him for not liking a man who could be so vulgar. He won't be pleased with the prospect of tearing up the Watchmen on Bowe's behalf."

Jake thought, *Jesus, I haven't seen a*

tap dance like this in years. Is this place bugged?

"I can absolutely understand that and so does the president," Jake said. Bureaucratic-speak: he could do it as well as anyone, or even better. "The president said, 'I trust Governor Goodman implicitly, but that doesn't mean that there might not be some rotten apples at the bottom of the barrel.' And that's all I'm asking: that you check for rotten apples."

"The governor can speak to that. But you must have heard that some of us think that Bowe has gone on a little vacation, and is letting us twist in the wind."

"We're looking into that, too," Jake said.

"Good." Goines looked at his watch: "One minute: let's go see the governor."

4

The governor's outer office was a large, cool room with gray fabric chairs and mahogany tables, decorated with bald eagles — wildlife paintings of the kind seen on postage stamps, eagles with talons extended, about to land on weathered branches, or soaring over lakes with white-capped mountains in the background. A two-foot-long bronze eagle launched itself off a stand in the center of the room; a bronze scroll of the U.S. Constitution was draped over the stand.

An elderly secretary and a blond college intern worked behind a double desk. The elderly woman called into the governor's office, and the intern smiled at Jake and didn't stop smiling.

"I'll tell the governor you're waiting," the older woman said.

Arlo Goodman was a friendly guy, big white teeth, blond hair falling over his forehead, flyaway, as though he'd been running his fingers through it. He was in shirtsleeves, the sleeves rolled up. He stuck his head out of his office door, something Danzig would never have done with a subordinate, and said, "Hey, Jake, come on in. You want some coffee or water?"

"Coffee would be good," Jake said. They did the Arlo Goodman left-handed shake — Goodman had taken a Syrian bullet in the right hand, and the bones had been shattered, leaving a knot of shrunken fingers.

To his secretary: "Jean, could you get that?"

She went off to get it and Goines said, "I'll let you guys talk."

Goodman nodded and led Jake into his office, asked, "What've you been doing about the limp, you gimpy fucker? You working the leg?"

"It's about as worked as it's going to get," Jake said. Goodman had done research on him; he pretended not to notice. "I keep stretching it, but it's maintenance. How's the hand?"

Goodman grimaced: "Same as with your leg. Not much point. Too much nerve damage. I can poke a pen through, to sign my name, so that's a benefit."

A minute more of physical-rehab chatter, then Jean arrived with the coffee — plain, heavy earthenware cups — and when she'd

86

shut the door behind her, Goodman said, "I'm scared to death about Lincoln Bowe, Jake. He's a fool, but I wouldn't want any harm to come to him — for my own sake, if nothing else. I've got all these rumors bubbling around me . . . I mean, Jesus."

"What's there to be scared about?"

Goodman was deadly serious now: "Come on, man."

Jake shrugged. "All right."

Goodman pointed him at a chair in a conversation group, slumped in one opposite. "Jake: I'm sure you've been researching me, so you probably know my stump speech. This country is at a crossroads. We are losing the thing that makes us American. The idea is what holds us together: the idea in the Declaration, the idea in the Constitution. But the people running the country now — not the president, he's a good man — but the Congress, and these people flooding across our borders, the South Americans, the Caribs, the Africans, the Arabs, they have one thing in common: they're out to rip this country for whatever they can get out of it. End of story. They don't care about freedom of speech, freedom of religion, all the rest of it . . . Well, like I said, you know the stump speech."

"I do." Jake waited.

"We're the counterpressure against those things. People are constantly trying to bring us down, to shut us up. Bowe was one of those people. And he wasn't fair about it — he wasn't willing to take you on in open debate. He'd use any little piece of dirt he could find, real or imagined, to malign anyone on the other side of the question. He'd do *anything* . . . which was one reason we'd never do anything aimed at him. We'd never give him an excuse. Now this." Goodman turned away and looked out his office window, toward the capitol. "Do you know Madison Bowe?"

"I've met her."

"So have I," Goodman said, grinning. "She's quite the little package. Tits and ass and brains and, worst of all, professional camera training. Did you know she used to be a reporter here in Richmond? Pretty hot, too."

"I saw something in her biography," Jake said.

"And now, she's your basic political nightmare, if you're on the wrong end of things," Goodman said. "If she'd married me, instead of Bowe, I'd be the president by now." He laughed and turned back to his desk. Chatter done. "So what does Bill

Danzig want? You're doing what? An investigation? An inquiry?"

"A search," Jake suggested. "Ordered by the president. Bowe is being used to hammer you and we're getting the ricochets. It's getting worse. We've got the convention coming up."

"If there weren't any ricochets, would they still be worried?" Goodman asked.

He was teasing, and Jake had to laugh. "Worried, but less worried," he said.

"That's what I figured. Danzig doesn't take his eye off the ball," Goodman said. "So, what specifically are you going to do?"

"I'm gonna find him — Lincoln Bowe — one way or another. I'm bringing in some FBI heavyweights. I may go to Homeland Security, the Secret Service, whatever. I'm going to squeeze. Some of your Watchmen, among other people."

"Mmm." Goodman peered at Jake for a moment, weighing him. Then, "We had nothing to do with the disappearance of Lincoln Bowe. You should convey that to the president."

Jake said, "Are you talking for yourself, or the whole state of Virginia?"

Goodman was irritated. "For myself and the people around me. I obviously can't speak for everybody."

"Mrs. Bowe says the Watchmen are involved. And after the incident at her house . . ."

"That was a mistake made by a low-level Watchman, and he has been thoroughly counseled on his mistake," Goodman said. "I've sent a letter of apology to Mrs. Bowe, with my personal guarantee that she can return to her farm with no fear of any interference. She has an absolute right to do that as an American. The Watchmen are not thugs, and we don't tolerate any thuggishness."

"You can understand her fear . . ."

"And perhaps you can understand ours, and why that poor dumbass Watchman did what he did," Goodman said, now with some heat. "She has been throwing mud at us, just like her husband did. Calling us Nazis, telling people that we're no better than the Klan. Slandering fine people who are only trying to heave this country up out of the mess that people like Lincoln Bowe got us into. Now, she's trying to claim that we kidnapped her husband and probably killed him. It's utter, errant nonsense."

"Governor, nobody ever thought you would have given an order to get rid of

Lincoln Bowe. You're far too smart for that . . ."

"I'm too *moral* for that," Goodman interjected.

"I'm absolutely willing to believe you," Jake said. "But what if some Watchman somewhere decided that he'd had enough? Who thought he'd be doing you a favor? Like this guy who went to Mrs. Bowe's house? Somebody who believes in direct action?"

Goodman: "You know John Patricia? The Watchman director?"

"I know who he is."

"We've had him looking for exactly that. We've had him talking to our organizers at the county level and even at the town level. Looking for anything that might point to a Watchman involvement with Bowe. So far, nothing. So far, we've been chasing our tails."

"So you're looking."

"We are looking and we will continue to look," Goodman said.

"If you find anything, you will get in touch with me?" Jake asked.

"We will. Or the FBI, if that's appropriate."

They talked for another ten minutes, the governor adamant that Bowe's disappearance must, in some way, have been brought about by Bowe himself — or maybe, though he didn't believe it, was a routine crime gone bad, a robbery that turned into murder, with the body dumped in the woods.

"But that . . ." He shook his head. "I don't believe that. These guys he drove away with . . . they sound like feds, to me. He didn't do anything that'd get him picked up by some, you know, intelligence organization, did he? I mean, he was on the Senate Intelligence Committee, he'd know all kinds of weird stuff."

"I don't think so. Mrs. Bowe sort of agrees with you on this — she says the cause is close by. It's no big international conspiracy."

"She's right," Goodman said. "But she thinks I did it, and I think Bowe did it. He's involved somehow. He engineered this, and it's working."

"You have no proof."

"No. Of course not. If I had it, I'd be shoving it down their throats." Goodman smiled again, quickly. "Even if I didn't have it, but I was pretty sure about it, I'd stuff it down their throats. But I got nothin'."

End of interview. They both stood up

and Goodman reached out to shake hands again. "If you need *anything,* call Ralph. Any time of day or night," Goodman said.

"Thanks," Jake said, and moved toward the door.

Goodman asked to his back, "Would you do it again? The combat?"

Jake stopped and nodded. "Yes. I would."

"Did you like it?" Goodman was grinning at him.

"Yes. Judging from your question, you did, too."

"We're a couple of unfashionable motherfuckers," Goodman said, walking over to his desk. "Stay in touch, Jake."

Goines gave him a private cell-phone number and left Jake at the elevators. Jake was almost out of the building when a woman's voice called to him: "Mr. Winter."

He looked to his left. The intern from Goodman's office was standing in a side hallway. She held up a hand and folded her fingers toward herself. Jake stepped over. "Can I help you?"

She was a tall blonde, a southern belle, busty, long legs, pink tongue touching her puffy lips. Her skirt and blouse cost somebody a couple of hundred bucks each, he thought, and her silk vest looked like Hermès. "There's a man named Carl V. Schmidt in a town called Scottsville," she said. "He's a Watchman. Goodman and Patricia and Goines are worried about him. They're trying to find him and they can't. They think he might have something to do with Lincoln Bowe."

"Carl V. Schmidt."

"That's right. I printed out his name and address." She handed him a slip of paper. "My name's on there, too. You can call me at the house."

"Why are you telling me this?"

"Because I don't like Arlo," she said. "He's crazy. He wants to be president, and that wouldn't be good. He also wants to sleep with me. Which he won't get to do."

Jake smiled at her. "You're not worried about all this?"

She shook her head and smiled back. "My old man's got more money than Jesus Christ and he's a big contributor. Arlo won't lay a finger on me."

"But you *work* for Arlo . . . ," Jake said, picking up her use of Goodman's first name.

"Because I'm a poli-sci major," she said. "He's nuts, but he's the governor. He's an opportunity. Anyway, check out Carl V.

Schmidt, and if it comes to anything, remember my name, and get me a job. I'll take anything in the White House. I work really hard and I'm really smart."

Jake nodded: "Thanks. If anything happens, I'll call."

"Thank *you*." She turned and tripped away, down the side hall. Jake looked after her for a moment, watching her ass, and she knew it without turning around. She lifted a hand and twiddled her fingers at him, good-bye.

Very attractive, Jake thought, as he headed toward the door, and so *young,* for such treachery.

In his office, the governor picked up a phone, tapped a number, said, "Give me a minute."

Darrell Goodman arrived two minutes later, from his cubbyhole office on the floor below. "I talked to Winter," the governor said. "He's doing what he said he was going to do: he's jacking people up."

"Want us to track him?"

"I can't decide. There are some risks . . ."

After a moment of silence, Darrell said, "I could probably get online access to Winter's cell-phone account, the billing records. We wouldn't know what he was saying, but we'd know where he was, and who he was talking to."

"What are the chances of getting caught?"

"Nil. We monitor from a phantom account and do the access from public hot spots."

"Fuckin' with a White House guy is different than fuckin' with Howard Barber," Arlo Goodman said.

"Be a very light touch," Darrell said.

"Then do it," Goodman said. He picked up a soft rubber exercise ball from his desk, pushed it between the fingers of his ruined right hand, tried to tense the fingers. "We're getting behind here. We need somebody we can squeeze. We need him now."

Out on the street, Jake got on his cell phone and called Novatny at the FBI.

"I've got a name for you. Could you run it? And could you find out where a town called Scottsville is? I think it's over by Charlottesville, maybe south?" He explained about the tip, without identifying the girl who had given it to him. On the note, she'd given her name as Cathy Ann Dorn, along with a local Richmond phone number.

While Novatny ran the name, Jake walked back to his car, edged back onto the streets, looking for an entrance to the interstate. Novatny called back: "Do you have any good reason to think this guy might be a problem?"

"No — just that my source said that Goodman and Patricia are looking for him, and think he might be involved."

"So what are you going to do about him?"

Jake frowned, said, "Hey, Chuck — what's up? What'd you find?"

"We found quite a bit on him. One of the things is, he's got more guns than the National Guard."

"What else?"

Carl V. Schmidt was a failed entrepreneur, Novatny said. He'd failed as an upholsterer, a dry cleaner, a cosmetics salesman, a limo driver, a lunch-van driver for construction sites, owner-operator of a security service, and twice as a real estate agent. Fifteen years earlier, he'd been given a general discharge from the navy, which wasn't good. He tended to drink and fight, the navy reports said.

He'd had property attached both by Virginia and the U.S. government, for failure to pay taxes. He'd worked off the debts, eventually, and currently was up-to-date. He'd once been charged with fraud, but apparently paid back the victim, and the charges had been dismissed.

"He worked the MacCallum campaign, in the Senate election two years ago," Novatny said. "There's a notation in here . . ." He paused, apparently looking for it, then read, "Quote: Both the Murray and the Bowe campaigns complained that cars with their bumper stickers were systematically damaged. That seven houses in Lexington with Bowe yard signs were splashed with paint, apparently from paint balloons. Police questioned Schmidt and several others. All were released for lack of proof."

"The Macs were bad news, some of them," Jake said. "Fruitcakes."

"He's a member of a gun club and the NRA. He owns, let's see, sixty-four guns," Novatny said. He counted them out: "Fifteen rifles . . . ten shotguns . . . and thirty-nine handguns. Yeah, sixty-four. Jeez. The guns, let me see . . . mmm, they're not collector items, they're shooters."

"So what do you think?"

"There's nothing that suggests he ever had anything to do with Lincoln Bowe,"

Novatny said. "If you think the tip is real, we could track him."

Jake hesitated, then said, "Let me think about it."

Novatny: "There's a tendency for you political people to keep things off-the-record. I understand that, given your job. But if you're gonna look into this yourself, take it easy. I've seen bios like this before. The guy could be a problem."

"Maybe if I eased up on him," Jake suggested.

"I don't want to hear about it. Stay in touch. If you actually find a single thing that could tie him to Bowe, call us."

"Talk to you tonight," Jake said. "Could you e-mail me that file? Like, right now?"

"You'll get it in two minutes," Novatny said.

A well-tended fiftyish matron was waiting at a stoplight and Jake pulled over, stepped out of the car: "Excuse me? Do you know if there's a Starbucks around here?"

She checked him out for a moment, looked at the Mercedes-Benz star on the front of the car, then smiled. Somebody of her own class: "If you go three blocks straight up this street, you'll see a Pea-in-the-Pod shop. Turn right and go one block."

"Thanks."

The Starbucks was a hot spot. He parked, went inside, got a croissant and a grande latte, took his laptop from his briefcase and went online.

The file was there. Along with the information on Schmidt, Novatny included a map of the Scottsville area, pinpointing Schmidt's house just off Highway 20, and across the James River south of the town. Scottsville was, as Jake thought, south of Charlottesville.

He finished eating, closed down the laptop, went to his car and pointed it out onto I-64.

There is no easy way to get from Richmond to Scottsville. Jake took I-64 west to Zion Crossroads, then south through Palmyra to Fork Union, and then west into Scottsville. When he saw the town, he remembered going through it on trips south of Charlottesville along Lee's route of retreat from Richmond to Appomattox, which was farther southwest.

He actually didn't remember the town so much — it had seemed to be a depressing place when he'd gone through before — as he remembered the bridge, a humped structure over the normally turbid James. Now, with all the rain they'd had in the spring, the river was rolling heavily against the bridge, showing some power.

The bridge was on Highway 20, south. Schmidt lived on County Highway 747, which was more of a lane than a highway, running in a loop off Highway 20. The house itself, painted a faded turquoise with a dirty blue trim, was not much better than a shack, and was sited almost beneath a line of high-tension electric wires.

An unpainted tin carport stood empty on the left side of the house, except for an old washer-dryer and a stack of two-by-fours. An ancient Ford tractor with rotting tires sat in a clump of weeds behind the house. An iron stake in the front yard, surrounded by a circular bald spot in the overgrown grass, suggested a large dog sometimes kept on a chain.

No dog visible. The front blinds were open. Could be a dog inside. From the road, he could see a sheet of white paper hanging on the door.

In training for Afghanistan, Jake had taken a course in burglary — what the army called surreptitious entry — from an ex-burglar hired by the CIA. It turned out that surreptitious entry was not particularly practical in Afghanistan, but the training had been interesting.

After three passes, he slowed and turned into Schmidt's driveway.

Just to knock, and maybe get a look at the door . . .

The paper on the door was from the Watchmen: *Carl: Please call in. We'll be at headquarters until 5 o'clock. This is super-important. Dave Johnson, District Coordinator, Watchmen.*

The paper was limp with humidity, as though it had been on the door for a while.

Jake knocked: no barking — but the door was probably the newest piece of the house, a solid chunk of wood with two small view windows and a big Schlage lock. His elementary burglary skills were not going to work with it.

He walked around to the front. Same thing: old house, new door.

He walked around to the carport again, knocked, called: "Anybody home?"

The house was isolated, the occasional car buzzing by on Highway 20, out of sight, and the occasional bee from the weed patch out back. He took a quick trip around it. The house was set on a concrete-block foundation, so there might be a basement, but if so, it was windowless. The house windows were fairly high — Jake was tall, but their lower sills were almost chest high on him. The window glass was dirty enough that he couldn't see much. Still, no barking, no sound from inside.

The carport entry was obviously the main one. Jake remembered one more thing from the surreptitious-entry course. The instructor said, "A lot of people hide a key outside the house. If they're going to do that, it's gonna be in about one of nine places: repeat after me . . ."

He found it in the wrecked washing machine, in the lint filter.

The house was dim and smelled of old moldy wallpaper. The floorboards creaked underfoot as he walked through it. Once inside, there was no point in being casual: he hurried through, calling, "Hello? Hello? Mr. Schmidt?" No answer.

The house had two bedrooms, a small living room, a kitchen with a breakfast nook, a bathroom, and a basement that smelled of dirt and propane. One of the bedrooms had four Browning gun-safes lined up against a wall. There was no chance that he could have opened them, if he'd had to; but he didn't have to, since the safe doors were standing open, and all four were empty.

He started looking for paper, or blood, or anything that would tie Schmidt to anything relevant. He went through the kitchen, checked the area around the telephone, the kitchen counter drawers, the stove drawer. He found paper, all right, but all of it was routine. Four phone bills, all old, all checked off with an ink scrawl, which probably indicated that they'd been paid. He stuck them in his pocket.

The kitchen cupboards were bare: they'd been completely cleared out. The refrigerator was empty and unplugged.

He went into the bedroom, found a three-inch stack of porno magazines under the bed, with maybe fifty gun magazines. Nothing under the mattress. There were still a few shirts hanging in the closets, some shoes on the closet floor, a few T-shirts and golf shirts in the bureau. He patted through them, found nothing. He did a tap dance on the floorboards, looking for a hidey-hole.

Noticed that there was no suitcase in the house; there were no bags at all.

The living room was spare. He gave it a

minute, rolling an old couch up to look at the lining, rapped the floorboards and moldings, then gave up. A hallway showed a hatch that led up into the eaves. He pulled out a chair, pushed on the hatch, pushed harder. Dust began to fall out, and he let it go.

Into the basement, feeling the pressure of time. Damp. A jumble of cheap tools, rusting pliers, a five-dollar socket set, a broken coping saw, were strewn on a chest of drawers used as a workbench. A reloading bench sat in a corner, with a rack of brass and powders above it. A furnace and a water heater. Nothing much. He was about to head back up the stairs when he noticed a circular mark on the concrete floor: one end of the workbench had been rotated away from the wall. He listened for a moment, tension building — he'd been inside too long — then grabbed a corner of the bench and pulled it out from the wall.

Nothing behind it. Then he looked up: an aluminum heating duct was fastened between two joists. There was a space between the duct and the first floor's subfloor. If you stood on the workbench . . .

He climbed up on it, slipped his hand up and down the top of the vent. At the far left side, he touched something, pulled his hand back. Couldn't see. Tentatively touched it again. Felt like . . . rags. He gripped it. Heavy. Pulled it out.

A bundle of rags. He knew without looking what was inside: a gun. He carefully unwrapped the bundle and found a Colt .45. One of Jake's personal favorites . . .

All right. The guy had four gun safes upstairs, once presumably full of guns, now all gone — and he'd hidden a .45 in the basement? What was that about? He weighed the options for a moment, then put the gun back, jumped down, pushed the bench back against the wall.

He'd have to think about all this, but first, he had to get out. The burglar/instructor suggested that you never stay inside a house more than four or five minutes: even if nobody comes, you begin to screw up, you leave behind prints, you give people a chance to see your car.

Jake hurried upstairs, peered through the windows. Nobody there, nobody coming. He slipped out, let the door latch behind him, put the key back in the washing machine. Picked it up again, wiped it, and still holding it in his shirtsleeve, dropped it back in place.

Walked back to his car, feeling self-righteous: *Nope, I wasn't in there, just knocked on the door. . . .*

Got in the car and let out a breath. Damn: he hadn't been that tense since Afghanistan. But he was smiling when he backed out of the driveway. He could feel the rush coming on. Feel the rush . . .

Schmidt was running. He might have expected to come back, but not anytime soon. All the perishable stuff was gone, the clothes left behind were all older, worn out, or showing wear. No suitcases, no guns. Had he sold the guns? Maybe the ATF could check; sixty-four guns would be worth at least twenty thousand.

If he'd sold all his guns, he probably was digging a deep hole. If he hadn't, if he'd stored them someplace, then they'd have a lead on Schmidt's best friend . . .

Jake was ten minutes in the car, already north of Scottsville, heading in to Charlottesville, heading home, when Novatny called.

Novatny was running, out of breath, shouting. "Where are you? Jake? Where are you?"

5

"We're moving!" Novatny shouted.

"What? I can't hear you."

"Sorry, I've been running up some stairs . . ." Novatny took a deep breath. "We're getting a helicopter, heading out to Virginia. Are you still in Richmond?"

"I'm down south of Charlottesville."

"Then you're a hell of a lot closer than we are," Novatny said.

"What happened?"

"The Buckingham County sheriff's office has a body out in a rural area, a state forest, all burned up," Novatny said. "They found a charred ID near the body. The ID belongs to Lincoln Bowe."

"Ah, man."

A moment of confused shouting at the other end, then, "We've got a chopper coming, oughta be off the ground in five, ten minutes. There's a place down there, called, let me see, on my map it's called Sliders, but it doesn't look like there's anything there. Here. Head south on Twenty . . ."

"Hang on, hang on, let me pull over."

Jake pulled into a driveway, got a notebook from his briefcase, and jotted down Novatny's instructions. ". . . take a left on 636. You go in there a way, couple of miles, and you'll come to the Appomattox-Buckingham State Forest headquarters. They're telling us that's the best place to put down a chopper."

"Have you talked to Danzig?"

"No. I can't get to him direct, I'd have to go through some routing. If you can call him direct . . ."

"I'll call him. See you at the park."

Jake backed out of the driveway, floored it, and the Mercedes took off like a scalded rabbit. He was forty miles away. He had to slow down going through Scottsville, but he didn't slow much and turned heads as he went through. *No cops,* he thought, *no cops, please no cops . . .*

Over the bridge and out on Highway 20, past Schmidt's place again, he swerved around a log truck, pushed it to eighty. The countryside was rolling, the road was curvy: perfect for a high-speed run in a German car if you didn't mind killing the occasional housewife out to get her mail from the roadside mailbox.

He worried about that, a little, but didn't

slow. Instead he compounded the sin by punching Gina's number on his cell phone. She came up and he said, "I need Danzig right now."

"He's talking to the president," she said.

"Go get him."

"Really?"

"Go in and get him. Get him!" Jake shouted.

"I'm going to put you on hold . . . hang on."

Danzig came up, a worried cut in his voice: "What?"

"The FBI has a burned body down south in Virginia. There's a possibility that it's Lincoln Bowe."

"A good possibility?"

"A charred ID was found nearby and it's his. The FBI's moving on it. I'm forty miles away in a car, heading down there fast as I can. We might need somebody to sit on the sheriff's department, if it's not too late. You gotta tell the press office, get them working."

"Charred?"

"I don't know what that means. But apparently, the body's pretty badly burned."

"Why are you only forty miles away?"

"I'll tell you about it later. It might not

be a coincidence," Jake said.

"All right, all right. You go, I'll take care of it at this end," Danzig said. "Call me back for anything significant. Anything, even if you think I might already know about it. Call me."

He kept the car at eighty, screamed through Dyllwyn, a fast right, then another right onto Highway 60 at Sprouse's Corner, seventy miles an hour past the county courthouse at Buckingham — hell, none of the cops would be there, he thought — a left on 24, six miles, a helicopter overhead the last mile of it, rolling through the intersection of 636 and coming up on the forest headquarters complex as the black helicopter put down in a graveled parking area.

Three Buckingham County sheriff's cars waited on the edge of the parking area, their light racks turning. As Jake pulled in, Novatny and Parker did the weird getting-out-of-a-helicopter hunched-over high step that everybody did. They were trailed by a senior citizen who clutched a hard plastic briefcase. A sheriff's deputy got out of one of the cars and jogged toward Jake, who parked just inside the turnoff.

"Sir, this is a restricted area."

"I'm with them," Jake said, pointing at the chopper.

Novatny and Parker were talking to another uniform, Novatny waving Jake over. He and the cop walked over and Novatny nodded at the senior citizen and said, "Jake, this is Clancy, he's with our crime-scene unit, and this is Sheriff Bill Winsome, his people are working the scene right now." Then Novatny asked, "What the heck did you do? You start talking to people and we get a burning body the next day."

Jake said, "Hey, I just put out the word."

Parker said, "Somebody sure as shit got it. We'll want to know who you talked to."

All the cops looked at Jake for a beat, then Novatny turned back to Winsome. "You were saying . . ."

"Somebody tried to burn the body with brush and gasoline. You can still smell a little gas," Winsome said. He was an elderly man, with a round pink face and white hair growing out of his ears. He had the sad liquid eyes of a bloodhound. "The wood is still damp from all the rain and didn't burn. They had it stacked around the body like one of them pyres."

"What about the head?" Parker asked.

"Still no head," the sheriff said.

"What about the head?" Jake asked.

"The head's missing," Winsome said. "It's hard to tell what happened, exactly, because . . . well, if you've ever seen a burned body, they sorta melt. This one's pretty bad, the hands are gone, most of the feet . . . but there should be a skull, or indications of a head, and there isn't one. A head. Of course, we haven't been all the way through the ashes, but I don't think there's gonna be anything there."

"Who found the body?" Jake asked.

"Guy who lives down there — Glenn Anderson — saw a fire last night. Where there shouldn't be one —"

"He didn't go over and check it?" Parker interrupted.

"No, that happens from time to time, you get people out on them hiking trails. Anderson was out working in his shop, changing the oil in his brush cutter, and he heard this whoosh, and he looked, and here's a fire as big as a house. It died down pretty quick, and wasn't any threat because it's been so wet. He figured some camper poured white gas on his campfire and got more than he bargained for. But then he got to talking to a neighbor this morning — they could smell something bad — and they went over for a look."

"Roast pig," Novatny said.

"Where's the scene?" Jake asked.

"Mile or so up the road, there's a trail head, a hiking trail goes back into the woods," the sheriff said. "It's pretty narrow up there, lots of trees, thought it'd be better to put the chopper down here."

"Who knows about this?" Parker asked.

"Nobody, except the people out here," the sheriff said. "Won't nobody find out about it until I say so, either, or somebody'll wind up with their ass kicked up around their ears."

Jake drove, trailed by the two cop cars, Novatny, Parker, and the sheriff riding with him. Clancy rode in one of the sheriff's cars. The sheriff, in the backseat, said, "I think maybe they got more of a fire than they expected, panicked, and ran. People think you sprinkle a gallon of gas on a bunch of wood and you get a campfire. What you get is more like an explosion. You can burn your ass off if you're not careful."

The road was narrow, snaking through the woods, past a clear-cut the size of a couple of football fields, then over a hump and down a barely noticeable incline to the trailhead.

A half dozen cop cars with LED racks, a couple of unmarked cars, and a van were pulled into the trailhead parking area. A farmhouse stood on the other side of the road, most of a half mile away, Jake guessed. Maybe a couple of city slickers thought they could get away with a fire, that far from anything. Maybe . . . But why didn't they just bury the body?

Two uniformed deputies and two men in civilian clothes were leaning on car fenders; when Jake pulled in, they straightened up and looked toward the newcomers. Jake got out with his cane, followed by Novatny, Parker, and Winsome. Clancy got out of the sheriff's car and joined them. The odor of roast pig was thin, but definitely in the air. They all turned their noses toward it, looking back into the trees.

Winsome introduced them as FBI investigators, and one of the plainclothesmen, an investigator with the Virginia BCI out of Appomattox, whose name was Kline, said, "Better come on back."

The body was fifty yards into the woods, a small end-of-the-trail clearing, clumps of old toilet paper in the brush, a few bottles and cans, a collapsed plastic trash barrel.

The odor of burned pig was thicker here, with the smudgy underscent of petroleum. Though he'd seen people incinerated by napalm, Jake didn't immediately recognize the body when they stepped into the clearing. It looked more like a rotting tree stump, with a new tree growing up out of the old roots.

"Jeez," Novatny said. They all sidled toward it. The closer they got, the more the body looked like a stump, until the last few feet, when they could see bloody raw fissures in the blackened flesh. It still didn't look human, until Jake went a bit sideways and saw the shoes. The shoes were badly burned, but still recognizable. The victim had been bound with wire to the tree, in a kneeling position, one foot on each side of the tree.

No head.

"Not just wire," Novatny said. "Barbed wire. Wonder if we could trace that? Where they got it."

"Could've just clipped it out of a fence in the night," the sheriff said. "That's what I would've done — if I was going to do this."

"Was he alive? Were they torturing him?" Jake asked.

"Have to wait for the autopsy," the

sheriff said. "But nobody heard anything. No screaming, or shouting. No commotion. I don't know why you'd wire him up if he was dead — why not just lay him down on a big stack of wood, and pile some more up around him?"

"Nobody saw a car?"

"No. After the fire died down, Anderson went back to changing his oil, he never saw a car leave. They must've come in here with a car, though. Didn't see much in the way of tracks, it's all gravel and bark in the parking area."

"You done with the photos?" Clancy asked, looking at the sheriff.

"Yeah . . . got video and stills both. We were waiting for you before we did any more."

Clancy walked once around the body, then stepped close, knelt on a bare patch of ground, took a short metal rod out of his case, and began pushing a shoe off the remains of a foot. The shoe fell apart, exposing a patch of reddened flesh. Clancy took another instrument from his case, a nine-inch-long polished steel tube that looked a bit like a syringe, cocked it by sliding the barrel, as if it were a tiny shotgun, pressed the tip against the red flesh, and squeezed. The instrument snapped, they all jumped, and Clancy pulled it back and stood up.

"How long?" Novatny asked.

"Pretty good sample. Ten minutes," Clancy said. He put the sampler in his case and snapped the case. "I'll go back to the car and do it."

"Ten minutes?" The sheriff's eyebrows were up. "How reliable?"

"With a good sample, ninety percent," Clancy said. "I've got a digital DNA record in my laptop."

"How come that doesn't get down to us?" the sheriff asked. "On-scene DNA could be handy."

Clancy shrugged. "You could have it if you wanted it — but the machine costs seventy grand, and it's about two grand per test, counting amortization on the equipment. Regular's what, a hundred and fifty bucks, for a two-day wait?"

"No head," Jake said, as Clancy disappeared back down the track. "No blood? Any sign of a struggle, any . . ."

"What you see is what we got, other than the ID," Winsome said. "We've already bagged the ID. We could do some soil tests, but we wouldn't learn much. The autopsy ought to tell us if he was alive."

Jake looked at Novatny: "Christ, I hope it's not him."

Parker said, "Chuck, it's him. You know it, I know it. The media is gonna go exactly berserk. This is gonna be worse than a Hollywood murder. This is gonna be worse than anything we've ever seen."

They all looked glumly at the body for another ten seconds, and Novatny said, "Well, at least we're not gonna be bored."

"Don't usually smell the gas afterward," Jake commented.

"What?" The sheriff looked at him.

"The gas usually burns up and the smell of the fire cloaks whatever is left. This smells like they either spilled some that didn't burn, or they deliberately sprinkled it around where it wouldn't burn."

"Why?"

Jake shrugged. "I don't know. I'm just telling you that you usually can't smell gas afterwards. At least, you can't smell jellied gas — napalm. Not the day afterwards."

"Well . . ." The sheriff looked for a moment at Jake, then turned to the state investigator and said, "Make a note, I guess."

Jake said, "When the Klan was big, a hundred years ago, they'd lynch black guys they thought had raped or killed or smart-assed a white woman." He nodded at the body. "Sometimes they'd use barbed wire and wire the victims to trees, or light posts, and set them on fire. They often castrated them. I never heard about them taking a head, though."

"Is that right?" the sheriff asked.

"That's right," Jake said. "The barbed wire was kind of a *thing.* It's also the kind of thing that'll get the attention of the TV people."

The sheriff said, "Huh."

Jake said, "So it's possible that they poured the gas on him and got more fire than they expected. But why didn't they just bury him? They could have put him two feet down, two guys working hard, in the time it took to pile up that wood. If they'd done that, he might not have been found for years. Was the fire really meant to burn him up? Or was it an advertisement? This whole scene looks to me like it was designed to get the media to freak out."

The sheriff looked at him closely, starting from his shoes, then asked, "What exactly do you *do?*"

Novatny said, "You know, if that's what it is . . . Jake, fifty people are going to look at our reports, the crime-scene stuff. It's gonna leak."

"That's what I'm thinking," Jake said.

The smell of the body had become intolerable, and there wasn't much to do other than look at it. They were walking out of the woods and met Clancy halfway, coming in.

He nodded. "It's him."

Evening was coming on, and with it, the mosquitoes. Jake walked down the road, kicking up little puffs of gravel dust, working his cell phone; Novatny walked the other way, working his.

Danzig said to Jake, "Jesus Christ. Hang on, Jake, Jesus Christ . . ."

Jake heard him, apparently on another phone: "It's him. Yeah, ninety percent, they did DNA on him. Naw, naw, it's him." Talking to the president.

Then he was back: "Does that leave you anywhere to go?"

"Ah . . . maybe."

"Do I want to know about it?"

"No. It's not necessary — yet. And I'm on a cell phone here."

"Okay. Tell me when it's necessary to tell me. Has the FBI detailed anyone to talk to Madison Bowe?"

"Not as far as I know."

"Tell this Novatny guy that I'm calling the director. I want somebody with some rank to do it. I don't want a goddamn sheriff's deputy calling her on the phone. Tell Novatny to coordinate it with the director's office. I'll call the director right now."

"Yes, sir."

Novatny, Parker, and the sheriff were standing in the parking area, waiting for Jake to get off the phone. When he did, Novatny asked, "Now what?"

"The case is yours," Jake said. "Full-court press. You're to coordinate with the director's office on informing Mrs. Bowe. Danzig's calling the director now. He may send the director himself over to tell her."

"That'll put him in a good mood," Parker said. "The director being such a warm human being in the first place."

"This is gonna be the mother of all task forces," Novatny said to Parker. "And we got the gun. We need a full crime-scene crew down here right now. We need guys debriefing the Virginia cops. We need everything."

The sheriff turned up his hands: "Then I'm out of it. Anything you need, call me."

"You don't sound that unhappy," Parker said. "You don't mind a bunch of feds trampling around your jurisdiction?"

An excessively thin smile from the sheriff: "I got five hundred eighty-nine square miles to take care of, that don't have anything to do with U.S. senators getting decapitated and burned at the stake. I'll take care of the five hundred eighty-nine, you take care of the senator. Of course, anything we can do to help, we'll do, you poor fuckers."

Back in the car, heading toward the helicopter, Jake said to Novatny, "About that tip, the guy with the guns."

"Schmidt," Novatny said. "I've been thinking about that, but I didn't want to mention it around the cops. What'd you find?"

"I went by the house, nobody home. I looked in the windows. There are four gun safes in one of the bedrooms, their doors are open, they all look empty. Doesn't look like there's been anybody home for a while. There's a note on the door from the Watchmen, asking him to check in. He apparently hasn't."

"All right." Novatny nodded. "You didn't go inside?"

"Of course not. But I was thinking, you might want to have some of your people take a look at it."

"I'll do that," Novatny said.

"I mean right now. Because I'm gonna call the governor and tell him about the body. He's gonna find out pretty quick anyway, and I want to be on his good side. Just in case that might be useful. If we have to approach the Watchmen . . . Anyway, you might want to have a couple of your guys on the scene before the Watchmen have a chance to go over the place."

Novatny nodded again. "We've got two Richmond guys at a Holiday Inn in Charlottesville, they've been working the case from there," he said, as they pulled up to the chopper. "Give me Schmidt's address and a ten-minute head start."

When Jake was back on the road, he called Goines again, told Goines to find the governor and to have him call back.

"I don't know how fast I can find him," Goines said.

"Make it as quick as you can. Make it an urgent priority," Jake said.

Goodman was back in ten minutes, as Jake was coming into Buckingham, this time at the speed limit. "Mr. Winter? This is Arlo Goodman." A little less friendly than he had been; more formal, as if he were expecting trouble.

"We found Lincoln Bowe's body," Jake said.

Long pause, the airwaves twittering through the cell phone. Then, "Here, in Virginia?"

"Down by Appomattox, between Buckingham and Appomattox."

"Ah, no." He sounded genuinely surprised.

"I thought you'd want to know," Jake said.

"I appreciate it." A little warmer now. Goodman could turn it on and off, even over the phone. "Who else knows?"

"Some cops. The FBI. The president. We're moving to tell Mrs. Bowe. The FBI has taken over the scene, a full crime-scene crew is on the way in. Your BCI guys are already on the scene."

"They didn't call me," Goodman said.

"The sheriff was discouraging calls, knowing that the FBI was on the way," Jake said. "Everybody is walking on lightbulbs."

"They should have called me," Goodman said. His voice was quiet, but suffused with rage. Somebody was in trouble.

Jake asked, "You know anything about this, Governor?"

A pause — a shocked pause? — then,

"What are you talking about?"

"I'm talking about a panic-stricken bunch of Watchmen looking for a gun guy named Carl V. Schmidt. I'm talking about the search being run from your office. Your Watchman even left a note hanging on Schmidt's front door. The feds are closing in on Schmidt's house now. If you guys know anything . . . I mean, it'll all come out in the investigation."

"What's the name again?"

"Carl V. Schmidt."

"I don't know it. The Watchmen are looking for him?"

Jake ignored the lie; it was routine politics. "Yes."

"I'll talk to John Patricia. Right now," Goodman said. "Will you be on this phone?"

"I will."

"I'll get back to you."

Out through Buckingham, at Sprouse's Corner, Jake stopped, looked left. He could take Highway 20 back through Charlottesville, and then north. He could be home in two and a half or three hours. Or he could go straight down Highway 60, back into Richmond. If he went north, he could stop at Schmidt's place and see what the feds were doing. On the other hand,

Danzig would want him doing political assessment, not crime-scene work, about which he knew nothing.

He thought about it for a few seconds, then went straight through the intersection, down 60, back toward Richmond.

Back toward Goodman.

6

Howard Barber arrived late, cursing the traffic, the cops who wanted ID, who might have doubted that he could be both a friend and a Republican, who suspected he might be a media interloper of some kind

Barber disabused them quickly enough. He had an officer's voice, a CEO's voice, the voice of a man who ran one of the hottest high-tech start-ups. They waved him through when he used the voice, pointed him at a parking spot next to a stand of azaleas. Before he got out of the car, he got on his cell phone, checked in with his office: "Hold everything for me, don't put anything through. I'm at the Bowes', it'll take a while."

His secretary said, "You're meeting Price and Walton at six o'clock at the Hay-Adams. You're still going?"

"I'll be there. And call Colonel Lake and tell him what's happening, that I can't get out of this. I'll call him first thing tomorrow."

He clicked off, sighed. He'd dreaded this. He got out of the car, went up the walk, said hello to a couple of people on the porch, got a biceps squeeze from one of them, then pushed into the scrum of people standing in Madison Bowe's living room. Madison was talking to an old friend from Lincoln Bowe's golf club, but broke away and came to Barber and hugged him. "Thanks for coming, Howard."

"Jesus, Maddy . . ."

"We need to talk." People were watching them from around the room, the late senator's wife hugging a strikingly tall, handsome black man who was wearing what appeared to be a five-thousand-dollar suit. You could almost hear the *hmmm.* Madison said, "Let's go, ah, God, not in the kitchen, there are a hundred people in there, let's go somewhere."

He followed her past the stairs to the study. The door was closed, and she opened it and poked her head in, saw that it was empty. "In here."

They stepped inside and she pulled the door closed: "Linc . . . Was it Goodman?"

"I assume so," Barber said.

"Did they torture him? I don't think he could have taken any pain . . ."

"Maddy, I just don't know," Barber said. "Most of my contacts are at the Pentagon, not with the FBI. I called some staff people over on the Hill, but they haven't been able to find out much. I assumed . . . What did the FBI tell *you?*"

"They don't know anything," she said. "This Winter, the guy I told you about — he was apparently there. I tried to call him at home, but he's not answering. I left messages."

"You said he was with Danzig's office."

"That's right. I assume he went down there with the FBI. He said he was going to kick some FBI bureaucrats, get them going. I pointed him at Goodman."

"I doubt that Goodman himself is involved — probably some Watchmen, maybe Darrell Goodman," Barber said. "But Arlo Goodman is too smart . . . Actually, I don't know what I think." He shrugged, and glanced away.

And Madison thought, *He's lying about something.* She said, "I'll try to talk to Winter. I'll try him every fifteen minutes until I get him. He's like you, he was in Afghanistan."

"I know about him," Barber said. "He wrote a book about the Pentagon."

She nodded. "Johnnie Black told me. *Winter's Guide to the Inside.*"

"I think I ought to talk to him," Barber

said. "At some point, we might want to . . . influence the investigation. It'd be better if I did it, than you."

"Okay. When I get him, I'll tell him to call you."

"It'd be better if he called me," Barber said. "And I think it'd be a good idea if you told him about Linc and me. You know, the whole thing. That'd bring him in for sure . . ."

"Oh, Howard . . ." She was appalled.

"Look, it's gonna come out. Better to come out that way."

Barber turned away from her for a moment, staring at the window that was covered with blinds, as though he could see through it. "God bless me." He rubbed his face and then turned back and asked, "How are you holding up?"

"I'm sad, I'm tired, I'm really angry."

"And you're really, really rich."

"Howard . . ." Hands on her hips.

He shook his head, held a hand up, a peace gesture: "Hey, Maddy. Linc once told me that of all the women he'd ever met, you were the only one who'd never thought about his money. I think that's why he went after you."

She teared up, turned away, wiped the tears with the heels of her hands. "God, I hope he wasn't alive. I hope he was dead before they burned him."

"I'm sure he was," Barber said. "I'm sure he was. You gotta believe that, Maddy." After a second, he added, "Talk to Winter."

Jake was on the highway, coming up to Amelia Court House, when Goodman called back and asked, "Where are you?"

"Passing Amelia Court House, heading into Richmond."

"I talked to Bill Danzig. Now I need to talk to you," Goodman said.

"Are you at the office?"

"I'm at the mansion. When you came into the office, did you come in from the capitol side of the building? Down a brick walkway?"

"Yeah."

"The mansion is about, what, seventy-five yards from that. Yellow house, white pillars. There's a gate to the mansion that faces the back entrance of the Patrick Henry. You'll see a guardhouse, right there at the front. I'll put you on the list."

Jake found a parking spot faster than he had in the morning, couldn't read the meter clearly enough to see whether it needed money, plugged it with quarters, tapped along the deserted walkway in the growing darkness. The governor's mansion was a two-story brick house, painted yellow, with four white columns over the front steps. The place was smaller then he'd expected, with a modest lotus-flower fountain in a front parking circle.

At the guard gate, a uniformed guard was talking to a second man. The second man was dressed in a black raincoat, black shirt, black trousers, and black canvas Converse All Stars. He was wearing a khaki tennis hat. He was lean, with a face too weathered for his age, which was about the same as Jake's. With his long nose and black clothing, he had the aspect of a crow. He saw Jake coming, watched him for a moment, then turned away and played with a television at the back of the guard-house.

The guard said, "Jake Winter." Not a question.

"Yes."

"I'll take you in," he said. He popped a latch on the steel gate and led the way across the parking circle, up the steps, and through a double door.

Through the doors, the mansion seemed to expand. A fasces-styled chandelier hung overhead, with a long hall leading to a couple of big public rooms. A portrait of the Virgin Queen looked down the hall at them. The guard pointed to his left: "In here."

A parlor. Goines was standing just inside, leaning against the doorjamb. Three other men, none of whom Jake recognized, were lounging on two long leather couches in a conversation area, briefcases at their feet. Legal pads were strewn across a coffee table in front of them, along with two coffee cups, two bottles of beer, and a silver bowl, shaped like a maple leaf, full of peanuts and M&M's. One man had his feet on the table; another had taken off his shoes to show a pair of dark brown dress socks. A hint of cigar smoke rode on the air; a portrait of George Washington looked down from above.

The room vibrated with cronyism: this was the inner circle, no question about it. And Goodman was the chairman of the board. He sat, squarely, in a huge leather chair, at the head-of-the-table position between the two couches.

"Jake," Goodman said. He stood up, gestured to a smaller, lower leather chair in the foot-of-the-table position. As Jake took it, Goodman said, pointing with his bad hand, "You know Ralph; and John Patricia, Handy Rice, Troy Robertson. Men, Mr. Winter is former special forces, got shot up in Afghanistan."

Robertson said, "You look sort of bureaucratic."

Jake shrugged. "I sit in an office, I'm outa shape. It'd probably take me . . ." — he made a little show of surveying Robertson — _". . . seven or eight seconds to snap your neck."

The staff members laughed, and Goodman smiled down at him. Robertson said, "Snap Goines's. He's getting to be a major pain in the ass."

Rice asked, "You want a beer?"

Jake took the beer, and they went to business.

Goodman said, "Jake, I swear to God, I swear on the bodies of my dead friends in Syria, I swear on anything you want — I had nothing to do with Lincoln Bowe's death. Neither did the Watchmen."

Jake nodded, and waited.

Goodman leaned forward, took a few peanuts from the bowl, rattled them in his fist, like dice. "So . . . now we get to the part where I sound like the psychotic that Madison Bowe says I am. I believe this whole thing is a carefully constructed conspiracy to bring me down. I believe Lincoln Bowe was involved, and probably Madison Bowe. She's been too good at ripping me. It seems scripted. Does that sound insane?"

Jake raised his eyebrows a bit, and then said, "It doesn't sound insane. I don't know whether it's probable."

"Good. That's all we want from you, that attitude," Goodman said. "Danzig says you're the best when it comes to developing information about a confusing political situation. We need information. We're trying desperately to figure out what's happening. Can you see that?"

Jake nodded. "Yeah — because that's what I'm trying to do, too."

"I want to suggest that you do two things at once. Make any assumptions you want. Assume that I did it myself, that I set Senator Bowe on fire after cutting his head off in the kitchen. Okay?"

Jake nodded: "I'm sure the FBI will do that."

"But I want you to make another assumption, too," Goodman said. "*Assume* that there's a conspiracy against me. Start from that point. If you make that assumption, if you look at it that way, too, maybe you can see what we can't. Because I'm telling you, we seem to be getting wound up tighter and tighter in this thing. Like this Carl V. Schmidt. Like Bowe getting immolated here in Virginia. But we didn't have anything to do with it. We are being set up. We can feel it. And it could have serious, serious consequences."

Jake blew a soft note across the top of the beer bottle. "But why? Governor, I don't want to seem insulting, but you're in the last year of your term. You can't succeed yourself. You're about to leave politics, at least temporarily. So why should they bother? A guy is dead — is somebody gonna murder a former senator in a weird conspiracy to get you out of office? I mean, even if they found Lincoln Bowe's head in your bedroom, you'd probably be out of office before they could get you to trial. Or is there something else going on? Something I'm missing?"

Goines jumped in, jabbed a finger at Jake: "That's what we can't figure out. That's exactly it."

"Maybe just pure revenge," Robertson suggested to Goodman. "After your showdown with Bowe. I mean, you really hurt him, there."

"So they kill Bowe to get revenge for

what I did to Bowe?" Goodman shook his head. "You need to spend more time thinking about that, Troy."

"I wouldn't be surprised if that body in the woods isn't Lincoln Bowe at all," Patricia said.

"They did DNA," Jake said.

"For DNA, you have to have two good samples," Patricia said. "Where'd they get the first one? Who was the guy who did the test, and what are his politics like? Did they do backup tests?"

"Forget that, forget that," Rice said to Patricia. "It's Bowe. It'd be too crazy not to be Bowe. Asking those questions makes us sound like we *are* nuts."

"Yeah, but the head's missing," Patricia said. "Why's the head missing? I'll tell you why — they couldn't match the dental."

Jake said, "I hadn't thought of that. That might be something."

Goodman raised a hand, shutting down the argument. "I personally believe it's Bowe. When they finish with the postmortem, we should know. I understand that they are taking hair samples off his pillows, out of his car, and so on. Maybe from his mother. They will know."

Jake broke in: "I have to ask the hard question, Governor. Who's Schmidt, and why have you been tearing up the state looking for him?"

There was a quick interlocking exchange of glances around the room, then Robertson said, "We haven't been tearing up the state."

"There's a letter on the door . . ."

"I'd like you to prove . . . ," Robertson started.

"We looked around for him," said Goodman, closing Robertson down with a finger. "He used to hang around with some Watchmen in Charlottesville. He was never inducted, never trained, never accepted. Our people up there always thought he was a little questionable. Then . . ."

Goodman shrugged and looked at Patricia.

"He mentioned a couple of times to our guys that something should be done about Lincoln Bowe," Patricia said.

"Ah, Jesus," Jake said.

"Yeah. The thing is, he was not one of our guys," Patricia said. "But when we heard about this, we knew we could take the fall for it. So we were trying to find him."

"Why didn't you tell somebody?" Jake asked. "Why didn't you tell me, this morning?"

"Because at that point, it was all politics," Goodman said. Jake nodded: they all
swam in a sea of politics, and the tide
never went out, not even for murder. "Nobody knew where Bowe was. He might
have been skiing in Aspen for all we knew.
There was no evidence of a kidnapping,
there was no evidence of anything. But we
were nervous, and so we looked. Now this.
We feel like we were . . . sucked into
looking for him. Like somebody's been
working hard to set us up."

Jake nodded, and thought about the gun
in Schmidt's house. That did have the feel
of a setup. Why would he empty his gun
safes, and leave one gun stuck away in the
rafters, where an amateur burglar quickly
found it?

"Look at the Bowes," Goodman said, urgency riding in his voice. "Madison and
Lincoln. Look at their friends. Look to see
if you can see anything. Hypothesize something. Suspect something. Try to figure out
what happened. What happened?"

They all sat and looked at each other,
and then Jake said, "I need everything
you've got on Schmidt."

"You'll get it," Goodman said. "So will
the FBI, for that matter. They've already
asked. They're at his house."

"When can I get it?"

"Give us an e-mail address and we'll get it to you tonight or tomorrow morning. So — you're going to do this?"

"I'll talk to Danzig," Jake said.

"Talk to him and get back to us. Ralph will be your liaison." He flipped a finger at his assistant. "He'll be available twenty-four hours a day. If you need anything — anything — call him. Research help, legal advice . . ."

"Muscle . . . ," Patricia said with a grin.

"Muscle won't help," Jake said.

Patricia: "Bowe got his head cut off and then his body was burned. Think about it."

Goines said, "I wonder if this Schmidt guy was the same size and weight as Bowe?"

"That *is* goofy," Robertson said.

"Hey, nobody has any ideas," Goines said. He sorted some M&M's from the silver bowl, tossed them into his mouth. "The way things are, nothing is too far-fetched."

"There's one thing that worries me; one line," Jake said. *Who will rid me of this meddlesome priest?"*

"That's what worries all of us," Goodman said. "If some goof thought he was doing it on my behalf, the murder'll stink like a mackerel in the sunshine and screw up our lives forever."

They talked for a few more minutes, then Jake stood up and said, "I'm going to take off. I need to get back tonight. I've got lines out everywhere, and I'm waiting for people to call."

On the drive back, Jake thought about the group gathered at the governor's mansion: all male, all veterans, all had been in a combat zone. He liked that kind of company, as a general thing.

But there was something not right about Goodman's group. They sparred with one another, like any group of vets; but with Goodman, they behaved as though they were still in the military, and they were subordinate officers. They deferred to him. More than that, they were obedient, subservient. Not like the usual political relationship — not the same relationship of the president to his staff — but a kind of abjectness, concealed beneath a hail-veteran-well-met bonhomie.

But they also projected a genuine air of confusion. They didn't know what was going on, he thought. Bowe's death had them panicked.

Darrell and Arlo Goodman talked in the

first-floor kitchen. "We went through the security tapes. He talked to your intern, the blond chick."

"Cathy . . ."

"Yeah. She stopped him in the hallway when he was coming out of the elevator. He seemed surprised, I don't think he knew her. She gave him a piece of paper. We're up and running on his cell phone, and he made a call from a cell in Scottsville, right by Schmidt's house. He went straight there when he left here."

"So it had to be her."

Darrell nodded. "Unless he talked to somebody in the elevator, and . . . that didn't happen. It's her."

"I sometimes thought . . ." Goodman shook his head. "I wonder what else she's been selling?"

"No way to tell," Darrell said. "What else you got?"

"It'd all be political stuff. Nothing that'd be trouble."

"She doesn't have access to your computer?"

"Not unless she's broken the password," Arlo said. "Besides, she doesn't have a key to the office, and there's always somebody around, even when I'm not. She wouldn't have much time with it."

"Wouldn't need much, if she knew what she was doing," Darrell said. "Slip in a piece of software . . . a keystroke register."

"You want to look?"

"Yeah, I better. I'll get a guy, I'll do it tonight," Darrell said. "Even if it's clean, it'd be better if she were out of your office."

"Can't fire her," Goodman said. "She works hard, she's pretty good. Her old man helped with fund-raising during the campaign."

"I'll take care of it," the man said. "Maybe she gets robbed."

Goodman's eyes narrowed. "Not robbed dead."

"No, no. Dinged up a little."

Jake called Danzig from the car, filled him in on the meeting.

"Goodman wants me to look around on this thing. He says he talked to you."

"Yeah, he did. When I told you to find Bowe, I didn't think you'd find him quite that fast. Or that way. We're all sorta freaked out."

"I hope I didn't trigger an execution. I'd put out word that we'd be looking for him."

"We don't even speculate in that direction," Danzig said. "Goodman is right about one thing, though — we don't know what's going on. We need to know. Right now. If it's something that we can pin on Goodman, something that doesn't impinge on national politics, then we can do that and forget about it. Let Goodman deal with it. If there's more, we need to know about it."

"I've got lines out."

"Keep working them. This is out of control now. It's wall-to-wall on CNN. It's like that hurricane, Katrina, or Katinka, or whatever it was, and nine/eleven."

Jake was tired when he got home, a little hungry, fighting the illusion that he could still smell Lincoln Bowe's roasted body, that the odor hung in his clothes, in his hair. He took a shower, changed into jeans and a T-shirt, padded barefoot down to the kitchen, and poured a bowl of cereal. Two minutes until eleven o'clock. He carried the cereal bowl into the den, turned on the television to catch the beginning of the news cycle; at the same time, he brought up his laptop and linked into the Net.

The television news was all Lincoln Bowe. There were shots of Madison Bowe with a group of senators, standing on the front porch of her town house, swearing for the cameras that the government would hunt down her husband's killers. There was a helicopter shot of Bowe's body being carried out of the woods in a black bag on a stretcher, and of cops working the site.

Madison Bowe said she had no idea why her husband had been killed, other than his ongoing clash with the Virginia Watchmen. "He saw in them a revival of the Ku Klux Klan," she said to the cameras. "A group supposedly of volunteers, whose real purpose is to intimidate the public. He hated that, and he challenged it . . ."

She looked terrific in black, Jake thought.

With one eye on the television, he checked his e-mail. He had a dozen messages, all routine. He hadn't checked his phone since Novatny called, and got him running toward the crime scene: he did it now, found a message from Madison Bowe: "Call me. Please. Anytime before midnight."

He also had a dozen hang-ups. He frowned at that: a dozen was too many. He checked the missed-calls register, and they'd all come from the same cell phone. He dialed the number, but the phone had been turned off.

He thought about calling Madison. He

and Danzig were shuffling between pools of quicksand, and everything they did had to be considered in the light of possible criminal proceedings. On the other hand, he *was* coordinating with the FBI. . . .

She picked up quickly: "Yes?"

"Jake Winter returning your call."

"You live someplace near me, right? Could I come over to talk to you?"

"Mrs. Bowe, things are getting complicated," Jake said.

"I know that. I talked to Novatny," she said. "I need to talk to you. This whole thing may be more in your area than Novatny's."

"The two areas have become somewhat the same," Jake said.

"Listen, can I come over and talk, or what?" she asked.

While he waited for her, he clicked around the cable news channels. They had hardly any real news — aerial tapes of the crime scene, with FBI vehicles clogging the narrow road, Madison Bowe's accusations from *Washington Insider,* taped interviews with the last persons to have seen Bowe alive — but they ran them in an endless loop, interspersed with interviews with prominent politicians and a couple of conservative movie stars.

Madison Bowe arrived at ten o'clock. He'd left the back gate open, and she nosed up to his garage. He let her in the back door, and she walked slowly through the house, appraising the kitchen, touching a table in the hallway that led to the living room, stopping to examine a watercolor, and peered at the newsreader on Fox, on the television in his den.

"She's barely got any clothes on," she said.

"She won't have, if CNN's ratings keep going up," Jake said. "I'm looking forward to the day."

In the living room, Madison settled into an easy chair next to the fireplace.

"This day . . ."

"I can imagine."

"A nightmare. I've got people I don't like all over the place. I've got the media, I've got the FBI . . ."

"It's the only thing on the news," Jake said.

"Yes." She shuddered. "Somewhere, though, Lincoln is laughing. He would have hated to go as an old man with tubes dripping into his veins. He'd have wanted something spectacular. He once told me that if he lived to be eighty-five, he'd buy the fastest Porsche he could find, wind it up to two hundred miles an hour, and aim it at a bridge abutment. The only thing he wouldn't like about this is that Goodman lived longer than he did. He would have hated the thought that he hadn't managed to take Goodman down."

"You don't sound . . . mmm."

"As upset as I might? Dead is dead. I was expecting it, to tell you the truth. I knew he hadn't just wandered off." She exhaled, slumped another inch; her eyes looked tired, with undisguised crow's-feet at the corners. "Do you think this Schmidt person killed my husband?"

He said nothing for a moment, considering her, then said, "I don't know. I'm not trying to avoid the question. I just don't know."

"Are the Watchmen involved?"

He thought about the five men in Goodman's parlor. "I don't know that, either. My inclination, at this moment, is to think they are not."

Now it was her turn to consider him. Finally she said, "They are. Somewhere along the way, somehow, they're involved."

"I don't know that," he said. "I do know that they are running around like chickens over there. Between you and me, I can tell you that Goodman and all of his top people are personally involved in trying to figure out what happened."

"You talked to him?"

"Tonight, at the governor's mansion. They're worried. They believe there's a conspiracy against them. They believe that your husband was part of it, and that you may be."

She shook her head, then asked, "Is it safe to walk here? The streets?"

"Sure."

"So let's take a walk around the block. I mean . . ." She flushed. "If your leg . . ."

"My leg's okay," he said. "Let me get my stick."

They walked down the back stoop, past her car, out the alley to the sidewalk. She said, "Something happened today. Maybe. Everything was moving so fast, everything is so foggy."

"What happened?"

"Let me think about it for a minute . . ."

They'd gone to the left, out of the alley. The corner house had an old-fashioned front porch, and a couple was sitting in a porch swing. Jake tapped along with his stick, and the man called, "Is that you, Jake?"

"Yeah, going for a walk. How're things?"

"Very quiet, when they aren't ripping up the street on your block. You can hear the jackhammers all over the goddamned neighborhood."

"Ought to be done in a week," Jake said. "Then my house will be worth a lot more money."

"But not mine," the man said.

"Suck it up, Harley," Jake said. The woman laughed, and Jake and Madison continued down the sidewalk.

When they were out of earshot of the couple on the porch, Madison said, "I'm telling this to *you,* and not the FBI. The FBI would pretend to hold the information, but there'd be leaks, it'd all be the most cheesy kind of thing . . . I'm telling you because you're political, but you're still in a position where maybe you could get justice for Linc."

"Okay."

They walked along, and then she said, "Lincoln is not — was not — one hundred percent oriented toward women. Sexually."

"Ah, jeez," Jake said, and stopped in his tracks.

"It's not unheard of, even for U.S. senators," Madison said.

"It could have a bearing on the murder,"

Jake said. "It could be a purely personal matter. In fact, if he was romantically active, then there's better than a fifty-fifty chance . . ."

They were facing each other and she reached out and put a hand on his chest. "Gay doesn't mean violent."

"Of course not. But given any kind of secret sex life, and then a disappearance, there's usually a connection. That's just the way it is," he said.

"What, you're the big crime historian now?"

"No. But I read the papers, for Christ's sake."

"If that's what it is, then it will come out. But that really isn't the way it is — I know some of his friends, and they're a good bunch. They're also very, very private, and very sophisticated. They would not murder anybody over an infidelity."

"You can't know that for sure," Jake argued. "All it takes is one crazy guy."

"That's not it," she said. She sounded positive.

"Ah, boy . . ." They turned together and started walking again. Then, "If he was gay, why . . ." He waved his hand, taking her in.

"Did he marry a woman? Because he

wanted a political career. All of his family is involved in politics, one way or another, and a conservative Republican gay was not going to get elected in the state of Virginia."

"That's not what I was going to ask. Why did *you* marry *him?*"

He could see her turn her face away from him, one hand going to her cheek. After a moment, "I wasn't entirely aware of his . . . preferred orientation . . . when we got married. Also, I was tired of bullshit. Especially from men. I'd been in a long relationship that didn't work out, and then I did some running around, and finally . . . I was tired of being chased by men who were more interested in my ass than they were in me. And here came Lincoln. He was smart, good-looking, powerful, he was rich, he was *commanding*. My mother picked up the gay thing, hinted at it before we got married, but there really wasn't a performance issue on his part. We got together okay in bed."

"And . . ."

"After we got married, the sex just drifted away," she said. "Then I became aware that he had other attachments. There was usually an assistant or a political associate whom he was a little too fond of, whom he spent too much time with. Maybe that's why I'm not as out of control as I should be. Linc was more like a favorite uncle. He hadn't been a lover for years. There wasn't that tie."

"Where are we going with this?" Jake asked.

"Well, if it's going to break, we'd like it to break in some civilized way. Not to leak. Not drizzle out. Not with all kinds of denials . . . Maybe, I don't know. It doesn't seem like the kind of thing that you just announce . . . I was hoping you could help."

"Jesus."

"Years ago, the French president had a longtime mistress. Everybody knew, including his wife. They invited the mistress to his funeral, the public pretty much thought that was cool . . . maybe something like that would work with Linc."

"No. Because Linc was murdered. His body was burned in the most spectacular way. If this comes out . . . ah, man."

"Linc had a lover, for a year or so, a few years back. Then they stopped being lovers and got to be close friends, almost like brothers. His name is Howard Barber. He's a tough guy, one of you ex-servicemen, Iraq, and he's very successful. He started a company that sells electronics to the military. He came over this afternoon, after I got the news about Linc. He said it was going to come out. He said there was no way to contain it. He was hoping to find some way to . . . You know."

"Be civilized about it."

"Yes."

"This is not a very civilized country when it comes to stuff like that," Jake said. Then he revised himself: "Actually, the country is civilized, it's the media that're not."

She walked along a little farther, and then she asked, "Can you do something?"

"Let me think about it. I need to talk to Barber."

"Of course."

"And you trust him."

She hesitated, then said, "Yes."

Jake picked up the hesitation: "You *don't* trust him. I could hear it."

"I do trust him . . . or I did trust him." She paused, then added, "When he came over today, he was looking at me. He was checking me out. He kept talking about the Watchmen, and then he was watching me, watching how I reacted."

"I don't understand what you're saying."

"I had the feeling — just a feeling — that he knows more than I do, maybe knows what happened. He was checking me to see what I'd been told about it. To see where the investigation was going. And somehow, he was priming me to be angry. To point me at the Watchmen."

"That's not good," Jake said.

"I might be misreading him. He's got to be freaked out — as I said, he and Linc were really close. When this gay thing comes out, people are going to look at Howard. Big, good-looking guy, always single . . . he hangs out with all the important colonels at the Pentagon, plays poker with them, goes on fishing trips down the bay. You know, the people who buy his products. They're probably not what you'd call gay-centric."

"Probably not," Jake agreed.

They'd turned two corners, and now walked across a street, Jake's street, but went ahead, down another block. Nice walking in the night, humid, cooling, quiet.

"What do you want me to do?" Jake asked.

"Talk to him, talk to Howard. Not as a policeman, but as somebody who knows what the FBI knows . . . and who also knows about this. See if there's anything."

"I can talk to him. But if anything serious comes out of it, I'd have to tell the FBI."

"Of course — if it looks like there's reason to believe that Howard had something to do with it. But he didn't. He wouldn't. He and Linc really were like brothers. He's the last person in the world who'd hurt Linc."

"That makes me suspicious. If somebody told Miss Marple that so-and-so couldn't possibly have done it . . ."

"You'd know who the killer was. I'm not Miss Marple, and Howard didn't kill Linc."

Twenty yards in silence; he could smell her, the scent of flowers, with some spice. Chanel, maybe? Had she put it on just before she came over? He pushed the question away and instead asked, "When did you last see Lincoln?"

"Two weeks before he disappeared. Sometimes I saw him every couple of days, sometimes I didn't see him for weeks at a time. Besides the farm, and the town house here, we have an apartment in Manhattan and a house in Santa Fe," she said. "He was always running around. He missed being in the Senate. He missed it desperately. That's why he hates Goodman, and hates this administration, because he feels that they assassinated him. Though, the last couple of weeks before he disappeared, he finally seemed as if he was a little happier. I don't know if something was going on, but it was as though he'd turned a corner."

"Huh."

They walked along for a while without talking, turning a corner and another one, finally ending back up at Jake's house. They walked down the alley to the backyard, and at her car, she said, "I've got to go. But let me ask you one more thing. Or two things. Personal things, if you don't mind. I talked to Johnnie Black about you . . ."

"Remember, he's on the other side. An evil Republican."

"Like me," she said. He could see her upturned face in the light from his back window. "He said you were in Afghanistan. He said that's where you got your disability. Is that right?"

"I was in the special forces for a few years," Jake said. "What's the second thing?"

"He said you were married to Nikki Lange."

"Yes," he said.

"The Queen of Push."

"I try not to think about it. You know her?"

"I know her. We overlapped a year on the Smithsonian board. I heard a comment about sex and violence." She sounded amused, peered at him in the dark. "That her husband provided the sex and she provided the violence."

He tipped his head back and laughed. "I heard the same comment. It's generally accurate. Looking back, I would have preferred an Afghani prison."

"How could you have done that? Married her?"

"Well, she's an attractive woman," Jake said.

"Big tits, small ass . . ."

"Come on, be nice." Jake said. "Anyway, our politics are generally the same, and like you and Lincoln, we got along pretty well in bed. I just didn't understand that she was the queen and I was the equerry."

"The what?"

"The equerry," he said.

"My, you have a large vocabulary."

"You ought to check out my conjunctions."

"Some other time, maybe," she said. "Do you ride? Johnnie said something about a ranch."

"I probably rode every day of my life from the time I was three until I was fourteen. Until my grandpa died and the ranch got sold. I've still got friends out there, I go out and ride when I can."

"You'll have to come out to my farm sometime," she said. "Of course, we ride the right way."

"We don't have that luxury. Our horses work for a living."

She laughed quickly, quietly, popped open her car door, and looked at him across the window. "Stay in touch with me. Talk to Howard. Help me."

"Mrs. Bowe, I work for Bill Danzig. I'll help you if I can, but my loyalty runs to Bill. And the president."

She nodded: "Then help me if you can."

She got in the car, backed carefully out of the drive. He made sure the gate locked behind her, then went into the house, dropped into the living-room chair, and over a couple of hours, had a couple of beers.

He didn't drink much, and he didn't drink often, and the beer left him a bit loopy.

He thought, *I could end it right now.*

If he called CNN anonymously, or Fox,

or any of the large newspaper chains, and simply said the word *gay,* they'd find out the truth in a matter of hours. And once that word was out there, the investigation would go in an entirely different direction. Politics would be out of it: the press would be hunting for a former lover, or a gay-hater, or somebody trying to cover up something else. . . .

But Madison wanted something "civilized," if that was possible. He could feel the request twisting in him.

He owed a certain loyalty to Danzig, and through him to the president. But they wouldn't care about civilized. If they found out that Lincoln Bowe was gay, their immediate instinct would be to get the word out, to create the greatest possible spectacle. The investigation of Lincoln Bowe's death would lurch into a ditch — a gay thing, a sex killing — and both Goodman and the president would be off the hook.

It would no longer matter if Goodman or his friends were guilty of the killing, because nobody would be looking anymore . . .

He thought about Madison.

As they'd walked along through the evening, he'd felt the beginning of an intimacy. Not only had they told each other a few truths, he could remember the feel of

161

her arm brushing along his, and the smell of her. He wished he'd kissed her good night; wished he had that kind of relationship with her.

Since his grandparents had died almost twenty years before, he'd been alone. Alone even in his marriage. He sensed a similar loneliness in Madison Bowe.

He was caught; torn. Decided that he didn't have to release the information immediately, in either a civilized way or an uncivilized way. He could hold it for a while. Talk to Barber. See where the FBI investigation went.

Think about Madison some more.

7

The call came in two minutes after he'd gotten in bed. A male voice: "Mr. Winter? I understand you're trying to find out what happened to Senator Bowe."

"Yes, I am. Who is this?" He checked his caller ID, found the same number he'd seen on the hang-ups, but no name.

"I really can't tell you that. I'm sure you understand." Jake did understand — a whistle-blower, a backstabber, a do-gooder. The voice was soft, well modulated. A bureaucrat somewhere, or maybe a politician, somebody with a little authority. "I apologize for calling so late, I tried to call a few times earlier, but there was no answer. If you want to know about Senator Bowe, talk to Barbara Packer. She's staff with the Republican National Committee. Ask her what she and Tony Patterson discussed three weeks ago in their meeting at the Watergate."

"What'd they discuss?"

"They talked about nonconventional means of destabilizing the administration.

By nonconventional, I mean criminal."

"Give me one specific," Jake said. "Give me a can opener."

The man laughed. "You mean, for the can of worms? Okay. Tell her, 'We know all about the Wisconsin thing.' See what she says."

"You've got to . . ."

"What I've got to do is, I've got to go. Don't bother to trace the call. Or, for that matter, go ahead. I'm calling from a prepay cell phone. There's no name on it."

The man was gone.

Jake thought about calling Novatny to see if a trace might be possible. Maybe there'd be some weird way of figuring out who it was — security cameras over the cash register when the man bought the phone. Something tricky . . . and he thought, *Later.* Better to find Barbara Packer first, see what she had to say. Whatever it was, it'd be political, and usually it was a good idea to keep politics away from the FBI.

First thing in the morning . . .

He went back to bed, thought about his walk with Madison, and then drifted way.

His eyes snapped open four and a half hours later, and he was up. One benefit of a short night — short nights all his life — was that Jake got in a half day's work before anybody else was moving. He was in his office by five-thirty, NPR's *Sunrise Classical* running in the background, searching the federal databases for Packer, the Republican National Committee staff member, Tony Patterson, who apparently worked for ALERT!, a conservative political action committee, and Howard Barber, Lincoln Bowe's onetime lover.

Packer and Patterson had spent their lives in political jobs, everything from grassroots organizing to campaign strategy. They were both backroom types, never out front.

Barber was more interesting. He'd been in Iraq, a platoon leader with the Rangers, and had taken home a Purple Heart and a Bronze Star. He hadn't been badly wounded — he'd had light duty for two weeks, and then was back on the job. The Bronze Star sounded legitimate, won during an attack on a dissident strongpoint after an ambush.

Back in the States, he'd gotten start-up money from an American Express program, and had put together software that integrated digital radio receivers with mapping programs for low-level infantrymen. The receiver was worn on the wrist, like a large watch, and, among other things, could provide real-time aerial views of combat scenes at the platoon and squad level, as well as linked graphic displays to coordinate maneuvers at the company, platoon, and squad levels. Just like a video game, Jake thought, if you didn't mind a really bloody "Game Over."

By seven o'clock, he had everything that was nonclassified. If he needed more, he could go to Novatny, but he was reluctant to do that until he saw where things were headed. Satisfied with the morning's research, he went to his newspapers, journals, and mail.

The *Times* had a two-column right-corner headline on Bowe, while the *Post* stripped the story across the top of the front page. Neither story had anything he didn't know, except that an autopsy had been scheduled for last night.

At eight o'clock, he got Novatny on the phone: "What happened with the autopsy?"

"This is confidential," the FBI man said. He crunched, as though he were chewing a carrot.

"I'm a confidential guy," Jake said.

"I'm just saying . . ."

"Yeah, yeah . . ."

"For one thing, the chemistry will take a while. But: he was dead when they set him on fire, though recently dead. He'd been shot right dead in the heart. In the heart at least. We don't know about the head, of course."

"Did they recover any of the slug?"

"Yes, they did. Deformed, but useful," Novatny said. "A copper-jacketed .45-caliber hollow point. As it happens, we recovered a .45-caliber pistol in Carl Schmidt's house yesterday evening, hidden in the basement. It was full of copper-jacketed .45-cal hollow points with Schmidt's fingerprints on them. I would bet my mother's virtue that we're gonna get a match on the slug."

"Whoa."

"My thought exactly," Novatny said.

"When will you know?" Jake asked.

"A while. But today. Don't want to screw this up."

"I'm surprised that you didn't get a through-and-through."

"Well, you know, .45s aren't exactly speed demons. With hollow points, they're throwing a slug that looks like an ashtray, ballistically, and this one hit a vertebra after passing through the heart, and stuck. It's hard to tell because of the burning, but the autopsy showed some kind of unusual debris in the wound canal, so it might have gone through something else before it hit him."

"Weird debris? Like what?"

"Gotta wait for the chemistry," Novatny said. "But it wasn't a shirt, there were no fabric fibers. They're working it."

"Call me when you get it," Jake said.

"Could get some of it today. Won't get all of it for a couple of days."

After he'd hung up, Jake leaned back in his desk chair, closed his eyes, and thought about it. If Schmidt was the killer, not only was he stupid, but he'd dumped Arlo Goodman in a political trash can. The media no longer dealt so much in facts, which had become unfashionable, as in speculation. And once they started speculating on Schmidt's involvement with the Watchmen, and the Goodman-Bowe feud, combined with the sensational way Bowe had died . . .

He thought again: Should he make the call? An anonymous call about Bowe's gay lifestyle would stop the investigation short. The news media had always been thoroughly hypocritical about sex, publicly preaching tolerance for anything but child sex, while at the same time exploiting any sign of sexual irregularity by politicians or other celebrities.

Still: he hesitated.

Did he really want to stop the investigation? In terms of his job, it would certainly be expedient, even if it led to an incorrect conclusion. And he felt the pull of his loyalty to Danzig. He should tell Danzig.

And he would, he decided: but just a little later. Maybe after he talked to Barber, after he'd looked into a few more things . . .

Two phone calls, the first to Danzig, to bring him up-to-date on everything but the gay stuff. The second to Ralph Goines, Arlo Goodman's assistant.

Jake identified himself: "I need some information immediately, or as fast as you can put it together. I need to know when you first started putting out feelers about Schmidt and how you did that. Did anyone see or talk to him after you started putting out feelers? Is there any way to know whether or not Schmidt knew you were looking for him?"

He expected Goines to get back. Instead, Goines said, "Hold on. I'm going to put this phone down, I could be a minute or two."

Jake held on, heard music in the background. Country-western, he thought. Then Goines picked up. "We began talking about him on the first, April Fools' day. He was still around. We had a guy named Andy Duncan stop by and chat with him about Bowe's disappearance. Duncan went as a Watchman, but he's also an accident investigator for the highway patrol, and he knows what he's doing. He got back to us and said Schmidt seemed to have missed the news stories that Bowe was gone. Remember, the stories weren't that big, it was more like, 'Where has the senator gone to?' "

"Okay. The point being that somebody asked him specifically about Bowe after Bowe disappeared."

"Yes. Then he worked in a roadhouse down there, as a bartender. A couple of Watchmen talked to him the day after that, and probably the day after that, too, although we haven't nailed that down. This was what, ten days ago. Anyway, when the newspaper stories started getting bigger, and we got a couple more guys wondering about Schmidt, we went down to see him again, and he was gone."

"So this would be a week ago."

"Don't quote me, but it was about that. We can put a precise timeline together and e-mail it to you."

"Mmm. That's okay. Listen, I can't give you the precise information I have, because it's classified. But — everybody will know this in a next few hours — the hunt for Carl Schmidt is about to go big-time."

"They found something."

"Yes. Tell your boss. Way the media works, they could be holding his feet to the fire."

Jake kicked back in the chair again, closed his eyes. Schmidt. He needed to know more about the guy. Because Schmidt had struck him as a loser, but not necessarily a moron.

If he'd been warned that people were curious about Bowe's disappearance and his possible involvement, would he still have hidden the gun in the house? If he really wanted to keep it that badly, he could have put it in a couple of Ziploc bags and ditched it out in the woods. He could recover it in two minutes, but nobody would have found it in a hundred years . . .

And that scratched semicircle on the floor of the basement. He'd been pleased with himself for detecting the possibility that the bench had been moved so somebody could stand on it. But now that he thought about it, Schmidt might as well have painted an arrow pointing to the hiding place. Was he really that dumb?

He dug around in his briefcase, found the note that had been given to him by Goodman's treacherous intern, Cathy Ann Dorn. If he could catch her before she went to work, maybe he could get a little insight on the Goodman team's reaction. He dialed the number on the paper, and a young woman answered: "Delta-Delta-Delta. How can I help you?"

"What?"

"TriDelts. How can I help you?"

He was nonplussed. A sorority house? "Uh . . . do you have a Miss Cathy Ann Dorn?"

There was a second of ominous silence, then, "Are you a friend of hers?" The voice had hushed.

"I was supposed to call her back about a job," Jake said.

"Oh . . . God, I don't know what to tell you."

Suddenly, bad vibrations, thick as syrup. "Is she there?"

"Actually, let me have you talk to somebody else."

"Could you . . ." But the woman was gone, replaced fifteen seconds later by a sharper voice. "You're looking for Cathy Ann?"

"Yes."

"Could I ask who's calling?"

"My name is Chuck Webster. I'm calling her back about a political internship she'd applied for, a White House internship. Is there something wrong?"

The woman hesitated and then said, "Cathy Ann was injured last night. She's in the hospital."

"Oh, my God. Is it serious?"

"Pretty serious," the woman said. She sounded grim. "They beat her up pretty bad. At least she wasn't raped."

"Oh, my God," he said. Again. "Could you give me her parents' number, or at least their names? I really need to talk to somebody. This is awful."

He meant it, and the vibe got through to the woman on the other end of the line. "Of course. Sure."

"Could you tell me what hospital? I can promise you that this is official . . ."

He got through to David Dorn in his daughter's hospital room. Jake said, "I just talked to her about an internship and I was appalled . . . How serious is it?"

"She won't die, but she's hurt pretty bad. They got her doped up pretty strong right now, she's out of it. I'll tell her you called when she wakes up."

"Please do that. Tell her to call me. The White House fellowship. She'll know. Do the police have any idea who did it?"

"None. Not a clue. Took her purse, took her computer and iPod. She was a target, I guess, young woman at night carrying a briefcase. I warned her so many times . . ." His voice caught; a crying jag. "I'll tell you what, if I ever get my hands on these sonsofbitches . . ."

Jake got off and thought: *Goodman?*

A military unit doesn't take kindly to traitors. Had they picked up on the fact that she'd talked to him? He thought about the security cameras in Goodman's office building . . .

Nothing to do about it, not yet.

He picked up the phone again and called Thomas Merkin at the Republican National Committee offices. "Tom, Jake Winter here."

"Hey, Jake. I heard you were tangled up in the Lincoln Bowe thing."

"Yeah. Was. I'd like to come over and talk to one of your staffers," Jake said. "Barbara Packer?"

"Barbara? About what?"

"About Senator Bowe," Jake said. "What she's heard, if anything. She's a friend of his, I think."

"Well, hang on, will you? Let me see if she's in." He clicked away, and thirty seconds later, clicked back. "She's in, but she doesn't know anything about Senator Bowe."

"All I'd like to do is chat," Jake said.

"Hang on." He was gone again, longer this time, then came back: "Should she have a lawyer?"

"I'm not a prosecutor, Tom, I'm not an investigator." But he put a little steel in his voice. "I'm just trying to tidy things up. If she wants a lawyer, that's fine with me, but I haven't even started a file on this thing."

"All right." Merkin was wary. "Hour?"

"See you then."

He called Howard Barber at his office. A secretary said that he was out for the morning but should be back after lunch. Jake left a message.

To the RNC.

He decided to take a cab down to the Tidal Basin, check out the cherry blossoms, then walk on over. And the cherry blossoms were excellent, a pink so pale that it was almost white. In fact, he thought, scratching his chin, they *were* white. Had anybody ever noticed before?

The cherry blossom festival was starting, crowds of Japanese tourists with cameras, so he moved along, stopped at a café and got a bun and a cup of coffee, sat outside and watched the Washington women in their new spring ensembles blowing along the sidewalks. . . .

He tapped his cane as he walked, and whistled a little Mozart. The ice was breaking up; lock tumblers were turning. He'd be done with Bowe in two days, he thought. Then maybe he could talk to Danzig about doing something with the conventions . . .

There'd been a couple of unhappy events at the RNC, most recently a schoolteacher who claimed he had a dynamite belt and attempted to blow himself up on the committee's front porch, in protest of Republican educational policies. A protest, in Jake's view, that was fully justified.

As it happened, the teacher himself was poorly educated. He didn't have a dynamite belt, but a blasting-cap belt. He had confused the high-tech-looking caps, which he'd stolen from a quarry, with dynamite, and instead of blowing himself up, he'd blown off several hamburger-sized chunks of meat and fat, and had blinded himself in one eye.

In any event, the RNC had installed

heavy-duty security, and now was protected almost as well as the White House. Not that a passerby would know it. A glass wall showed off a plush lobby, with an unprotected woman sitting behind a wooden desk, friendly and open. The wall behind her, though, was a couple of feet thick — a blast wall — and between that wall and another inner, concrete wall was an airport-style scanner system.

He walked through the security, the guard raised an eyebrow at the cane, X-rayed it, gave it back, and passed him through the inner wall to the real reception area, with a less expendable receptionist. She recognized him, though he'd never seen her before — she was one of the smiling, chatty women who were always out front. She'd pulled his bio, of course.

"Mr. Winter. Good to see you, sir. Tom and Barb and Jay are waiting for you."

Merkin and Barbara Packer and Jay Westinghouse were sitting in a conference room at the back of the building; Jake knocked and stepped inside. From their faces, he suspected that he might have interrupted a heated discussion. Merkin he'd met several times, and Merkin introduced Packer and Westinghouse: "Jay is our lawyer. We thought, what the heck, he might as well sit in."

Yeah, what the heck. "Fine with me," Jake said.

Merkin was thin but soft, a guy who didn't eat much, but who never worked out. Westinghouse was polished, a little too heavy, a man who liked his martinis.

Packer looked harried. She was in her late forties, dark complected, with an efficient hairdo. She wore an efficient blue suit, as close to a man's suit as she could get without being obvious about it, and a cobalt-and-gold silk scarf for a tie. They spread around the rosewood conference table and Jake webbed his fingers and smiled at Packer and said, "Do you have any idea of why Senator Bowe might have been killed? Some kind of political or personal issue that might have resulted in violence?"

The other two men looked at her and she said, "No, of course not." She had a grim mouth, a thin line turned down at the ends. At the same time, she seemed genuinely puzzled.

Westinghouse said, "Is this . . . What's the status here?"

Jake shrugged. "I'm asking Ms. Packer about Senator Bowe. If she has no idea of why he might have been murdered, then okay. If she does, she better say so, or she

better be prepared to kiss the kids good-
bye for a few years."

"I don't want to hear that," Westinghouse said.

"Hear it from me, unofficially, or hear it
from the FBI when they cart her out of her
house," Jake said, half to Packer, half to
Westinghouse. "We've been hung out to dry
on this Bowe thing and we're not putting
up with it. The only people who are bene-
fitting are you guys. The press is gonna
start whipping Goodman, and by implication us, with Judge Crater stories, with
black helicopters, with conspiracy theories.
When we've worked our way through it,
somebody's going to pay. If there's some
kind of political thing going on . . ."

"Jake, that's crazy talk," Merkin said,
pushing his chair back. "You've got to
know that."

"No, I don't know that," Jake said. "What
I'm afraid of is that somebody at a low
level, an operator — Ms. Packer, for in-
stance — knows that something's going on,
and they think they're being smart. I don't
really believe that *you* guys know about it,
because you really *are* smart." He nodded
at Merkin as he said it, the flattery prin-
ciple, ". . . but somebody, somewhere does.
And if it's somebody who thinks he, or she,

is being smart . . . well." He shrugged.

Merkin looked at Packer: "You don't know?"

"No, I don't." She looked at neither Merkin nor Jake, and Jake felt a tingle. She knew *something.*

"What did you and Tony Patterson talk about, over at the Watergate three weeks ago?" Jake asked.

Her face turned white. She looked at him for a moment, as though he'd turned into a viper, then shook her head and pushed her chair back. "Oh, no." She turned to Westinghouse. "I won't talk to this man anymore."

"What the hell is going on?" Merkin asked.

Jake had pushed the situation to a breaking point: now he could back away. Now he *had* to back away, since he didn't have anything else, other than the one cryptic suggestion.

"The Wisconsin thing could blow up on you. There's a murder now," he said. "At this point, none of this has to go anywhere. It's just a bureaucratic dance. But, Tom, I suggest that you and Jay sit down with Ms. Packer and have a talk. She's been acting in your name and you've got enough problems already. This Bowe thing is a nightmare. There's going to be serious trouble, and even if you're on the very far fringe of it, it could still be the three-to-five at Marion, Illinois, kind of trouble."

"Ms. Packer hasn't been acting in our name. If she's been acting in any way, it's on her own. The RNC has nothing to do with . . . anything."

Jake smiled: "I wish I could take a tape recording of that back to Bill Danzig. He'd put you on TV."

Merkin didn't smile back: "We'll have a chat about this, and I'll get back to you. Soon."

"Do that."

On the way out the door, he gave Merkin his private phone number.

"If you hear anything, call me anytime. I mean it: three a.m." He said good-bye, nodded at Packer without smiling. They were already snarling at each other when the door closed behind him. He backed out through the building security, and figured that about the time he got to the bottom of the steps, they were putting the red-hot rebar on the soles of Packer's feet.

Maybe something would bleed out; and maybe not.

But from the way Packer was acting, he thought it probably would.

8

Jake hadn't expected to hear from Howard Barber until after lunch — but Barber called back as he was on his way home.

"Can you tell me what exactly you want to talk about?" Barber asked.

"Not on a cell phone," Jake said. "Basically, I spoke to a friend of yours last night, and she said that I should get in touch with you. About her husband."

"Ah." Pause. "I'm in Arlington. Where are you?"

"Burleith, north of Georgetown."

"Why don't I come there? One o'clock?"

Jake would have preferred to see Barber at his office, to get a look at it, to make a judgment, but couldn't turn the offer down. "That'd be great."

Jake had one egg left, so he fixed himself a last egg-salad sandwich, then went out to his stamp-sized backyard to swing a golf club, working on his hip release. Get ready for summer. He made fifty swings, struggling not to lose his bad leg on the follow-through, and was sweating when he finished. He'd just put the six-iron away when Barber arrived.

Howard Barber was a tall black man wearing a steel gray suit, a black golf shirt, and opaque blue-glitter sunglasses with a phone bug dropping to one ear. Jake saw him clambering over the ditch in the front yard, and went to get the door. Barber had just rung the bell when Jake popped the door open.

Jake said, "Mr. Barber? Come in. I should have told you about the construction. I should have had you come around back. . . ."

Jake took him into the study, pointed him at a reading chair in the corner. Barber sat carefully, looking around the office, then crossed his legs and leaned back. "Nice place," he said. "That new sidewalk ought to kick the value up."

"That's what my neighbors tell me," Jake said.

They chatted about real estate values for a moment, then, "I talked to Maddy this morning after I called you back," Barber said. "She filled me in on what you're doing. I don't understand how I can help."

"She said you were Lincoln Bowe's

closest friend. Bowe may have been kidnapped and murdered . . ."

"What do you mean, *may have been?*" Barber said, frowning, and leaning forward. "The boy's dead. Decapitated. Burned. I mean, Jesus Christ, what do you want?"

"It's not all that clear," Jake said. "The FBI is chasing a suspect, but there are problems, quite frankly."

"What problems?" Barber asked, frowning.

Jake shrugged. "Anomalies. Like the fact that he had a huge collection of guns, but left one where it would be found, and it may be the gun that ties him to Lincoln Bowe. Like the fact that he's become invisible. Can't find him, nobody's seen him. In the opinion of a number of people, the suspect was set up and is probably dead himself."

Barber said, "Huh." Then, "I could think of reasons for all of that. If I was trying. I mean, the guy obviously ain't the brightest bulb on the Christmas tree."

"Yeah, but I'm not trying to alibi him," Jake said. "I'm noticing anomalies."

"Okay." Barber lifted his hands, slapped them down on his thighs. "All I can tell you is, Linc and I talked the day before he disappeared. We were going to play golf the next week, but by that time, he'd been gone for four days. I didn't know he'd disappeared until I saw the first story in the papers. Then I called Maddy down at the farm, and she told me."

"Was he . . ." Jake hesitated. "Look, I'm trying to ask if he had any gay friends that you may know about, who were passionately involved with him. I'm trying to figure out if this could have been a relationship thing."

"Gay murder." Barber settled back, shaking his head.

"Yeah."

Barber exhaled, said, "Shit," looked at the ceiling, then said, "I can't tell you for sure. He was not, mmm, monogamous. But I don't think . . . I think if he was involved in something really hot, really difficult, he would have told me. The sex cooled off for him the last few years. Gays get older, too, you know."

"Never thought about it," Jake said.

"Well, it's true. Anyway, I could call a couple of people and ask."

Jake smiled. "I'd really prefer to do it myself."

Barber shook his head. "Linc moved in political circles. Political gay circles. Some of the people are already out, but some absolutely couldn't afford to be outed. You're doing staff work for some Bible-thumper from Alabama, you get outed, you lose your job."

"I wouldn't out them."

"I might believe you, except . . . what would you do if it became expedient to out them? If it helped the cause?" Barber asked. "I don't know you well enough to trust you on it."

"Okay. But you'll ask around."

"I'll ask, and I'll get back to you."

"I'll take it, if that's the best I can do," Jake said. "But if it's a relationship thing . . ."

"Then I'll call the FBI. I'm not going to let somebody walk on Linc's murder."

Jake: "So who do *you* think did it?"

"The Watchmen," Barber said, without hesitation. "One way or another. Linc had a lot of influence, both through his family and through his political contacts, and he couldn't keep himself from going after Goodman. Couldn't help himself. Looked at Goodman's combat records, made some comments he shouldn't have."

Jake broke in: "There's a question about Goodman's records?"

Barber shook his head again. "No. That was one of the problems. Linc thought there was, and couldn't keep himself from saying so. He believed there were problems with his Silver Star and with the Purple Heart. But there were twenty guys there when Goodman got hit, and several of them actually saw it happen. They were down in a road cut, some Iraqis were lobbing RPGs at them. Goodman was directing traffic, running on his feet, and whack! He gets it in the hand. A couple of guys actually got sprayed by his blood. And Goodman stayed on his feet and kept directing traffic until his guys got on top of it."

"So there was no doubt."

"None. Not only that, the guys in his unit say he was a pretty good officer. Took care of them. But you know how it is when a politician has a medal and a war wound — there are always people ready to piss on them. Linc bought into the stories, repeated them. Goodman proved they weren't true, but Linc wouldn't shut up."

"Really bad blood, then."

"They hated each other," Barber said. "Goodman took Linc's Senate seat away in a dirty campaign. Linc went out of his way to smear Goodman every chance he got, and with his family connections and old Virginia loyalties, he's caused Goodman some problems. Social problems. Not getting the old-boy invitations he should get, not playing golf with the old money."

"Status."

"Yup. Status. Goodman thinks he's terrifically important, and he wants to be treated that way."

"When Senator Bowe vanished, did you think he'd been kidnapped?" Jake asked. "Or did you think something else was going on?"

"At first, I thought something else might be going on," Barber said. "Then two, three days went by — that wasn't Linc's style. A week out, I thought he was probably dead."

So there it was: Barber had thought Bowe was dead, as Madison suspected . . . but the way Barber put it, the feeling was purely rational. Nothing to lie about.

"So, shoot. I go back to my boss and tell him it's a straight kidnapping case," Jake said.

"That's what it looks like to me," Barber said.

Jake laced his fingers, rubbed his palms together, thinking, then, "What do you think of the Watchmen? Could somebody say that you've got a reason for pointing us in their direction? Is there something personal . . . ?"

"I think two things. First, when we — the Bowes and I — say Watchmen, we're not really talking about the guy on the corner in a jacket helping an old lady across the street. We're not talking about the Boy Scouts. When Goodman was still a prosecutor, he put together a group to do intelligence work. Half dozen guys, maybe. John Patricia was the first guy . . ."

"I've met him."

"Patricia was air force intelligence. He brought military interrogation to Norfolk. And Darrell Goodman joined up. He's Arlo's brother and he's a crazy mother. He'd take a guy apart with a pair of wire cutters if he needed some information. There are stories down in Norfolk about Goodman's boys fuckin' up some people pretty bad. Of course, they cut way down on prostitution and street crime about disappeared, and drugs went away. Everybody was happy to look the other way, 'cept the druggies and the stickup men."

"Okay . . ."

"The thing is, Arlo carried those same guys over to his campaign for governor. Dirty tricks, spies, disinformation, the whole works. Intelligence operations, in other words."

"I saw a guy outside the governor's mansion," Jake said. "He had a special forces look about him — he was wearing a raincoat and one of those floppy-brim tennis hats, black tennis shoes. Looks like he had some kind of complexion problem, like really bad acne . . . but then I thought, maybe a burn, maybe service-connected."

"That's Darrell Goodman," Barber said, snapping his fingers, then pointing his index finger at Jake. "Always that raincoat. You ought to look him up. Take a look at his military records. I mean, there's nobody in the Pentagon who really wants to know what those guys did in Syria. They might think it needed to be done, but they don't want to know about it."

"So. An asshole." Jake made a note.

"Yes. A major asshole."

"You said you thought two things about the Watchmen. What's the other one?"

Barber nodded. "Okay. From what Maddy told you, you know that I'm a gay black man. The Watchmen are a proto-fascist group, with their own little charismatic führer. What should I think about them? I'd like to see them run out of the country."

"They don't seem to have a problem with blacks," Jake said. "Or gays, for that matter. Not that I've read about."

"Give them a while," Barber said. "Being

antiblack or antigay or anti-Jew isn't useful to them yet. But they'll get to it. Right now, they're against immigrants. That's not going to be enough, not when Goodman runs for national office. You know that thing he says, about how he never met a Commandment he didn't like? Well, do not fuck your brother is in there somewhere."

"You're a pessimist, Mr. Barber."

Barber smiled and spread his hands: "Hey. I'm a gay black guy. Pessimism keeps me alive."

"Last question, then," Jake said. "I don't know if you'll know what I'm talking about, so I'm going to come at it obliquely — because if you don't know, I don't want you to guess."

Barber studied him for a moment, then: "Okay."

"Did you know that your friend Lincoln Bowe was involved in an effort to . . ." Jake hesitated, hoping he'd leave the impression that he was groping for the right word, though he'd spit at Barber exactly what the unknown man had told him on the phone, ". . . that he was, uh, what shall we call it: examining nonconventional means of destabilizing this administration. Does that mean anything to you?"

Barber's eyes went opaque: "No. What the hell does it mean?"

Jake thought: *He knows.* "All right. I really can't tell you . . ."

They talked for a few more minutes, and Barber, as he was leaving, promised to get back on the question of Bowe's ongoing love affairs. At the door, Barber said, "When is the gay thing going to hit the streets?"

Jake shrugged: "I haven't told anybody yet. I'm afraid it'd derail the investigation. You want a call before I do it?"

"I'd appreciate it . . . and if you could take it a little easy?"

"I'll try. But it's going to be out of my hands at that point."

Jake let Barber out the back door, then spent an hour making notes of the conversation and listing questions. He'd noticed how Barber's language switched easily back and forth from a street-flavored lingo to postgraduate sophistication. From *Goodman's boys fuckin' up people* at one moment to *proto-fascist charismatic führer* the next.

And he'd been lying about Bowe and the destabilization thing. Bowe had been into something. Now Jake had to work through it. Whatever it was, how did it tie in to Goodman? Or did it?

He made another call about Cathy Ann Dorn — he got the nursing desk and was told that she had been awake, had eaten some cottage cheese, and was asleep again.

He talked to Novatny.

"Bowe was alive when he was shot, but he was full of drugs. Enough painkiller to knock him on his ass. They may have kept him sedated to control him. Shot him in the heart. The debris in the wound canal was newsprint. The thinking is, they may have tried to use a wad of paper to muffle the sound of the shot."

"That's weird."

"Shooting a drugged guy is weird," Novatny said. "Cold, ice-cold, murder. Don't get no colder than that."

Jake went online, into the federal records. He had only limited access as a consultant, but he found a file on Darrell Goodman. The file was informative in an uninformative way — parts of his military record had simply been removed from the unclassified files. And that meant, almost certainly, that he was a snoop-and-pooper. Goodman had himself a hit man.

Jake was thinking about it when Merkin, the contact at the Republican National Committee, called back.

"Jake, we gotta talk. Where are you?"

"I'm home. Is this about Packer?"

"About Packer and Tony Patterson." Merkin sounded worried.

"Okay. I can come there, or you could come here. . . ."

"No, no. How about at the National Gallery? Like in the nineteenth-century French paintings?" Merkin suggested. "I could walk over. Meet you outside in an hour?"

"I should be there by then. If not, pretty quick after that." And he thought, *Doesn't want to talk to me at his office . . . doesn't want to be seen with me.*

Barber called Madison Bowe on her cell phone, caught her on the way back from the funeral home. "I talked to Winter," he said. "He says he hasn't told anybody about the gay thing."

"Huh. I was all braced."

"He's afraid it'd derail the investigation."

"Ah, jeez," she said. "I feel like I'm . . . It makes me feel rotten. I'm not made for this."

"I know, I know. Maybe you oughta just

get out of it, get away from Winter. The guy is pulling stuff out of the air. I didn't even want to *look* at him. I was afraid he could read my eyes."

"He is that way . . . ," Madison said.

"I'll tell you, it doesn't really make sense. He should have told Danzig by now," Barber said. "I'm wondering . . . Maybe Winter is trying to do right by you."

"He likes me," Madison said.

"I could tell. And you like him back."

"Mmm." She realized it was true. She hastened on. "About the other issue . . ."

"Not on the phone," Barber said. "Tell you what. I'll stop over and see you when we both have time. We can talk it all out."

The National Gallery looks like a WPA post office. Jake found Merkin on the main floor, morosely examining Cézanne's *House by the Marne.*

"In Cézanne's day, the Marne wasn't *the* Marne," Jake said, taking in the painting.

"Looks like a creek," Merkin said. "Not like a million dead men, or whatever it was."

"I didn't know you were an art fan, Tom."

"Ah, it calms me down, coming here," Merkin said. "I never see anybody from work."

"Probably be better if you did," Jake said. "I mean, for the Republic."

Merkin nodded. "Let's walk."

They walked toward the American wing, talking in hushed voices, Whistler's huge *White Girl* peering at them down the long hall. Merkin said, "As far as I know, nobody did anything illegal."

"Then what're we talking about?"

"Patterson had worked with Packer in North Carolina on the Jessup campaign, and out in New Mexico on Jerry Radzwill's. They saw each other around. Patterson is with ALERT! right now. He was an advisor on the Bowe campaign. He was set for a decent job if Bowe won, but Bowe didn't, so he wound up at ALERT!"

"He's a Bowe guy."

"Was. Anyway, he got in touch with Packer and said he had a hypothetical for her. If, hypothetically, somebody had a package that would dump Vice President Landers off the ticket, when would be the best time for the package to be delivered?"

"What's in the package?"

"Don't know. Neither does Packer. Here's the thing, here's what Patterson was saying. He was saying that somebody has a package that's so specific, so criminal, so irrefutable, that as soon as somebody respectable gets it, he's gonna have to turn it over to the FBI or face criminal charges himself. But until then, it's a figment of the imagination, floating around out there."

"The implied question was, when did the Republicans want the package dumped to do the most damage?"

"That's about it," Merkin said.

"What was the answer?"

Merkin's shoulders slumped, and he shook his head. "Jake, you know how the talk goes on these hypotheticals. People talk about this stuff all the time. Dump it October first, there's plenty of time for the scandal to blow up, not enough time to recover . . . but who knows, maybe it could be suppressed until it's too close to the election. So maybe September fifteenth. And maybe . . . Hell, you pick a date."

"Sometime in the fall."

"I would say that."

"And you're telling me this now because . . ."

"Because now that it's out there and somebody knows about Patterson and Packer, we don't want to get caught in the obstructing-justice squeeze," Merkin said. "We're reporting this to you, as the president's point man on the Bowe investigation. I'm going to make a record of our talk here, and date it, get it notarized, and stick it in a safe-deposit box. If I never need it, that's great. If I wind up talking to a Senate panel or a grand jury . . ."

"All right," Jake said. "This information, whatever it is . . . Patterson got it from Senator Bowe?"

"I don't know. You'll have to ask Patterson." He swung his sport coat off his shoulder, dug in a side pocket, and came up with a leaf torn from a desk calendar. A phone number and address were written in the memo block. "I happen to have his name and address with me."

Jake stuck the paper in his pocket. "I'll probably have to tell the feds."

"We'll do everything in the world to cooperate. Packer understands that. We don't have anything to do with Patterson, so that's not our problem. Remember: the whole thing was presented to Packer as a hypothetical. And it was all so vague, what was she going to report? Anything we did could be interpreted as an unsupported and scurrilous attack on the vice president."

They walked to the end of the wing and stood looking at *White Girl*. She looked back with a boldness that was disconcerting, as though she were personally interested in their conspiracy. After a moment, Jake said, "Well, shoot, Tom. I was planning to sit in the tub tonight. Nice soothing soak."

"It's an election year, Jake."

"Yeah, it is. But let me tell you something, Tommy. If I were you, I wouldn't go leaking this around. If it's real, it'll come out. But there are elements of a conspiracy here — a conspiracy with a murder, and you guys are in it. We're not talking about six weeks in minimum security anymore."

"I know that."

"So don't mess with it. Talk to your people, too. Sit on them. This is gonna be . . . this is gonna be difficult."

Danzig would still be in his office: Jake said good-bye to Merkin and called. Gina picked up the phone.

"It's Jake, Gina. I gotta see him."

"He's done for the day. The president's back and they're talking."

"Get him out when you can. I'm down by the Mall, but I'm headed that way. Clear me through to the blue room."

"Can you give me a hint?"

"You don't want to know about it, Gina. Best if you asked the guy about it. I'm really telling you that for your own good, if we all wind up in front of a special prosecutor someday."

"Uh-oh. I'll clear you through."

Jake flagged a cab. Five minutes later, he was checking through White House security, heading for the waiting room. The place was crowded, but nobody spoke, simply sat and stared, poked keys on laptops, or browsed through week-old copies of the *Economist.*

He'd waited twenty-five minutes before an escort touched his sleeve: "Mr. Winter?"

Danzig's two junior secretaries were gone, their desk lights out. Gina sat in a quiet glow, working with pen on paper. When Jake came in, she touched a desktop button and said, "I hope it's not that bad."

"Bill can fill you in," Jake said.

The green diode came up, and she said, "Go on."

Danzig was standing behind his desk, frowning at a stack of paper. When Jake came in, he looked up and asked, "Is it bad?"

"It could be," Jake said. "Really bad."

Danzig pointed at a chair: "What?"

Jake sat down and said, "A low-level operator for the RNC has been talking to another operator, a guy who worked a bunch of Senate and gubernatorial campaigns, including Bowe's last campaign. He's a Bowe guy, now with ALERT! His name is Tony Patterson. He was making tentative inquiries about dropping a scandal on you. On us. Supposedly, a rock-solid accusation against Vice President Landers that would dump him off the ticket. The question he was putting to the RNC was, when to drop the package on us. The timing."

"Why would he ask the RNC?" Danzig asked. "Why not Bowe? Bowe would know."

"I don't know. I do know that he and this woman, the woman at the RNC, were old campaign buddies. So it was partially old-buddy stuff. And there was just a hint that the package might be *coming* from Bowe. That Bowe might be trying to distance himself from it."

"Goddamnit," Danzig said. They looked at each other in silence for a moment, then Danzig said, "If it's true, one obvious conclusion would be that Bowe was killed to stop this package from coming out."

"Yes."

"That'd be a disaster." Jake said nothing

and Danzig spun his chair away, thinking. Then he said, coming back around, "On the other hand, if we push the investigation into this hypothetical package, and it turns out that Bowe was killed for some completely unrelated reason, we're still in trouble. Because once anybody knows about the package, it's gonna leak."

Jake nodded. "If the package exists. If it's not part of some scheme by Bowe, including his disappearance, to mess with us."

"He had himself killed to mess with us?"

"I haven't worked out that part," Jake said.

Danzig smiled, a rueful smile, said, "Ah, God," twirled again in his chair, came back around, said about the vice president, "Landers is a crooked sonofabitch and we've known it from Day One. But he gave us Wisconsin, Minnesota, and Iowa, and we needed them."

Jake said nothing.

Danzig said, "He'll deny everything. He'll ride it right to the end. There's no way we could go to him and say, 'Is there anything in your past?' because we all know there is, and we all know he'll deny it. Deny, deny, deny."

"Want me to jack up Patterson?"

Danzig rubbed his face, suddenly looking old and tired. "Wait overnight. Let me sleep on it," he said.

"Okay."

Danzig leaned forward. "The problem is this: the RNC may be feeding you this rumor, knowing it will get to me. I talk to the president, we ask around. Even if we keep it secret, the RNC feeds it through the back door to some conservative sheet or cable station. The *L.A. Times*, maybe. Tells them that we know about it. Then we're in trouble, whether or not it's true. We can't even deny that we asked around. Landers gets investigated all summer, into the campaign."

Jake nodded. That's what would happen.

"If we have to dump Landers, we've got to do it before summer," Danzig said. He was talking to himself as much as to Jake. "We can't carry him into the convention. But if the accusation is bullshit, then Landers pees on us."

"We need some specifics," Jake said.

"Just like with Bowe," Danzig said. "If we could only get the specifics, we could move. Without them, we could be screwed no matter what we do."

"But if we don't look into it . . . we could

get into pretty deep trouble ourselves," Jake said. "I mean us, personally. Obstruction of justice and all that."

Danzig nodded: "Of course. But everybody would give us a day or two. Working through the bureaucracy."

Jake stood up: "I'll be on the phone. Call anytime."

"What about Schmidt?"

"Nothing new. Can't find him," Jake said.

"But we're looking."

"Novatny's tearing up the countryside. He's pretty competent."

Danzig picked up a pencil, drummed it, stuck it behind an ear, rubbed his face with both hands. Tired. Finally he said, "Best thing that could happen is, we find Schmidt and pin the killing on him. Or on the Watchmen," Danzig said. "Then we find the package and get rid of Landers, and never let anybody even hint that there might have been a connection."

"Gonna be tough," Jake said. "The media's running around like a herd of weasels, putting every rumor they can find on the air. Looking for somebody to hang, somebody to blame."

"When the going gets tough, the tough blame the CIA," Danzig said. He paused, then said, "But I don't think that applies here."

"Not yet, anyway," Jake said.

"Goddamnit. *Goddamnit.*" Danzig flipped a desk calendar: "Four months to the convention." He stared at the calendar, then said, "Listen: I'm going to talk to the president. We'll want you to see Patterson in the morning. Get some sleep. I'll call you early, one way or the other."

9

Jake left the White House, tapping along in the night with his cane, looking for a cab. Lots of traffic, not many taxis. He'd walked three blocks before he finally spotted a ride, flagged it. "Daily News, in Georgetown."

The driver grunted, and they drove wordlessly down M across the bridge, six blocks down. The driver grunted again, Jake passed him a couple of bills, and got out. The Daily News was a surf-and-turf joint, with enough light to read by, and an Amsterdam-style newsstand in the front entry, like a brown bar. He chose a battered copy of *New York*, ordered the mangrove snapper and the house white, and settled into a quiet booth to read some gossip and enjoy the fish.

Was nagged by the thought that he should have told Danzig about Bowe being gay. The issue was one of loyalty: he was taking Danzig's money, and he even generally agreed with the president's program, versus that pushed by the Republicans. Bringing up the gay issue would advance the cause. Yet . . . whether or not Madison Bowe knew it, she'd be trashed. And she'd blame him, and he didn't want that. Actually, he thought, he wanted Madison Bowe: honor versus testicles. The thought made him smile at his own foolishness . . .

He had a second glass of wine at the end of the meal, something with an edge to cut the sweetness from a crème brûlée, then gathered his case and stick and went outside. Nice night. He decided to walk, a little more than a mile. He ate at the Daily News twice a week, and the walk was just right for his leg.

The light was dying as he strolled along the uneven sidewalks, puzzling out the problem of what to do. He took twenty-five minutes to get home.

The front walkway to the house was still torn up, so he automatically continued around to the back, to the alley entry.

He heard the car doors open. Paid no attention to it until he got his key in the gate lock, realized that he hadn't heard them close again. Not that it was odd, exactly . . . then he saw the man coming, too fast, way too fast, too close, something raised above his head. And a second man, coming in a rush, a step behind the first. They were big, rangy, fast, one black and one white, he thought, and then they were on him . . .

Somebody shouted and Jake raised his cane and flinched away from a movement and took the first stroke of what might have been an axe handle — or maybe just a stick, but he had axe handle in his mind's eye — on the side of his cane and his arm, and he shouted, heard himself shout, more like a scream, then the second man swung at him, another ax handle or stick and Jake caught the blow with a push of the flat of his left hand, and then the first man caught him on the back of the neck, then on the head, and dazed, he went down, flailing, rolling, rolling, rolling, trying to make them miss, trying to get back in the fight, off the defensive. The two men were flailing at him, one of them saying, "Git him, git that mother, git him," a kind of chant, and he tried to stay faceup so he could see the blows coming, fending with his cane and hands, and he heard a man scream, *Hey you sonsofbitches* and he was hit again and again and then there was a powerful, shattering blast and a flash of light and the man closest to him froze for just an instant and Jake slashed his knee with the steel handle of his cane and felt it crunch home, saw the man stagger, then a woman was screaming and another flash of light and another blast, a gun, he thought, and then he was hit one last time and he was gone . . .

Jake woke up in an ambulance, rolling hard downtown. "What happened?"

He struggled to sit up, but couldn't. A phlegmatic black man looked down at him and said, "You rest easy. You got mugged."

"Mugged?"

A few minutes later, he woke up in the ambulance, struggled to sit up, couldn't, and asked a phlegmatic black man, "What happened?"

"You got mugged."

"Mugged?"

The doc told him later that he asked the question twenty-five times over the next hour, both in the ambulance and in the OR. Then he woke up in an intensive care unit, still in his street clothes, minus his shoes, and looked at a young Indian doc and asked, "What happened?"

"You got mugged."

"Mugged? Where? My house?"

Now the doctor smiled: "Ah. You're awake. Yes. As I understand it, you got mugged at your house. You have a concussion, of course, but not too bad, I don't believe, and a whole bunch of bruises. Good bump on your head, and a cut. It's going to hurt in a while. Your skull is in one piece — we took a picture — but we had to cut some hair away from the head wound. After it stops hurting, it's going to itch like fire. You have five stitches there. A couple of your neighbors are outside, by the way. Would you like to see them? They witnessed the event, I believe."

"Yeah. Sure. Mugged? I can't believe I was mugged."

A woman came in and said, "Mr. Winter?"

"Yes."

"Mr. Winter, do you have health insurance?"

"Sure."

She seemed to step back. "Really?"

"Why wouldn't I have?"

"Well, that's nice." She seemed skeptical. "Rami, the doctor, said you had good shoes and I should check. Would you have the card?"

She went away, clutching the card; seemed amazed at the turn of events.

A moment later, Harley Cunningham, his across-the-alley neighbor, pushed through the door, trailed by his wife, Maeve. Cunningham sold home bars and pool tables for a living. He did a double take, said, "Man. They beat the hell out of you, Jake."

"What happened?"

"My back window was open, I heard you come tapping up the alley, I looked out, and I saw these assholes get out of a truck and I could tell they were coming after you. They had these clubs — they might have been pool cues — but I had my shotgun in the bedroom closet and I yelled and Maeve yelled and they were beating the shit out of you and I ran and got the shotgun and let off a couple of shots up in the air and they run off."

"Who were they?"

"Fuck if I know," Cunningham said.

Maeve gave her husband an elbow and said, "Watch the language, he's all beat up."

"He's not gonna hurt any worse because I said 'fuck,' " Cunningham said.

"Didn't hit you in the face," Maeve said to Jake. She patted him on the arm. "That's a blessing."

"The doc said I was mugged," Jake said. Now that he was awake, he was beginning to feel the ache in his back, arms, legs, and one hip. "Just a couple of guys . . . ?"

Cunningham shrugged. "They were layin' for you, man. That truck was parked there, and they jumped out when they saw you comin'. You been playin' around with somebody's wife?"

Maeve: "Harley, my God."

"You see the car?" Jake asked.

"Yeah. It was an SUV. I think, like, a Toyota maybe. Dark in color. I told the cops. They're gonna come see you. I think one guy was black and one guy was white. Salt 'n' pepper."

"Harley, that's bigoted," Maeve said.

"That's what they call them, black and white guys together," Cunningham said.

"Maybe in nineteen fifty-five," Maeve said.

Cunningham to Jake: "I liked firing that twelve-gauge, man. It made a wicked flash in the night. Scared the hell out of 'em."

"You say they were laying for me?"

"Oh, yeah. That truck was there for a while, I noticed it earlier on. Didn't know anybody was inside. When I heard you in the alley, I was going to yell something down about those jackhammers on your sidewalk, and I saw them coming after you. I'll tell you something else — that wasn't no cheap SUV. It was brand-new, from the looks of it. They weren't looking for a quick fifty bucks."

"Did you tell the cops that?"

"Sure. But they didn't pay too much attention to me. They were too busy typing stuff in their computers."

The Cunninghams left after a while — they'd picked up Jake's briefcase and cane, and left them with him — and the cops did come. Jake had nothing to tell them, partly because he couldn't believe that anything he was doing would get him beaten up, and partly because talking to the cops wouldn't help track down the guys who'd jumped him. They had nothing to go on, except that the men were driving a dark SUV, maybe a Toyota.

"Ten percent of the trucks on the street meet that description," one of the cops said. "At least you managed to hang on to your wallet and your briefcase."

"Maybe they picked you out because you're disabled, homed in on that cane," the second cop said. "Believe me, some of these assholes like nothing more than seeing a well-dressed disabled person."

They went away, leaving the strong impression that they would file a report but that nothing would be done.

The headache arrived a few minutes later. The doc came in, said they would keep him overnight, and, "I can give you a little something for that head. When you get home, you can take a Tylenol when you need it, but no aspirin or ibuprofen. You want to stay away from any blood thinners for at least a couple of days . . ."

When he woke up, at five in the morning, he was embarrassed. Embarrassed that he'd gotten beaten up, hadn't managed to defend himself better. He enjoyed a decent fight, but what happened the night before, he told himself, hadn't been a fight. It *had* been a mugging, cold and calculated. He thought about Cathy Ann Dorn. Not a coincidence?

But why would Goodman want to slow him down? He'd been cooperating with Goodman . . .

Another thought popped into his head. They'd known he used the back door, because of the sidewalk. Howard Barber had had trouble with the front door . . . if he remembered right, he'd said something to Barber about using the back.

Barber? But why?

Overnight, in the back of his bruised

brain, he'd filtered out a few more conclusions.

The attackers had been large, tough, and in good condition. One of them had a hill accent, Kentucky or eastern Tennessee, like that. They were good at what they did. They hadn't meant to kill him — they could have done that with a single gunshot, or even a couple of axe-handle or pool-cue strokes to the back of the head.

Instead, he'd taken two glancing blows to the head, another on his neck, and a dozen on his back, legs, and one hip. They'd meant to do what they had — to put him in the hospital. If Harley hadn't been there with his shotgun, and if they'd had another minute, Jake might have been in bed for a week, or a month, or a year. They'd hit him hard enough that if they'd hit bone, squarely, instead of meat, they would have broken the bones . . .

He'd never had a chance: and he was still embarrassed.

And he thought that if he encountered the two men again, in a place where he could do it, he'd kill them. The thought made him smile, and he drifted away on a new shot of drugs, not to wake until eight.

At eight o'clock, he rose back to the sur-

215

face, thrashed for a moment, and a nurse came in and asked, "How are we feeling?"

"We're feeling a little creaky," Jake said. He could feel the bruises, like burns. "Could you hand me my briefcase?"

"The doctor will be here in a minute."

"Yeah, but my wife is probably going crazy, wondering where I am," he lied. "I just want to call her."

He got the phone. When he switched it on, he found four messages from Gina, starting at six-thirty, all pretty much the same: "Jake, where are you? We're calling, we can't get you. Call in . . ."

He called. Gina picked up and he said, "You won't believe what happened, where I am . . ."

Danzig came on a moment later, his voice hushed: "Jesus Christ, Jake, how bad are you hurt?"

"Ah. Not bad. I'm bruised up. I got a few stitches in my scalp, got a headache. They say I'm fine."

The doc came in to hear the last part of it, pulled on his lip, and shook his head. Jake said to Danzig, "The doctor just got here. I'll call you from the house. I'm still working."

"You think, I mean — the Watchmen? Or just muggers? Or what? I mean, it's a pretty big coincidence."

"Yeah, I'm thinking about that. Give me an hour or two."

"What about this Patterson? We wanted you to go see him, but maybe Novatny . . ."

"No, no. Keep Novatny out of this part, or you're gonna see it all over the papers." He glanced at the doc. "Listen, I can't talk right now, they're about to do something unpleasant to me."

"Okay. Okay. Well, Jesus, take care of yourself. Call me." Danzig sounded like his father.

"I'll call."

He punched off and the doc said, "Not *that* unpleasant. Get a light shined in your eye, pee in a bottle, give up a little blood. Is it true that you have health insurance?"

He was on the street at ten o'clock, a vague ache in his brain, a hotter, harsher pain where the stitches were holding his scalp together. Sunlight hurt his eyes; he needed sunglasses. And he was really beginning to hurt now. He got a cab, had it drop him at the alley. Cunningham came out on his back balcony and shouted, "That was quick."

Jake called back, "I owe you, Harley. Big-time."

"Ah, bullshit, man, glad you're okay."

"Couple bottles of single malt, anyway."

Cunningham threw up his hands. "Now that you mention it," he said, "you *do* owe me . . ."

Inside, Jake did a quick check of the house, then went into the bathroom and looked at himself. They'd cut a bit of hair away from the scalp gash and put a piece of tape over the stitches. That didn't look so good. He peeled off his clothes, turned to look at his back. He had a row of cue-width bruises on his shoulder blades, back, butt, and legs, already in the deep-purple stage, with streaks of red. They'd be a sickly yellow-black in a week.

If Cunningham hadn't been there with his shotgun, if they'd had time to really work on him, he would have needed all the insurance that he had . . . or none at all.

Despite the headache and the bruises, he got Patterson's home phone number and called. He got an out-of-office phone message that said he was in Atlanta and would be back in the office in four days. The message gave his e-mail address and said that it would be checked daily.

Uh-uh. No waiting in modern times. He

went online, got a list of Atlanta hotels, and started calling, beginning with those he thought a political consultant might patronize.

He hit on the third try: Patterson was at the Four Seasons.

He called Gina, told her his problem, got routed through to the White House travel office, and booked on a jet leaving National at one o'clock. He'd have to hustle.

He cleaned up, shaved, showered, dressed, shoved a Dopp kit and a change of clothes in a carry-on bag, called a cab.

The cabdriver was named Charlie, a morose man so fat that he'd crushed the front seat in his aging Chevy. Charlie's head barely protruded over the back of the seat, showing an untidy mop of hair that looked like a stand of ornamental grass, yellow-white and erect. He worked eighteen-hour days, and was Jake's cabbie of choice. Charlie took his cab calls in the back room of a twenty-four-hour newsstand, and so could provide a summary and commentary on news from around the country.

He had a disaster that Jake hadn't heard about: "Big shoot-out between the Border Patrol and the coyotes, down around El Paso. There were some Chinese involved, I guess they were coming across, and somebody started shooting. Two or three dead Border Patrol, a bunch of dead Chinamen. I don't know about the coyotes. They say the Border Patrol crossed the river chasing them . . ."

"Ah, boy."

"Well, what you gonna do?" Charlie asked. "Gotta keep them out somehow."

"The penalty for crossing the border isn't death," Jake said. "What else happened?"

"Mostly bad weather. Lots of tornadoes out in Oklahoma and Kansas. Some small town got it, but nobody was killed. Still on strike in Detroit. The Canadian prime minister got a nosebleed during a press conference and he's at the hospital for a checkup. One of the jurors in the Crippen trial got thrown out because he got caught watching trial news . . ."

Charlie concluded with, "By the way, you look terrible. What's the story on your scalp?"

"Got mugged last night. Beat the heck out of me."

"You all right?" Charlie asked. "You think you ought to be flying?"

"They gave me some pills. I'm okay."

"Huh. Tell you what — you got a Frankenstein vibe going, them stitches sticking out like that. You ought to buy a hat."

He arrived at the gate at National with fifteen minutes to spare. He bought a couple of hunting magazines, and *Scientific American*, and a ball cap to cover the scalp wound. There wasn't much in the way of ball caps at the gate, and only one that fit: a pink cap with a *Hello Kitty* logo on the front.

He took the cap, got on the plane. A headache had been lingering in the background all morning, and in the plane, it got worse. Bad enough that he couldn't read for the first half hour of the flight. He had the window seat, and kept the window shutter closed to avoid the light. Tried to relax, took a pill that the doc said wouldn't make him too woozy. That helped a bit.

When the headache backed off, he punched up his laptop and read the information he'd pulled on Patterson. The quality was poor, mostly on the level of gossip, but he could read between the lines.

Patterson was a political hack, number two or three in a campaign management team, the guy who did the stuff that had to be done but nobody wanted to admit to.

The disinformation guy; the fixer. He'd worked on both of Bowe's senatorial campaigns, one winner and one loser, and two dozen other campaigns scattered around the country. A photograph, from *Washingtonian* magazine, showed a man in his midforties, in a suit that was rumpled but expensive, a drink in his hand, a glassy smile on his face. There were a dozen people in the photo, three posing, including Patterson, the rest just milling around, most with drinks, at a charity ball.

There were, Jake thought, a hundred thousand people like Patterson within thirty miles of the Capitol.

Like Elizabethan courtiers with machine-readable IDs.

Madison Bowe had just gotten off the shuttle and was walking through LaGuardia in New York, when she turned on her cell phone and found a message: Call Johnson Black.

She pushed the speed dial, and when she got through, Black asked, "Did you hear about Jake Winter?"

She stopped for a moment, turned to face a wall, plugged her opposite ear with her fingertip — traveler's privacy — and said, "What happened?"

"He got beaten up last night. One of my guys heard it from a cabdriver, and I called a friend downtown. He was in the hospital overnight, but he's out now."

"Goodman?"

"I don't know. The cops have it as a mugging. But Jake — I'm not sure he'd let himself get mugged."

"Oh, God. I'll call him," she said.

But when she called, she got a cell-phone answering machine. She said, "Jake. Call me. It's important. Here are the numbers . . ."

She took a cab to the apartment, worrying about him: *How bad, how bad, how bad?* Then thought, *Why am I worried about him?*

10

The Four Seasons was an ungainly building, pale gray, with an acre of marble floor inside, white pillars and crystal chandeliers and what looked, against the odds, like it might be a decent bar. Jake called up to Patterson's room from the house phone, expecting no answer, prepared to wait.

But Patterson picked up on the third ring, his voice stiff, cranky, as though he'd just gotten up. "Patterson."

"Mr. Patterson, my name is Jake Winter. I work for Bill Danzig, the president's chief of staff. I need to talk with you. Right now."

Patterson was confused. "Bill Danzig? Who?"

"The president's chief of . . ."

"I know who Bill Danzig is. Who are you again? Where are you?"

"I'm downstairs. I work for Mr. Danzig. If you want to call and check, you can do that. I need to talk."

"Okay . . . Do you want to come up, or should I come down?"

"Better that I come up."

A "DO NOT DISTURB" light was still blinking at Patterson's door when Jake knocked, then knocked a second time. As he waited, he adjusted his cap, then saw an eye at the peephole. The door opened on a short chain, and Patterson, still in pajamas, looked out: "Do you have some identification?"

Jake dug out the White House ID. Patterson looked at it for a moment, then said, "Let me get the chain . . ." The door closed a couple of inches, the chain rattled, and then the door opened fully and Patterson said, "Are you sure you got the right guy? I'm in the other party."

"Yeah. You're the right guy."

"How'd you find me?"

"I got the message on your answering machine, and called all the Atlanta hotels that a political consultant might stay at."

Patterson smiled at that. "Okay. Come on in. I was up all night last night, didn't get to bed until after six this morning. Raising money." He yawned, rubbed the back of his neck, led the way into the small suite. "I was afraid the CIA had planted a bug in my toenails or something. The way you tracked me."

He was taller than he'd looked in the

magazine photograph, and heavier. His double-extra-large burgundy pajamas were printed with thumb-sized black-and-white penguins. He dropped into a chair, pointed at the sofa across the coffee table, asked, "What's going on? You want some coffee?"

"You know about Senator Bowe?"

"Of course. You couldn't avoid it. What does that have to do with me?" But Jake picked up the defensive note in his voice. Patterson suspected what was coming.

Jake said, "A while back, you met with Barbara Packer at the Watergate and asked her what would be the best time, from a Republican point of view, to drop a scandal on the vice president. Was the scandal provided by Senator Bowe?"

Patterson stared at him for a moment, calculating, then said, "Give me a minute." He stood up, went into the bathroom, and closed the door. A minute later the toilet flushed, and a minute after that, his face damp from splashed water, he came back out of the bathroom, sat down heavily, and asked, "Is the FBI on the way up?"

"Not yet; but they may be later," Jake said.

"You said you work for Danzig. Are you a cop, or not?"

"I'm not a cop. Technically, I'm a research consultant. I will tell you, though, that the FBI is all over the case. If I think that what you know is relevant to the Bowe investigation, I'd have to give you up. Sooner or later."

Patterson studied him for a minute, then said, "Maybe I should get a lawyer and talk straight to the FBI."

"You could do that," Jake said. "But the FBI is nervous. The more heat that's put on them, the more likely they are to find somebody to send to prison. I'm just looking into the politics, not the crime."

After another moment of silence, Patterson said, "The truth is, it's all politics."

"So what about Bowe? Was he retailing this scandal to you?"

He leaned back on the couch. "Yeah. Essentially."

"What does that mean?" Jake asked.

"Linc knew about this package — I don't know who's got it now, and I didn't even see all of it. There are papers, e-mails, bank records, even a video recording involving the construction of a four-lane highway in Wisconsin. Highway sixty-five. It runs between the Twin Cities area and a resort town up north. The state and federal government spent three hundred and fifty million dollars on it. If the package is accurate, quite a bit of the money stuck to the vice president and his friends. Seven, eight million, anyway. Probably more."

"Where'd the documents come from?" Jake asked.

"The general contractor. The overall management contract went to a company called ITEM, and somebody with ITEM apparently documented the graft. Why, I don't know. Who, I don't know. The fact is, it could be a very clever forgery, one of those little Internet assholes gone crazy. But if it's real, and if it gets out in public, the vice president is gone. Maybe the president with him. Depending on the timing."

"The timing."

"Yeah. The timing. Think about it," Patterson said. "If somebody drops the package now, there'll be a huge stink and in a month or so, the vice president goes away. Everybody starts maneuvering for a trial, but that won't come for a year or two. We — the Republicans — squeal and holler, but the administration says, 'Look, we didn't know he was a crook, it happened before we picked him. We're gonna put him in jail now that we know.' You lose thirty points in the polls, then pick a good man to replace Landers. You have a big happy convention, talk about the fact that the vice presidency doesn't mean shit anyway, you recover the thirty points, and us Republicans are back at square one."

Jake crossed his legs. "Okay . . ." When you got somebody rolling with a story, you let them roll.

Patterson continued: "If we dropped the package in the first week of October, the scandal would peak on election day. It'd take you two or three weeks to get rid of Landers. You know how that goes, he denies it, he maneuvers, his wife cries for the cameras and defends her man. But this stuff is undeniable, if it's real. So a week before the election, Landers is dumped, and you're down thirty points in the polls. Nobody wants the VP nomination because the Dems are about to get creamed. You wind up with some loser on the ticket, which makes everything worse — makes you look weak — and the president goes down."

"All because of the timing."

"Oh, yeah. If this thing is real, it'll come out, sooner or later. But the timing is absolutely critical."

Jake stood up, limped around the suite, over to the window, and looked out over Atlanta. Turned back and said, "You don't know where the package is?"

"Nope. Linc took that information with him. Some place in Wisconsin, obviously. Maybe Wausau, that's where ITEM's headquarters is. But they've got several offices around Wisconsin."

"None of this connects to Senator Bowe's last campaign, does it?"

Patterson looked away, touched his fingertips together, rubbed them for a moment, and then said, "No. Not exactly."

" 'Not exactly'?"

"He would have loved to fuck this president, and to have gotten word back about who did it to him, after what they did to him," Patterson said. "Linc had a mean streak. Big mean streak — but then, he was a U.S. senator. You don't get that job without a mean streak."

"Huh. But no involvement with Arlo Goodman."

Patterson produced a rueful smile. "Arlo Goodman," he said. "How long did it take you to find out about this package? Track me down? After you started looking?"

Jake shrugged: "A couple of days."

"Right. I bet fifty people have had a sniff of it by now. It's like a great big Easter egg, and everybody's hunting for it. I will bet you one thousand American dollars that Arlo Goodman and his boys have heard about it. I will bet you that that's the reason they snatched Linc."

"You think Goodman . . ."

"Damned right, I do. A couple of those Iraq veterans that Goodman has hanging around, those special forces assholes, took Linc out in the woods and drilled holes in his head until he told them about the package."

"That's . . . quite the statement."

Patterson made a helpless gesture with his hands. "I can't prove it. I don't have a single atom of proof. But I bet that's what happened. If Landers gets dumped now, who better for the vice presidency than Arlo Goodman? He's popular, he's good-looking, he's a hell of a campaigner, he's the governor of a big swing state, and he can't succeed himself. He's available. In four years, he's got a shot at replacing the president."

"And for that to work, Landers has to get dumped now," Jake suggested.

"Absolutely. Goodman needs that package out there now, or in the next month. If it doesn't come out until October, he's outa luck. The Dems lose, Goodman's out of his governorship next year, with nothing political available. And he has no real claim for the presidential nomination in four years."

They both thought about that for a

minute. "If your guess is right, about Goodman and Bowe," Jake said, "I'd think you'd be a little worried."

"I am — but not as worried as somebody else must be," Patterson said. "I was downstream from the package. I never had it. Linc was the only guy who could point you upstream, to whoever has it now."

"Does Madison Bowe know about it?"

Patterson scratched his head. "You know, I just don't know about that. They were . . . separate . . . although they liked each other okay. And he was pretty protective of her. I don't know if he would have told her about it. This thing could be real trouble for people who know about it."

Jake said, "Huh." Then, "Have any idea where I could look? Who I could ask?"

"I'd find Linc's closest asshole buddy, and ask him. Somebody both in politics and in bed with him. But it's just possible that he didn't tell anyone."

Jake thought: *Barber.* And, *Patterson knew that Lincoln Bowe was gay.*

"How many people knew about Lincoln Bowe's sex life?" Jake asked. When Patterson hesitated, he added, "I don't need a number, I'm just looking for a characterization."

"So you know?"

"That he was gay? Yes. Madison told me."

Patterson nodded. "So who knew? Anybody who knew him for a while — knew him well. If you were close enough to see who he was looking at."

"Quite a few people."

"Yeah. He was careful, but people knew. Two dozen? Three or four dozen? I don't know. I don't know if his parents knew . . ."

"Would Goodman know?"

"Ah . . ." Patterson ruffled his hair with one hand, squinting at the bright light from the window. "That's hard to tell. I would be surprised if Goodman hadn't put a spy or two in our campaign, but it'd be at a pretty low level — a volunteer, somebody running our computers. If Goodman knows, it's probably only at the rumor level. And then you look at Madison, and you think, 'The guy's gay? With pussy like that in the house? No way.'"

They talked for another twenty minutes, with Jake trying to nail down every piece of information Patterson had about the Landers package. When they were finished, Jake stood up, dropped his legal pad back in his briefcase, and asked, "What're you going to do?"

"Keep my mouth shut, for the time being," Patterson said. "Until I find out where the trouble is coming from. If I talk to the FBI, they're gonna want to know why I didn't bring this up right away. Then the whole Landers thing will blow out in the open, and you guys get what you want — Landers is off the ticket, and we're fucked. If I don't talk to them, I might still be in trouble, but there's a possibility that I can slide through. Right now, at this moment, I think I'll try to slide. But that could change."

"You gonna let me know?"

Patterson showed a shaky smile: "Maybe. I might need a little help. I've given you a little help, I might need a little help in return."

"Call me," Jake said. "Things can always be done."

As Jake headed for the door, Patterson called after him: "Have you got something going with Madison?"

That stopped him: "Why?"

"Because when I said 'pussy,' your eyeballs pulled back about two inches into your head. I thought you were gonna jump down my throat."

"I talk to her," Jake said.

"Sorry about the 'pussy,' then."

"Yeah . . . well. You were right about the thought, anyway."

"One more thing," Patterson said. "What's with that goofy *Hello Kitty* cap?"

Jake touched the cap: "Short version, I've got a cut with a bunch of stitches and a white patch of scalp where they shaved it. A cabdriver told me I was giving off a Frankenstein vibe. I was on the run, and didn't have time to get a different hat."

Patterson smiled again: "The hat . . . I've never been questioned by a guy wearing a *Hello Kitty* hat. Kinda scary, in a chain-saw-massacre way."

When he left, Patterson was still on the couch, drinking a Coke from the minibar, staring at the television. Jake walked down to the front desk, asked the bellman to get a cab for him, saw an *Atlanta Braves* hat in the gift shop, bought one, shoved the *Hello Kitty* hat into a trash can, walked out on the front steps, and punched Danzig's number into his cell phone. Gina put him straight through.

"We've got to be really careful," Danzig said, without preamble.

"I know. I talked to Patterson. We need to talk, tonight, if I can get a flight. Could be late."

"Call the travel office."

He called the White House travel office and found he was already being booked on a seven o'clock flight back. He'd had his phone turned off during the first flight and his talk with Patterson, and when he checked messages, he found a voice mail from Madison Bowe.

"Please call me. It's important." She left both her home and cell-phone numbers. The cab came, and he put the phone away until he was at the airport. He got a ticket, walked through security, and called her from the gate.

She answered on the first ring: "Hello?"

"Madison, Mrs. Bowe — this is Jake Winter."

"Jacob. Jeez, I've been trying to get you everywhere," she said. "Johnson Black heard that you were beaten up last night, and they took you to the hospital. Where are you?"

Interesting. She seemed concerned. "Atlanta."

"Atlanta?" She seemed less concerned. "How did you get to Atlanta?"

"By air," he said.

She laughed and said, "No, stupid, I didn't mean, I meant — oh, fuck it, I don't know what I meant. You're not hurt?"

"Bruised. Got some tape on my head." He felt himself sucking for sympathy. "Are you . . . mmm, the funeral is tomorrow?"

Somber now: "Yes. One o'clock. It'll be a circus. Listen, does Danzig still have you looking around, or are you all done?"

"We'd still like to know what happened," Jake said.

"Good. You're still looking. I've got more problems."

"What happened?" He let the alarm show. "You don't think, I mean, you haven't seen anybody . . ."

"No, no. I'm in New York, I'm about to head back to Washington. We better talk face-to-face. I'm getting really paranoid."

"Will you be up late?" he asked.

"Probably. When do you get back?"

"I'm scheduled in at nine o'clock," he said. "I've got to stop to talk with Danzig. I don't think I could be any earlier than ten or ten-thirty at the earliest."

The airport had universal wireless, and while he was waiting for the plane, he went online to the State of Wisconsin website, and then to federal DOT records, adding file information to what he'd been told by Patterson. The road project had been real enough, and the money was just what

Patterson had said it was. Much of the money had come from the federal government — which meant that if the Landers package was legit, then Landers had committed federal felonies.

The flight was called on time and the trip back was as quick and routine as the flight out: short, boring, noisy. When he got out of the seat in Washington, he had a little trouble standing up: his bruised muscles were cramping on him, and he stopped in the terminal to stretch a bit.

Nothing helped much: he simply hurt. Outside, he grabbed a bag, took a cab to the White House, called ahead, and had an escort waiting at the Blue Room. Gina was in Danzig's inner office, shoes off, twitching her toes in her nylons. The other two secretaries were gone. When Jake walked in, she asked, "How's your head?"

"Little ache. Could be hunger, though." He had to explain exactly what had happened.

Danzig: "So after you were down and before your friend fired the gun, they didn't go after your wallet? They didn't get your briefcase?"

"No. That worries me."

Gina shivered: "I don't like the sound of it." Then she stood up. "You want coffee? I could get you a sandwich?"

Jake said, "Yeah. Both. That'd be great."

"Ham and cheese? Tuna?"

When she was gone, Danzig said, "She's relentless . . . So?"

Jake dropped into a chair across the desk from him, dug in his case, brought out a yellow legal pad, looked at his notes. "In Wisconsin, under the Landers administration, the state began work on a ninety-one-mile improvement of Federal Highway 65. The improvements began at I-94 east of the Twin Cities and ran up to a resort area called Hayward, in the Wisconsin north woods. There were about three hundred million federal dollars spent on it, plus about fifty-five million in state money. Landers and his friends allegedly stole about eight million dollars of it."

"Jeez, more'n two percent. That's pretty good," Danzig said. "How'd they do it?"

"Don't know. There's this package . . ."

Halfway through the briefing, they heard Gina come back, and Danzig put a finger to his lips, a "be quiet" signal. Gina came in with the sandwiches and coffee, and Danzig said, "Gina: take off."

"Oh, if you've still got things . . ."

"Gina: go home. Say hello to your husband. I'm going to talk to Jake, get this whole project out of the way, then I'm going home myself. Tomorrow, I want to set up a daily report process for the convention, so get me a list of anyone critical that we need to bring into it."

"I could start that tonight."

"Gina: go home."

When she'd gone, reluctantly, Danzig turned back to Jake. "You were saying . . ."

Jake finished the briefing, then Danzig asked, "How many people know about this package?"

"Patterson thinks that quite a few have had a smell. If he's right about Goodman . . ."

Danzig was shaking his head. "That Goodman stuff sounds phony. Goodman's way too smart to get mixed up in a kidnapping and murder. Or in beating you up, if you were thinking that."

"I don't know," Jake said, shaking his head. "They seem to have a thing going on down there. Goodman develops a wish and somebody does something about it."

"Like killing Lincoln Bowe?"

"I don't know," Jake said. "But if this package is out there, and Goodman knows about it . . . I can see why Patterson's worried. Goodman likes power. He's going to lose it. He's got a year left. He might see this package as a way back."

"Yup." Danzig twiddled his thumbs: elementary.

"The question is, do I take all this to Novatny, or do I keep looking around, or do we just forget about it?"

Danzig studied him for a minute, then said, "This is the thing, Jake. Patterson was right about Landers, for sure. If we need to dump him, we need to do it soon. And *we* need to do it. We don't need the *New York Times* or the *Washington Post* to break this on us. We need to look proactive."

"We need the package."

"Yes. Landers won't go if we don't have it. He'll just dig in."

"Maybe we could . . . Never mind."

"You were going to say?" Danzig asked.

"I was going to say, maybe we could replicate it. Put it together independently. But that would take an investigation, the word would bleed out, and we'd be twisting in the wind."

Danzig nodded: "Exactly. If there's a package, we need it now, and we need it all. If there isn't a package, we need to know that. What we don't need is a long investigation, a special prosecutor, a controversy. We don't need a long-brewed scandal. We need either to get it over with, or buried for good."

"You want me to keep looking?"

Danzig said, "Jake, I do want you to keep looking — but I don't want to have anything to do with it. I'm going to tell Gina tomorrow morning that we're all done, to tote up what we owe you on the consult. I want you to continue on your own hook, and if you find the package, I want you to deliver it." Another moment of silence, then Danzig said, "You get my drift."

Jake said, "You want me to be deniable."

"Took the words right out of my mouth," Danzig said. "I want the best of both worlds. I want you off the payroll, so we don't have any backfires. I want you to keep looking, so that if there is something we need, you'll find it and we'll get it. Us, not anybody else. And I want it so if you get caught doing something unethical or criminal, we can throw you to the wolves."

Jake smiled: "Thanks, boss."

"You're not a virgin."

"One part of me is. I wouldn't want that changed in a federal prison."

"I can understand that," Danzig said. "But believe me, there's a terrific upside if you pull this off."

"What upside?"

"What do you want?"

The question hung there. Jake stared at him, then said, "You're serious."

"Absolutely."

"I might want a lot," Jake said.

"I can't give you a billion dollars, but I can get you something good."

Jake thought about it for a minute, then nodded. "You'll pay off this consult?"

"As of tonight."

"Should I stay in touch?"

"Call me if you get it," Danzig said.

"And if I don't?"

"Then don't call me. But Jake: you gotta get it."

Jake stood up, leaned on his cane for a moment, then took a slow turn around the office, looked at the Remington bronze that sat on the credenza, touched the buffalo head, turned back, and said, "The whole thing, the package thing, started with an anonymous tip. A guy calls in the middle of the night and says, 'See what Packer and Patterson talked about at the Watergate.' So — who was that, and what was the motive? There's somebody else out there. I can't see him. I can't see what he wants."

Danzig tapped on his desk with a yellow pencil, staring at Jake but not focused on him, and finally sighed and said, "Shit, Jake, there's *always* somebody out there. What he wants . . . he might want anything. The simple pleasure of knowing he took down Landers. Maybe there's a better job in it for him. Maybe he figures they'll make a movie about him, he'll get to go to Hollywood and fuck Brittany West."

"Patterson suggested that Goodman could benefit. Take a big step up," Jake said.

Now Danzig's eyes snapped. "Well. We'll see how things work out. I know why he'd say that, though. God help us."

Jake headed for the door: "I'll see you."

"You're gonna do it?"

Jake smiled. "You don't want to know, right?"

11

Jake arrived at Madison's town house at 10:30, wrestled his overnight bag out of the cab, hung it over his shoulder, carried his briefcase on the other side, tapped his way up the walk with his cane. He'd called Madison from the cab. Halfway up the walk, the porch light came on and she opened the door.

"Mrs. Bowe . . ."

"Did you have a good time at the White House?"

"You hardly ever have a good time at the White House, unless you're the president," Jake said. He thought about Danzig, and the *What do you want?* "You *can* have interesting times."

"Gonna tell me about it?"

"No."

She had a black dress hanging on a hook in the entryway, still in a plastic dry-cleaning bag, and a shoe bag sitting on the floor beneath it. Funeral clothes, Jake thought, as he went by into the living room. She had a gas fireplace. The fire was on, flickering behind a glass door. He dropped his bags, sat on the couch, and she asked, "A glass of wine?"

"That would be great."

She was back in a minute, with two glasses. The wine was already open, and she held it up to the ceiling light and peered through it. "I started without you," she said. She poured and handed him a glass. "I talked to Novatny. They have no ideas, other than this Schmidt man."

"But Schmidt's a pretty good idea," Jake said. "What happened in New York? You said something odd happened."

"First of all, tell me what happened the other night. When you got mugged."

He told her, succinctly, trying not to show his embarrassment, nipping at the wine while he talked. She listened intently, and then said, "Doesn't sound like a robbery."

"I know," he said. "And I know what you're going to say. I don't think the Watchmen are involved. Goodman thinks I'm out scouting around for *him*. I was actually thinking that your friend Barber might be a possibility — though I don't see what beating me up would have gotten him."

She frowned: "He has a violent streak in him. I've seen that in the past. I think Linc

246

was attracted to it. But remember when you told me about *The Rule?* Who benefits from your getting beaten up?"

"The Rule doesn't say that the benefit has to be obvious. In fact, it usually isn't. We just don't know enough yet . . . So: New York?"

"Yes." She poured a glass of wine for herself, set the bottle on the coffee table, and perched on an easy chair, folding her legs beneath herself as women do. "I took the shuttle up early this morning and went to the apartment. To check it, make sure everything was okay, to look for some papers, to pay the maid. I needed to get Linc's will, for one thing, some insurance policies that Johnnie Black needs to see. I got everything I needed, but . . . his medical records were gone. There were two big folders, in the top drawer of the file cabinet, and they were gone. They aren't here and I know they aren't at the farm. I can't see why they'd be in Santa Fe, his doctor is in New York."

Jake thought about it and shrugged. "I don't know what that means."

"Neither do I. Except that underneath the bed sham, I found a bottle of prescription medicine, Rinolat. I looked it up online, and it's a painkiller. I didn't understand it all, something about monoclonal antibodies. Anyway, he was taking a heavy dose. The stuff would put a horse to sleep."

"I know . . ." He slapped his leg. "I have some experience with it. Was it dated?"

"Yes. A month before he disappeared."

"He was sick?"

She shook her head: "Not as far as I know. I haven't seen him for a while. The last time I saw him, he was a little cranky, but he wasn't in pain. Not that I could see."

"Huh. The stuff isn't of any use recreationally . . . Are you sure it was his?"

"The prescription was in his name, from his doctor."

Jake sipped the wine, swirled it in his glass. He didn't know much about wine, but it tasted fine; tasted like money. And he thought about the autopsy report. Novatny said that Bowe's body had been suffused with painkiller, possibly to keep him helpless. But was that what happened? "You think somebody stole the medical file? Have you talked to the maid?"

Madison nodded. "Yes. I did. This is the other funny thing. She saw his doctor. At the apartment. With medical equipment."

"What doctor?"

"James Rosenquist. He's an old friend of Linc's. One of his special friends, or once was. I called him, and he said he hadn't seen Linc for six months, since a physical. But James has a white streak in his hair — he's a little vain about it — and the maid said the man she saw in the apartment, the doctor, had a stripe like a skunk."

"Ah, man." Jake leaned back, rubbed his face, and yawned. Shook his head and admitted, "I still don't know what it means."

"Neither do I. It's just that there seems to be another mystery in New York and there shouldn't be two mysteries at the same time. Not unrelated ones," Madison said. "I was thinking about siccing Johnnie Black on James, but since James denies even *seeing* Linc . . ."

"Rosenquist is in New York City?"

"Yes. He has one of those practices on the bottom floor of a co-op, on the Upper East Side."

"One of the rich guys," Jake said, "who'll be all lawyered up."

"Absolutely."

Jake sighed, gulped the wine, bent forward to pick up his case, winced at the pain. "Mrs. Bowe. Let me check around, but to tell you the truth, I don't know what I can do."

"What if James, what if Rosenquist is hooked up with Goodman somehow? I mean . . ." She flapped at him.

"There's no reason to think that? That there's a connection?"

"No, but it seems odd. Linc didn't hide things from me. We no longer had a sexual relationship, but we were still married. We were certainly fond of each other. I didn't know anything about an illness. I didn't . . . I mean, what if Rosenquist drugged him somehow? Delivered him?" Her voice trailed away, and she frowned. "Am I being a dingbat?"

"Not at all," Jake said. "Nothing you said is crazy, I just don't see where you're going with it. Or where it can go."

She chewed her lip for a moment, looking at him, then said, "You don't trust me."

"I do, as far as . . ." He stopped.

"As far as what? You can throw a Toyota?"

"No. I do trust you." Another little lie. Or was it? She *felt* trustworthy. On the other hand, apparent trustworthiness was a quality that Washingtonians spent a lifetime perfecting.

He'd thought of asking her about the Landers package, but decided not to: he had to do more checking. If she had it, or knew who did, he didn't want to do something that might inadvertently pull a trigger, get the package dumped to the *Times*. Not until Danzig was ready for it, anyway.

He stood up, said, "I'll call you tomorrow. Let me think about all of this. I'll call you."

She leaned back in the chair for the first time, took another sip of wine, looking at him over the top of the glass, and then said, "All right. This probably won't help you learn to trust me, but I need to tell you something. I thought about it when we started talking about his sexual orientation."

"Okay."

"Linc had his outside relationships — but so did I. I've had two affairs in the last nine years. Both of them lasted about two years, with nice, discreet men, and then they stopped. They stopped basically because they weren't going anywhere. Linc knew about both of them, and it was okay with him. I mean, he was a little wistful — but he understood."

Jake said, "Mrs. Bowe . . ."

"You should call me Madison, under the circumstances."

"What circumstances?"

"The circumstances of me using you as a confessor. But let me finish. I thought you should know, because it's another thing about us . . ." Her forehead wrinkled, and she gestured with the glass, then, ". . . it's another thing, that if I hadn't told you, and you found out later, you'd wonder about. You'd wonder if there might be some reason that somebody would want to get rid of Linc. But: I promise you, I have had exactly two relationships, no more. Neither of the men involved would have any reason to wish harm to Lincoln. Neither affair continues. Everybody is more or less happy. So . . ."

He nodded now, and said, "You really didn't have to tell me. I don't think people do what was done to Lincoln because of *your* outside relationships. In the most extreme cases, somebody might get shot, I suppose. But in this day and age . . ."

"You're a little cynical," she said.

"I work in Washington."

That night, he lay awake for a while, considering possibilities. One seemed clear: all roads to the truth ran through the dead body of Lincoln Bowe. And he thought about Madison Bowe and the medical records . . .

He was gone before he knew it, awake again before five o'clock. He cleaned up, stretched, worked his leg. He ached from the beating, and the bruises, if anything, were darker, bluer. The lingering headache was still there, a shadow, annoying but not limiting. He'd been lucky.

Or possibly, he thought, he was being manipulated, not only by Madison, but by the men who'd beaten him up. Perhaps they'd beaten him for some reason that he couldn't even imagine, pushing him toward . . . what?

From his office, he used his access to government records to go online with the Social Security Administration. There, he checked the records of one Donald Patzo, a man from deep in his past. Patzo had skills he might need . . .

There were twenty-four Donald Patzos in the records, but only one fit by age and by employment. Patzo was sixty-six years old. He'd started drawing Social Security when he was sixty-two, and his employment record suggested that he wouldn't have much of a pension — he'd had twenty-four jobs in the forty years after he'd gotten out of the military, and hadn't worked at all for the fifteen years he'd spent in prison.

Jake noted his address, then looked it up on his laptop map program. At seven o'clock, he called Madison.

"This is Jake. I hope I didn't wake you."

"No, no, this is going to be a hellish day," she said. "I've been up since five."

"Can I stop by and pick up the key to your New York apartment?"

Pause. "What are you going to do?"

"I want to go over it inch by inch. I'll try to preserve your privacy, if there's anything you don't want me to look at."

"No, no." Another pause. Then, "I guess I'd rather have you tear it apart than the FBI. When are you going up?"

"Right away. I've got to do some running around, but I'd like to get the shuttle out of National at noon."

"Soon as you can get here."

He was at her door at seven-fifteen. Two television trucks were parked in the street, but neither bothered to film Jake. A man with a funny hat was just leaving, heading for a florist's van. Another woman was inside, Madison's best horsey friend from Lexington, she said. She gave him the key with a note to the doorman. "I called the doorman, told him you were coming and to let you in."

"Is there a computer in the apartment?"

"Of course." She was wearing jeans and a golf shirt, and was standing close to him, her voice pitched down. Jake could hear her friend talking on a telephone.

"Do you know his password? If it has a password?"

She rolled her eyes. "He was in Skull and Bones at Yale. It's 'Bonester.' "

"You gotta be kidding me . . ." He shook his head, smiled: the Ivy League. "Is there a safe?"

"Yes, but it's empty. I emptied it yesterday. It's in the kitchen, actually, under what looks like a built-in chopping block."

Her friend was in the living room. They'd walked out to the entry, and as he turned to leave, she caught his jacket sleeve, pulled his shoulders down, and kissed him quickly on the lips. "Be careful. Be careful, please."

Then he didn't want to leave; but he did. He stopped at a convenience store, made a call to Don Patzo in Baltimore. Patzo picked up on the fourth ring, sleep in his voice: "What?"

Jake hung up. He wanted to talk to Patzo face-to-face.

Traffic was bad, and all the way to Baltimore, he could feel the kiss.

There was, in his experience, a wide variety of kisses, ranging from Air, on one end of the spectrum, to Orgasmic on the other. Included were Affectionate, Hot, Friendly, First, Promising, Intense, Good-bye for Good, See You Later, Desperate, Mom, and French, not to be confused with French Officer.

Had this been a First — which implied a Second — or had it been an Affectionate or Friendly, which weren't necessarily good? Had she pushed up against him a little? Had he recoiled? He didn't think he'd recoiled, but he'd definitely been surprised. Should he have taken hold of something? Like what?

He remembered the old Irish joke, and smiled at it: "Sweet lovin' Jesus, Sweeney, didn't you have nothin' in your own hand?" — "Nothing but Mrs. O'Hara's ass, and though it's a thing of beauty in its own right, it ain't worth a damn in a fight . . ."

Like being fourteen again.

He was in Baltimore a few minutes after nine o'clock, used the car's nav system to find Don Patzo's house. He got lost, even with the nav system — the maps showed streets going through where they didn't — wandered around for a half hour, and finally found the place down a dead-end street not far from the water, but with an unpleasant fishy smell about it.

Patzo was the man who'd tried to teach him burglary before Jake left for Afghanistan. He'd been in prison a half dozen different times in three states, before taking the contract with the CIA, and in class said he didn't know the exact number, but thought he might have done better than two thousand burglaries. "Quality jobs: wasn't stealin' no fuckin' boom boxes or video games."

Jake asked him how he'd gotten caught so often. "Percentages, sonny. Just like in gambling. You figure the odds are a hundred to one against getting caught, then you go in a hundred times, and guess what? The percentages just ran out."

Patzo lived in a small, frame house with shingle siding, a concrete-block stoop, and a neatly trimmed lawn. A dozen freshly planted petunias struggled for life in a window box. Jake knocked, knocked again. Patzo came to the door. Jake recognized him, but only because he'd known who he was.

The Patzo he'd met ten years earlier was a thick-necked, buzz-cut hood in his middle fifties. This Patzo had shriveled, although the hood was still there in his black eyes. His face was gray, the color of heart trouble, and his nose was large and soft. He was wearing a shabby flannel shirt and jeans with a too-big waist, and white athletic socks.

He pushed open the screen door and said, "Yeah?"

"Don Patzo," Jake said. "You once taught a burglary class to a bunch of special forces guys."

"Yeah? So what?"

"So I was one of those guys. I need a little help."

"Ah, fuck you, pal." Patzo started to pull the door closed. "And I didn't teach no gimps."

"I wasn't a gimp back then," Jake said. "I got to be a gimp later. What I want you to do is easy, not dangerous, will be all done by tonight, and will get you a thousand bucks in tax-free cash and a couple of decent meals. The best part is, it's legal."

Patzo didn't shut the inner door. "How legal is that?"

Jake fished the apartment key from his pocket: "The owner gave me the key and called the doorman to clear the way. You're more of a consultant than a burglar."

Patzo pushed the door open: "I'll give you five minutes to talk to me."

They talked, and Patzo agreed. Jake loaded the old man into his car, headed back to Washington. Stopped at Riggs, opened his safe-deposit box, took out ten thousand of the twenty-five thousand he kept there, just in case; stopped at a drugstore, bought a package of vinyl gloves; and drove them both to National. Patzo kept his mouth shut, but he watched everything. The only emotion he showed was a tightening of his fists when the plane took off, and again when it landed.

They were in New York at one o'clock, a cab across the Triborough to the Upper East Side. The doorman had a note from Madison, and sent them up to Bowe's apartment.

They stepped inside, facing an oval, gilt-framed mirror above an antique table with a cut-crystal bud vase.

Patzo said, "Jesus Christ, that fuckin' table is worth thirty grand."

"You know antiques?"

"Enough. Used to do a lot of woodwork. You know — when I was working for the state." He touched the table gently. "How the fuck would I get it out of here?"

"Don't even think about it," Jake said.

The apartment had two bedrooms, but was bigger than that implied. The kitchen was long and narrow, but complete. The living room was expansive, oak floors and three Oriental carpets, contemporary abstracts on the wall, including, over the fireplace, an excellent Rothko. A den opened off the living room; and down a hall were two bedrooms, a master bedroom suite and a smaller guest room. The master bedroom had a bathroom that contained a tub big enough for three or four people. All of it was wallpapered in delicate pastels.

Jake gave Patzo a pair of the vinyl gloves and a short instruction: "Look, but don't leave any prints. If you find anything that looks like it's been hidden, or interesting — legal papers, medical documents — come get me. The owner had all the stuff inventoried for the IRS, so if anything goes missing, it's gonna be embarrassing for us both."

"Place like this has a safe," Patzo said.

"It does," Jake said. "It's empty — the owner emptied it yesterday. See if you can find it."

"Like a test."

"Yeah."

As the older man prowled the apartment, Jake sat on the floor and started through the filing cabinets. There were two, in the den, under a built-in computer table. He checked each individual file folder and found paid bills, financial records, co-op apartment records, tax forms, receipts and registrations for automobiles, and account papers for mutual funds at Fidelity and Vanguard. He totaled it up in his head, and found that Bowe's accounts at two banks, at U.S. Trust, at Merrill Lynch, and the mutual fund companies totaled some eighty-five million dollars.

He checked every file folder, looking for hidden papers. Found none.

Patzo came by: "There's a gun hanging off the headboard of the bed in the big bedroom."

Jake went to look. The revolver looked like a self-defense piece, an old blue hammerless .38. The gun was in a black rubber holster that had been screwed to the headboard. Jake said, "Keep looking."

As Madison said, there were no medical records at all. He checked the bank accounts, and there had been several large checks cashed in the months prior to Bowe's disappearance, but the records didn't indicate whom the checks were paid to.

He pulled up the computer, signed on with the Bonester password, and started reading e-mail. The e-mail, both incoming and outgoing, was remarkably bland. Too remarkably. He went into the address book, found addresses for fifty or sixty people, including Howard Barber. Yet when he looked for mail involving Barber, either outgoing or incoming, there was none.

The e-mail had been purged.

Patzo came back. "The safe is under the cutting board in the kitchen. It's open. You want to look?"

Jake went to look. As Madison had said, it was empty. "Now, what does this teach you?" Patzo asked.

"Beats the heck out of me," Jake said.

"It teaches you that the guy who put the security in this place knew what he was doing," Patzo said. "He knows he won't fool a pro, if you give the pro all day to look, but no goddamn junkie on this green earth is ever going to find this safe. Not except by accident. So, if there's more stuff hid, it's gonna be clever, and you're gonna have to look for spaces where there shouldn't be spaces."

"That's why I dragged your ass up here."

Jake went back to the computer and

checked the history setting. The history had been wiped, and the time period for saving documents had been set to zero.

Bowe, Jake thought, was wiping out traces of himself right up to the time he disappeared. He could get Madison to go to the banks, and find out whom Bowe had written checks to, but that usually took a few days, and it might take longer, and involve lawyers, in the case of a dead man.

But if Bowe wasn't worried about all the personal financial records he'd left behind, why was he so worried about e-mail, about websites he'd visited, about his medical records? Why had this skunk-striped doctor denied seeing Bowe? Jake was thinking about the doctor when Patzo came back.

"Got another one."

"Another safe?"

"Another something."

This one was in the living room, in a built-in DVD-CD case. "You see the way it looks like this is a trim panel, on the side, but it's not a panel?" Patzo said, tracing the wood with his hands. "There's eighteen inches of space there, a foot high, a foot deep. It could just be a measuring mistake, except everything here is done too well. Everything is very tight, and then you have this . . ."

He kept probing at it, but finally gave up. "I don't know how it opens. But if you went after it with a crowbar, I think you'd find something."

"Maybe it opens remotely," Jake said. "A button, or you think the TV remote?"

"There'd have to be an electric eye for a remote. Probably not that. Probably . . . Let's see, they'd have to wire it, they probably wouldn't want to run the wires all over the place, so it'd be close."

They looked at the edges of the paneling, under the shelves, around the edges of the fireplace, groped behind the TV. Then Patzo said, "Huh," put his foot out, and pressed a piece of base molding. A drawer slid silently out of the DVD case, and Jake said, "Holy shit," and Patzo said, "Like one of them pyramid movies, where the tomb opens," and they both went over to look.

A few worn pieces of paper on top. Jake lifted them out. Below them, they could see a jumble of leather, with the flash of gemstones. Peering in the drawer, Patzo said, "Your friend is a fagola. Or something. A freak."

"My friend is the guy's wife," Jake said. He pointed. "What *is* that?"

"I used to know a fella in the adult novelty business, he had a whole caseful of this stuff," Patzo said. "That thing is a dog collar for people, and that's the dog chain. I don't *know* what that thing is, but I ain't gonna touch it."

"Ah, Jesus," Jake said.

"Other cultures," Patzo said.

"What?"

"Other cultures. The fagola is other cultures. They do what they do."

Jake looked at the paper he'd lifted out: three photographs, a hippie couple perhaps from the sixties, a young girl on a swing, a young boy. The photos were smooth, aged, but with a certain curve to them. They'd been in a wallet.

There was also a three-by-five card with a phrase written on it with a felt-tipped pen: *All because of Lion Nerve.* Nothing else.

"I never seen a dog collar with diamonds in it," Patzo said. He was holding it up by the buckle. "But that's what it is."

"I doubt they're real diamonds," Jake said. "They're too big."

"In a place like this? They're real. And that dog chain is eighteen-karat gold," Patzo said. He looked at Jake. "Can I have them?"

"What?"

265

"The dog collar. The chains. And that other thing. I mean, it's gonna be really embarrassing if your friend finds it, the wife. I couldn't help noticing that the wife is Mrs. Lincoln Bowe and her husband is the dead senator, so if this stuff is his . . . I mean, I could get rid of it. Nobody would ever know. I couldn't tell anybody, because they'd send me back to the joint."

"How much is it worth?"

Patzo said, "Less than Bowe's reputation."

They finished combing the apartment, and Jake called Madison on her cell phone just after six o'clock.

"You okay?"

She'd been alone after the funeral. "I couldn't stop crying. It got on top of me, Jacob."

"But you're okay now?"

"No. I'm pretty messed up," she said.

"Ah, jeez," he said. After a moment of silence, he said, "I need to brace Dr. Rosenquist. Would that cause you an endless amount of trouble?"

"No. He's not my doctor," she said. "I don't even know him very well. What'd you find?"

"It's what I didn't find. Your husband seems to have prepared for his disappearance. He destroyed his personal e-mail, he wiped the history off the computer. All of his tax records and bank records are intact, though, and very neatly filed, as though he was getting ready for an audit — or an estate examination. The question is, Why did he remove the medical records, and why did the doctor deny seeing him? That's one mystery we need to clear up."

"Go ahead. Do it, Jake. But please, please, be careful."

"Yes. I'll figure out a way to keep you out of it. There's one other thing. We found another hideaway in the apartment and there were some items related to your husband's sexual life. Leather stuff, chains. I'm wondering, my consultant says they may have some value, maybe even substantial, but given their nature . . ."

"Get rid of them," she said.

"There were three photos in the same drawer. They're flat and warped, like they were in a wallet. There's a picture of like a hippie couple back in the sixties or seventies, probably, the guy's wearing plaid pants . . ."

"Oh, no," she said. "There's one of a young girl, and a young boy."

"Yeah. Are they important?"

After a long silence, she said, "He'd

never take those out of his wallet. Those are . . . If he left them behind, they're a suicide note."

"A suicide note?"

"Yes. He would have known that I would know. He was sending me a message. They're pictures of his parents, his sister, and himself. They were personal icons. He never would have left them behind, any-where. They're a suicide note."

"A suicide note only works if somebody finds it," Jake said.

"There'll be something in his papers, somewhere, that'll tell me where to look. Or maybe his mother knows, she's still alive. But Jake: he knew he was going to die. Either he was being stalked, or he'd do it himself. But he knew."

He opened his mouth to tell her about the three-by-five card, and then stopped. He'd rather see her face-to-face for that. If *all this* meant his disappearance, he wanted to see her face when he gave her *Lion Nerve*. To see if it registered . . . *What's this, Jake? You don't trust her?*

They talked for another two minutes, and Jake said, "I'm going to see Rosenquist."

"Call me tonight. Tell me what he says."

★ ★ ★

When he got off the line, he said to Patzo: "Your lucky day. I'd like to see your buddy's face when you ask him to get rid of a diamond-studded dog collar."

Patzo's face broke into a beauteous smile. "Jesus, man. I mean, this is my *life*, right here. This dog collar . . ." He held it up, half wrapped in a piece of toilet paper. "I got a *retirement.*"

"You think you can get back to Baltimore on your own?" Jake asked.

"Sure. Lemme make a few calls, maybe take a train back. Could you gimme a couple hundred bucks? I don't like those fuckin' airplanes," Patzo said. "What are you going to do?"

Patzo made his calls, gave the antique table a long, lingering look, patted it goodbye, and left Jake alone in the apartment.

When he was gone, Jake found the most comfortable chair, pulled it over to a window, where he had a clear view down Park Avenue, and thought it all over. All of it, from the circumstances of Bowe's disappearance, to Schmidt and the poorly hidden gun, to Barber, to the mystery call that led him to Patterson, to the missing medical files.

269

To that morning's kiss.

Everything that had happened ended in a mystery. He had almost no resources to solve any of them . . . with one exception.

He sat until it was dark, working it out. And when it was dark, the red taillights streaming up Park Avenue, electronic salmon on the way to spawn, he pushed himself out of the chair, turned on a single light, went into the master bedroom, and got the gun and holster from the back of the headboard.

He pulled the gun out, checked it, ejected the five .38 shells from the cylinder.

When they'd gone through the apartment, they'd found a toolbox in a kitchen drawer. Jake used a pair of pliers to pull the slug out of one of the .38s, dumped the powder down the sink, washed it away.

He loaded the empty case back in the pistol, turned it until it was under the hammer, found a knee-high woman's boot in the closet of the second bedroom — part of Madison's New York clothing cache — shoved his hand in the boot, holding the gun and the boot between two pillows, and pulled the trigger. There was a muffled crack, and the smell of burning primer.

"Hope the cops don't do any forensics up here," he muttered to himself, as he was putting the boot back in the closet. He opened a couple of drawers in Madison's dresser, took out a pair of black panty hose. He pulled them over his head, asked the mirror, "How do I look?" He considered himself for a moment, then said, "Like some moron with a pair of underpants on his head."

He took them off, refolded them, put them away. He couldn't wear them past a doorman anyway.

He went back to Madison's dresser, sat down, looked at himself in the mirror. He looked all right, he thought. Like a bureaucrat or a college professor just back from vacation, who hadn't had a chance to get his hair cut, who stayed in shape with handball.

There was nothing he could do, without a makeup expert, to make himself look like a thug. He didn't have the scars under the eyes, he didn't have the oft-broken nose, he didn't have the shiny forehead. He did have the scalp cut. If he combed his hair just so . . .

He could definitely go for the insane look, he decided. He half smiled, thinking that he should have kept the *Hello Kitty* hat.

He went through Madison's drawers, then through Lincoln Bowe's, found a comb and a tube of hair gel. Went to the bathroom, gelled his hair, swept it straight back. Gelled it some more. The gel made his face look thinner, his head smaller, like a Doberman's. And it made him look a little trashy. Expensive trashy, a street guy who'd lucked into a thousand-dollar suit. Better.

Stared at himself in the mirror again, took a quarter out of his pocket, put it between his upper right gum and his cheek. Talked to himself in the mirror, while holding the quarter in place with cheek and lip pressure: "Hi. I'm a killer for the CIA, and I'm crazy. I'm here to put a bullet in your head . . ."

No. He was being cute. He didn't want cute, he wanted cold. He rehearsed for another moment: "Get your fuckin' ass on the couch, fat man . . ." More gravel in the voice: "Get your fuckin' ass on the couch . . ."

Rosenquist lived on the twelfth floor of a co-op apartment in the Park Avenue six-hundreds, a bulky granite building with a liveried doorman. One of the residents, leading a dog only slightly larger than a hoagie, went through ahead of Jake. The doorman nodded and she took the elevator. When the lobby was clear, Jake walked in. The doorman straightened and Jake asked, "Dr. Rosenquist?"

"Who's calling?"

"Andy Carlyle." No point in going on record with the doorman. "A friend of his died and I helped clean out the apartment. I found some, mmm, personal items that I believe belong to Dr. Rosenquist."

The doorman called up. After a brief chat, he handed the phone to Jake. Jake took it and said, "Hello?"

"This is James Rosenquist. What do you have?"

"Your friend's wife asked me to clean out, mmm, his apartment." Ostentatiously not using the name. "I found some, ahh, jewelry. There were some personal papers, plus a note that said that you should get the jewelry. One of the pieces is leather with diamonds, two are separate gold chains."

"Give the phone back to Ralph. I'll tell him to send you up."

In the elevator, Jake said aloud, "Tough and mysterious. Tough and mysterious. CIA killer. Movie killer, movie killer, movie killer . . ."

Looking at himself in the elevator

mirror, he did a quick recomb of his hair, baring the shaved strip and the stitches. The Frankenstein vibe. When he was done, one lobe of the greased hair had fallen over his forehead, and he liked it, a vague Hitleresque note to go with the Frankenstein. He put the quarter between his gum and his left cheek and said, "Here's lookin' at ya."

No. He was being cute again. No cute. He needed crazy.

Rosenquist was a blocky, round-faced man dressed in sweatpants, a half-marathon T-shirt that said, run for your life, and slippers. A soft man, fifty pounds overweight. He had a glass in his hand. Dance music played from deeper in the apartment. Jake bobbed his head and held up his cane and the briefcase, tried to look like a polite CIA killer, and asked, "Dr. Rosenquist?"

"Better come in. You recovered these things from Linc's apartment?"

Rosenquist had closed the door and Jake took two quick steps down the hallway and looked into the living room. Empty; music playing from a stereo in the corner. Jake turned back and said, his voice as hard and clipped as he could manage, "Yes, but we disposed of them. I used them as an excuse to get in here. I want to know what you did with Bowe's medical records."

Rosenquist stopped short, his lips turning down in a grimace, and he growled, "Get out."

"No. We no longer have room to fuck around." Jake stepped closer to him, and then another step, and Rosenquist stepped backward. "You're right in the middle of this, Rosenquist, and people are getting hurt. I need the records."

Rosenquist moved sideways, his hand darting toward an intercom panel. "I'll get . . ."

The gun was in Jake's hand, pointing at Rosenquist's temple. "You don't seem to understand how serious this is, fat man," he said. "I've been told to get the records. I will get them, one way or another."

Rosenquist's hands were up, his eyes wide: "Don't point the gun at me. The gun could go off, don't point the gun."

"The records . . ." The quarter slipped and Jake caught it with his upper lip: a snarl, a sneer.

"There are no records, there are no records," Rosenquist babbled. "Whatever records there are, are in my office, but they're meaningless. He never had any-thing wrong with him." But he was lying;

275

his eyes gave him away, moving sideways, then flicking back, judging whether Jake was buying the story.

He wasn't. Jake waggled the gun at him. "In the living room. Put your ass on the couch, fat man."

"There are no records . . ." Rosenquist sat on the couch.

Jake said, "What were you treating him for?"

"I wasn't treating him, honest to God." Lying again.

Jake looked at him, then said, in a kindly voice, "I've had to kill a few people. In the military. And a couple of more, outside. You know. Business. I didn't like it, but it had to be done. You know what I'm saying? It had to be done. These people were causing trouble." He hoped he sounded insane. The quarter slipped, and he pushed it back.

"I know, I know." Rosenquist tried a placating smile, but his voice was a trembling whine.

"This is the same kind of deal, when you get right down to it," Jake said. He said, "If you move, I'm going to beat the shit out of you."

"Listen . . ."

Jake flipped open the gun's cylinder,

shucked the shells into his left hand, and Rosenquist shut up, his eyes big as he watched. Jake picked out the empty shell, with the firing pin impression on the primer. Held it up so Rosenquist could see it, slipped it back into the cylinder, snapped the cylinder shut.

"Now," he said. He spun the cylinder.

"Gimme a break," Rosenquist said. "You're not going to do that."

Jake pointed the pistol at Rosenquist's head and pulled the trigger. It snapped, nothing happened. Rosenquist jumped, his mouth open, his eyes narrowing in horror: "You pulled the trigger. *You pulled the frigging trigger.*"

Jake spun the cylinder: "Yeah, but it was five-to-one against. Against it blowing your brains out. Though maybe not. I can never do the math on these things." The quarter slipped, and he stopped to shove it back in place with his tongue. Drooled a bit, and wiped his lips with his hand; saw Rosenquist pick up on the drool. "It's supposed to be five-to-one every time, right? But if you do it enough, it's gonna go off eventually, right? How many times on average? You're a doctor, you should have the math. Is it five times to fifty-fifty? Or is it two and a half times to fifty-fifty? I could never figure that out."

He pointed the gun at Rosenquist's head again and the doctor's hands came up as if to block the bullet, and he turned his face away and blurted, "He had cancer."

"Cancer." Jake looked at him over the barrel. "Where, cancer?"

"Brain. A tumor."

"How bad?" Jake asked.

"Untreatable."

"How long did he have it when he disappeared?"

"He'd had it for probably a year, but we'd only known about it for a few weeks. Growing like crazy. Nothing to do about it. When he went, he was already showing it. He was losing function, physical and mental. He had some deep pain. We could treat that for a while, but not for long."

"Was he planning to suicide?"

"I think so. I don't know. I don't know what happened with this . . . beheading. I don't know. He told me to keep my mouth shut. He was my friend."

Jake stepped back, flipped the cylinder out again, reloaded the gun.

"You're going to kill me?"

"I don't have to," Jake said. "If you say anything about any of this, it'll all come out. Prison's not the best place for a fat soft gay guy. You'd have to deal with it for a long time."

"I can't believe Madison had anything to do with this," Rosenquist said, his Adam's apple bobbing.

"Jesus Christ." Jake laughed, his best dirty laugh, shook his head, drooled again, wiped his lips. "You're just so goddamned dumb, fat man. This is *way* past Madison Bowe. You don't know what you've done with this little game. You don't know what you've stepped into. The FBI's in it, the CIA, God only knows what the security people are doing. I know the Watchmen are working it and there're some guys working for Goodman you wouldn't want to meet. They'll cut your fuckin' legs off with a chain saw. Madison Bowe? You fuckin' dummy."

"If you're not with Madison . . ." Rosenquist was confused. "Who are you with?"

"Best not to know," Jake said. He smiled the crooked coin-holding smile. "It's one of those deals where I could tell you, but then I'd have to kill you."

Old joke; Rosenquist recognized it, at the same time he seemed to buy it. Jake pushed on: "So. Mouth shut, ass down. Maybe you'll live through it — though I don't know what the other side's thinking. Wouldn't destroy any records, but you might put them someplace where your lawyer can get them if he needs them. They're about the only chip you've got in this game."

And he was out of there.

On the street, clear of the building, walking fast, he called Madison. "I think I should come and see you," he said.

"Come on," she said.

Then he started to laugh. If his grandmother had heard him up there, using the language, she would have washed his mouth out with soap.

So he laughed, and the people on the sidewalk spread carefully around him; a man, alone, laughing aloud on a New York street, in the dark. Not necessarily a threat, but it pays to be careful.

12

On the way back in the plane, Jake tried to work through what he knew: that Lincoln Bowe had been dying, and that Bowe had known about a scandal, a package, that would unseat the vice president of the United States, and, if delivered at the right time, probably the president as well.

They did not fit together. He kept trying to find a way, and not until they were coming into National, the Washington Monument glowing white out the right-side window, did one answer occur to him.

He resisted the idea. Struggled again to find a logic that would put all the pieces together — but Occam's razor kept jumping up at him: the simplest answer is probably the right one.

And the simplest answer was very simple indeed: they weren't related at all.

Jake got out of the cab at Madison's a little after midnight. The front-porch light was burning, and Madison opened the door as he climbed the stairs.

"What happened?" she asked. "Come in . . . You look exhausted."

"I'm fairly well kicked," Jake admitted. "The days are getting long."

They drifted toward the front room. "Tell me," she said.

"I'll tell you, but you can't ever admit knowing, all right? It could put you in legal jeopardy. If you have to perjure yourself, and say you didn't know, that's what you do," Jake said.

"What happened?"

"Rosenquist didn't want to talk. I faked a Russian roulette thing, using a pistol of your husband's. I pointed it at Rosenquist's head and pulled the trigger. That's a felony, aggravated assault. But he started talking. I hinted that I was from some political group, maybe even an intelligence organization. I told him I didn't know you."

"Jeez, Jake." She was standing close to him, and put her hand on his elbow.

"We had to know," Jake said. "Here's the thing: he told me that your husband had brain cancer. He was terminal. Rosenquist said there was no chance he'd make it. When he died, he was already showing functional problems, both physically and mentally. That explains the press reports

282

that he'd been drunk in public. That he seemed to be on the edge of control . . . He was medicated. I think he killed himself — had himself killed — and tried to hang it on Goodman."

Her hands had gone to her cheeks. "My God. But . . . his head?"

"He might not have known the details, might not have worked through the logic of it. On the other hand, maybe he did. They couldn't leave the head. They had to know that it would be destroyed, completely, or an autopsy would have shown the tumor. Best way to get rid of it would be . . . to get rid of it."

"That's unbelievable." She was pale as a ghost.

"You don't believe it?"

"No, I sort of do — but I can't see *anybody* planning that. It's too cold."

"I was told by somebody who knew him that Lincoln had a mean streak . . . a mean streak can mean a coldness. Maybe he could do it."

She walked away from him, both hands on top of her head, as if trying to contain her thoughts. "I just, I just . . ."

"Novatny told me the autopsy indicated that Lincoln had been drugged — painkillers. We thought it was to control him; it was actually for the pain. I'd bet he was unconscious when they did it and I'll bet you anything that Howard Barber set it up. He was Lincoln's best friend, they share both a sexual orientation and a set of politics. They both hated Goodman, and Barber had done some rough stuff in the military. He had the skills, the guts, the motive, and Lincoln could trust him to do it right."

"The Schmidt man?"

"I think he was set up. By Barber. I didn't have a chance to dig for connections, but they were both in the military at the same time. Schmidt was given a general discharge, which usually means a kind of plea bargain. He did something, but they didn't want to waste time with him, or maybe they didn't want the publicity. I've got some access to military records. I can probably figure out what happened."

"But why can't they find . . . oh. You mean, Howard killed him, too? Killed Schmidt?"

"That's what I think."

"If Howard killed him, there had to be a plan, Linc would have to have known . . . I don't think Linc . . . Linc wouldn't go away without feeding the *cats*, he wouldn't kill a man who was innocent."

"Your husband didn't have to know the whole plan," Jake said. "May have preferred not to."

"Another thing . . ." He fished the note out of his pocket. "I found a note in the second safe. It says, 'All because of Lion Nerve.' Do you have any idea what it means? It was right on top of the safe, with the pictures, like it was important."

She looked at it for a moment, and a thoughtful frown wrinkled her forehead. "I don't know what it means, but I know what it *is*. It's an anagram for something. Linc talked in anagrams — he could come up with an anagram for anything, off the top of his head. He used them as mnemonics."

Now Jake smiled: "You're the first person I've ever heard pronounce *mnemonics*," he said. He took the note back. "The 'Lion Nerve' is the anagram?"

"I'd think so."

He tucked the note in his pocket. "One last thing . . ."

He told her about the package, about the attempt to push Vice President Landers out of his job, about Patterson, about a Wisconsin connection. She listened carefully, then asked, "I know Tony Patterson from the campaign. He's a smart man —

so why couldn't it be Goodman? How do you know Goodman *didn't* take Linc, to get this package? You say that's what Tony Patterson thinks. That makes perfect sense to me."

"Because then, Schmidt doesn't make any sense," Jake said. "What I think is this: I think we have two groups fighting it out in the dark. Goodman's people have gotten a sniff of the package, and they are desperately trying to find it, to push it out early. Maybe even to make an explicit deal that would get Goodman into Landers's job. Barber's group has the package, or knows where it is, or who has it, and they don't want it pushed out until the last minute, when it'll do the most damage."

Madison thought about it for a minute, then said, "Wisconsin."

"That's where the package is supposedly coming from."

"There's a man there named Alan Green," Madison said. "He runs a polling company called the PollCats, something like that."

"You think?"

She nodded. "He was an aide to a congressman here for ten years or so, before his guy lost and Alan went back home to make some money. He's gay. He and Linc had a relationship. They've always been tight politically. If the package is coming from Wisconsin, Al knows everybody in Wisconsin. He could be the tie between Wisconsin and Lincoln."

Jake thought about it for a few seconds, then, "I'll go out there. Tomorrow."

"Can I come with you?" she asked. "I know Alan fairly well, he'd talk to me."

Jake was shaking his head. "You're too visible. If there's ever an investigation, you don't want to have been anyplace around Wisconsin. You want to be able to claim that even if your husband was involved in the package deal, he didn't tell you, specifically to protect you. If you've gone to Wisconsin . . ."

"What about you?"

"I'll go to a little trouble to cover my tracks, though nothing's ever perfect. You have to hope that the tracks get lost in the clutter."

"All right." She put her hands to her face and rubbed. "What will you do if you find the package?"

"Break it out," Jake said. "I'll have no choice."

"You could just walk away," she said. "Right now. Go back to the university. Write another book."

"I could. But there are two factors here. If the Republicans — you guys — have it, you'll break it out anyway, and wreck someone I like. The president. He's a pretty good guy. But the other thing is, as long as there's a scramble going on, *you're* going to be near the center of it. Everybody's going to at least check you. Both sides, Barber and Goodman, have people who I suspect would kill for it. I don't want you to become a target."

She shook her head. "Howard wouldn't hurt me. We've always been sympathetic . . . *simpatico*."

"This isn't a friendship thing anymore," Jake said. "Listen, I've got to . . . mmm . . . I don't want to think that you're playing me. That Madison Bowe is playing Jake Winter. Because there are some real problems. They've got lethal injection in Virginia. Even if Barber could beat the charge of killing Lincoln, making it out to be assisted suicide, he's got the Schmidt thing hanging over his head. I'll bet you a hundred dollars that Schmidt's buried out in the woods. If you know about it, you could be in trouble with him. You could be part of a murder conspiracy. If you don't, you could still be a serious danger to him, and he to you. Either way, you could be in trouble."

She stared at him for a second, then stood up and dusted the seat of her pants. "Maybe I should go to New York. Or Santa Fe. Tell a couple of people I can trust, and just split."

"That might not be a bad idea, going to New York," Jake said. He looked at his watch, stepped back toward the door. "I'm going to try to work this through. You — don't isolate yourself. The more people you keep around you, the safer you'll be."

She walked him back to the door. "What you said a minute ago . . . whether I'm telling you the truth about Schmidt."

"Yeah?"

He turned on the porch, his stick and briefcase in hand, hoping for a good-bye kiss, and she said, "You don't trust me."

"Not yet, not entirely," he confessed. "But I'm trying as hard as I can."

"Try harder." She closed the door, and he walked down to the curb to wait for the taxi.

The governor was asleep when Darrell walked through the front door, punched a code in the burglar alarm, flipped on a hall light, and climbed the stairs to the second floor. He tripped another alarm, a silent alarm, on the way up, and a strobe began blinking at the governor's bedside.

Goodman woke and heard Darrell call, "It's me, Arlo." Goodman sat up, turned on the bedside lamp. "Come in. What happened?"

Darrell pushed into the bedroom. "Sorry. It's important. I want you to know what I'm doing."

"What?"

"We've got a lead on the package. Winter was in New York, he came back to talk to Madison Bowe, we got the whole conversation. They must've been sitting right under the bug."

"What's the lead?"

"Bowe thinks it might be with a guy named Alan Green, out in Madison. Should have thought of him, but I didn't know he was from Wisconsin. He was a staffer on Bowe's last campaign."

"Holy shit." Goodman jumped out of bed, took a turn around the bedroom. "This is fuckin' wonderful. Get the package, Darrell."

"We're trying to get out to Madison, me 'n' George. Winter's going tomorrow morning, I don't think we can beat him out there. We've lined up a state plane, we're getting the paperwork done now, but we can't take it right to Madison. Somebody might see it. So we're flying into Chicago, we'll drive from there. It'll be close."

"Get the package, okay? That's what you're for. Get the package," Arlo said. "You get it, I've got one foot in the White House."

Darrell smiled a thin dark smile. "If Winter gets it, do we take it away from him?"

Goodman pondered for a moment, then said, "No. If you're *sure* he's got it, we can float a rumor that the administration has it, and that'd force their hand. But we've got to be *sure* they have it."

"There's another thing," Darrell said. "Bowe had brain cancer. He probably planned his own murder — it was probably carried out by Howard Barber."

Goodman whistled. "How sure?"

"Ninety-five percent. That's why the body was full of painkillers. If we do an analysis of the people around Barber, we could probably pick out the ones who helped pick up Bowe. We could grab one of them, stick a battery up his ass, and get enough detail to hang Barber."

Goodman said, "The package first. We can handle Barber later. Was Madison Bowe in on it? The killing?"

The man shrugged. "We don't know that yet."

"If we could find out . . ."

"Grab a guy, stick a battery up his ass."

Goodman was irritated. "You're a little too quick with that, Darrell. We're not talking about cats. When people disappear, other people ask questions."

"If the guy disappears, we could probably hang that on Barber, too. A smear of blood in the trunk of his car . . ."

"Get the package, Darrell."

13

Jake was moving early. The fastest way from Washington to Madison was through Milwaukee, driving the last ninety miles into Madison. He got a car from Hertz and headed west, a drive of an hour and a half, including the time spent fighting traffic going out. He'd gone back into the end of winter — the trees were just opening up, the wind was from the south, warm and smooth, telling of spring.

The car's navigation system took him off I-94 down into the city, to Johnson Street, two or three blocks from the Wisconsin capitol. He must not be far, he thought, from the university — the sidewalks were full of buzz-cut students with book bags. Undoubtedly, he thought, full of that fuckin' Ayn Rand and Newt Gingrich.

The PollCats' address was a shabby two-story brick-and-glass professional building left over from the 1970s. The narrow parking lot, in back, had only four cars in it, with grass and weeds growing through a jigsaw pattern of cracks in the blacktop.

Jake got his cane and his case, walked in the back door through a long dim hallway smelling of microwave chicken-noodle soup, to a cramped lobby, and found a listing for PollCats on the second floor.

He went up, stepped off the elevator: PollCats had an office at the end of another gloomy strip of carpet, one of eight doors off the hallway. The hall was silent. Two of the doors had signs next to them, six did not, and through the glass door-inserts, appeared empty.

At PollCats, through the glass door panels, he could see a blond receptionist reading a *Vanity Fair*. Jake turned the knob and went inside. The receptionist dropped the magazine into a desk drawer when she heard the doorknob rattle, perked up, and smiled at him. He smiled back and said, "I'm here to see Alan Green."

She was pretty, peaches-and-cream complexion, blue eyes, hair done in a French twist. "Do you have an appointment?"

"No, I don't. I'm a government researcher, visiting from Washington. It's quite important."

She picked up her phone. "What branch of the government?"

"The executive," he said. He took his White House pass from his wallet and handed it to her. She looked at it for a second, then put the phone down and said, "Just a moment."

She disappeared through a door into the interior. Jake waited, ten seconds, fifteen, she was back. "He just has to get off a phone call."

At that moment, they both heard, faintly, the flushing noise from a toilet, and she got a little pink: Jake said, "I would have told me the same thing."

"It seemed better than the alternative," she said. Then, "When was the last time you were at the White House?"

"Last night."

"Did you see the president?"

"No. But once I did, and he nodded at me."

"Must give you a feeling of power," she said, tongue-in-cheek.

"I repeat the story whenever I can," Jake said. "I've been to a half dozen dinner parties on it."

They were still chatting, the girl a little flirty, but way too young, Jake thought — twenty, maybe, twenty-two — when Alan Green popped through the interior door. Green was short, bald, and burly, wide shouldered and narrow waisted, like a former college wrestler or gymnast. He wore khaki slacks, a white dress shirt, and striped tie, the tie loose at his thick neck, and a corduroy jacket with leather patches at the elbows. He smiled and asked, "Mr. Winter? Can I help you?"

"I need to speak to you privately," Jake said.

"Could you tell me the subject?"

"Lincoln Bowe."

"I heard the news. The news was terrible," Green said. "What is your involvement?"

Jake glanced at the receptionist, then said, "I can tell you here, or privately. If I tell you here, you may pull this young lady into what's about to happen."

Green's smile faded. "What's about to happen?"

"You should know that as well as I do, Mr. Green. The, mmm, package is about to break into the open. A number of people think it may be the motive for this murder."

The blood drained from Green's face, and Jake knew that he'd connected. He looked at the receptionist, who shook her head, confused, and Green said, "You better come in. Katie, stop all my calls. Call Terry and tell him I can't make it. I'll call him later. Tell him I had an emergency."

Green's office was a twenty-by-twenty-foot cubicle furnished with a cheap Persian rug over the standard gray business carpet, leather chairs, and photographs: the faces of fifty politicians, ninety-nine predatory eyes and one black eye-patch worn by the former governor of Colorado, all signed. There were ten more of Green with two presidents and a selection of Washington politicians; and three personal photos, all of striking young men.

"What about this package?" Green asked. He picked up a short stack of paper, squared it, put it in an in-box.

"I have a general outline of what the package is, the highway deal," Jake said. "I don't yet have it. The package has apparently caused at least one and perhaps two murders. Very likely two. I'm coordinating with the lead investigator for the FBI on this, a man named Chuck Novatny. You can call him if you wish."

"I don't know this package," Green said.

Jake let the annoyance show on his face: "Don't bullshit me, Mr. Green. I got your name from one of the principals in this case. And if you really didn't know, we'd still be talking out in the hallway."

Green blinked. He'd felt the trap snap. Jake continued: "We can handle it as a political issue or we can handle it as a criminal matter. Once this package gets out there, nobody's going to much care about the route — but they will care about who tried to suppress it, who tried to keep it undercover, because those are the most likely motives for the murders."

"I don't know . . . What murders? Lincoln Bowe, I've heard there's some question . . ."

Jake shook his head: "There's no question. There are people who'd like you to believe it was a suicide, but he was alive and heavily drugged when he was shot through the heart, and that makes it murder. The killers tried to frame a second man, a Virginia man, for the murder — and the second man is missing and we believe he's also dead. You are playing with fire, Mr. Green. You are in deep jeopardy, not only from the law, the FBI, but from people with guns . . . unless you're one of the gunmen yourself, or are cooperating with them."

"Don't be absurd," Green snapped. They stared at each other for a minute, then Green asked, "Another gentleman came to see me about this. I told him that I had no idea where this package might be."

"Who was that?"

He shook his head: "I won't tell you that, if you don't already know."

"I probably know, but there are several possibilities," Jake said.

"A black gentleman."

"Yes. I know him. A good friend of Lincoln Bowe's, and possibly of yours." Jake's eyes flicked toward the pictures of the young men, and then back to Green. "The black gentleman shares a cultural . . . choice . . . with you."

Green said nothing.

"And he doesn't have the package?" Jake asked.

"Apparently not. He didn't when he was here."

"Mr. Green, I'm sure you've done the calculations that we've all done. I know from your background that you'd like the package to be broken out later in the year. That's not going to happen now. I don't care how it comes out, only that it comes out soon. So that we can have a fair election, straight up. If I leave here without it, I am going to sit in my car and call my FBI contact on the telephone, and tell him about it. I think you'll almost certainly be in jail tonight. I don't think you'll be getting out any time soon."

"Jesus Christ," Green said. He pulled a

Kleenex out of a box in his desk drawer and patted his sweating scalp. "You don't mess around, do you?"

"There's no time. There's just no time," Jake said. "There are some violent people looking for this package, and I'm afraid more people will wind up dead if they keep struggling to find it."

"That goddamned woman," he said. "If she hadn't put that paper together . . ."

"What woman?"

Green took a cell phone out of his coat pocket and began working one of the buttons with his thumb. As he did, he said, "Mr. Winter. I don't have the package. I know about it. I've actually been through it. I'll probably tell you who has it, but I've got to talk to her first. I can't just have you show up . . . I mean, what if you're the guy with the gun? I've never seen you before. And maybe the best thing would be if she went to the FBI. I've gotta have some time. I've gotta think."

Jake looked at his watch. "How much time?"

"I don't know if I can get her. If she's out . . . she doesn't have a cell phone. Anyway, she didn't the last time I talked to her."

"So try her," Jake said.

"Not with you sitting here. We may have to *talk* . . ."

"I'll come back in an hour," Jake said. "Get in touch with her."

"I'll tell you right up front that she was hoping to get a little something out of the package," Green said. "Linc suggested that she could get a decent job, if the package came out at the right time. Maybe I could . . ."

"Our friends get taken care of," Jake said. "Nothing illegal, or unethical, but they get the attention they deserve. They wind up with decent jobs and benefits and pensions."

"Okay . . . I'll try to call her," Green said. He looked at the cell-phone screen, then laid it on his desk, pulled out another tissue, and patted his scalp again. "Jesus Christ."

Jake got up, stepped toward the door, said, "See you in an hour."

Green called after him, "You've seen the FBI reports on Linc?"

"I have not — but I talk to the lead investigator every day."

"There are rumors . . . barbed wire, no head, that sounds like he was tortured," Green said.

"I wouldn't want you to pass this around . . ."

"No, no, of course not."

"We think that was an effort by his friends — your friends — to increase publicity," Jake said. "I can't tell you everything behind the supposition, and you might know more about it than I do . . ."

"I do not," Green protested.

". . . but he was definitely dead before he was decapitated, and before he was burned. The whole burning scene seems to have been set up to imply that the Watchmen were involved somehow . . . it was set up to resonate with the idea that the Watchmen are Nazis, or Klan, who kill people and burn them as examples."

"And they don't? How about the Mexican kid . . . ?"

Jake held up his hands, shutting Green off: "I don't want to get in a political argument. The Watchmen may be Nazis, for all I know. But the scene itself seems to be a setup, managed by Lincoln Bowe's friends. That's what we believe."

He left Green staring at the cell phone. In the outer office, the secretary ditched the *Vanity Fair* again and stood up. "All done with the secret talks?"

"Nope. I'll be back. Could you tell me where I could get a bagel and a book?"

She drew a quick map on a piece of printer paper, pointing Jake toward the campus and the campus bookstore, at the far end of State Street. As she gave him the directions, she patted him on the arm: a toucher, he thought. She was nothing but friendly, smiling as she sent him on his way. If he'd been fifteen years younger, he would have been panting after her.

Might be panting a little anyway.

Of course, there was Madison — the woman, not the town. Madison, who'd once kissed him. And then didn't. He thought about that as he got oriented with the hand-drawn map, and started toward the campus.

The girl's map was accurate enough, but didn't have a scale. He had to walk nearly a mile; flinched at the sight of a big GMC sports-utility vehicle with blacked-out windows, rolling along beside him. Remembered the beating he'd taken. If God gave those guys back to him . . .

He smiled at the thought.

The day was a nice one, the beginning of warmer weather, and the college girls were coming out of their winter cocoons, walking along with their form-fitting jeans and soft breast-clinging tops. Excellent.

Maybe get a novel, Jake thought: he'd just read the first of a series of novels about British fliers during World War I, by Derek Robinson, and was anxious to get another. And, of course, university bookstores were the most likely place to find his own books; like most authors, he always checked.

The store was a good one. He found *The Goshawk Squadron* and copies of both of his books, though only one of each, in what he thought was an obscure location. When he was sure nobody was looking, he reshelved some outward-facing books so that only their spines showed, and then faced out his own book. The shelf was still too low, but there was nothing he could do about that.

Nevertheless, two copies. With a sense of satisfaction, he walked across the street, got a bagel with cream cheese, and sat on a bench in the sun and started reading about the Goshawks . . .

Madison Bowe stood behind the etched-glass insert in the front door, watching as Howard Barber climbed out of his car, straightened his tie, patted his pockets as though checking for keys, then headed up the walk onto the porch. He was wearing the usual wraparound blades–style sunglasses and dark suit. He was reaching for the doorbell when she opened the door.

He stepped inside, took his sunglasses off, said, "Maddy, what happened, you sounded . . ."

She hit him hard. Not a slap, but with a balled-up fist, hit him in the cheekbone as hard as she could; but she was not a big woman, hadn't thrown many punches, and he twitched away before the punch landed and that took some of the impact out of it.

She tried again, but he was ready this time, brushed her off. "Hey, hey, what the hell?"

She shouted at him: "You killed Lincoln and you killed Schmidt and now the whole thing is coming down on us."

"No, no, no . . ." He had his hands up now, backing away from her.

She was spitting, she was so angry, the words tumbling out of her. "Don't lie to me, Howard. I know about the brain tumor, I know about the medication. I stayed up all night, trying to work out explanations, and there aren't any. You killed Howard and you killed Schmidt. Now Jake Winter knows about the package and he's looking for it."

"Ah, jeez," Barber said, dropping his

305

hands. She took a step toward him and he said, "Maddy, don't hit me again. That hurt like hell. Just listen for a minute, huh?"

"Howard . . ."

"Linc died at . . . a friend's place. He'd worked out the whole thing, the whole thing involving Schmidt. When he'd died, we took him down to the basement and shot him. We shot him in a way that would keep the slug in the body and we planted the pistol at Schmidt's place."

"And killed Schmidt," Madison shouted: but she was pleading for a denial.

He gave it to her. "We didn't kill Schmidt. Schmidt's in Thailand, screwing twelve-year-olds. We're not gonna kill some innocent guy."

"Thailand?"

"Schmidt has a thing about hookers," Barber said. "Young brown hookers. He's also tied to Goodman. They were on the same base at Latakia, at the same time, and he kept trying to get into the Watchmen. And he likes guns."

"Guns . . ."

"Guns. On top of it all, he was desperate for money. We told him about a job possibility in Thailand, tending bar in an American place down south of Bangkok. He took the job. We'd fixed it up through a pal of mine — had to pay most of his salary, so the Thai guy who runs the place essentially has a free American bartender for a couple of months."

She wasn't sure whether or not to believe him, but she pushed ahead. "Lincoln was dead?"

"I sat with him until he stopped breathing. He took an overdose of Rinolat."

"And Schmidt?"

"Schmidt's in a beach town about the size of my dick," Barber said. "We told him he was hired to play the part of an old expat China hand. He's grown a beard, makes drinks, he's getting along pretty well for the first time in his life."

"Why don't they know this? Why don't the police know this?"

Barber shrugged. "You don't have to check out of the country yet. You just have to check in. We gave him the ticket, so there's no financial record."

"Howard, if you're lying . . ."

"I'm not lying. Schmidt has no idea of who we are, of who bought him the ticket, of how it worked," Barber said. "He just saw a good deal being handed to him by a guy in a bar, and he took it. If somebody thinks we killed him, if there were ever any legal question . . . he'll be 'discovered' by an American tourist."

"Jesus, Howard. How can you keep this shut up? There must be so many people involved . . ."

"The same people who've kept their mouths shut about Linc and friends all these years."

She stepped back to think about it; reeling from information overload.

Barber said: "Now tell me about Winter. How'd he hear about the package?"

"I don't know how he heard about it, but he tracked down Tony Patterson, and Tony gave him the outline," Madison said. "He doesn't know where it is, or who has it. He doesn't even know if it's real. I told him about Al Green out in Wisconsin. A wild-goose chase. I mostly wanted to get him away from here. Away from you. You guys are the ones who mugged him, right? You could have killed him . . ."

"Listen, listen . . . He goes to see Green, that's another day or two. Maybe I can talk to a couple of people, get him shunted off again, in another direction."

"You didn't answer the question. You're the guys who mugged him . . ."

Barber's eyes shifted: that was an answer.

She stepped toward him again, lifted her fist, but he stepped sideways, one hand up to block, and asked, "Is he the one who told you about the brain tumor?"

"Yes. He . . ." She started to tell him about Rosenquist, but suddenly shifted, suddenly thought she might not want to. She still wasn't sure about Schmidt, what Barber might have done to him. And her feelings about Jake were confusing: Wasn't he the enemy? "He apparently found a computerized medical record somewhere. He's got all kinds of computer access, intelligence services, the FBI."

"That sounds a little hinky," Barber said.

"That's what he told me."

"You gotta manage the guy, Maddy," Barber said, his voice urgent. "He's talking to you, he's coming to you, you gotta manage him."

"I'm trying. That's why I sent him to Wisconsin."

Barber nodded: "That was quick thinking. If I hadn't grilled Green myself, I would have said he'd be the guy who'd know . . ."

"I just hope he doesn't," Madison said. "I just hope he wasn't lying to you."

"Nah. He would have told me. He knew about me and Linc . . ."

"So where is it? Why can't you find it?"

"We're still looking, but we've decided that if we can't find it, we wait until after the convention, and then we leak what we've got. We get people looking at that highway project. We have enough details that we can redo it — maybe even force the guy with the package out into the open."

She pressed her fingertips to her forehead. "How did this ever start? How could you and Lincoln . . . What could possibly be worth it?"

Barber examined her for a moment, as though he were puzzled, and then said, "We're talking about the presidency, Maddy. We *might be* talking about changing the history of the country. If people like Goodman get their way, this place could go down like Rome. A hundred years from now, two hundred years from now, people will look back . . .

"Spare me," she said. "I don't need any historical analysis. I need to get back to the farm. I need to go riding. I need to get away."

"Hang on, baby. We're almost there. Hang on."

The whole thing had gone to hell, and Darrell Goodman didn't quite know how to get out of it. He and George had flown to Chicago on a state plane, on Watchmen business. At O'Hare, they'd rented a Dodge van, the most inoffensive and invisible car that he could think of, and had headed north for Madison.

The trip had taken longer than he thought. Both he and George were wasted from the overnight flight, and the stress; and Darrell was annoyed with George, because George kept having to stop at roadside rests and gas stations to pee.

George had been an operator with the CIA, a contract guy, but wasn't the sharpest knife in the drawer. Arlo Goodman had once said to Darrell, "Even the CIA needs guys who carry stuff. That's what George did."

Darrell had driven: George had ridden silently along, half asleep, waking up every hour or so to ask if they could stop. George thought he had an infection, Darrell thought it might be his prostate, but whatever it was, George couldn't drink half a Coke unless he was standing next to the can.

And that seemed wrong; that simple problem had unbalanced Darrell. You didn't have a mission fouled up because a guy had to take a leak. That wasn't the way the pros did it.

They'd gotten to Madison later than they'd hoped, but had just spotted the PollCats building when they saw Winter walk out the front door, tapping along with his cane. "Knew he'd beat us," Darrell said. They watched as Winter turned away from the building, going on down the street. George, sleepy eyed, said, "Want to take him?"

"No. No, for Christ's sake. We find out if he got it, and if he didn't, who's got it, and we take it away from *them*."

They watched until Winter was out of sight, then pulled into the parking lot in back. From the parking lot to the PollCats front door, everything went fine. They saw nobody, heard nobody. George said, "This place is a ghost town."

Then they opened the door and everything went to hell.

Now the blond-chick secretary was pressed back against the office wall, eyes wide with fear, George in front of her, dressed all in black like a movie villain from *Batman*, not letting her move. Darrell pointed a leather-gloved hand at Alan Green and said, "If you don't give me that fuckin' package, you fuck, I'm gonna break your fuckin' weasel neck."

He knew that wasn't the idea. There

should have been an urbane approach, an understated threat, a sly blackmail, and instead, it had gone straight in the dumper, and here he was . . .

And then he made the mistake of pushing Green in the chest. Green didn't just look like a wrestler: he'd been one, at the University of Wisconsin, twenty years earlier. He was scared and angry and strong. He caught Goodman's arm and made a move, so quick that Goodman, good athlete that he was, was spun off balance and found his arm locked and bent and choked off a scream and Green said, "I oughta throw your ass out. . . ."

Nobody found out where he was going to throw Goodman, because George, in one quick motion, pulled a silenced .22 from a shoulder holster and shot Green in the back of the head. The gun made a spitting sound, clanked as the action moved, and Green went down like a load of beef.

Goodman twisted in surprise, said, "Jesus Christ," looked at George, looked at Green. The blond secretary looked at both men, looked at Goodman's eyes, knew she was dead: she launched herself at him with her fingernails, slashing, as quick as Green had been, cutting Goodman at the neck and down his arms, and Goodman said,

"Jesus, Jesus," trying to fend her off, and there was another quick spit and the blonde went down, bounced, landed on her back, naked blue eyes staring lifelessly at the ceiling.

Goodman was breathing hard, stunned, astonished, looked at George, gasped, "We gotta get the fuck outa here," and he led the way out, said, "Put away the fuckin' gun, we gotta get out," and panic clutched at him and he shook it off, and they were out, the door locking behind them . . .

Jake lost some time with *The Goshawk Squadron*; glanced at his watch and was shocked to see that it was after one o'clock. He got up, put the novel in his case, and headed back to the PollCats office.

Up State, down Johnson, watching the ass on a tall slender blonde, and when she turned, thought, my God, you've been watching the ass of a *child.* She stopped at a curb to cross the street, caught his eye and smiled a bit; not a child's smile.

In the old brick building, the smell of rug and flaking paint, up the stairs, to the PollCats door. It was locked. He rattled the handle, then knocked. No answer. And he thought, *Ah, man.*

They'd run on him, and he hadn't seen it

coming. He rattled the door again, exhaled in exasperation. The critical thing was, *time,* and Green must know that. All he had to do was stay out of sight for a while. . . .

He was turning away from the door when he noticed the shoe. The shoe was in the open doorway of Green's private office. He couldn't see all of it, just a heel and part of the instep. It was a woman's shoe, upside down, the short stacked-heel in the air, and there, in the corner, an oval, that might be a toe in a nylon stocking.

Jake backed away from the door. Wondered what he'd touched. Thought, *Maybe it's not what it looks like.* Thought, *What if somebody's not dead, what if I can save a life by calling the cops?* Thought, *The big GMC with the blacked-out windows.*

Thought, *That's ridiculous, there's gotta be a thousand of those trucks in Madison . . .*

But he knew what was in the office. Felt it like an ice cube in his heart.

He walked to the end of the hall, searching the corners of the ceilings, listening for voices. Heard nothing; but did see a woman in one of the offices, hunched over a stack of paper, working with a pencil. No cameras. But: he'd not tried to hide his approach. He'd used his cane, carried his case, hadn't worn a hat. If anybody had seen him, they'd remember. And he'd for sure wrapped his fingers around the arm of a chair in Green's office.

"Shit. Shit, shit, shit." He walked back to the PollCats office, knocked once, then again, rattled the door. Nothing. The shoe sat there. "Goddamnit."

He used the steel grip on the cane to punch a hole in the glass panel. He punched out enough that he could get a hand through, didn't try to hide the noise; but then, there really wasn't much noise.

He stepped inside the door, crossed to Green's office.

The blond secretary lay on her back, a palm-sized spot of blood under her head. Green was also on his back, a stain on the rug beneath his head. There was a spatter of blood on the glass of the pictures on the wall.

Jake looked for a moment, then took out his cell phone and dialed. Novatny came up: *"Yes?"*

"Chuck, this is Jake Winter. We've got a hell of a problem, man." He looked at the blank dead face of the young secretary. "Jesus, Chuck, we've got, ah . . . ."

"Jake, Jake . . . ?"

316

Novatny told him to walk out of the office and wait in the hallway, not to let anyone in the office. "I'll have somebody there in five minutes. I don't know who yet."

Jake hung up, took a step toward the door. Hesitated. Stepped back to Green. Reached beneath him, toward his heart. Felt the cell phone. Slipped his hand inside, took the phone, put it in the phone pocket of his briefcase. Looked at the office phone for a second, then took a tissue out of a box of Kleenex on Green's desk, picked up the desk phone and pushed the redial button. The phone redialed and a man answered on the first ring, "Domino's." Nothing there — not unless Domino's Pizza was delivering the package.

He hung up, stepped toward the door, caught the glaze on the secretary's dead, half-open eyes. The rage surged: the same rage that he'd felt in Afghanistan when he'd encountered dismembered civilians, killed by dissidents to make some obscure point. The secretary had been a kid. Probably waiting to get married; probably looking forward to her life. All done now. All over.

His hands were shaking as he turned away and stepped past her, out into the hallway.

An agent from the Madison FBI office arrived one minute ahead of the Madison cops.

14

The FBI man took a look and backed away, pointed a finger at Jake and said, "Wait."

The first cops walked in and walked back out, shut the door on the PollCats office, faced Jake to a wall, checked for weapons, read him his rights, and sat him down in the hallway, on a chair they borrowed from one of the occupied offices.

Jake told them that he didn't want a lawyer, but he did want to talk to Novatny privately, and wouldn't make any other statement. The FBI man went away for a while, then came back and said, "Agent Novatny will be here in three hours. He's flying straight in from Washington."

The Madison homicide cops, who arrived ten minutes after the patrolmen, were pissed, though the lead investigator, whose name was Martin Wirth, allowed that Jake probably wasn't the killer, since he'd reported the crime. "But he knows something about it and I want to know what it is," Wirth told the FBI man. "This is my town, this is my homicide, and the entire

319

FB fuckin' I can kiss my ass. This guy's going nowhere until I say so."

The FBI man put his sunglasses on, looked at the investigator, and said, "Uh-huh."

Wirth asked Jake, "Where'd you get that cut on your head?"

"I was mugged, in Washington."

"Right."

"I have a copy of the police report in my briefcase," Jake said.

"You know, these guys are getting away . . ."

Jake said, "Look: Nothing I know can get you to anyone. Everything I know is background. I didn't see anything you haven't seen. I don't know who might have done this."

"Then how come you won't make a statement?"

"I can't tell you why I won't make a statement, because then you'd know something I'm not sure I should tell you," Jake said. "Okay?"

"Fuck no."

"I will make a statement to agent Novatny and then agent Novatny can either tell me to make a statement to you, and I will. Or he'll tell me not to, for national security reasons, and I won't," Jake said. "I'm probably saving your life. If I told you what I know, the FBI might have to come in here and kill all of you."

"You're being a wiseass," Wirth said. "We don't like wiseasses in Madison."

"Marty," the FBI man said, "Madison is the national capital of wiseasses. What are you talking about?"

The police kept Jake sitting outside Green's office as their crime-scene people came and went; investigators talked to everyone in the building, but nobody had seen any strangers coming or going at the time of the murders. Nobody had heard any shots. The building, it seemed, was more than half empty, and the offices that were occupied were mostly sedentary businesses without much traffic: two book-keepers, a State Farm agent, an insurance service bureau, the office for a medical waste-disposal service.

In the end, to make the city cops happy, Jake had to go down to the police head-quarters and sit in a conference room. He felt as if he should be sitting on a stool, with a pointed hat on his head, facing into a corner. On the other hand, the cops were exceptionally mellow, and gave him coffee, doughnuts, and magazines.

Novatny showed up four hours after Jake called him, Parker trailing behind. Wirth was still working, bared his teeth at Jake when he showed the two Washington FBI men into the conference room, and said, "I'll be waiting."

Parker nodded and pulled the door shut.

"What happened?" Novatny asked. He took a seat across a conference table, while Parker braced his butt on a windowsill.

"I was following up a possibility on Bowe," Jake said. "Just cleaning up. I thought it was thin. Then this. Either it's not related at all or somebody killed Alan Green to shut him up."

"Keep talking."

"Bowe was gay," Jake said. "He was also dying of brain cancer. That's why he was full of drugs, for the pain. I think — but I don't know — that Bowe and a group of his gay friends plotted a way to make his death look like a murder, and to blame Arlo Goodman for it."

They both stared at him for a moment, then Parker, his forehead wrinkling, asked, "Why?"

"Because they think Goodman is the point man for a fascist political movement — or a populist movement, whatever. Profamily, prochurch, semisocialist, antigay, intolerant, authoritarian. They set up Schmidt for the fall, because he was linked to Goodman. Then, I think, they killed Schmidt. But I don't know that. That's just what I think."

"Green was in on it? I saw the pictures in his office . . ."

"Green was gay, a former lover of Bowe's. He might have been about to fold up. I mentioned Schmidt to him, how he disappeared. He sorta freaked. I got the feeling that he looked on the whole Bowe-death thing as a complicated political joke. Certainly didn't think murder was involved . . . Anyway, I came out to talk to Green about it and scared the hell out of him. He said he had to talk to some friends about what to tell me, so I walked down to a bookstore, bought a novel, ate a bagel, and when I came back . . . there they were."

"Sonofabitch," Parker said.

"How long have you known this, Jake?" Novatny asked. "That Bowe was gay? That the whole thing might have been a setup? Why in the hell didn't you tell us?"

"I've known Bowe was gay for a couple of days. Madison Bowe told me, asked me not to pass it along if I didn't have to, but left it to my discretion. She was afraid that it would leak — and it would have — and that would have ended the investigation. It would have become a gay thing. She still believes that her husband was murdered, and that Arlo Goodman was involved. And she had a point."

"But now . . ."

"Now things have changed," Jake said. "I didn't think it was a gay thing. That was too far-fetched and that's why I didn't tell you about it. Nobody cares about gay anymore — and Bowe wasn't even in office. Then I got Madison Bowe's permission to go to New York and look at Bowe's apartment. I found an empty pill bottle there — it's still there — and tracked it back to Bowe's doctor, who told me about the cancer."

"And then you thought . . ."

"I thought it was all too much: Nobody can figure out where Bowe went. He was smiling when he disappeared. His body is found in this spectacular way with an arrow pointing straight at Schmidt. Why did Schmidt get rid of every gun in the house, except the one that could convict him of killing Bowe? That was goofy. I started thinking that the whole thing was faked. And I'll bet you something: I bet if you look at Schmidt, that you'll find some kind of tie to Arlo Goodman. One that

Goodman might not even know about, but that would look suspicious if somebody got tipped off."

"So it's all a fraud. The Bowe murder," Parker said.

"Yes. I started to think it was basically a suicide, and it occurred to me that, if that's what happened, that his friends had to be involved. People he could trust absolutely — and that suggested it might be this group of gay lovers, people who'd kept the secret all those years. And who had reason to fear Goodman."

Novatny and Parker looked at each other, then Novatny rubbed his face with his hands and said, "On the way out here, I figured out twenty reasons why you were here and there were dead people, and how it might be related to Bowe. Nothing I thought of was this weird."

"Is Madison Bowe in on it?" Parker asked.

"No." Jake shook his head. "She and Lincoln Bowe haven't been together for years. She's just been a cover for him. And she's the one who's been pushing the investigation. She got me started in this direction. She gave me Green's name. She gave me the key to her apartment, pointed me at the doctor. I think that Lincoln

Bowe deliberately kept her in the dark. Maybe because she wouldn't have gone along; or maybe to protect her."

Novatny was skeptical. "You have no idea who the killers might be."

"Bowe's gay friends. You could ask around, you'll turn them up. Madison still thinks that Goodman is involved. She thinks the idea of a bunch of Bowe's friends getting together to kill him is ludicrous. Your guess is as good as mine."

"Assuming that you're telling us the truth — and I think you are, even if we're not getting all of it — then the killer's somebody from here in Madison," Parker said. "Got to Green inside of an hour."

Jake scrubbed at his hair with the palms of his hands, then said, "That doesn't seem right. That just doesn't seem right. But that's what happened."

"Have you figured out how it went down in Green's office?" Jake asked.

Novatny frowned. "We think the killers were professional — nobody heard any shots, but the shots were probably fired from a .22. Those are not so quiet, so it must have been silenced."

"How do you know it was a .22?"

"Took a slug out of a wall," Parker said.

"The base was intact, looks like a .22."

"Could be a .22 mag. The damage was pretty big," Novatny said.

"They were executed, then," Jake said.

Novatny brightened: "Not exactly. We think that the secretary tried to resist, tried to fight them off, went after somebody with her nails. She got some skin and a little blood, so we've got DNA. If we can find the guy, we can nail him."

"And Green . . ."

"He took it right in the back of the head. He was executed. We think the secretary tried to resist, that's when she lost her shoes, got her hands on someone, and Green just stood there and *boom*."

"What now?" Jake asked.

Novatny got a tape recorder, read Jake his rights, and got him to repeat the statement. Jake did, but insisted that most of what he said, other than the basics about Bowe's sexuality and the cancer revelation, was speculation. "I just want out of this," he said. "I'm a research guy, not a cop. I just want out."

Novatny talked to the Madison chief, but didn't tell Jake the outcome. They did cut Jake loose, at seven o'clock. "Are you going back to D.C.?" Novatny asked.

"Yes. But first, I'm going to check into a hotel and get some sleep," Jake said. "I'm really screwed up."

"One thing," Novatny said. "Do not go back to Madison Bowe. She's going to be a critical witness. Don't mess with her."

"Believe me. All I want is out," Jake said.

Jake walked down to State Street, through a couple of alleys, in and out the back of a pizza place, and found a phone near the restrooms in a sports bar and called Johnson Black, Madison's lawyer. He got lucky, made the connection, talked to Black for a moment, then ordered a beer at the bar and stood next to the phone. Madison called him back twenty minutes later from a phone in an M Street lounge. "Listen to me," he said. "There's been a disaster."

He told her about it, then said, "So the feds are going to come to you. You confirm the homosexual angle and you tell them why you didn't want that made public — that you were pushing the investigation into Goodman, and were afraid the homosexual angle would end it. You tell them that sexuality is a private matter, and you had no reason to think that it was involved in Lincoln's death. You tell them that you had no idea that there was a setup . . ."

"I didn't," she said. "But now you're telling me . . . I caused this girl's death somehow. If I hadn't sent you there . . ."

"You didn't cause her death," Jake said. "Somebody else did. You can't anticipate the outcome of everything you do; you can go crazy trying. Somebody else killed them, not you."

"But if I hadn't sent you . . ."

"Madison, get a grip. It's really critical right now. If you're going to feel guilty, feel guilty about something you actually did."

"But you don't know . . ."

"Tell me later," Jake said. "Not on the phone . . . Has anything happened there that I should know about? Is anybody pushing you?"

"One thing, but . . . ah, jeez, I can't keep the girl out of my head."

"Focus, goddamnit. What happened?"

"I talked to Howard, I confronted him. He killed Linc, but it was essentially a suicide. Linc had already taken an overdose. He claims that Schmidt is in Thailand, working as a bartender. That Schmidt is obsessed by brown hookers. Those are Howard's words. He says that they can bring him back anytime they need to."

"Ah, jeez. Listen, stay away from Barber. Stay away from him. He's about to become the eye of a hurricane. He might be involved here . . ."

"Jake . . ."

"Tell the truth, but don't tell them about the package," Jake said. "Not yet. Just omit it. Don't tell them what Barber said. And don't tell them about this call. This never happened."

"What are you going to do?"

"I've got to think. Listen, call me tomorrow, on my cell phone, from a public phone. At noon. If anything's happened, I'll let you know then. I can't call *you,* because if there's an investigation, they're going to pull the phone records to see who was talking to whom."

Off the line, Jake walked back to his car, found a Sheraton hotel, checked in, and began working Green's cell phone. He'd been talking about a *woman* who had the package, and had automatically taken the cell phone out of his pocket, as though her number was there.

The phone was unfamiliar, but it took him only a minute to figure out the menu system. The call log showed one outgoing call after Jake's arrival, lasting twenty-four minutes. The call was to the 715 area code.

Jake found a Yellow Pages in the closet, checked area codes. The 715 code covered most of the north half of Wisconsin. Now for the three-number prefix after the area code.

He signed on to the hotel's wireless service, went out on the Net, found a listing for Wisconsin prefixes. The three-number prefix was in Eau Claire. He checked an online map: Eau Claire was probably three hours away by car. If the killers had gotten a name, somebody in Eau Claire might already be dead. In fact, if the killers had gotten either the phone number or the name, that person almost surely was dead . . .

He didn't want to use the FBI search service to find the name behind the number; that could be tracked back to him.

But . . .

He lay on the bed, covered his eyes with his forearm, tried to think about it. If the killers had threatened Green and his secretary to get information on the package, did the killers get the information and then do the killing? Is that why the girl resisted, attacked a gun with her fingernails? Maybe she saw the bullet coming . . .

But if they'd killed the secretary to force the information from Green, there wouldn't have been any percentage in giving it to them, because Green would have known at that point that he was doomed.

So maybe the killers *didn't* have a name . . .

He needed to know whom Green had called without leaving obvious tracks. A thought popped into his head: the public library. Could it be that easy? He went back online, looking for an address of the local public library. When he found it, on the library website, he also found a list of telephone references available online. He worked through the menu, tracking the number: and found it. The Eau Claire number went to a Sarah Levine. He checked another directory and had an address. He said her name aloud, tripping a memory: "Sarah Levine, Sarah Levine . . ."

Lion Nerve. He picked up a pen, crossed out letters. He had Levine, plus o-n-r. Ron Levine.

Back online, using his government access to Social Security records. Ran Ronald Levine against ITEM: Got an immediate hit. Ronald Levine worked for ITEM for seventeen years. Retired, started collecting Social Security, then showed a change-in-status. He checked: Levine had died.

Okay. He knew who had the package — Ron Levine's widow, Sarah. If she was still alive.

If whoever had killed Green had done it to get the package, and if they had gotten Sarah Levine's name, then she was probably dead. They'd had more than eight hours to get to her. If they hadn't, then what? Then, Jake thought, they didn't get her name, and they could be watching me. Or coming for me.

The Dane County airport had an all-night Hertz car rental service. He called, gave them the rental information on his car, told them that it sounded funny to him — the engine would hesitate when it downshifted, after it got warm. Wondered if he might trade it for another. No problem. He told them he'd be in early.

Tried to sleep. He got his four and a half hours, but he was restless, waiting for something to happen. At two-thirty he was up and moving. He cleaned up, packed, did the on-screen checkout, and carried his overnight bag and case down to the car. Moving fast. If they were going to try to take him, they'd have to catch him in the hundred feet between the hotel and the car, and at three o'clock in the morning, they might be a little slow to react.

He saw nobody in the parking lot, but felt the chill in his spine as he was backing the car out. He made it to the Dane County airport, did the paperwork, upgrading to a Ford SUV, saw nobody out of place. As he was waiting for the Hertz guy to finish the paper, another thought popped into his head. If the watchers were good, and trained, he *wouldn't* see anybody.

But now, at least, he wouldn't be driving a car that he'd been seen in, that might even have a locator hidden on it; maybe a change of cars would throw them.

Out on the interstate, he headed north, driving a little too slow, watching for headlights that stayed back. Got off at a rural highway intersection, watched for lights behind him, saw one car getting off. Took another left, and another quick one, waited, then headed back to the interstate. If they had a team, they could still be with him. If they were in the air, they could still be with him.

But he could do more loops on country

roads all the way up, and even, in the last few miles, maybe wrap up a trailing team in the streets of Eau Claire. Whatever: it'd have to be good enough.

All the way north, whenever his headlights swept across the black backdrop of trees, like a projector's light in a darkened theater, he could see the flickering face of the dead secretary. The face would stay with him for a while, he thought. Cruelly, he found himself wishing she'd fallen facedown, so he wouldn't have to see it.

Darrell Goodman, worn and scared, put a finger to his lips, hooked Arlo Goodman's arm, and pulled him toward the staircase. Arlo Goodman followed him down and around to the concrete tunnel in the basement.

"We had a big problem in Wisconsin," Darrell whispered.

"Not too big," Arlo said.

"Pretty big. The Green guy went after me, and George shot him. The secretary . . . we had no choice with the secretary. We had no choice."

Goodman peered at his brother as though he'd gone crazy. "Are you telling me you killed them?"

"There was no choice," Darrell protested.

"Sweet bleedin' Jesus." Arlo stared for another few seconds, trying to grasp it. "I should have strangled you when you were a kid."

"Listen. Nobody knows," Darrell said. "We rented the car in Chicago. We put a little mud on the plates, so they're not on any camera. We went into a parking lot at the back of the building, and nothing faces the back except a brick wall and a door. We went up, nobody saw us. No cameras, we checked. We went in. We put the guns on them to scare them, I slapped Green a couple of times, and the next thing I know, he's all over me. Then the chick . . . but we got out. Not a sign of anybody looking at us. Went right straight back to Chicago, fast as we could, dumped the weapons on the way, turned in the car and got out of there. I'm going to root the IDs out of the license bureau, nobody'll ever know."

"You dumb sonofabitch," Arlo groaned. "No guns, no guns. Why'd you take guns? You were supposed to blackmail him, for Christ's sake."

"He came after me, man. And then George . . ."

Arlo waved him silent. "Where's George?"

"Sitting in my office."

"George has to go away," Arlo said.

Darrell licked his lower lip. "That can happen."

"Make it happen soon. The next few days. I don't want to see him anymore."

"Don't worry about that . . ."

Arlo slapped his brother on the side of the head with his good hand. "This might screw us for good, dummy. I take it you didn't get even a sniff of the package?"

"Not a sniff. But Green knew something, I think. We might've had a chance, until he came after me. Things just got out of control, you know?"

Goodman said, "Ah, jeez . . ."

"There's something else — good news," Darrell said. "We've been listening to the tapes again. Howard Barber told Madison Bowe that he was the one who shot Lincoln."

"What?"

"I just found out. I don't know what's happening in Madison — maybe we can find some way to point the cops at Jake Winter. We know he was there in the morning. And then, if we leak the news about Bowe being gay, and if we leak Barber to the FBI . . ."

"Fuck the FBI. You always want to stick a battery up somebody's ass. Okay. Check around, find out who Barber's three closest pals are. Pick one. If he confirms it, we'll nail Barber ourselves. Nail him to a cross. Maybe we can find a way to get Bowe at the same time."

"I don't think she knew."

"Who cares? She knows it now," Arlo said. "She's obstructing justice by not telling the FBI. You just get that going. Figure out who Barber's pals are. When we pick him up, nobody'll sweat a couple of dead people in Wisconsin — or they'll figure Barber did it."

At a gas station just south of Eau Claire, Jake stopped for coffee and to plug Sarah Levine's address into the car's navigation system. After a few loops and dodges, seeing nothing unusual, he followed it to her house behind the Eau Claire Country Club. Still before seven o'clock. Prayed that she was home. Looked up in the sky, for airplanes.

Paranoid, he thought.

Sarah Levine was home. She came to the door in a housecoat, a short, square woman with a square face, blue-green eyes, pearly white hair, and worry lines on her forehead. Jake thought she was in her early sixties. She pushed open the glass storm door, peered at him nearsightedly, and said, "Yes?"

Jake held up his White House ID. "Mrs. Levine, I'm a researcher with the White House. I'm here to talk to you about a package of evidence about possible corruption involving a state highway project. I'm very serious. There have been some terrible things happening, possibly because of the package."

Her mouth worked a few times, and she looked up and down the street, as if for help, and then she said, "What kind of terrible things?"

"Did you hear about the murders in Madison?"

"Omigod," she said. "Who?"

"Al Green and his secretary. They were shot to death, yesterday, possibly by men looking for this package. There's no way to know for sure, but you might be in danger yourself. We need to talk. And I need to establish my identification with you. That I really do work with the White House."

He tried to look helpless. He saw her hesitate, then look at his walking stick. He leaned on it a little more heavily.

She said, "Al was shot? I just talked to him yesterday."

"Yes, he was shot. The FBI is working the case now."

"Are they coming here?" she asked.

"You'll eventually have to talk to them, if they determine this package is relevant. But . . . Mrs. Levine, I really need to look at it, and talk to my superiors in Washington."

Alone inside the house, she seemed more nervous about him. Jake took out his cell phone, called Danzig's office. Gina answered: "This is Jake. I need to talk to the guy."

"I thought you were all done?"

"I am. But something came up, and this is pretty urgent."

Danzig came on the phone a minute later, his voice cautious. "Jake? I've been hearing some rumors about Madison . . ."

"The city, or the woman?"

"The city . . ."

"Yeah. I was there. Things are rough. But: I've made contact with the package in question. I need you to establish my bona fides with a woman here . . . It's important." He glanced at Levine and smiled. "She doesn't necessarily trust me, given the circumstances. I would like to have her call the White House, and have her switched up to your office so she could talk to you for a second."

"Is this absolutely necessary?" He didn't want to do it.

"I think so, sir. We'll have to talk to the FBI, though. There's another copy, somewhere in Madison."

Silence, then, "Tell her to call."

"You can call the White House?" Levine asked doubtfully.

"Sure. It's basically an office building with a big lawn," Jake said. "This is the only way I could think to prove that I'm okay."

She called Washington directory assistance, got the main number for the White House, and at Jake's instruction gave her full name: "This is Sarah MacLaughlin Levine, calling for Mr. Danzig."

She had to wait a minute, then said, "Yes . . . yes." Another few seconds, then, "Yes. Yes I do." She looked at Jake. "Okay, thank you. I'll talk to him. Okay. Thank you."

"They said you're official." She was more confident now. "They said you were coordinating with the FBI."

"I am — but before we get too far down that road, we have to assess the contents of the package. We don't want to get caught up in a fraud; we have to make sure that everything is legitimate; that they're for real."

"One thing, though," she said. "This is about your . . . vice president. How do I know you just won't throw them in the river?"

Jake tried to look as pious as he could: "Mrs. Levine, this package is going to come out, sooner or later. There are copies. Once I have it, there's no way I can bury it. If I did, I'd go to prison. But we have to make sure that it's real."

"It's real," she grunted. "Landers is crookeder than a hound dog's leg. The whole bunch of them are crooked."

The package was almost exactly that: a cardboard box that said Xerox on the side, and that had once held ten reams of 92-bright white printer paper. Inside the box was a stack of notebooks, some files, and three DVD disks in a Ziploc freezer bag.

"We hoped . . . ," Levine said tentatively, as Jake began thumbing through the paper. "You know, my husband passed away three years ago. He had an infarction. I hoped that maybe because I helped out, you know, that I could get help getting a job. They took my husband's pension away, those people at ITEM, those big shots, they said he elected to get more money early, or something like that."

"We can talk about your help," Jake said. "I think you'll be okay. If you tried to get to the authorities."

"I tried, Lord knows I tried," she said. "I knew Al from when he was fund-raising, I knew he was well connected in Washington. I thought that was the best way to get this to the proper people."

She put Jake in the living room to read, brought a package of Oreos and glasses of orange juice as he worked.

The package described a standard piece of corruption, notable only for the arrogance shown by the vice president and his friends, and the size of the return. The highway project involved reconstruction of about ninety miles of Wisconsin's federal Highway 65, from its intersection with Interstate 94 a few miles east of the Minnesota line, to the town of Hayward in the north woods.

"Highway Sixty-five is the main road from the Twin Cities up to the Hayward Lakes resorts," Levine said. "My husband worked on the project for six years, it was a big deal, you bet." She dug around in the kitchen cabinet, found a Wisconsin road map, and traced the line of the highway

343

with a finger. "The project was on the up-and-up. The project saved lives . . . It was only later that the trouble started. My husband was a comptroller on the project, and there was trouble right away with equipment. That's all on disk one, the books."

The general contractor, ITEM, subcontracted with several dozen smaller independent companies to do the planning, environmental studies, equipment and materials supply, earthmoving, and paving.

The key was in the heavy equipment. One of the companies, Cor-Nine, leased twenty-odd pieces of heavy equipment, mostly heavy dump trucks, along with a few graders, to ITEM over four years, for a total package price of $7.3 million. They also paid Cor-Nine $210,000 for maintenance and repairs.

"That's what really made me laugh, when Ron told me about it," Levine said. "The maintenance, that was hilarious."

"Too much, or not enough?" Jake asked.

"I suppose you'd say too much, since the equipment didn't exist," Levine said.

"Didn't exist."

"Didn't exist. Ron said you couldn't see it, even at the time. The equipment could always be somewhere else . . . You're only talking about one piece for every five miles or so of the road, and there were so many little contractors coming and going that nobody but ITEM knew who was doing what."

"They did the whole highway at the same time? They didn't just do ten miles at a time?"

"Normally, a project would be staged, maybe over fifteen years or so. To maximize the return, they had to do the whole thing while Governor Landers was in office," she said. "They already had a two-lane highway going up, so they constructed another two lanes beside it, all at once. After that was done, they coordinated the old highway with the new highway in stages — essentially, cleanup work, building intersections. That was legitimate, too. It minimized the traffic and business disturbances in all these small towns along the way . . ." She tapped the small towns on the map.

"And Cor-Nine was Landers and his pals."

"No, no. Cor-Nine was some people you never heard of, a bunch of Frenchmen."

"Frenchmen?"

"Yeah. They were a French-based equipment-leasing corporation that, after you traced it to France, came back to the

Bahamas and then disappeared," she said. "If anybody asked, ITEM could say that all they knew was that they were leasing equipment at a good price. If the money disappeared, it was some kind of French tax-avoidance deal. Couldn't blame ITEM for that."

"You seem to know an awful lot about it," Jake commented.

"I was a bookkeeper before I got married," she said. "I know about money."

"So how did the money get to Landers?"

"Through his brother. Sam."

"The guy in Texas," Jake said. The vice president's colorful sibling, big hat and big boots, a lime green Cadillac with longhorns welded to the hood.

"Right. Sam Landers goes down to Texas, a hot real-estate market for retirees — no state income tax, warm weather. He sets up a development company. The vice president and his friends own about seventy-five percent of it and Sam has the rest. The key thing, though, is the financing. The Landers family had no money — but Sam managed to get financing for his Padre Island apartments from . . ."

"A Bahamas bank," Jake said.

"Yes. He builds the apartments — they

346

are quite nice, I understand — repays his loans, and walks away with a nice profit. A very nice profit. The profit is nice because the Bahamas money is buried in the construction. For the money he supposedly puts into them, the apartments should sell for $450,000. But, because he's not actually repaying the loans, he's building $550,000 apartments. Nothing else can compare. And they're snapped up by retirees who can see the deal they're getting, but which is invisible on paper. He pays his taxes — no state income tax in Texas, remember — and the money is back in the United States, all legal and tax-paid."

"But they lose forty percent to the feds."

"Not really. They actually made some profit on the construction. They came out of it with probably five to six million. And then, with a perfectly good development company, and with some experience and a track record, they started doing real projects. They've been making money ever since. The vice president is probably worth fifteen million. Maybe twenty."

"How did your husband know about all the different parts of the deal?"

"He watched the whole thing get set up. There's a man named Carson, Ron's boss, he told Ron to keep his nose out of it. That stuff goes on in any big state project. But Ron knew there'd be trouble sooner or later, and he didn't want to be the one who went to jail, so he made copies of everything. On the sly. Carson's still one of the big shots at ITEM. He held Sam Landers's hand through the first couple of apartment projects. And he kept books, on the computer, you know, and Ron made copies. Those are the DVDs."

They spent an hour sitting on the frontroom couch, looking at paper, loading the DVDs into Jake's notebook, going through the notes, the records, the bank documents, the real estate titles, and tax documents. Altogether, the package was as devastating as advertised. If true.

"If true," Jake said.

"Well, Al Green said that the thing is, everything here has a public record behind it. Records that the Landerses can't dodge," Levine said. "It's all visible, but nobody could ever tie it together without inside knowledge."

Jake looked at his watch. "I gotta get you out of here."

Now she was nervous again. "What's going to happen?"

"I think, because of what happened in Madison, that you should take a trip," Jake said. "Do you have any place that you can go? A friend's, or a sister's, that's away from here? Somebody who doesn't have the same name?"

"I have a sister in Waukesha."

"Would she put you up for a few days?"

"I'm sure she would," Levine said.

"Then you should go. Right now — I'll wait until you're ready. Leave me a phone number and I'll get back to you. I've got to talk to some people back in Washington."

"The president?'

"I don't actually talk to the president that much," Jake said. "But I'll talk to some people and see what can be done. If you've been straight with us."

"I've been straight," Levine said. "I knew it was going to cause trouble, but . . . after they took Ron's pension away, I have no money. I mean, we had some in Fidelity, but it's mostly gone now. I need to get a job. I can't work at Wal-Mart, that's the only thing I can get here, there aren't any jobs. I might have to sell my house . . ."

Tears were running down her cheeks; Jake wanted to pat her on the shoulder, but he didn't know quite how to do it. "Let me get you out of here, and get this package to Washington. We'll figure something out. This is gonna work for you, one way or another."

She took forever to get dressed and pack: more than an hour, by Jake's watch. Jake suggested that she call her sister from outside the house.

"You think I'm bugged?"

"I don't want to take any chances with anything," Jake said.

When she was ready, she got her dog, a nervous gray whippet, and Jake helped wedge it into a carrying case and carried it down to the tuck-under garage and put it on the front seat of her car.

He carried three more suitcases down, told Levine to give him a week.

"You'll hear from me, or from somebody with the federal government, in no more than a week. We have to get experts to evaluate the package — you can understand, this is really, really sensitive stuff."

Jake also gave her a thousand dollars from his stash. "Personal loan," he said. "Pay it back when you can."

He followed her out to the Wal-Mart that she didn't want to work at, watched as she made the call to her sister, then waved good-bye.

The package was in the back of the SUV. He called Gina again and said, "It'd be really helpful if you could get me a ticket back. From Eau Claire, Madison, Milwaukee, or the Twin Cities."

"Just sit right where you are," she said. "We've got a plane on the way."

15

On the way to the Eau Claire airport, Jake stopped at a Kinko's, spent a half hour making a duplicate of the package, and FedExed it to himself in Washington. His next stop was at an OfficeMax, where he bought a cheap plastic briefcase and stuffed the original copy of the package inside. The plane was due at twelve-fifteen; Madison called promptly at noon.

"I talked to the FBI this morning. Your friend Novatny. I didn't tell them that Howard killed Linc. I was afraid to," she said. "Although, I think they know. I gave them some names, including Howard Barber's. I called Howard from a pay phone after I talked to you last night, and told him that the FBI doesn't know about the package."

"Okay. I don't know what's going to happen, but I've been thinking about it," Jake said. "Can you come to my place tonight? Bring an overnight bag? I've got a guest room."

"Well . . . Why?"

"I don't want you staying at your house, alone, but I need you in Washington," Jake said. "I'd rather explain it to you face-to-face. Try to settle this."

"Then I'll do it. What time?"

"I ought to be there by seven or eight. Say, eight o'clock. If I can't make it, I'll call you," Jake said. "Madison: don't talk about anything sensitive in your living room. Don't use that phone in the hallway, by the kitchen. Just don't."

"You think? I'm bugged?"

"It's a definite possibility. Keep people around you, don't get isolated. If you call me, call from a pay phone. When you come tonight, just bump up to the back gate, the way you did last time, and I'll let you in."

The jet was assigned to the Department of Homeland Security. It wasn't fancy, but the turnaround was quick. Jake spent the air time reviewing the package, putting together a presentation. Every once in a while, he'd look out at the countryside below: most of the time, he saw the eyes of Green's blond secretary.

They flew into National at four o'clock in the afternoon and taxied down to a government hangar. Jake found a driver, from the White House motor pool, waiting on the tarmac, and followed him out to a nondescript Daimler station wagon that smelled of onions and motor oil. He walked into the Blue Room a half hour after the plane touched down.

A navy lieutenant was waiting to escort him up to Danzig's office. Inside, Gina waved him through.

Danzig was standing beside his desk with his hands in his pockets. He looked like he'd been doing nothing but waiting.

"Did you get it?" Danzig was usually intense; now he was actually vibrating.

Jake nodded, dropped into a chair, his briefcase on his lap. Tired. Stress beginning to bite at him. "The only question is whether it's real. I'm almost sure it is. I think research will prove it. But I've gotten tangled up in a murder investigation, and to tell you the truth, my statement to the FBI and the Madison cops wasn't exactly complete."

"How not complete?"

Jake patted the package. "This thing is involved in the killings. We've got to give it to the feds as soon as we can. We don't have more than a few days. I can already feel an obstruction charge out there."

"If you deliver it to them, the most they can say is that you were late," Danzig said.

"Yeah, bullshit. If they want me, they can get me," Jake said. "What I'm going to need is the silken breath of the president blowing down somebody's back. Words like *national security, Someone's ass is grass,* like that."

Danzig nodded, avoiding Jake's eyes: "Anyway."

"Yeah." Jake started unpacking the cheap briefcase. "Here's the stuff. Here's how it worked. . . ."

Danzig wanted to review each piece of paper, to crawl through the books on the DVD disks, to find inconsistencies. They took two hours, the longest time Jake had ever spent in Danzig's office. They found inconsistencies, but they appeared to be paperwork mistakes, rather than logical errors that would suggest a fraud. When they were done, Danzig stood up, walked around the room in his stocking feet, sighed, and said, "Shit."

"What do you think?" Jake asked.

"They're real. I've seen stuff like this before, and they have the feeling of reality about them. The grit. A few pieces are missing, but that's what you'd expect if it was real. The inconsistencies are consistent with reality."

"I agree. You could get somebody else, maybe, to do some specific checks on the public records, to nail it down."

Danzig nodded. "Of course. We'll start that tomorrow. Tonight, if we can, maybe some of the stuff is online."

"I'd want to see the actual paper, where it exists . . ."

"So would I," Danzig said. Then, "Okay. You wait here for a minute. I'm going to get the boss."

"There's another thing, somewhat related," Jake said. "And it's about to pop. Lincoln Bowe was gay. His death was a conspiracy that Bowe set up himself, carried out by a close friend, or a few close friends, in an effort to embarrass Goodman."

Danzig's face didn't move for a moment, as though he hadn't heard. Then he said, "Holy shit."

"I had to tell the feds. They're now investigating Bowe's gay friends. It's gonna leak in the next day or two, and the whole investigation is going to lurch that way, away from the package. But it'll come back."

Danzig ran one hand through his oily

hair and then said, "You're a hell of a re-searcher, Jake. I hope you never come after me."

Danzig padded out of the office, re-turned five minutes later, trailed by the president. The president was a tall, white-haired Indianan, a former governor and senator, a middle-of-the-roader chosen to lead the ticket when the Democrats de-cided to get serious. He was wearing a dark suit and white shirt, without a tie, and like Danzig, was in his stocking feet. Jake stood up when he walked in.

"Hey, Jake," he said. They shook hands and the president asked, "What the heck did you drag in this time?"

They spent another twenty minutes combing through the package, and finally the president said to Danzig, "I believe it. What do you think?"

Danzig glanced at Jake, then back to the president, who said, "Go ahead. He's in deeper than we are."

"We've got to do some verification and then we talk to Landers," Danzig said. "He's in town. We'll get his ass over here, stick this thing up it. Come to some kind of agreement."

The president looked at Jake. "You say

there's another copy?"

"At least one more — probably in the dead man's safe-deposit box," Jake said. "The FBI will get to it sooner or later. Probably sooner, since Novatny's working the case."

"I don't know him," the president said.

"He's pretty good, sir. Also, there are quite a few other people who know about it, know enough details to cause trouble, even if they don't have the package. It's possible that the package could be replicated, at least a good part of it, from public records. If the Republicans talk to the *L.A. Times*, and they put a couple of investigators on it, they'll hang the vice president; and maybe get us in passing."

"All right," the president said. To Danzig: "Get Delong and Henricks here tonight. We want to get this taken care of, and I want to turn this over to the FBI by the end of the week. I want Jake to do it. We need to cover him." Delong was Landers's chief of staff; Henricks, the president's legal counsel.

"We've got a lot to talk about," Danzig said to the president. He was tense, but seemed happier than he usually was. He liked an outrageous problem, Jake decided. And this would make a hell of a scene in a what-really-happened book, five years after the president left office.

"We do," the president said. "We don't need Jake to do that."

"Mr. President, I do have one thing to suggest," Jake said. "When you're talking about the other stuff, don't spend too much time thinking about Arlo Goodman as a replacement for the vice president."

The president nodded, but asked, "Why not?"

"Because there are strings floating all over this mess and I suspect some of them lead back to Goodman. Maybe even to the murders in Wisconsin."

"I'll keep it in mind," the president said.

Jake went out the White House gate, stood in the street for a moment or two, then walked down a block, flagged a cab, and went home.

He was home at seven-thirty. He took a shower, shaved again, just to feel fresh, brushed his teeth, put on clean jeans, a black T-shirt, and a sport coat. Then he went down to the study, pulled some books out of a shelf, found the green-fabric pistol case, took out the .45, slipped a clip into it, and dropped the gun in his jacket pocket.

At ten minutes to eight, he went out and

sat on the back stoop. At five after eight, a car turned down the alley. He recognized it as Madison's, opened the back gate, and she drove into the yard. She got out of the car and asked, "Are you okay?"

"Yeah. Come on, let's get you out of sight."

Inside the door, she asked, "Is that a gun in your pocket, or are you just happy to see me?"

She had a soft leather carry-on bag and a briefcase. Jake took the bag, led her into the house, up the stairs to the guest room. "Bathroom, first door down the hall," he said. "Come on: I'll get you a glass of wine or a beer and tell you the story."

She took a beer, settled into a chair in his living room, while he sat on the couch across from her. "Tell me about the gun," she said.

"The two people killed in Madison were executed. They were killed in an office building and nobody heard any shots," Jake said. "The gun was probably silenced, and the killers are probably professional — at least, they'd done it before. The only reason there weren't more dead people in the building is that nobody happened to bump into them in the hallway."

"Why didn't they come after you?"

"I was behaving unpredictably, maybe. Or maybe they didn't know I'd been there already," Jake said. "After I found the bodies, I called the cops, and then there were cops all over the place."

"That's why you're carrying a gun," she said. "You're afraid they might come here."

"Yeah. Or to your place."

"You think my house is bugged. Why wouldn't you think this place is?" Madison asked.

"Because somebody followed me out to Wisconsin, or maybe even tried to get there before me. We talked about it in your living room. That's the only place I talked about it. The thing is, I was on the earliest plane to Milwaukee and there was no way to get into Madison faster than I did, unless they'd rented their own jet and flown directly to Madison. That would leave too much of a trail."

"If they come here, you plan to shoot it out?" She sounded skeptical.

"I've got alarms. The woman who used to own the place thought she might be raped and murdered at any minute, and she covered everything," Jake said. "If anybody comes, we'll know it. The gun would give us a chance to call for help. A little time."

She pushed off her shoes, curled her feet beneath her, and said, "It's not Howard Barber, Jake. I know him well enough to tell you that he wouldn't have executed a secretary."

"How about Schmidt? I know what he told you, but I want to see the guy."

She looked away from him, her tongue touching her bottom lip, and then she said, "We're coming up on that trust thing. I made you feel bad the other night, when I asked if you trusted me, and made you admit that you weren't quite there yet."

"You *did* make me feel bad," he admitted.

"Well, you were right . . . I've been lying to you a little. I didn't know about Linc. That was a shock. But I knew about the package. I didn't know the details, but I knew it was out there, I knew that it might bring down this administration. I didn't tell you about it when you really needed to know."

Jake watched her for a moment, suppressing reaction. The truth was, he'd known that something wasn't quite right. He *hadn't* trusted her. "Then why did you send me out to Madison?"

"I thought I was sending you on a wild-goose chase. I'm sorry. Howard had already talked to Al Green, and Al denied knowing anything about the package. We wanted to get you out of the way for a few days, hoping the whole hunt for the package would die down, so we'd have more time to find it. We sort of expected the gay thing to get out . . ."

"You expected me to put it out to the media?" She'd expected betrayal of what she'd portrayed as a personal confidence.

"Well, yes. It would have solved some of your problems."

"Thanks," he said, his voice dry. He felt as though he should be angry, but he wasn't — not yet.

"We just wanted . . . delay," Madison said. She knotted up her hands, twisted them. "We wanted the package to come out in the fall. Or if not that, just before the convention, to ruin the convention. But Howard didn't think Green had it. Green swore he didn't."

Jake peered at her for a moment, then said, "Now you're telling me the truth."

"I didn't want to mislead you," she said. "I really didn't. But you were working for Danzig and we were working against him."

"Why tell me now?"

"Because I'm tired of lying to you," she

said. "I just want this to stop. I want the girl in Madison to be alive again. And I don't want to be . . . on the other side from you."

Jake thought about it, then said, "If Howard Barber didn't do the killing, it must have been Goodman. Or somebody acting for him."

"That's all I can figure out. Unless there's a third party that nobody knows about. The CIA, the DIA."

"Ah, that's not it. Outside of the movies, they don't murder all that many people."

"I've got more bad news," Madison said. "I didn't know that Howard had been involved in Linc's disappearance until you told me. I accused him of it, and he admitted it."

"So that's clear."

"The problem is, I did it in my living room. Which you think is bugged."

"Ah, man."

They were working through the implications of her confrontation with Barber when the phone rang and Jake stepped into the hallway to pick it up.

"Jake, this is Chuck Novatny. When did you get back?"

"This afternoon. What's going on?"

"Have you seen, or spoken to, Madison Bowe since we talked yesterday?"

"Yes. She's here. I'm not plotting with her, I just don't want her to be alone with these killers out there. You want to talk to her?"

"Jake, goddamnit."

"Hey, pal, if you want to put a few FBI bodyguards in her house, I'll send her back home. But I'm not going to have her sitting there like a big goddamn jacklighted antelope while the FBI tiptoes around, trying to get its protocols right."

"Fuck you," Novatny snapped.

"Yeah, well, fuck you, too."

Silence. Then, "All right. Let me talk to her."

Jake carried the phone into Madison, said, "Novatny."

Her eyebrows went up and she took it and said, "Hello? Yes. I can do that. Can I bring Johnson Black with me? Okay."

She handed the phone back to Jake. Novatny said, "We need her here tomorrow for another statement. We need to talk to her about who else is in this gay ring . . ."

"I'm not sure it's exactly a ring."

"You know what I mean," Novatny said.

"Yeah, I do, but I'll tell you what,

Chuck. 'Ring' sounds bad. It sounds like a supermarket tabloid. And if I were you, I'd start choosing my words carefully. This thing . . ."

"I know. It's run completely off the tracks. Officially, I don't like the fact that you've got Madison Bowe at your place. Unofficially, keep an eye on her. You've got a gun?"

"Yup."

"Okay. She's got an ocean of money, I could give her the name of a good security outfit if she needs it — all ex–Secret Service guys."

"I'll tell her," Jake said.

"And, Jake — best of luck."

Jake had to think about it for a half second and said, "Yeah, fuck you again."

Novatny laughed and hung up.

Jake told Madison about the security service and suggested that she might try it: she said she'd think about it. "It might be inconvenient to have those people underfoot," she said. "What about the bug? If there is a bug."

"Leave it. I have an idea for a pageant."

"A pageant?"

"You know, a play," Jake said. "A drama. We'll need the bug."

"What are you talking about?"

"I'd have to trust you to tell you," he said.

"I know . . . ah, God. Jake: you can trust me. Not before, but now you can. I don't know how I can prove it."

They sat in silence for a while, and then another idea popped into his head. He said, "Hang on a minute," went into the study, dug in his briefcase, and found a hospital room number for Cathy Ann Dorn.

She picked up the phone and said "Hello" with a broken-tooth lisp. "My dad said you called," Dorn said when he'd identified himself.

"Are you okay? Are you getting back?"

"No. I'm really, really messed up. Not hurt bad, but my nose is broken . . ." She started crying, caught herself, and then said, "And they broke my teeth so I look like some kind of fu-fu-fu-fucking hillbilly or something. . . ." And she started crying again.

"Can I come and see you?"

"Yes. I'm just sitting here, with this thing in my arm. I have to go to imaging to-morrow morning, but I'll be back before noon. A dentist is coming tomorrow after-noon . . ."

"I need to see you privately. Is there any possibility . . . ?"

"Dad comes in the morning and then he goes to work, and he and Mom come for lunch about twelve-twenty. If you were here after ten, it should be private."

"I'll be there," Jake said.

"Don't look at me weird when you get here," she said. "I'm ugly now, so don't look at me weird."

"Cathy, I've got a friend who was hit in the face with a piece of shrapnel the size of a butcher knife and it almost took his face off. We folded it back over and got him to the hospital, and today he's got this little white scar. You can't even see it unless he's got a tan. The docs can do anything. In a couple of months, you'll be looking great, and I'll introduce you to the president."

She hiccuped, then said, "Really?"

"Count on it."

"Now I'm going to have to trust you," he told Madison, back in the living room. "I have a possible source into Goodman."

He told her about Cathy Ann Dorn: "I'd love to get her into Goodman's office, take the hard drives out of his computer."

"Jake: think," Madison said. "She nearly gotten beaten to death. That's not a coincidence. You'd send her back in there?"

Jake frowned: Cathy Ann wasn't exactly in the army. "Okay, that's not the best idea. But she's a resource. I'll think of something."

"Interesting job you have . . ."

Madison asked him how he came to work for the president. Jake filled her in, told her about his grandparents' ranch, and the distance between himself and his parents. Then, "You want another beer?"

"Sure. One more couldn't hurt."

She came back to his grandparents, and he talked about working the ranch, about how his grandfather resisted the transition from horses to ATVs. "I used to envy those kids with the big Hondas and Polarises riding around in a cloud of smoke, tearing up the countryside. I'd be sitting up there on some mutt, take me fifteen minutes to get somewhere you could get in one minute on a Honda," Jake said. "Now, I'm nothing but grateful. Would have been nice if the family had been a little tighter, you know, my parents, but hell. I had a pretty good childhood, all in all. Thought I'd die myself, though, when Grandma went . . ."

She told him about her childhood, in Lexington and Richmond. Her father had been a lawyer, her mother a housewife. Her father committed suicide when he was fifty.

"I hated him for it," she said, getting out of her chair, wandering around the room with the bottle in her hand. "I was in college, and we'd had some growing-up troubles, and some arguments, and they got pretty hot and I did some screaming and I never had a chance to make it okay before he went out in the backyard and shot himself."

"Was there . . . ? Did you know why?"

"Yes. He was depressed. Major depression of the medical sort. He wouldn't go to a shrink, because he still thought he might run for a serious political office — he was on the Richmond City Council twice. He didn't want a 'mental illness' brought up. So he had some pills from his M.D., but they weren't working . . . And one day, a really nice day, he went out in the yard and sat in a swing for a while, and then *blam*. A neighbor heard it and came running . . . Maybe that's why I married an older guy. Maybe I was trying to get back to Daddy."

She sat down again, but when she sat down, she sat on the couch with Jake. Feeling precisely like a teenager in a movie theater, Jake let his left arm fall along the top of the couch. He started thinking about his breath, and what he'd eaten. Beer should cover it, he hoped.

She was talking about riding, and did a little butt-hop closer on the couch, and he thought, *Man, she's sending out semaphore signals, just go ahead and do it.* And he thought about Novatny and his *good luck*. Amazed at his own boldness, he moved a little closer to her himself, reached a hand behind her far shoulder, and pulled her a bit closer and kissed her. She sank into it, leaning against him, said, mmm, and when he started to pull away, caught him, and they kissed again.

The conversation grew confused.

After a minute or two, Jake's hand wandered down her body, and the conversation grew even more confused. And he realized that with the second beer in him, he was going to have to pee, and fairly soon. He also realized that he would cut his legs off before he'd leave the couch.

He thought, *What small heads women have,* when his hand was behind her head, and at another moment, when his hand was wandering from one breast to another, she misinterpreted it as a fumble and said, "Here, wait a minute," and helped him un-button her blouse. He popped her bras-siere one-handed and she mumbled, "I see you've had some training in brassieres," and he said, "I was just lucky," and she said, "Right . . ."

After that, the conversation seriously languished until she laughed, a little breathlessly, and said, "Jake. Stop. Jake, I really, really have to pee. Let me up, you oaf."

She ran up the stairs to the bathroom. Jake hurried into the first-floor bathroom, flushed a few seconds before she did, washed and dried his hands, checked his hair in the mirror, gargled some water, just in case, and was standing in the living room with his hands in his pockets when she came back down the stairs.

"Hi." He took her hand and pulled her in and kissed her on the forehead and said, "This brings up the whole question of sleeping arrangements."

"My God, Jake. Do I have to do *all* the heavy lifting?"

He slept his four and a half hours. He woke up and felt the weight and remembered she was beside him, listened to her breathe, and then thought about the evening. He should, he thought, quit trying to work the problem. He should take Madison on a trip to London, or Paris, and lie low until the whole thing was done. Then they could come back and go wherever the relationship took them.

Ride horses.

But that wasn't what he was going to do.

He could close his eyes and see the face of the dead girl in Madison. Cold, bloody, cruel murder.

16

They ate breakfast together, English muffins, marmalade, and coffee, and Jake said, "You can either come with me or I can ditch you with a friend. I know a retired professor at Georgetown, you'd be pretty secure at his place."

"Silly goose," she said. "I'm coming with you."

He called Gina at the White House and asked, "What's my schedule, if I have a schedule?"

"Jake, it's a nightmare here," she said. For the first time since he began working for Danzig, Jake could hear excitement in her voice. "The guy wants to talk to you, but he hasn't had time. Let me see if I can interrupt him."

He listened to electronic noise for a minute, then two, and then Danzig came up abruptly and said, "Stay in touch. I'll want you on two hours' notice. Not today or tomorrow, but maybe the day after . . . or the day after that. We'll want you to talk to Novatny, give him a deposition on the retrieval of the package."

"Things are proceeding?"

"Yes. We should have it wrapped up in forty-eight hours. Sixty at the outside." And he was gone.

They took Jake's car, leaving hers behind in the garage, moving slowly with the congestion across the bridge into Virginia, fighting traffic every inch of the way, a full hour before they broke into a steady flow.

They were in Richmond a little after ten, followed the navigation system to the hospital. As they came up to it, Jake said, "It might be better if she didn't see you. If you want to shop for a few minutes or maybe talk to your mother."

She shook her head: "I couldn't visit Mother for less than four hours. Give me the car, I'll run over to a bookstore."

Jake had gotten a room number from Dorn, and went straight up to the surgical-care center on the third floor. He'd spent a lot of time in hospitals, and the smell of the place brought it all back: everything from the scramble to get him to a med unit, to the flight out to Germany, to the hospital in Bethesda, and the small stuff —

the sound of the overhead speakers, the beeping of monitors, the hollow sounds of voices in tile hallways, and all the drawers; drawers everywhere.

Cathy Ann Dorn was being wheeled into her room as Jake came down the hall. She lifted a hand and said, "Mr. Winter, I think it'll be a minute."

"We have to get her into bed," the nurse said.

"She's afraid my ass'll show," Dorn said.

Dorn and the nurse went into the room, and two minutes later the nurse came out and said, "She's got a mouth."

"Yes, she does."

Dorn was propped up in bed, a bottle of water in her hand, with a bent straw sticking out of it, sunlight slanting through the window across the bed and her covered toes. Jake said, "Hi," and checked her out, let her see it. Her face was a mottled black, blue, and yellow, with small healing cuts still showing black. Her upper teeth were ragged: broken or completely missing.

She said, "The surgeon this morning said that they could fix my nose pretty much, but it might not be perfect."

"Mmm," Jake said. "How about the rest of you?"

"They kicked me pretty bad, they were afraid my liver might be lacerated, but they didn't have to go in." She'd started picking up the surgeon talk.

"So you'll heal," Jake said, pulling a chair toward the bed. He sat down and said, "When the oral surgeon finishes with you, your teeth will look better than new. You can even pick your shade of white. You ought to tell them to take it easy with the nose. Keep a little bit of a bump."

"What?" She was amazed at the thought.

"You're a pretty girl, but prettiness — no offense — straight prettiness can be bland. I could see you with a little bump on your nose; you'd be gorgeous. You'd be network-quality."

A light popped up in her eyes. "You think so?"

"I know so. And I wouldn't have minded getting a look at your ass — from what I saw down in the hallway, the first time we met, it's pretty terrific. Another network-quality asset."

"It is pretty terrific," she said. "I work on it."

They sat in silence for a moment, and then Jake asked, "What do you think happened? A robbery?"

She rolled her eyes. "It wasn't a robbery,

Jake. Arlo did it. His fuckin' brother, Darrell. Somebody told him I talked to you, and then when you knew about Carl V. Schmidt, they knew I told you — so they caught me and beat me up. Arlo visited and patted my hand and said they miss me."

"Did you tell your father that? Did you tell Goodman?"

"No . . . I'm still thinking about what to do."

"Don't tell anyone," Jake said. "I was just in Madison, Wisconsin. You'll be hearing about this in a few days probably . . ." He told her about the killings in Madison. "Things are seriously screwed up, Cathy Ann. Right now, you're okay. But I wouldn't mess with Goodman and I wouldn't have your father mess with him. I would not mention Darrell Goodman to anyone."

"They're just going to get away with it?" She was horrified, in the plain-faced way that young people sometimes were.

"They'll get away with it because you can't identify anyone, and the people in Madison are dead. Knowing he did it, and proving it, are two different things," Jake said. "On the other hand, we can get the word around to the right people, and absolutely fuck them. They won't be able to get

Goodman nominated as dogcatcher."

She looked at him speculatively, and then said, "You're here for something. Other than to cheer me up."

"You said you were smart," Jake said.

"I *am* smart."

Jake had decided that the best way to ask was to go straight ahead: "I'd like to get something out of Goodman's office. I'd like to copy the hard drives on his computer. It'd probably take ten or fifteen minutes. I was hoping you might know somebody, or know some way we could do it."

She was shaking her head. "I'd do it, but they won't take me back. Arlo said that I should take it easy and get back to school and concentrate on my studies. Even if I got back, Dixie — that's his secretary — watches everything like a hawk."

"Shoot." He scratched his head. What to do?

"What do you think's on the hard drives?" Dorn asked.

"I don't know. But there'd probably be a lot of e-mail in and out, and I'd dearly love to see it," Jake said. "I'd like to see who he's involved with, so that maybe we can catch a couple of them in the net, and get them to talk about Goodman."

"That'd be illegal, wouldn't it? You

couldn't copy his computer and then use it as evidence."

"If you know something for sure, the details of it, then it makes it a lot easier to find evidence outside the original source," Jake said. "If I can do that, I could give it to a friend of mine in the FBI."

She thought for a moment and then smiled and said, "There's a tunnel between the governor's mansion and the capitol. I used to go down there with a friend and smoke. But . . . that's impossible. There are guards, and there's an alarm system that even covers the inside of the house. We weren't allowed to go in before a certain time, because the system had to go off."

"And his office is impossible."

She nodded. "Yeah. It really is. There are the outside guards, the Watchmen, and the inside guards, and alarms. I mean, he's the governor. And since I left, his secretary is the only other person in there, and she's in love with him."

"All right."

"Would you have a problem breaking into a police car?"

"A police car?"

"Arlo gets driven around by a highway patrolman. Several of them, actually. They have this big black Mercury. He goes to lunch at Westboro's almost every day, a little after noon." They both looked at a wall clock. Ten-thirty. "It's where all the legislators hang out. He goes there and meets people and they have lunch and do politics. He takes his briefcase and his laptop with him and he usually leaves it on the floor of the backseat when he gets out. The cop leaves the car in a parking garage. It's pretty dark in there."

"You're saying . . ."

"You might be able to grab the bag and run. You wouldn't be able to copy it without him knowing."

"Where's the cop?"

"In the restaurant," she said. "He's also a bodyguard, he eats across the room from Goodman. I ate with him a couple of times. The cop."

Jake thought about it for fifteen seconds. "That's pretty iffy."

"That's all I can think of," she said. "I'm sorry."

Jake slapped his legs, said, "Well. Time to go to Plan B."

"What's that?"

"You don't want to know. But I'll tell you what: you keep quiet about this visit, get well, stay away from Arlo, go to school like a good girl, and when everything quiets down, give me a call. I'll get you something you'll like."

"You promise?" The light in the eye again, just like when he told her that she'd be gorgeous.

"We take care of people," Jake said.

Back in the car, Madison asked, "Get what you needed?"

"Maybe." He thought about it for another moment, and then asked, "Do you know a place called Westboro's? A restaurant?"

"Sure. Everybody in Richmond does. Political hash house."

"Let's go over there," Jake said. "I'd like to look at a parking garage."

"Who're you meeting?"

"No one, I hope."

He told her about the laptop. She said, "That's pretty iffy," picking the word right out of his head.

"We're hurting pretty bad here," Jake said. "We need a way to break something out."

"Jake, there'll be alarms . . ."

"It's all in the timing," Jake said. Thought about the package. "Everything's in the timing."

"Well," she said, "whatever happens, it'll be a heck of a rush."

Westboro's was a low red-brick building four blocks from the capitol, with an old-fashioned lightbulb marquee out front, and under that, a red neon script that said, the capital's best steaks, chops, seafood. The parking structure was an ugly poured-concrete lump fifty yards farther down the block. Jake looked at his watch: almost eleven.

He took the car into the garage, saw the entrance, but no gate. "How do you pay?" he asked.

"Parking meters inside. The meter guy enforces the meters."

"Excellent."

He turned into the ramp. As Cathy Ann Dorn had said, it was dark inside. He could see no cameras. The ramps were two-way; you went out the same way you went in. The first upward-slanting ramp was full; the next, around the corner, was only half full. A man walked past them, down the ramp, and out. Jake went onto the next four ramps, then turned around and started down again. On both the back and front walls of the ramps, there were staircases going down.

He pulled into a parking space, let the engine run, stepped into one of the back staircases, walked down two floors and out. The door opened on a sidewalk along another street, less busy than the front, but still with cars moving along it.

Jake went back up, got in the car, and they drove back out. Madison asked, "What?"

"We could do it," he said.

"If we get caught, Goodman'll put us in jail," she said. "If the cop hasn't shot you."

"I might be able to blackmail my way out of it. If the cop hasn't shot me."

"Tell me . . ."

He outlined his idea, and she said, "If anyone sees you going in, they'll tell the police that it was a man with a limp. They'll know who it is."

"If I walk on a left tiptoe, I don't limp. I can't do it for long, but I can do it for a few hundred yards."

"So what am I supposed to do?" she asked. "Wait at Mom's house until I find out whether you're dead?"

"That would be the pessimistic version of it," Jake said.

"Bullshit. I'll drive."

He smiled at her: "I was hoping you'd offer."

He got a ball-peen hammer at a Home Depot on Broad Street and a pair of cotton work gloves. They drove back to Westboro's and parked a block away, where they could see the front of the parking garage.

"There'll be a lot of traffic, starting just before noon," Madison said. "People grabbing the good seats that aren't reserved."

Jake looked at his watch and yawned nervously. She picked it up and yawned back. "We could neck for a while," he said.

"I'm too scared."

"You don't have to drive . . ."

"No-no. I've been talking big," she said. "I'll do it. But I'm still scared."

"Good. Scared is realistic. Just don't freeze and leave me on the street."

Now she nodded: "Maybe you'll learn to trust me."

Tried to make conversation as they watched politicians and hustlers streaming into Westboro's: "Was Howard Barber the guy who had me beaten up?"

"I hope not," she said.

"I'm not asking what you hope," Jake said. "I'm asking what you think. At that point, Goodman had no reason to go after me. You guys did."

"Kind of narrows the range, doesn't it." She pursed her lips, looking out the windows, and then said, "I asked him. He didn't say 'yes,' but he never said 'no.' He avoided the question. And he definitely knows people who'd do it. You scared him. He wanted to slow you down."

"I'd like to get his people alone. One at a time. With my stick."

"I'd like you to stay over tonight," Jake said. He yawned again, and she yawned back. Both nervous. The hands on the car clock seemed to be plowing through glue. "You know, mostly because . . . I'd like you to stay over."

"We could talk about the role of NATO in the new Europe," she said.

"Yeah, yeah . . . but tomorrow, I want you to go home. Carry on as usual, don't do anything cute, don't play to the bug, if there is one. Just carry on. There's gonna be a lot to talk about anyway. The shit is already headed for the fan."

"Where are you going to be?"

"Running around," he said.

"You're not going to get hurt?"

"Certainly hope not."

"Maybe I ought to run with you."

"That won't be . . . uh — here's a Mercury."

Cathy Ann Dorn would have made a good spy, Jake thought. The Mercury was right on time, six minutes after twelve. The car disappeared into the parking garage, and four minutes later, Arlo Goodman walked out, trailed by a big man in a dark suit and sunglasses. Both were empty-handed.

"The bottom of my stomach just dropped out," Madison said. She started the car.

"Don't leave me on the street."

"You do it, and get out in a hurry," she said. "What . . . what if there's some kind of booby trap?"

"There's not even a booby trap in the president's car," Jake said.

"What if there's a camera or some-thing?"

"There won't be a camera . . ." But he reached into the backseat and found the *Atlanta Braves* hat he'd bought in Atlanta. He put it on and popped the door.

She said, "Wait. Wait for five minutes, so we know Goodman hasn't sent the cop back to get something."

They sat for three minutes, then Jake

popped the door again. "Gotta go. Don't take any phone calls."

"Wait." She was digging in her purse, pulled out a silk scarf, said, "Put this over your face. Like a bandanna. In case there's a camera."

"Jesus." But he took the scarf. "My biggest worry is that a car'll turn in . . ."

"There haven't been too many . . . ," she said anxiously.

"I'm going."

This time he went, walking on one tiptoe. He was ten yards from the garage when another car pulled in. "Shoot." He stopped and walked back down the block, past Madison, forty yards, fifty yards, then headed back toward the garage. Two men walked out into the sunshine, turned away from him, toward Westboro's. He closed into the garage, was twenty yards away, his tiptoe foot getting tired, when they went into the restaurant.

A minute later he was inside, walking up the ramp, feeling the hammer heavy in his pocket. Watching behind for another car. Hurrying now. Up the first ramp, around the corner. He thought about the scarf, thought *fuck it,* then got it out anyway, did a quick wrap around his lower face. Pulled on the gloves. Between that and the hat, nothing would be visible but his eyes. And it *was* dark.

He got the cell phone out, pushed the button, heard it start to ring. Madison would be moving.

He took a deep breath, listened for a car, heard nothing, started counting, "One-thousand-one, one-thousand-two . . ." stepped quickly over to the Mercury, pulled the hammer out of his pocket and hit the back window with it. The glass exploded inward, and the car alarm went. He knocked out the rest of the glass with the hammerhead, reached through the window into the screaming wail of the alarm, pulled open the back door, spotted the briefcase on the floor, grabbed it, and ran.

Down to the back door. Nothing coming up the ramp at him. Down the stairs and around, counting, "One-thousand-nine, one-thousand-ten . . ."

He stopped at the door, pulled down the mask, pushed it under his shirt collar, and stepped out. Madison was just cruising along the street, pulled over. Jake got in the car, still counting, but now, aloud. "One-thousand-fourteen, one-thousand-fifteen."

He looked out the back window.

Nothing moved around the parking

garage. They turned the corner and were gone.

"I had a thought," she said. She was cool, contained, but with a little pink in her cheeks. "If Arlo thinks about this and thinks, 'Jake Winter,' what if he has the Highway Patrol look for us? Stop us on some phony drug charge? Search the car."

"Huh." He considered the idea for a minute, then said, "We can't take a chance. Let's go to the airport. We can rent another car, you can follow me back. If you see me get stopped, you can keep on going."

"I'm so scared I could pee my pants," Madison said.

"Those are obscenely expensive leather seats you're sitting on," Jake said. She started to laugh, and then he started, and he said, "I'm sweating like a horse myself. Let's get the fuck out of Virginia."

17

Russell Barnes was a double amputee with a mop of red hair tied in a ponytail with white string. A long, thin red beard straggled down the front of his green army T-shirt. He met them at the front door, took a long look at Madison, and said, "Jake, nice to see you. How's the leg?"

"Not bad. How's the pain?"

"I'm so hooked on the drugs that even if it goes away, I'm gonna have to deal with the drug problem. I don't know if I can do that," he said.

As they talked, they followed him, in his wheelchair, back through the dimly lit tract house to what had once been a family room, now jammed with computer equipment. A ten-foot-long wooden workbench, littered with electronic testing equipment, three keyboards, and a half dozen monitors of different sizes, was pushed against one wall, under a photograph of a man in an army uniform posed as the Sacred Heart of Jesus. The workbench was low, made for a man in a wheelchair; the room smelled of

Campbell's tomato soup.

"Whatcha got?" Barnes asked.

"Laptop," Jake said, taking it out of his bag. "Password protected."

He handed Barnes the HP laptop. Barnes looked it over, plugged it into an electric strip on the top of the workbench, brought it up. "This might take a couple of minutes."

There was no place to go, no place to sit, so Jake and Madison stood and watched as Barnes played with the computer. He said, "Commercial password program. That's not good."

"You can't get around it?"

"I can get around the password, but I suspect that a lot of the stuff on it is going to be encrypted. Encryption is part of the program."

"Can you beat the encryption?" Madison asked.

"Sure, if I had a computer the size of the solar system, and five or six billion years to work it . . . Let's look at the drives."

He flipped the laptop over and started pulling it apart, moved a black box from one part of the workbench to the laptop, connected a couple of wires into the guts of the laptop, pushed a switch. A monitor lit up, and a program started running down the screen. He stared at it for a while, tapped some keys on one of the keyboards, and unencrypted English began running down the screen.

"Whatcha got is a small amount of encrypted stuff, looks like e-mail, and a fair amount of unencrypted stuff. The encrypted stuff is only accessible if you get me the key. The unencrypted stuff I can print out for you. Most of it looks like crap, though. Some of it's part of programs he bought . . . you know, illustrations from Word, that kind of thing."

"The encrypted e-mail . . . are the addresses encrypted? The places they were sent from?"

"No. I can tell you where incoming messages originated and where outgoing messages were sent to."

"That'd be good. What we need are e-mails, letters, any text that appears to be, you know, independently generated."

"Take a while," Barnes said. "I got a fast printer, but there's quite a bit of stuff in here. Probably, mmm, I don't know, could run eight hundred or a thousand pages."

"We can wait," Jake said.

Madison took the car and went out for coffee and snacks, while Jake and Barnes watched the pile of paper grow in the printer tray, talked about Afghanistan and hospitals and drugs and old friends, including some who were no longer alive.

"This chick you got with you, is this serious?" Barnes asked.

"Hard to tell," Jake said. "She lies to me sometimes."

"She's Madison Bowe, right?"

"No. Just looks like her," Jake said.

Madison came back and said to Jake, "CNN has the gay story. I saw it at the Starbucks."

"Oh, boy. I wonder where it leaked from?"

"What's that?" Barnes asked.

Jake explained briefly, saying only that Lincoln Bowe had gay connections. Barnes shook his head and smiled at Madison and said, "They'll be on you like fleas on a yellow dog. The media."

"Yes. I'm sure."

"Doesn't bother you?"

"The possibility that people would find out, that there would be a story . . . it's been out there for a long time. Lincoln and I talked about it, how to handle it. I'll be okay."

They were out of Barnes's house an hour later, carrying two reams of paper and the restored laptop, blinking in the sunlight; Barnes had kept a copy of the hard drives, and would continue working through it. "What next?" Madison asked.

"Back to my place. Read this stuff. Figure out what you're going to do."

"I'm going to call Kitty Machela at CBS. Next week, I think. We'll arrange for one of her famous interviews."

"Woman-to-woman chat."

"Dark set, conservative clothes, sympathy," Madison said. "She'd sympathize with Hitler if she could get him in an exclusive interview. It'll kill the story. My part of it, anyway."

At Jake's, they got comfortable in the study, flipping through the paper, while the television ran in the background, the gay story blossoming like a strange fungus. There were shots of the outside of Madison's town house, pictures of reporters knocking on the door.

"Every network has to show its guy knocking on the door, even when they just saw another guy knocking on the door," Madison said.

"Keep reading," Jake said.

In a thousand sheets of paper, they

found one thing, and Madison found it.

"The murders in Madison happened . . . there's . . . mmm . . . there's a note, a duplicate receipt for a private plane flying from Charlottesville to Chicago for two passengers, charged to a state account, early in the morning, five a.m., arriving back in Richmond at nine p.m. Charged to a state police account. I wonder why the cc would come back to Goodman?"

Jake took it, read it, then looked up. "Because Goodman ordered the plane, or had it ordered. Had to approve something. Somebody flew into Chicago, which must be three or four hours from Madison by car, the morning Green and his secretary were killed. They were back that night."

"But why a state plane? There'd have to be a pilot, there'd be paperwork."

"Because you can't carry weapons on a commercial flight, not without registering them," Jake said. "And they're not going to register weapons with silencers, huh?"

"Why didn't they fly into Madison?"

"Because the name might come up in a search, if someone like the FBI looked for flights going into Madison or Milwaukee, or anywhere in Wisconsin. They had to take a risk, but they minimized it by going to Chicago. Without this note . . . digging

396

this out of the woodwork would be impossible, believe me. This is in the bottom of a computer file somewhere, and nobody will ever look at it again, without somebody asking for it. But since we know about it, they can't escape. Because the paperwork is there."

"But they'll have some kind of story about what they were doing in Chicago," Madison said.

"Probably. But this is a piece of the puzzle. And it tells *me* something. It tells me that your pal Barber probably didn't do it."

They locked eyes for a moment, but she didn't say it: *I already told you that Barber didn't do it. Don't you trust me?*

"I trust you enough to plan a murder with you," Jake said. "I wouldn't even do that with Russell Barnes."

She asked, "What murder?"

He said, "Just a minute. I've got to call Russell."

Jake went to the phone and called. "Russell. Look at the encrypted stuff, the encrypted messages. See if you can find one for the day before yesterday, originating in Chicago or anywhere in Illinois or Wisconsin."

"Hold on. I'll queue them up."

Barnes was back in four minutes: "There's one from Chicago at eight a.m., very short. There's another from Madison, Wisconsin, at two o'clock, even shorter."

"They did it," Madison said. "You think his brother . . . ?"

"Yeah. Darrell."

"Is that who we're going to murder?"

"Let me tell you about my idea for a play," Jake said. "For a pageant . . ."

"You mentioned that, but you didn't tell me what you were talking about."

"That's before I hired you as a wheelman," Jake said.

He told her about it, about the drama that he was planning for her living room. "If you do this, and I'm not telling you not to, you have to think it out like a chess game," Madison said. "Right down to the last little move. You have to have a backup story in case anything goes wrong . . ."

"But you're not saying 'no,' " Jake said. "You're not arguing against it."

"No, I'm not," she said. "Sometimes, justice isn't enough. You need revenge."

"So. You'll do it."

"Yes."

They stared at each other for a moment, then Jake said, "Call Johnson Black, have him come here to pick you up. You stand on your porch, make a brief statement about the gay stories. You go inside and talk to Black about whatever. When the TV people are gone, probably after the evening news, you call me. I'll come over and we'll do the drama."

She nodded. "Now I'm scared again. That's twice in a day."

"We're all in trouble here, Maddy," Jake said. "This whole thing has been so complicated. But if there's a bug — and there's gotta be a bug, I'd bet on it now — Goodman knows that you know what Barber did to your husband. If he can find a way to make the tape public, you could go to prison. Maybe for a long time. You know what judges do to celebrities, just to prove that they're not above the law . . . And if I don't get that package to the FBI, I'm in trouble for the Madison shootings, myself. The drama might settle it."

"But we're going to kill somebody. We're premeditating."

"Yeah." Again, they stared at each other for a bit, then Jake said, "Look. We've got a huge problem: we've got a psycho on our asses — or on yours, anyway. I might still skate. Sooner or later, though, they'll have to do something about you. The new vice president can't have any vocal opposition that alleges any kind of scandal, any kind of problem. If they're thinking about Goodman, and you're out here screaming that Goodman is a killer and a Nazi . . . it's easy enough to choose somebody else. Arlo Goodman needs for you to go away, or to be discredited, or humiliated. And they've got a psychotic killer willing to do the heavy work."

"But there's a hole in your idea. The way you set it out."

"Yeah?"

"Yeah. What are you going to do with the other car?"

Jake blinked. Then, "God. I'm a moron."

"You're not a moron. You just need somebody to go with you. You need a wheelman, again."

He blinked again. "Oh, no. No, no, no . . ."

"Oh, yes. It's the only way."

They argued, went around and around, and finally she said, "I'm going, and that's it; I'm going, or you're not." Then she called Johnson Black. Black arrived an hour later, took her away.

Ten minutes later, Jake watched CNN as

Madison made her statement from the front porch. She said that there had been an assumption that sexuality was private, but that the FBI were apprised of the situation with Lincoln Bowe, and that it was part of their investigation. That she was distressed that people were pounding on her door, hounding her, and that one certain way of NOT getting any information was to pound on her door.

She would refuse to answer anyone who came to the door, and the thrill-seeking reporters should be ashamed of themselves. More information would be made public at an early date.

With a bunch of reporters yelling "When?" at her, she went inside. Then a ranking D.C. cop took the microphone and said that anyone who stepped on Mrs. Bowe's yard or any of the other yards down the block, without permission, would be arrested for trespassing. That all the TV trucks were a hazard in case of emergency, and they would have to leave the street. That anyone not leaving would be ticketed and the trucks would be towed, and the bill would have to be paid before the trucks were released. That towing a big truck would cost upward of $2,000. He added that once the tow truck was there, as in all police tows, there would be no last-minute decision to leave — if the tow truck showed up, the TV trucks would be towed.

After a flurry of cell-phone calls, the trucks began leaving. An hour after the porch statement, a reporter from the *Post* stood alone on the sidewalk, shifting from foot to foot.

An hour after that, the sidewalk was empty.

18

Darrell Goodman stepped into the governor's office, around the departing maids. The first maid was carrying a silver coffee service, the second a basket of scones, the remnants of an appropriations meeting with the leaders of the statehouse and senate. Darrell hooked one of the scones out of the basket and said to his brother, "Rank has its privileges. Free bakery."

Arlo Goodman made a flapping gesture at the door. Darrell closed it, and Arlo made a "What?" gesture with his open hands.

Darrell held up a finger, said, "I've been talking to Patricia, the numbers of the Watchmen are up pretty strong this month. We're starting a new chapter in D.C."

"That's great," Arlo said. "There's a chapter out in California now, I just saw it on the Internet."

"Yeah. The leader over there, in D.C., may have been in Syria at the same time you were . . ." He rambled on about D.C. numbers as he opened his briefcase, took out a folded piece of paper, and pushed it at Arlo. Arlo took it, looked at it. A laser printout, a letter:

I'm so sorry. I didn't know what I was getting into. I was one of the four people who helped take Lincoln Bowe away. The other three are Howard Barber, Donald S. Creasey, and Roald M. Sands. I thought it was a complicated political joke on Arlo Goodman. We were supposed to look like Goodman's hit men. I didn't know that they were going to shoot Linc. Now I read in the newspapers that he was still alive when he was killed. I don't know. He was supposed to commit suicide, not be shot. I don't know what happened to his head. Howard Barber would know. Howard Barber organized this. He's responsible. Roald and Don don't know anything. Now everything is coming apart. I'm so sorry, but I can't stand the thought of prison. I know what would happen in there.

— Dan White

Arlo read it and his eyebrows went up. Darrell bent over the desk and whispered in his brother's ear, "He committed suicide with his own gun after writing the note. The original is signed with his own pen. The pen's in his coat pocket. An anonymous call went to the Fairfax cops, and Clayton Bell got another anonymous call, supposedly from a Fairfax cop, and he's there now. Bell will almost certainly call us. He'll want some guidance."

Arlo nodded and pulled his brother's head down, whispered back, "Nobody else knows anything?"

"George was there with me — but next week, I'll settle that."

"He can't feel it coming," Arlo whispered. "I don't want him to leave an envelope somewhere."

"We're okay," Darrell whispered. "After I take him, I'll go through everything he's got, just to double-check. But there's nothing. One thing he is, is loyal."

Arlo breathed, "Excellent."

Lt. Clayton Bell, a state police officer who'd been running the Bowe investigation, read the note through a plastic envelope put on by the crime-scene people; he was reading it for the third time.

"I'll need some advice on how to proceed," he told the Annandale chief. "I think we pick up the three of them, handle them separately, see what their stories are. But I'm going to talk to the prosecutor's office first. Maybe call . . . I don't know, maybe the governor."

"That's up to you, Clay. We don't have a crime here, so there's nothing for us. If you just want to handle it . . ."

Bell nodded. "We'll handle it. I'll get a crime-scene crew here, just in case. If you guys can keep the scene sealed off, I'd appreciate it."

"We can do that."

Roald Sands called Howard Barber on his cell phone.

"Yes — Barber."

Sands was screaming. "Howard, Howard. I just went by Dan's place, there are cops everywhere. There's a crime-scene truck there, the state police, the local police. Something's happened."

"Whoa, whoa . . . take it easy." But even as he said it, Barber's heart sank. "Where are you?"

"I'm headed home. I'm afraid the police will be there. I think they know."

"How far are you from home?"

"Five minutes," Sands said.

"Call me just before you get there. Let me know if the police are there: I'll be at this number, just hit redial. If they're there, remember your story. That it was voluntary, you were just picking him up and dropping him with me. You were bodyguards . . . Bring it back to me. I'll handle it."

"Okay, okay. Jesus Christ, Howard, I'm scared."

"Take it easy, man. Take it easy. Call me in five."

Barber ran through the list on his cell phone, picked out Don Creasey's number, touched it. Creasey's secretary answered, and Barber said, "This is Howard Barber. Let me talk to Don, if you could."

"Um, he's indisposed at the moment . . ."

"You mean, in the bathroom?"

"No, I mean, I mean I just don't know what to tell you, Mr. Barber. There's just been some kind of trouble. I don't think I'm supposed to talk to people about it."

"Well . . . okay, I guess. I'll catch him later."

He kicked back in his chair, laced his fingers behind his head, thought it out. The cops had broken it down somehow. He'd known it could happen. He'd taken every possible precaution, and nevertheless, here they were. He laughed, then looked around his office. Been good for a long time.

Sands called back, said, "There are cars across the street with people in them. I can see them from here, they're looking down toward me."

"Remember your story, Roald. Just remember the story."

He hung up, thought about it some more, then opened the office blinds and looked down at the parking lot. Nothing yet. He ran through various permutations of the story: that Lincoln Bowe had been frightened of Arlo Goodman, and that he, Barber, had sent the other men to act as bodyguards, that they'd brought him north to Barber's office, and that Barber had secretly driven him to New York, and he'd disappeared from there . . .

But that wouldn't hold, he thought. Too many things didn't happen. He couldn't answer questions — what car had he taken, where had he stopped for gas, had they stopped to eat anything . . . He flashed to the last time he'd been to Rapid Oil; they'd put a mileage sticker on the window of his car, with a date. Maybe he could run down . . .

No. One way or another, they'd poke holes in it. They'd hang him. Huh.

And they might hang Madison Bowe

along with him. Somehow, the Goodmans were involved in this — and if they pushed the cops to play Madison against him, the two of them would be stuck. Whatever else, Madison didn't deserve to go to prison.

Barber went back to the window and cranked the blinds fully up, walked to his office door. His secretary sat in a bay off the main room; in the main room, four women and two men sat in cloth cubicles talking on phones and poking at computers, like high-tech mice in a maze. To his secretary, he said, "Jean, I need you to run an errand. Could you drive over to Macy's and pick me up a dress shirt, white or blue? I'll give you cash . . ."

"You mean, right now?"

"If you could," Barber said. "I've gotten my ass in a bind, I'm going to have to run out of town tonight . . ." He fumbled four hundred dollars out of his wallet and gave it to her.

"But you've got the Thirty-first Project Managers at ten o'clock tomorrow."

"I should be back," he said. "Just get the shirt, huh? If you've got stuff that has to be done here, I'll pay overtime anytime you have to stay late."

"That's not necessary . . ." She got her

sweater and purse and went mumbling off, and Barber went back to his office windows just in time to see the cops arrive. There were two cars, both state police. Not FBI. The Goodmans, for sure.

He could go with them, stick with the story. Another guy was going to pick up Lincoln Bowe, so he merely transferred him . . . but the other three, Creasy, Sands, and White, all knew bits and pieces of the story, and the cops would play them off against one another, and sooner or later, one of them would fold.

Barber had always been an outside guy, a guy who liked to move around. A cell the size of a bathroom. He rubbed his face with his open hands and looked back into the parking lot. Had an idea, smiled at it. He wore a gold Rolex on his left wrist. He reached into his desk drawer, took out a paper clip, straightened it, and using the edge of the Rolex bracelet as a guide, scratched his wrist until it bled, in two small scratches both back and front. He changed the watch to the other wrist and did the same thing.

He was putting the watch back on his left wrist when he heard the voices in the outer room: cops asking for his office. He walked around and sat behind his desk.

Calm. More than calm: cold.

A plainclothes cop stuck his head in the office door and asked, "Mr. Barber?"

"Come in. Close the door, please."

Three cops. One of them pushed the door closed with his foot. The plainclothesman said, "Mr. Barber, I'm Lieutenant Clayton Bell, Virginia State Police . . ."

Barber stood up.

In the outer office, a saleswoman named Cheryl Pence was standing in her office pod when the screaming started: "No, no, don't, don't, help, help . . ."

There was an impact like an explosion, and without thinking, Pence ran to Barber's office door and yanked it open, the other five office employees all standing, staring. When the door came open they saw three Virginia state cops looking out through a broken window. Pence screamed at them, "What did you do, what did you do . . . ?"

Bell, shocked, white-faced, turned and muttered, "We didn't do anything. We didn't do anything."

He was talking to air. Pence had backed away and then started to run for the outer door, the other five stampeding behind her. Bell said to the other two cops, "We didn't do anything."

Outside, three television crews, tipped by what they believed to be local police, had been waiting to film the arrest. They hadn't been ready for a man to come hurtling out through the wall of glass, five stories above them. One cameraman, saddled up and ready to roll, got a shot of the three cops at the window, looking down.

The three reporters stood there openmouthed, and then one of them said, "Holy shit." He turned toward his cameraman: "You get that? Tell me you got that?"

"I got the cops," the cameraman said.

A hundred miles away, Arlo Goodman screamed, "What? What?"

19

Madison Bowe heard about Howard Barber's death from Johnson Black, who heard about it from a television reporter who was calling Black to ask him to call Madison for a comment. She turned on the television, watched for a moment, then found the maid and said, "Harriet, I'm going shopping for a few minutes. I'll just run down the hill, I'll be back in half an hour."

Afraid reporters might already be lurking, she put on a hat, went out through the back door, cut through the yards of a half dozen neighbors, then out to the street, not quite running.

Jake was working on the script for the evening's drama when Madison called. "I'm down on M Street. Did you hear about Howard?"

"What about Howard?"

"He's dead." Her voice was hushed, nervous. "Three of Goodman's cops went to arrest him, they supposedly got some information that he was involved in Linc's disappearance. But something happened, and he crashed through his office window and fell five stories and he's dead. Some of his office workers told the television that he was screaming for help and then they heard the crash . . ."

Jake was astonished, groped for words. "Jesus. What do the cops say?"

"All three claim he threw himself through the window. Right through the plate glass. I don't know. I just don't know. The FBI is there, I guess they've taken over."

"I'll call Novatny, see what I can find out."

"What about tonight?"

"It's still on, unless the cops delay you . . . I'll come in, we'll talk about Barber, I'll tell you everything I know, you tell me what you found out — you should start calling people about it, because that's what you'd naturally do. Then we'll go into our play. Just follow my lead."

"What if there's no bug?"

"Then nothing will happen," Jake said.

"Should I make a comment about Howard? For the media? They're going to start calling. They were already calling Johnnie Black to see if I'd do one."

Jake scratched his forehead, thinking for

a minute, then said, "I guess . . . That's up to you. It won't make any difference, one way or another, to the play tonight. But we can't have anyone else in the living room when we talk. We have to be alone, or we wouldn't do it."

"All right. Maybe . . . I'll tell Johnnie that I could have a comment tomorrow, but I want to wait and see what happens."

"What do you think about Barber? Could it be suicide?"

She hesitated, then, "Maybe. He's depressive. He's excitable. He could do it . . . I don't know."

"All right. Hang on: manage it. See you at nine."

Jake called Novatny, but the FBI man wouldn't talk. "You're too deep in this, ol' buddy."

"I'm not asking for a state secret — I just want to know if it was suicide."

"That's what the Virginia State Police say."

"What do you say?"

"Too early to tell."

"Thanks a lot."

Jake called Danzig's office and talked to Gina. "Tell Bill that there's a story on television about a guy who jumped, fell, or was thrown out a window over in Arlington. Virginia State Police were there and some of the witnesses say the guy was thrown. The thing is, this guy is mixed into the Lincoln Bowe disappearance. There's going to be a stink around Goodman, at least for a while."

"I'll tell him."

"You almost done over there?"

"I don't know," she said. "I really don't."

She knew everything, of course. They were building some distance between themselves and Jake, just in case. "Talk to you later."

They were getting into the endgame on Lincoln Bowe: Jake could feel it coming. In a week, there'd be nothing left to do but the cleanup. The cleanup, depending on who was doing the cleaning, could send a few people off to jail.

For the moment, there was still room to maneuver.

He climbed the stairs to his junk room, unlocked his gun safe, took out the Remington .243 and a semiautomatic Beretta 20 gauge with two boxes of shells. He'd last used the .243 six months earlier, on an antelope hunt in Wyoming. When he left Wyoming, he could keep three slugs inside three-quarters of an inch at a hundred yards, shooting off sandbags. It was sighted a half inch to an inch high at a hundred, so any shot he wanted to take, from muzzle-tip to two hundred yards, was point 'n' shoot.

Or back in Wyoming, had been. He'd traveled with the gun in a foam-padded case, but it generally wasn't healthy to assume that a scope sighted-in six months earlier, and moved two thousand miles, was still on.

He looked at his watch: he had just enough time to get to Merle's and back to Madison's at nine o'clock. He whistled a line from Eric Clapton's "I Shot the Sheriff," took the rifle, shotgun, and hunting-gear bag down to his bedroom, packed an overnight bag, and carried it all down to the car.

Made a mental note to stop at Wal-Mart.

Endgame coming.

Arlo Goodman was in the mansion's front parlor, feet up on an antique table donated by the Virginia Preservation Society, talking to Darrell. "Can we wall ourselves off? That's the only question that matters."

"Absolutely. Nothing points at us," Darrell said. "Nothing. Bell and the others swear to God that Barber jumped. I think the feds believe them. For one thing, his office would have been wrecked if a guy Barber's size was thrown out the window. He was like a goddamn weight lifter, and Bell's fifty-five years old and is fifty pounds overweight. He threw *Barber* out the window? He's lucky Barber didn't throw him out."

"The problem is, eighty percent of the equation is image," Arlo said. "They have an image they want. They want a guy who's an economic liberal, but who's in touch with the prayer people, who's in touch with the gun people. Right now, I'm it; but with just a little twist, I become Hermann Göring. Then I'm not it. Then my fifteen minutes are up." He stood up, took a lap around the room, gnawing at a thumbnail, tugging at it. He wrenched a sliver of it free, spit it into the carpet. "Look. We need a leak. We need to leak to the media that the feds think Barber killed Bowe. We need that out there right now. Everything's right on a knife edge . . ."

"We can do that. I can do it," Darrell said.

"If we can get that out for tomorrow —

even if the feds equivocate — we're in good shape. If we can get that out there tomorrow, it'll make suicide more reasonable. It'll take the story away from Bell and those other fuckups, no matter what they did."

"I'll move," Darrell said eagerly. "The *Post*, the *Times*, three or four TV channels . . . I'll talk to Patricia. He's got contacts everywhere. He's got the phone numbers. We can reel it back in, Arlo. They won't be naming a new guy until after Landers is gone, and that'll take a while. We're still good."

Merle's was a long, low concrete-block building painted an anonymous cream, buried in a block of warehouses in the flight path of Dulles International. The sign outside, an unlit wooden rectangle, said, merle's, and nothing else, in fading red paint.

Jake parked, carried the rifle around to the front door, pushed in, was hit in the face by the not-unpleasant tang of burned gunpowder. The shooting lanes took up the back of the building; the first fifteen feet in the front was the salesroom, isolated from the shooting lanes by a double concrete wall, with panes of double vacuum-glass on both walls. You could still hear the gunfire, but distantly.

Merle Haines was leaning on the counter, paging through a copy of American Rifleman, while Jerry Jeff Walker sang "I Feel Like Hank Williams Tonight" from a buzzing speaker mounted in the ceiling. Haines nodded at Jake, who was a seasonal regular, and asked, "How's it going?" Jake nodded back and said, "I need to tune up the .243." He handed over his car keys and Haines hung them on a Peg-Board and said, "Lane nine."

"And two boxes of that Federal Vital-Shok, the one-hundred-grain Sierra, if you've got it, and two targets."

"Goin' huntin'," Merle said. He took two boxes of 100-grain Federal off the shelf and two target faces from under the counter, and passed them over. Jake paid him, took his earmuffs out of his pocket, put them on, and pushed through the door into the range. The first eight lanes were for pistols, the last three lanes for rifles, with shooting tables. He walked past two fat guys shooting revolvers and one in-shape military-looking guy shooting a Beretta, down a short flight of stairs, to lanes nine, ten, and eleven. He was alone.

He'd be shooting down an underground

tunnel at fifty yards — not long, but long enough to get an idea of where the gun was. He sat down at a table, arranged a pile of sandbags on the table in front of him, took the rifle out of its case, pressed three rounds into the magazine, and jacked one into the chamber.

The .243 was a comfortable gun, accurate and easy on the shoulder, if a little slow to reload. He fired five shots slowly, carefully, breathing between shots, then pulled the target in. Four of the shots were tight and all over the bull, right where they should have been. The fifth was a half inch to the right; he'd pulled it. Nothing had moved since Wyoming.

He fired five more shots at the second target, and got one ragged hole three-quarters of an inch wide, across the lower face of the bull. He packed the gun up, collected the remaining cartridges, and walked back out through the salesroom.

"Short and sweet," Merle said, as he handed over Jake's car keys. "Good luck with them critters."

On the way to Madison's, she called and said, "I'm in the backyard. Johnnie Black is here, I'm calling on his phone. We're talking about Howard. Johnnie's got a source who said that the FBI crime-scene investigators have found something weird with the body. There were some scratches on his wrists like he might have been handcuffed and they've gone to the three cops and collected their handcuffs."

"Jeez. How could they, he wasn't . . ."

"The thinking is, they cuffed him, he didn't resist, then one of them hit him on the back of the head with something heavy, and they threw him out the window — but because he went out and landed on his back and head, there's no evidence that he was slugged. That's what the thinking is."

"The FBI's thinking?"

"No, no, that's Johnnie, trying to figure out what could have happened. But he's going to talk to a couple of his media pals, just pass the speculation around. It'll be on the air tomorrow — keep Goodman shuckin' and jivin'."

"All right. I doubt that's what happened, though," Jake said. "Too complicated — especially with witnesses right there in the office."

"Maybe . . . Listen, I really need you. I'm scared, I'm sad, I'm messed up by everything that's happened."

"I need you too," he said. "But if your place is bugged . . ."

"If the place is bugged, if the bedroom is bugged, then they've heard it all before. I don't care anymore, Jake. I'm going to send Johnnie home. But I need to spend some time with you. Right now."

"I'm on my way," he said.

He parked a block from her house, got his stick, tapped down the sidewalks, a glorious April evening, sunlight still warming the sky, but cool with a touch of humidity to soften the air. Another car was parked farther down the street, and when he turned in at Madison's sidewalk, a woman jumped out of the car and called, "Sir, sir, could I speak to you a minute? Sir, I'm from the *New York Times* . . ."

Jake called back, "I'm sorry, I really can't speak to you." On the porch, he knocked, saw the woman was still coming along the sidewalk, a notebook in her hand, and she called again, "Sir, sir . . ."

Madison opened the door. He said, quickly, "*New York Times* coming up fast." Madison looked behind him, grinned, said, "Come in, Mr. Smith. Good to see you again . . ."

"It's a sad day," Jake said, as the door swung closed. When he heard the *snick* of the lock, he pushed her back and said,

"Not so close to the glass . . ."

Then her arms were around his neck and his hands were on her hips, and he steered her toward the stairs. At the bottom step she broke away long enough to whisper, "There would be a certain *frisson* to know that Arlo Goodman was listening, but I freshened up the guest room . . ."

"Just hope the bed can take a beating," Jake said.

The first time they'd slept together had been one of the *first time* situations that combined curiosity with wariness and possibly courtesy, an effort both to discover and to leave a favorable impression. This time was a collision, with Jake pulling at her clothing, with Madison ripping at his shirt, falling together on the bed, no preliminaries, nothing but *in,* and consummation, Madison groaning with him, her short rider's nails digging into his shoulder blades, as he forced himself into her and pressed her down.

When they finished, she gasped, "God . . . bless me."

He was sweating, breathing hard, his heart thumping, and he wanted to do it again, right then, but was temporarily hors de combat. He rolled away, stood up, shook himself, crawled back to her, put his mouth next to her ear, and said, "No jokes about bugs."

She said, aloud, "I wonder if anyone has figured us out? The first time we met, Johnnie Black was there, he picked up a little electricity."

"Probably me," Jake said. He was on his back now, his arm under her head. "I was asking a million questions and all I really wanted to do was jump you."

"That's pretty romantic," she said.

"Hey. It's the truth. The first reaction was sexual. Only later did I begin to appreciate your fine mind and deep understanding of Arab culture."

She sat up. "My 'fine mind.' More like my fine ass."

"You *do* have a terrific ass," Jake said. "When Danzig sent me to see you, one of the things he mentioned in the briefing was your ass. I've noticed that a lot of serious women riders have great asses. Probably all the pounding. Anyway, I'm thinking of nominating you for Miss Ass, USA. We could create a pageant in Atlantic City . . ."

"We could call the contestants 'aspirants' . . ."

"Your spelling sucks," Jake said. "Anyway, we could have the Atlantic City Ass Parade, like the Rose Parade in Pasadena, but instead of flowers on the floats . . ."

"That's enough. Did Danzig really mention my ass?"

"Yes, he did. And your . . . breasts."

"Except he called them tits."

"Yes, he did." He rolled up on one shoulder. He lightly dragged his index finger from the notch of her collarbone to her navel, and on south. "It's a weird thing. With most good-looking women, you might want to play around a little. You know, get them up on top, or just . . . fool around. With you, all I want is *in*. And I want to stay in. I just want to be inside, be as close as I can get."

After a moment, she said, "That's nice, I think. After a while, you'll probably notice my fine mind."

"And your understanding of Thai culture."

"Arab."

"That's what I meant, Arab."

They made love twice more, and after the second time, with her arms wrapped around his neck, she whispered, "I think . . . we could be onto something here."

"At my age, I'm almost afraid to think that," Jake said. "But I hope so."

She pushed herself up on her elbows. "We have a huge tub in the master bath . . ."

They spent a half hour in the bath, which was big enough to float them both simultaneously, and then climbed out, retrieved their clothes. While Jake got dressed, Madison changed into jeans, boots, and a plaid shirt. She already had a bag packed. "You ready?"

"I'm ready." She touched her hair, as though for a TV appearance. "Let's do it."

"You're sure?"

"I think about the girl in Madison. You described her a little too well."

"I could figure out something with the car," Jake said.

"Nah — I'm going."

He trailed her down to the front room. Launching the play, she said, "You're sure you don't want another glass of wine? You have to go?"

"Yeah, I've got to get this done," Jake said. "I could use a Coke. It's a long drive."

They went out in the kitchen, still talking, and Madison got two Cokes out of the refrigerator and said, "Take another one for the road."

"Thanks."

They drifted back into the front room

and he twisted the top off the Coke bottle; Jake wondered if the *pfffttt* it made would be audible on a tape.

"I don't understand why you can't look at it here," Madison said. "I mean, in Washington, at your house."

"Because I'm tied into the Wisconsin thing. If Novatny smells a rat, the feds might come crashing through the door. And they must be getting frantic, with Barber going out the window. If I've got the package, I'm toast. I don't even know everything that's in it yet. It might be impossible to hold on to . . ."

"You've got to hold on to it, Jake," Madison said, urgency in her voice. He thought, *Not bad.* "You've got to. All of this will have been pointless if that thing gets out there now. All you have to do is hold it until after the convention. Or even just before the convention, that would do it. Just hold on to it for a few weeks."

"I'd like to. But I gotta find out what's in it, sugar," Jake said. "The cabin has everything I need — it's got Internet access, got a computer, and nobody's gonna find it. I talked to Billy and nobody'll be there all week. For the rest of the month, for that matter."

"When are you coming back? I might need you here."

"I need you, too." He kissed her, spent some time with it, then broke away, breathing hard again. "We gotta stop. I gotta get going."

"Please try to hold on to it," she said, an urgent, pleading tone in her voice. "If Landers gets knocked out now, they'll give the job to Goodman in a flash. He's the one they want. Landers won't do them any good this year."

"I will, I'll hold on to it." Sounding a little harassed now. "I'll try to hold on. If there's nothing in it that would push it out there right now, I'll stick it in a safe-deposit box, somewhere that's not obvious, and we'll break it out in October."

"Where are you going to be? Give me a phone number . . ."

"You can't call from here, if there's trouble, they could trace it back, they'd know you knew where I went."

"Only for an emergency. I'd call you from outside."

"All right. Got a pen? It's 540-555-6475."

"540-555-64 . . ."

"6475. Don't use your cell phone, either. We don't want any tracks that the feds can find later. For one thing, that might drag Billy into it, just for loaning me the place."

"What if I have to call you, and you're not there?"

"I'll be there. Or I'll be on my way back here. I'm gonna get up early and work on it all day; I won't be going for a walk in the woods."

In the doorway she kissed him a last time and whispered, "How was that?"

"Perfect." Though he wasn't sure about that: some of it sounded like dialogue from a bad novel.

He left her in the doorway, headed back down the walk, tapping along with his cane. He was twenty feet down the walk when he heard a woman's voice calling, "Sir? Sir, I'm with the *New York Times*."

He thought, *Damnit,* and turned back, scurried up the front steps to the house, rang the bell. Madison appeared at the door, puzzled, and Jake stepped inside, held her close, and whispered, "The *Times* still has the place staked out. I'll give you a single ring when it's clear."

"Okay. I'll start turning out lights."

Back outside, the *Times* reporter was standing on the sidewalk, carefully outside the property line. As Jake came down the front walk, she called, "Sir, could you tell me who you are?"

"I do paperwork for Miz Bowe and the law firm. You'll have to call Johnson Black, I'm sure you have his number."

"If you . . ."

"Miss, if I said one more word, they'd fire my ass. Think of the guilt you'd feel."

"I'd manage somehow," she said, but she was smiling at him.

"Call Johnson Black." He glanced back at the house. "Miz Bowe is going to bed. If you're planning to stay all night, I hope your car has a heater."

Inside the house, the lights were going out.

20

Jake cruised the neighborhood for half an hour before the *Times* reporter left. He saw her car pulling out of its parking space, followed the taillights until she turned left at the bottom of the hill, eased up to the stop sign, then far enough out into the street to make sure that she'd kept going. When she was out of sight, he touched the speed dial on his cell phone, let it ring once, then turned the car around. Madison came down the side of the house carrying her overnight bag.

"I hate doing this," Jake said when she got in the car. "This is way more dangerous than stealing that laptop. Maybe we just oughta call the cops."

"No. If it's the wrong guy's DNA in Madison, we'd never find him. And we'd look like morons for pointing the FBI at Goodman. We'd have no credibility left at all — and I don't have that much now."

"But hanging you out there . . ."

"I won't be hanging out. Besides, the car's a problem that you can't solve without me."

"If it weren't for that . . ."

"Did you bring me the shotgun?"

"Yes."

"Then drive."

They got out of Washington in a hurry, stopped at a Wal-Mart and picked up a box of contractor cleanup bags, kitchen gloves, and four infrared game-spotter cameras. From there it was west and south on Interstates 66 and 81, stars out, listening to classic rock on satellite radio, lights sparkling above them on the mountains as they drove down the length of the Shenandoah. As they went past Staunton, Madison said, "We're getting close?"

"Another half hour."

They could see the lights of Lexington when they cut right into the mountains, good roads narrowing to twisting black-topped lanes. Jake stopped at a dark place, a hillside looming to their left in the starlight, a deep valley on the right. "This is the trailhead for the park," he said. "It's three miles across the hill down to Billy's place. If they come in navigating with maps, I think it's about 90 percent that they'll leave their car here. It's what I'd do. They've got a straight shot across the hill and they'd come down on top of us. If they're good in the woods, nobody would ever see them."

"We can't be locked into this, though," Madison said. "We've got to work out some options."

"Yeah. They could leave their car along the road, but the problem is, it might attract attention. Might have a cop note the tag number. There's really no other place to park, and if you put it back in the woods, then it might *really* attract attention; you'd be trespassing. This parking area, you see a car in there fairly often. We just have to take care that they don't blindside us."

"Or send in the Virginia State Police. We don't want to shoot any policemen."

"That's a problem. But they won't. They won't want anybody to see the package until they get a look at it first. It's gonna be Darrell and whoever was with him at Madison."

"You're too confident, Jake," Madison said.

"I know how these guys think," Jake said. "That's how they'd do it. That's how *I'd* do it."

"What if they're already there?"

Jake smiled: "Then we're toast. But I

434

don't think they'd start shooting if they saw you. You'd be too hard to explain."

The question of Darrell Goodman's arrival was the one that bothered them most: they talked about it, off and on, all the way down to the cabin. If the bug in Madison's house was monitored often, Jake thought, they'd come in at dawn. If it was monitored less frequently, they might not come until evening, or the next morning.

"If they're not here by then, we'll have to pull out," Jake said. "Danzig will be going public with the package."

From the parking area to the end of Billy's driveway was a long loop of narrow blacktop. The driveway began with a nearly invisible indentation in the tree line. Fifty feet in, invisible from the road, was a locked gate and the beginning of a gravel track. "Billy's is the only place back here," Jake said. "We're on his land now."

"Dark," Madison said. Then: "What if they have those night-vision things? Darrell was military, he probably could get National Guard equipment."

"If they can't see us in the daytime, they can't see us at night. And if you keep yourself down, they won't see us." He got out and opened the gate with his key, drove the truck through, and locked the gate behind them.

The cabin was built on a wide spot of a crooked valley nestled in a series of steep, heavily forested hillsides. Just below the cabin, on the creek that cut the valley, Billy had excavated a three-acre pond and filled it with bass. The shallow, six-foot-wide creek trickled down over a rocky bottom, past the cabin, into the pond, over a concrete lip, and then down and out of the valley.

They came around the last turn in the gravel track, and the cabin glowed like a piece of amber in the headlights. A motion-sensing yard light flicked on. Jake parked, and feeling the hair rippling on the back of his neck, climbed the porch, unlocked the door, turned on the lights. Madison helped carry the gear bags inside.

Were they out there? Up the hill, arguing what to do about Madison? Hurried calls going out of the ridgetop? He didn't think so, but it was a possibility.

The cabin was big enough to sleep eight, with two bedrooms, a bath, and storage on the upper level. The first floor had two more bedrooms, a bath, a kitchen and a great room, and a set of high windows that looked out over the pond. A large-scale geological-survey map of the property was framed and hung on the wall of the great room.

Jake took Madison to the map. "This is probably the same map they'd be looking at, if they pull it off the Internet." He tapped a tightly bunched strip of contour lines south of the cabin. "Up here, we've got this really steep hillside — it's virtually a bluff. It's unlikely they'd come in over the bluff, because it's just too steep, and there are springs all along the side of it, it's pretty slippery in there. I don't think they'd come in from the west, because they have to cross too much of the open valley, and the creek, and it'd add a couple of miles to the approach. They could come north, up the drive, park far enough up the driveway that you couldn't see their car from the road. The thing is, they can't be sure from this map that there aren't any more cabins up here, or that we might not have a gate with an alarm."

"We have an alarm on our gate at the farm . . ." She peered at the map. "So the best way is over the hill."

He nodded. "From the east. From the

parking lot I showed you. That's right here." He tapped the map again. "They leave their car at the trailhead, cross the hill in the dark, taking it slow, watch the cabin for a while, then come in at dawn and take me out. They dump the body in a hole somewhere, then exfiltrate during the day, taking it slow again. One of the guys moves my car, dumps it in Lexington. Nobody would ever know."

"What if there are three or four of them?"

"That would be another problem," he said. "But this would be murder, so there won't be. They'll try to keep it as tight as they can. Could be only one guy. A pro that they bring in for the job."

"I'm worried that we're overconfident," Madison said.

"You keep saying that. But with this kind of deal, you do the intelligence and you make your play," Jake said.

"I hope you're not fantasizing that you're back in Afghanistan."

"So do I. Fantasy could get us killed."

While Madison unpacked the gear bags, Jake figured out the game-spotter cameras. They were cheap digital cameras with flashes, in camouflaged plastic, meant to be posted along game trails to check for passing deer. They worked on infrared motion-sensing triggers, and had been around for twenty years, long enough to become reliable. He put batteries in them and left them on the table.

"We've got walkie-talkies like these at the farm," Madison said. Jake had two Motorola walkie-talkies in his hunting gear.

"Put new batteries in and we'll check to make sure the channels are synced," Jake said.

"What if somebody hears them from the outside? The range is pretty long . . ."

"Not here. We're too deep in the valley. When we're turkey hunting, if we go over the top of the bluffs, we can't pick up a call from the cabin. And you can't call out from the cabin on your cell phone. You have to be up on top."

"Okay." She glanced at her watch. "You better change."

He got into his cool-weather camo, got his sleeping bag, put three power snacks and two bottles of springwater in his hip pockets. He took a full box of shells, loading four into the rifle, the rest into the elastic loops of the cartridge holders on the camo jacket; he'd never used the loops before, and fumbled the shells getting them in.

Nervous. And getting a little high on the coming combat.

Madison had taken the shotgun out of the case and was looking it over. "It's just about like mine," she said.

As Jake checked a flashlight, he watched her handling it. She knew what she was doing. "Snap it a few times, then load it up."

She dry-fired it, pointing it across the room at a framed photo of the hunting group, using a trapshooter's stance. Satisfied, she shoved some shells into the magazine.

"If one of them comes through the door, keep pulling the trigger until he goes down." She nodded, and Jake said, "I'm going to run outside. I'll be back in a minute."

He slung the rifle over his shoulder and picked up the game-trail spotters and the flashlight. If they were out there . . . but they wouldn't have been able to move that fast. If they'd moved deliberately, but hadn't done anything weird, like rent a helicopter, they'd arrive in perhaps four hours. He had time.

Outside, the night was cool, damp. The leaves would be quiet; he would have preferred a crisper, drier night. He carried the game cameras around to the west side of the house, the side he wouldn't be able to see, and began tying them into trees between the cabin and the pond. If they did come in from the west, they'd trip the infrared flashes, and he'd see the flashes . . .

Unless, of course, a deer came in. Then he'd get a false alarm. But the grasses on the open slopes around the cabin didn't pull many deer in. He'd have to hope for the best.

Back in the cabin, they synced the radios. Jake switched his to "vibrate" and said, "When you get up in the morning, turn the TV on, first thing. Change channels every few minutes, but news channels. Leave the one window open just an inch, so they can hear it. Keep the blinds down, except the one over the kitchen sink. Leave that half up. When I give you four chirps, that means . . ."

"Walk past the window," she said.

Jake nodded. "Not too fast, not too slow. You don't want to give them time to fire a shot, but you want them to see your body. For Christ's sake, don't look outside — they might see your face and take off. If they just see the flannel shirt, your arm, all they'll pick up is the movement."

She touched her lip with her tongue. She was nervous, too. "Okay."

"If they get me, then they'll have to come after you," Jake said. "That'll only happen if there are several of them. If there are several, you know what to do."

"I call for you, at the open window, so they can hear my voice."

"That should scare them off," Jake said. "If not, I'll take them on. You call nine-one-one, you yell at me that the cops are coming, so they'll know. Then you tip the tables as barricades, make them come through the doors to get you. If they think the cops are coming, if they don't have time to organize, I think they'll run, even if I'm dead."

She shivered. "Jake . . ."

"We'll be okay." He grinned at her. "Maybe."

When they were ready, Jake kissed her, said, "Keep shooting until you see them go down," and stepped outside. The porch light was on, and he hurried away from it, into the dark. Probably three hours before they'd arrive, at the earliest, he thought. At this moment, they'd probably be somewhere in the Blue Ridge.

If they'd monitored the bug at all. But,

he thought, they would have: too much was happening all at once, and the bug would be invaluable.

He walked away from the cabin in the narrow slash of light from his headlamp, the rifle slung over his shoulder, climbed the east hill on a trail he'd walked fifty times before, heading toward a crease in the hillside, hoping it wasn't too wet.

When he got there, he tested it with his bare hands. No more damp than the rest of the hillside, and not bad. He unrolled his quiet pad in the low vegetation, trying not to crush any more of the leafy plants than necessary, unrolled his sleeping bag on top of it, then slipped inside.

Inside the bag, he could move with absolute silence; and he'd stay loose and warm. He'd jacked a shell into the rifle's chamber in the cabin; he tested the safety, to make sure it was on, then snuggled up to the rifle, the muzzle just outside the top of his head.

And went to sleep.

He'd learned a long time before that sleep was protective; you were silent in your sleep, as long as you didn't snore, and if you were in an ambush, you didn't snore. You also woke up at any non-natural sound, and at fifteen- or twenty-minute intervals.

He did that for an hour, then two hours, then three, the minute hand on his watch seeming to jump around the dial as he went in and out of sleep. At four, he was done with the sleep. He'd heard several small animals in the dark — skunks, maybe, possums, raccoons — but nothing larger. There'd been no flashes from behind the cabin.

At five-thirty, he heard movement above him and to the south. Listening, hard. Turned his head that way, looking for a light. Moving in the dark was difficult in the Virginia woods; even a red LED lamp would help some, and shaded, pointed at the ground, normally wouldn't be visible. But since he was below them, he might catch just a random flash . . .

He saw nothing. The movement stopped, and he listened, breathing silently, his nostrils twitching, an atavistic effort to find a scent. Down below, the cabin porch lights, and the yard light near the shed, lit up the yard. There were two lights on inside the house, but no sound. Jake had told Madison not to turn the TV on until six o'clock, after turning on lights first in the upstairs bedroom, then in the bathroom, and finally in the kitchen.

After twenty minutes of silence, he'd begun to wonder if he'd actually heard the movement, if it might not have been a departing deer. But he always thought that when he was hunting. You'd hear the sound, then you'd doubt it, and then you'd hear it again, and then you'd figure out where it was going, the angle, the speed, the shooting possibilities.

Sunrise wouldn't be for another half an hour. If it had been Jake, he'd have gotten into a shooting spot before there was any movement in the cabin. If they were up there, they'd be watching the cabin and making last-minute plans. In a few minutes, they'd start down the hillside, probably a few yards apart. They'd go in as a team, he thought, rather than breaking up and circling against each other.

At a minute before six, he heard movement again, and at the same time got a single alert vibration from the walkie-talkie. Madison was up and moving. The light came on in the upper bedroom, and then in the bathroom. The movement stopped when the first light came on; it started again when the second light came up.

So they were here. A deer wouldn't have

frozen. And whoever it was, was doing it right, moving with almost imperceptible slowness, placing every foot carefully — but it was impossible to move through the woods without making some noise. If there'd been wind, Jake wouldn't have been able to pick out the footfalls; but there was no wind. They were pretty decent at it, he thought. He'd have to keep that in mind.

By six-fifteen, daylight was coming on, enough to shoot, and he'd heard the movement pass him to the south, heading down the hill. A moment later, Madison turned on the kitchen light, and then the television. He gave her four beeps on the walkie-talkie, and she walked by the half-open blind of the kitchen window, fast enough that he caught just a flash of shirt.

If the men below were watching the cabin, they should have seen it. And they should have focused on the idea that the quarry was inside . . .

Fixing on any specific idea was a killer.

Five minutes later, he saw them for the first time. For a moment, he thought there was only one, a man in military camo, complete with head cover, carrying a short black weapon. The gun had a fat snout, as big around as an old silver dollar: a special forces military silencer, a gun they'd bought from the Israelis.

Then he saw more movement ten yards away, a second man. There'd been no flashes from the cameras on the backside of the cabin. He hadn't expected any, because the approach was so much poorer on that side. There could be a backstop guy on the other side, but it didn't feel that way. This felt like a hunter-killer team, well coordinated, moving in on a target.

A scraping noise came from the cabin, the sound of a chair being moved. Madison was improvising. The TV channels, barely audible from Jake's position, changed. When they did, one of the men flicked a hand at the other. The other man scurried across the opening to the cabin, ducked down next to the porch steps.

They waited for a moment. Then the second man crossed the clearing, joining his partner. They both were wearing head and face covering, probably against the possibility of security cameras. Jake was tracking them both in the scope now, clicking the safety off, waiting for the shot. He wanted them on the porch. If he took the first one before they were on the porch, the second man might be able to roll under the cabin before he could get another shot off.

One of the men gave a hand signal, and they moved up the steps, slowly, slowly, ready to crack the front door, or maybe a window.

Window. One of the men slid toward the larger window looking into the cabin, while the other crouched next to the door. He was going to do a peek. Jake put the cross-hairs on him, watching the other man with his off-scope eye.

The man at the window did a slow peek, then moved his head back, gave the other some kind of hand signal; the man near the door may or may not have gotten it, but it didn't make any difference.

Because at that moment, Jake shot the window man in the back.

21

The window man went down and Jake tracked right to the second man as he worked the bolt, but the second man was already moving fast, up in the air, over the porch rail, onto the ground and rolling. Jake snapped a shot at him, had the feeling that the shot was a good one, but the man flipped under the cabin and disappeared.

Jake said into the walkie-talkie, "One down, but we've got a loose one, he jumped the railing, he's under you, watch the back."

Madison said, "Yes."

A moment later, a flash went off behind the cabin, one of the game-trail cameras. The loose man had continued under the cabin, putting it between himself and Jake, and was heading for the trees. Jake started moving as soon as he saw the flash, sideways across the hill, running. The walkie-talkie vibrated in his hand and Madison called, "He's crossing the creek, he's across the creek . . ."

Jake jacked another shell into the

chamber as he ran, saw the second man ten feet from the tree line, hobbling, straining for the trees. Jake pinned the rifle to a tree trunk to steady it, but had no time, no time, and wound up snapping another shot into the brush where the man disappeared.

On the walkie-talkie, Jake said, "There's one on the porch, I think he's gone. Be careful, though. I'm tracking the other one."

"Be careful, be careful . . ."

Now it was a game of cat and mouse. The man in the woods had big problems: he'd probably been hit, though it was impossible to tell how hard. But if he had been, he was bleeding and under pressure to get medical help. His car was three miles away, over tough country, and even if he was able to walk to it, he'd have to keep moving. If he stopped, he might bleed out; and he'd certainly stiffen up.

Jake had problems, too: he couldn't take a chance that the man might get away. He *had* to block him. If the other man realized that, he might simply hide, tend to the wound, and hope that Jake would stumble into him. If he killed Jake, he might not have to walk to his car: he might get Jake's.

Jake paused just long enough to press

three more cartridges into the rifle, then began jogging across the hillside. He was making a lot of noise, but he had to get in position to block. Once he was there, he could slow down into a stalking mode.

The walkie-talkie vibrated. He stopped, put the radio to his face, said, "Yes."

"He's moving south. He's going up the west side of the bluffs."

Jake started moving again, climbing higher on the valley wall. If the other guy was moving, he wouldn't be able to hear Jake. In his mind's eye, Jake could see a perfect ambush spot overlooking a deer-food plot with a shallow ravine running along its side.

From there, he should be able to see anybody coming along the top of the bluffs. The spot was two hundred yards away. He windmilled toward it, refusing to let his bad leg slow him, his own breath harsh in his ears. Brush lashed his face, tore at his body and legs, scratching his face. He kept moving, gasping for air, up a last short slope and into the nest at the top.

Billy had stacked tree branches in a two-foot-high triangle, an impromptu ground-blind looking down at the deer plot. Jake eased into it and settled down. Listening, listening . . .

★ ★ ★

The sound of the slug was unmistakable as it hit George Brenner, a *snap-whack* so fast as to be inseparable, but distinct from the sound of the shot, which followed a few milliseconds later. Darrell Goodman didn't think about it; he was too thoroughly trained to think, he simply moved, vaulting the porch railing, scrambling for the cover of the cabin. He felt an ankle go when he hit the ground, and he rolled toward the inviting darkness under the porch, felt the bite of a slug cutting into the same leg with the damaged ankle, never heard the second shot.

The shooter was quick.

He threw his weapon over his back on its sling and scrambled toward the right side of the cabin. The support beams were only eighteen inches over the ground, and in a few uneven places, even closer than that. Animals had been under the porch; he could smell them on his hands, in his face, and still he scrambled and dragged himself, ignoring his leg, out the other side, and then he was running toward the trees, staggering, his left leg weakening, the cabin between him and the assassin.

In the course of the scramble, his brain had processed the cabin as a trap. It provided immediate cover, but that wouldn't last. He had to get out. If he could make it to the trees . . .

He didn't think about being hit again. There was a bright flash to his right, and he dodged, thinking it might be a muzzle flash, but then he registered it as *too bright,* and a second later plunged into the tree line. As he did, there was another *snap-whack* four inches from his face, as a slug tore into a tree trunk.

Jesus!

He went down, on his belly, slithered into a depression, damp with dew on moldering leaves, and then he stopped.

Listened, trying to suppress his heavy breathing, his heart pounding. He could hear the other man — had to be Winter. Jesus Christ, he'd set them up, he must've known about the bug, how long had he known, what had he fed them? He groped into the leg pocket on his injured leg, took out a cell phone, looked at the connection bar. No connection. He was too deep in the valley. He'd had a solid link at the top of the ridge, three hundred yards away. He had to get to a spot where he could link up, had to move quickly.

Winter wasn't alone. There was at least one more guy in the cabin, then there'd been the flash on the hillside when he was running, so there might be two more. The fag group? Was Winter working with Barber's guys? No time to think: had to move. Couldn't let them pin him down.

He slid one hand down his injured leg, probing for the wound, came away with a wet red-stained hand. No first-aid kit. Still, he had to do something about the bleeding, soon.

If he could get to the top of the ridge, he could make a call, hunker down, wait. If they came for him, he could make them pay.

He pushed off from the depression, nearly groaned with the pain, and using his arms as much as his legs, began moving as quietly as he could toward the west side of the bluffs south of the cabin.

Jake heard him, but at first couldn't see him. The second man was probably no more than a hundred yards away, but the woods were so thick that he simply couldn't see more than a few yards into it. A good thing: the other man couldn't move quietly.

So Jake tracked him by the sound of his movement, and after two or three minutes, realized that the other man didn't seem to be getting closer. He seemed, instead, to be working toward a neighboring bean field, though that was five or six hundred yards away to the southwest, not far from where Jake had set up during the turkey season. Away from the car park, from the direction he'd come in from.

Why would he go there?

The walkie-talkie vibrated in his pocket, and he slipped it out, gave her a single beep of acknowledgment. "The first one is gone. There's blood on the ground where the second one jumped."

Jake muttered, "Okay," then, as quietly as he could, "You're out? Go back in."

"I'm okay here, I just came out to check. The runner was hurt."

"Get back in. I'm tracking him, he's well south of you."

And getting farther south, Jake decided a minute later. Then: *high ground*. The other man was looking for a place to make a cell-phone call.

He had to move. He slipped out of the makeshift blind, risked walking on the grass on the edge of the food plot, exposed, but too far from the second man to be seen, he thought. Still, the hair rose on the back of his neck, and some danger gland in his brain was shouting at him to get out of sight.

He paused inside the tree line. Listened, heard just a bit of movement, still heading up. Found a game trail, worn leaves and slightly thinner brush where deer had cut across the slope. Passed an old buck-rub, made a mental note. Moved slowly, slowly, still-hunting.

Stopped every six feet. Listened. When he heard nothing, he froze. When he heard movement, he moved. Five minutes into the stalk, he saw a tree limb shake; a little jiggle of new bright-green leaves, like a squirrel might make, but too low. Sixty yards out, two-thirds of the way to the top of the bluff.

From experience, he knew that the other man would have to get nearly to the top before the cell phone would work. Jake watched until he saw another leaf-jiggle, and then moved, sideways, across the hill, until he found a seam in the trees. Not a trail, not a gully, but simply a seam, the result of random seeding . . .

But it gave him a shooting lane.

He eased down, put the scope on the last spot he'd seen movement, and glassed the area.

He saw the first hard movement a

minute later. Watched, watched . . . green, brown, black: camo.

He fixed the scope on it, pulled the trigger.

Goodman heard him coming. Couldn't see him, but thought the footfalls were a man's — the sky was too bright, and the sound wasn't explosive enough to be a large animal. He was being stalked. He couldn't pick out an exact direction; but there was only one. Had he been wrong about another man in the woods, in addition to whoever was in the cabin?

He could feel that he was still losing blood, he was weakening. He had to do something.

Moving slowly, he slipped the weapon off his shoulder, cocked it, clicked it onto full-auto. There was a downed branch a few feet away. He edged over to it, pulled off his camo hood, snagged it over the tip of the branch, and slowly pushed the branch out in front of him. Before moving again, he dug into the damp earth around him, rubbed it over his face to kill the face-shine. Then he moved along for ten feet, the branch out in front, pushing the camo mask, another ten, another ten, climbing higher and higher. He might possibly be able to make a phone call from where he was, but couldn't risk turning the cell phone back on. If it rang, he was dead.

He pushed the stick ahead a fourth time. A sudden *crack,* a slug plucked at the hood, the gunshot from the trees no more than thirty or forty yards to his right. He snapped his gun over, pulled the trigger, and hosed the trees with thirty rounds of nine-millimeter, shredding leaves and vines and bark and twigs and dirt.

He flipped the mag out and slammed in another as he rolled away from his shooting position; another shot plucked at the ground behind him. Damnit, he'd missed. He fired three quick bursts and this time let himself roll back down the hill, scrambling, falling, turning, trying to control it as he let himself go, his gun pointed up the hill. He saw a flash of movement and fired another squirt, and then was scrambling right back to where he started.

He was fucked, he thought. They had him.

One last chance . . . He fired the last few rounds in a single burst into the trees where he'd seen the stalker, slammed his last magazine into the weapon, and burst out of the trees. He was weak, his eyes were going dark, but he only had to make it thirty yards to the shelter of the porch.

If he kicked in the door he'd be face-on with the guy inside, maybe, maybe the guy would be surprised enough, after the fight up the hill, that he wouldn't be ready. If he could get inside the cabin, if he could just get a break from the hunter, if he could barricade himself, if he could do something about his leg, if there was a hard-wired phone inside that hadn't been disabled.

If . . .

He ran.

The burst of full-auto didn't hit Jake, but it knocked him down. The slugs were shredding the landscape six feet away from him, uphill, then swung toward him, tearing up the tree branches overhead, and he was on his face, jacking a round into the rifle.

Another burst behind him, not loud, more of a chattering sound: the weapon was silenced, it had looked like one of the Israeli commando jobs, meant for killing terrorists in a quiet way . . .

Two more bursts, and then he registered the guy moving, snapped a shot at the movement, got another burst in reply, jacked another round, lay flat listening, realized that the movement was fast now, and farther away. He lifted his head just in time for another burst, thought, *He's heading for the cabin,* pulled out the walkie-talkie and shouted, "He's coming right at you, I think. He's coming right at you . . ."

Jake was on his feet now, listened for one second, heard the continuing thrashing below, and started running. Blood on the ground: the other man had been hit. He must be desperate, he was going for the cabin. Jake had to get clear of enough brush to take the shot, he'd have just one, if the man could still run, but getting clear would be a struggle . . .

With the woods all around him, it would be possible to see the other man, but impossible to get a decent shot. He'd see him as flashes between trees, but as he swung the rifle barrel to track the target, he'd be as likely to hit a tree as anything else. He needed a shooting lane.

But when Goodman broke out of the trees, running for the cabin, Jake was too far up the hill. He saw him, saw the movement, had no shot . . .

Goodman was fifteen feet from the cabin

when he saw the movement, then registered the face.

Madison Bowe, wearing a flannel shirt. And in her hand . . .

Madison dropped the walkie-talkie, picked up the twenty-gauge, and stepped out on the porch. She heard, rather than saw, Goodman break from the trees. She leveled the shotgun and let him come.

Saw him then.

And from fifteen feet, fired a single shot into his face, and he went down like a rag doll.

Was stunned by the act. Stood, motionless for a moment, then said, "Oh, God," to nobody.

Jake got there a minute later, flailing along on his bad leg. He stopped next to Goodman, his rifle pointed at Goodman's heart, probed him with a foot, but there was no point in probing: most of Goodman's head was gone.

Jake came up on the porch, his face almost as hard as hers.

"What'd I tell you?" he asked.

"What?"

"I told you to pull the trigger and to keep pulling it until the gun was empty. I

don't need any of that single-shot bullshit."
He glanced back at Goodman's body, then
stepped close to her, touched her forehead
with his. "You did good." He started to
laugh, high on the rush: "You did so
fuckin' good."

They saw it differently, but to the cops,
it probably would have been murder —
hard to explain that first shot in the man's
back. Jake checked the body where it was
still lying on the porch. He'd died instantly,
hit in the spine and the heart. The slug had
passed through his body, digging into a
four-by-four upright next to a window.
The bullet hole was smaller than his
smallest fingernail, and looked like a routine defect in the wood.

"What do I do?" Madison asked.

"Pick up all the brass you can find — the
shells thrown off by Goodman's gun. I'll
point you at the spots, and there's a blood
trail going up the hill. You'll need gloves to
pick it up. Don't touch it with your bare
fingers."

He showed her where Goodman had
climbed the hill. "I don't think I can get it
all," she said. "It's all scattered around, in
the trees."

"Get what you can."

While she did that, he searched the two

dead men, got car keys, put the bodies in two of the contractor cleanup bags, dragged them to his car, fitted them in the trunk. When they were out of sight, he got a bucket and soap and washed the blood off the porch. That done, he hosed down the places where Goodman had been hit and then had died, eliminating as much of the blood trail as he could find.

Now would be a time for a good solid rain, he thought, looking up at the sky: and it was possible that he'd get it.

Madison came back down the hill with a bag of brass and two magazines. Jake counted them: eighty-eight out of ninety shells accounted for, assuming that all three mags had been full.

"Now what?"

"Now's the dangerous part," he said. They had to move the bodies and the other car.

"You're not still going to Norfolk?" she cried. "You said we might be able to do something else. I mean, it's crazy, Jake, if anything goes wrong . . ."

"But it'll work for us, it's the only thing that'll really work for us."

Madison was adamant, and so was Jake; they snarled at each other as they drove out to the car park. Goodman had been driving an SUV: they found it in the park, just where Jake had thought it would be. When they clicked the remote control at it, the taillights blinked.

There were no other cars in the parking space, and Jake moved the bodies from his own car trunk, and threw the guns, the empty mags, and some of the clean empty shells in the back with them, then pulled one of the contractor's bags over the driver's seat.

Madison was pleading with him. "Jake: don't do this. It's not necessary."

"It is," he insisted. "Just stay on the other route. You'll get there quicker than I will, because it's shorter. I doubt that I'll see a cop all day . . ."

He did see cops, two of them. Neither one gave him a glance. He saw one near Farmville, and another near Franklin, both on back highways. He stopped only once on his way, to empty the bag of 9mm brass into a creek on a back road. The bag he threw out the window when he was sure there were no cops around.

Norfolk is a complicated place, and not easy to get around. He took it slowly, ultracautious through traffic, and finally found a spot to dump the truck. He left it on a grimy industrial back street, in a collection of other trucks from a nearby light assembly plant.

Before he left it, he took the plastic bag off the driver's seat, stuffed it in his pocket, closed the truck's doors, and locked them. Madison picked him up at a gas station six blocks away.

"Still think it was foolish," she said.

"It's not. We've given them a story. We've given them something they can work with. Darrell was involved in cleaning up the gangs down here, and there are stories about his interrogation techniques. Stories about bodies that went in the Atlantic. We gave them the payback story."

"What about the slug in the cabin?"

Jake shrugged: "Means nothing. First of all, it'd be almost impossible to find. The hole is tiny and I rubbed it over. Neither guy has a slug in him, so there's nothing to match. Goodman's full of shotgun shot, but that's not diagnostic. We'll get rid of the rest of the shotgun shells, buy new ones of a different brand, clean the guns."

She looked at him for a long moment. "I didn't mean to get on you for driving to Norfolk, but I was pretty scared. I haven't done this before."

"Neither have I. Not like this," Jake said. "Are you pretty freaked out about the dead guys?"

She shook her head. "No. They were killers and they were coming to kill us. As for the blood . . . I've got two hundred head of angus. They get butchered and sold for meat. Blood's not a new thing if you raise farm animals."

They left Norfolk, headed back to Washington. Jake drove, fast now, seven miles over the speed limit, and after a while, she said, "Actually, we're pretty good at this."

"It ain't fuckin' rocket science," Jake said. "The only problem is the stakes. You make a mistake, you go to prison. Or worse."

"Even if Arlo Goodman knows what happened, what can he say about it?" Madison asked, building her confidence. "That he knows we did it, because he sent his brother to kill us?"

"And if they investigated, what could they prove? Nothing. On top of all that, there's the credible alternate story: hoodlums did it, in Norfolk. I think we're good."

She straightened herself in the passenger seat, pulled down the vanity mirror, and checked her face. They'd heard the stories about Howard Barber; television was waiting for her in Washington. "You're gonna be hard to train," she said.

"My first wife said the same thing."

"She was right." She pointed out the windshield. "Now shut up and drive for a while. I've got to think about what we might have missed."

Arlo Goodman sat at home and waited for his brother to call. He expected a call around seven o'clock in the morning, or maybe eight, depending on how long it took to get through the forest above Winter's hideout. But Darrell had warned him that it might take longer, and it would be unwise to use cell phones from the site of a murder . . .

Especially with the murder victim in bed with Madison Bowe, and Bowe so willing to make accusations.

Darrell had also suggested that after they did Winter, and got him in a suitable hole, he might put George in with him. That'd take some extra work.

At eight, with no call, Goodman still wasn't too worried. He sat in his office and watched television, the breaking story on Howard Barber — the FBI was investigating the possibility that Barber had killed Lincoln Bowe, with Bowe's own connivance, the anchors said, with convincing excitement. The media was camped outside Madison Bowe's house, waiting for a statement.

At ten o'clock, he was apprehensive.

At a little after ten, he learned that Madison Bowe was not in her town house, although she'd been there at midnight the night before, and the first newsies had arrived by 5 a.m. Had she slipped out? they asked. Had she gone into seclusion? Where was Madison Bowe? The last person to be seen at her house was a man with a cane.

Arlo Goodman heard that and thought, *Uh-oh*. If she'd slipped out to be with Winter, if Darrell had killed them both, if something had gone wrong . . . He continued working: the state of Virginia doesn't stop for a simple news story, or a missing brother.

At eleven, he tried Darrell's cell phone, and it rang but cut out to an answering service. Where the hell was he?

At noon, now seriously worried, he was working at his desk when a thought popped into his head. Darrell and George had only gone to Wisconsin, where the pollster and his secretary had been killed, because of a conversation they'd overheard on the bug in the ceiling of Bowe's town house. A conversation between Winter and Bowe, with no other witnesses.

Winter hadn't known the pollster's name. Had never heard of him. When the killings were done, and Winter had a chance to think, might he have asked, "How did these people get here so fast?"

If he was smart — and he was — he might have suspected a bug. If he suspected a bug . . .

Had he set them up? Jesus Christ: had Winter dragged them into a trap?

By six o'clock, he knew something had happened, but he didn't know what. He could ask somebody to check on the location of Darrell's cell phone, but he was unsure whether he should make the request. Better to wait until Darrell was obviously missing, let somebody else notice.

The TV was still on, and he caught Madison Bowe, escorted back to her house by her attorney: she had been talking to the FBI, she said from her porch. She refused to believe that Howard Barber had killed Lincoln; refused to believe that it was all a fraud. Broke into tears for the first time: refused to believe that Lincoln could have done this without giving her a hint; done it to *her,* as much as anybody else.

A good performance, Goodman thought. In fact, he was riveted.

Not by Madison, though.

The camera swung across the crowd of newsies, clustered on the porch. On one of the swings, it picked up a man leaning against a Mercedes-Benz, a half block away. One arm was braced against a cane.

"That fuckin' Winter," Arlo Goodman said aloud to his television set. "That fuckin' Winter."

Darrell, he thought, was dead. So was George.

He suspected that he should cry, that he should feel some deep emotional choke at the loss of his brother. He didn't. He didn't feel much at all.

What he did do was smile ruefully at the television and think, *Darrell's dead — and that's not all bad.*

22

They got back to Washington late in the day, went to Jake's house, unloaded the car, turned on the television. Jake went up to the junk room and got a gun-cleaning kit. When he came back down, Madison, pale faced, said, "There's a story out that Howard killed Linc and that the FBI knows it."

"Then they're probably looking for you," Jake said. "The media, anyway. Let me check my phones."

He'd had a call from Novatny early that morning: "Get back to me if you know where Madison Bowe is. We need to talk to her."

"What do you think?" she asked.

"People may have seen you here," Jake said. "Neighbors, when we came in. I should call Novatny — but you should call Johnson Black first."

"That'll make it look . . ." She paused, shook her head. "Never mind."

"What?"

"That'll make it look like I'm trying to

hide something — but that's silly. Everybody in Washington would call their lawyer first."

Johnson Black arrived thirty minutes later. The guns had been put away, they'd taken showers, the clothes from the cabin were running through the wash cycle. Black was beaming when he came through the door, kissed Madison on the cheek, shook Jake's hand, said, "Now it's getting interesting. Jake, if I could talk to Madison alone for a minute?"

"He can stay here," Madison said. "What do you want to know?"

Black peered at Madison for a moment, then said to her, "I have to warn you that your interests might not be identical. Maybe it'd be better if I talked to you alone."

"Forget that," Madison said. "I want him here."

Black shrugged. "All right. The FBI will ask if you know anything about Howard Barber killing Linc."

"I guessed. Howard came over, I accused him of it. He more or less confessed, and I threw him out."

"You didn't tell the FBI or anyone else?"

"It was two days ago, Johnnie. I was

going through a nightmare."

"All right. When the FBI asks, I'll advise you to stand silent. If they really want to know, they'll take you before a grand jury, but they'll have to give you immunity."

"If I won't talk to them, then they'll know . . . I mean, they'll *really* know."

"Having them know, without going to prison, is better than going to prison. Period. End of story."

"All right."

"Besides, if you and Barber had a private conversation, well, Barber's dead — so who's there to contradict you?" Madison glanced at Jake, and Black caught it. "What? Who else was there?"

"Nobody. But Jake thinks my house might have been bugged."

"Uh-oh." Black looked at the ceiling. "How about this place? Who would have given them a warrant. You think Homeland Security . . . ?"

"We think it's Goodman," Jake said. "No warrants, just the Watchmen. Every time Madison has a conversation in her living room, it seems to wind up in the papers the next day."

"Huh. Well, I know the people who can find it, if it's there," Black said. He looked at his watch. "Let's go. First to the FBI, then home. You'll have to make a statement to the press."

He looked at Jake, then back to Madison: "Did you tell Jake? About Barber and Linc?"

"No. Not then. Not until we heard on the car radio that the FBI was looking into it."

"What exactly is your relationship with Mr. Winter?"

Madison shrugged, then said, "Intimate."

Black said, "That may not have been wise. To have become . . . intimate . . . under the circumstances."

"I would have said 'athletic,' " Madison told Black, hands on her hips. "And screw the circumstances."

Black said, "Okay. Now, let me phrase this next question as carefully and fully as I can. Was Howard Barber suicidal because of his relationship with Linc? If he was, and if you were willing to say that, we might be able to smooth over some embarrassment that everybody's feeling about his death. We might be able to . . . apply some political salve. Can you say that Howard was suicidal?"

Madison didn't hesitate: "I pleaded with him not to do anything rash. He seemed absolutely despondent. He had a history of clinical depression. He told me that he'd thought about going along with Linc — when Linc died."

Black showed a smile, then said, "Let's call the feds. Jake, you've got the connection . . ."

Novatny picked up the phone and asked, "Have you seen Madison Bowe?"

"She's here, hiding out," Jake said. "She's afraid a Watchman will find her and throw her out a window."

"That's about eighty percent bullshit," Novatny said. "I think Barber jumped."

"That's not what they're saying on TV — and the FBI's not talking to us, if you remember. Ol' buddy."

"Yeah, well . . . Is she going to talk to us?"

"She'll talk to you or a DOJ lawyer. Her attorney's with her now," Jake said. Across the living room, Johnson Black wiggled his thick eyebrows. "I don't know what they're talking about, but they've been in the study for a while."

"We're talking about Johnson Black?" Novatny asked.

"Yup. They told me to call you. Do you want to come here, or do you want them to come there?"

"Really?" Novatny was skeptical.

"Really."

"It'd be more convenient if she came here."

"Give her half an hour," Jake said. "Where do you want her exactly?"

"My office. Call ahead — I'd like to take a walk around the block with you, before we go upstairs."

"With me?"

"Yup. A chat. Nothing sworn, no wires, no games. Just talk. Two ol' buddies."

"See you in an hour," Jake said.

They went in two cars, Johnson Black leading in his limo, Madison and Jake following. They called ahead and found Novatny waiting at a pull-in parking strip, accompanied by what looked like an intern or possibly a random teenager. Novatny said, "Park where you are."

"The signs say that's illegal," Jake said; a row of signs warned of heavy fines and immediate towing.

"Joshua here is going to guard the cars. He'll shoot anybody who objects," Novatny said. "C'mon, Jake. Two hundred yards."

They went off together, Jake tapping along with his stick, Madison moving up to

Black's limo for a last-minute conference. Jake said, "So. What do you need?"

"I want to know what the White House is doing," Novatny said. "If we're about to have nine million pounds of shit land on our heads."

"Judging from the television . . ."

Novatny stopped and turned. "Fuck the television, Jake. I want to know if we're going to get hammered. If I'm on my way to Boise, if Mavis is going to get shuffled off to a basement somewhere." Mavis Sanders was Novatny's boss. "If I should quit and get a security job before it's too late."

Jake shook his head: "Chuck, I honest to God don't know. The White House cut me loose a couple of days ago, closed the consulting contract. I may be on my way back, though. Something else came up."

Novatny was interested. "Having to do with this case?"

"Having to do with something serious. Maybe related, maybe not. I can tell you, just between us ol' buddies, it's not this penny-ante shit you've been dealing with so far. Lincoln Bowe and Howard Barber."

Novatny rubbed his forehead. "Not like this penny-ante shit? *This penny-ante shit?* Jesus Christ, Jake."

"I'm telling you this because we've worked together, and I like you, and I like Mavis," Jake said. "Get yourself braced for something coming from an entirely new direction. Political. You should know about it in twenty-four hours, forty-eight at the outside. I'll try to get them to bring it directly to you and your office. You'll be a star for bringing it in. You'll go in a history book."

"What do you want? For doing that?"

"Consideration," Jake said.

"Consideration?"

"Yeah. We want some consideration. If we don't get it, somebody's going to shove some consideration up your ass and break it off. With what's coming, you can look at it two ways — you can decide whether every niggling little procedure's been followed, or you can go for the substance. If you go for the substance, you'll be okay. I think. But that's just me doing the thinking."

Novatny licked his lower lip. "They've got some good hunting out of Boise."

"Didn't know you hunted," Jake said.

"I don't. That's what I hear from the guys who've been there," Novatny said. "That's what they always say. 'There's some good hunting out of Boise.' "

"Well, that's one thing."

Novatny looked up and down the block. Joshua was guarding the cars like a hawk. "I'll tell you, Jake. I've never worried too much about procedure. I've always been a substance guy. So's my whole office."

"You're speaking for the office? For Mavis?"

"I am."

"Substance is good. This new thing that's coming, it has everybody so scared that we've literally been hiding out," Jake said. "I'm afraid to let Madison out of my sight. I'm afraid somebody's going to kill her, like those people in Wisconsin."

"Ah, shit. The new stuff has to do with that?"

"It might. I'm not sure. You'll know soon enough."

They finished their walk and Novatny said, "Do what you can, man." He collected Madison and Black and disappeared into the building, Madison turning to give Jake a finger wave before she went in. Novatny walked beside her, awkwardly straightening and restraightening his tie. If you didn't know better, Jake thought, you might have thought Novatny was the one being investigated.

Jake got on his cell phone, called Gina in Danzig's office.

"I need to talk to the man."

"Things are intense right now," Gina said. "Let me see if I can find him. I'll call you back."

"Tell him it's critical. He has a real need to know this."

"I'll tell him," she said. Her voice was absolutely neutral.

Fifty-fifty, Jake thought when she'd hung up. Fifty-fifty that they'd call. If they didn't, he'd really been cut loose.

But Danzig got back in five minutes. "What's going on?"

"Things are moving. There may soon be a settlement in the FBI/Madison Bowe/guy-thrown-out-the-window situation. My guy Novatny says he's not interested in procedural matters. Only in substance."

"You think that'll hold?"

Jake nodded at his phone. "I do. It's in everybody's interest." The Rule: *Who benefits?*

"You better get over here. I'll have Gina put you on the log."

Gina was five degrees on the warm side of neutral when Jake got to Danzig's office.

She shipped him straight through: "He's tired. Take it easy."

Danzig was wary: "There are rumors that you've gotten close to Madison Bowe."

"They're true," Jake said. "But I'm still working for you — my loyalty runs to you. You don't want to know everything that's happened, but I think we're in a place where everybody can be accommodated."

Danzig nodded, and waited. He wasn't giving anything away.

Jake said, "We need to get the package to the FBI. To Novatny, specifically. Novatny is willing to argue a particular view: that they should stick to the substance of the package, and not nitpick the procedure that got the package to them. So the question is, Where are you with the vice president?"

Danzig exhaled, relief showing on his face. "If they'll do that . . ."

"We're in a position to insist on it. I've already had a preliminary talk with Novatny, and he agreed; he said he was talking for Mavis Sanders, his boss. They have no idea of what's coming and we're delivering it to them. We had an absolutely solid reason for holding it for a few days, to check and make sure that it wasn't a complete election-year fraud. When we realized it wasn't, we acted as swiftly as anyone could expect . . . as long as we get it to them soon."

Danzig nodded. "The vice president will resign tomorrow night. At one o'clock tomorrow afternoon, he's going to call a press conference for seven o'clock, and he'll announce that he's leaving immediately. He wanted time to consult with his brother, which he's done. If you were in a . . . condition . . . to take the package to the FBI, we thought you should do it, accompanied by the president's counselor."

"When?"

"Well, I think before the one-o'clock announcement. Word will start leaking about that time."

Jake nodded. "I'll need the originals."

Using Danzig's telephone, Jake called Madison on her cell phone. "Are you still talking to Novatny?"

"He's here. We're just finishing. And we're not talking. We've offered to talk to a grand jury, if there is one, if we get immunity."

"Are they going to go for it?"

"Nobody knows yet," she said. She was crisp, controlled.

"Let me talk to him."

He could hear Novatny fumble the phone: "Yeah?"

"Tell Mavis that we have a hot political package coming to you tomorrow, just after noon. She should alert the director, but don't let it outside that circle. That's absolutely critical. I'll be at your office at noon, and you should have a lawyer with you to receive the package."

"Is this the thing we were talking about?"

"It is — and Chuck, this is going to be the biggest deal since Bill Clinton's blow job. You've got to be ready. You've got to be ready to brief the director, you've got to be ready for a media blitz."

"I'll move. I'm sending Mrs. Bowe home now."

"Let me talk to her." Madison came on and Jake said, "There'll be about a million reporters at your house. I think it's better to face the music now, rather than hide out."

"I can handle it," she said.

"I'm going to come by — I'd like to watch. From a distance."

Late evening, Jake dealt the cards. They were at Jake's house, in the living room, the shades drawn. Somebody had tipped the media, or part of it, anyway, and three media trucks were parked in the street at the side of the house. "I'd have a hard time in prison," Madison said. She picked up her hand, looked at it, picked three cards and tossed them in the discard pile, and added, "Give me three."

"You're not going to prison," Jake said. He dropped three cards in the discard pile, dealt three to Madison, took three for himself.

"That's really comforting." She showed her hand to Jake: "Two sevens."

Jake said, "Two jacks."

Madison said, "Damnit, I can't win with these cards." She stood up, blew a hank of hair out of her face, and took off her blouse. "The TV people probably think we're in here plotting strategy."

"I am plotting strategy," Jake said.

He collected the cards and shuffled. He hadn't lost a hand yet. Madison watched him shuffle and her eyes narrowed: "Hey, are you cheating?"

"Would I cheat?" He shuffled a second time, glanced at her. She was watching his hands, and he thought how solemnly she was doing it. She was solemnly playing strip poker. He'd seen her laugh, frown, cry, groan — had seen any number of expressions, including a really nice snarl — but he'd never seen her smile with simple pleasure.

Late morning. One of Johnson Black's assistants brought over two sacks of groceries, mostly vegetables, and Madison began making veggie chili, which she told Jake that he'd love. At noon, dressed in a blue suit with a green tie — not an intuitive match, Madison said, but it looked terrific — he got in the car and headed for the White House. The moment he backed into the alley, he was surrounded by shouting reporters. He eased through them and headed east.

Danzig, Gina, and the president's counselor, a sober middle-aged woman from Indianapolis named Ellen Woods, were waiting in Danzig's office. Woods had the package in a black leather portfolio. She was dressed in a blue power suit; her eyes were like black flint. "We want you to inventory the items before we go over," she said, glancing at her watch.

Jake went through it quickly: it was intact. "It's all here."

"Then let's do it," she said.

They went in a presidential limo. Danzig called twice while they were en route, though the trip took only five minutes. "Just wondering if we were there yet," Woods said dryly.

Novatny, Mavis Sanders, and three other high-ranking FBI functionaries and lawyers met Jake and Woods in Sanders's office. Woods pointed Jake at a chair, gave the feds a brief oral explanation of the materials, and then handed over the package.

Though he'd been warned, Novatny was astonished. He asked Jake, "Wisconsin? Wisconsin? You knew about this when Green and his secretary were killed?"

"There were rumors here in Washington of a package like this. I was checking them out — I went out to Wisconsin because I'd learned that Green and Bowe had been lovers, and that Green was well connected around the state," Jake said. "My feeling was, if he didn't know about the package, he might be able to point me at somebody."

"And he pointed you at this Levine woman? Wait a minute . . . I don't understand the timeline."

Jake took him through his arrival in Madison, the morning interview, the afternoon discovery of the bodies, and then he began to lie a little.

"Green told me he didn't know about it but he could make some calls," Jake said. "I gave him a specific name: he denied knowing it. Later, when I tracked the woman down — this was the next day — she admitted that she did, in fact, know Green. By that time, I had the feeling that I was in the grip of a political conspiracy to damage the administration, and that it might all be a fraud set up by Lincoln Bowe. I brought the package back for evaluation, and the instant we realized that it might be valid, the president ordered me to turn it over to you guys."

The FBI people all sat back. "You're willing to talk to a grand jury?" one of them asked.

"Absolutely. But I don't have a lot of information. All I have is fragments. I pressed Madison Bowe on the subject and she knows even less than I do. It appears that Mrs. Bowe was deliberately kept out of the circuit by her husband, as a way to protect her."

"I understand from media reports that you and Mrs. Bowe are friendly," one of the feds said.

"Yes. We are. But most of this developed

before we became . . . friendly."

"And you think there *was* a conspiracy," one of the suits said.

"Yes, I do. I think — I'm not sure — that it was set up by Lincoln Bowe, when he found out that he was dying from brain cancer. I think it was carried out by Howard Barber. I think the body was burned to attract the kind of intense press attention that it got, and I think the head was removed so that an autopsy would not show the cancer. I think if he is exhumed, an analysis of his spinal fluid would show the presence of cancer cells. Mrs. Bowe knew none of this — she never even saw him after the cancer diagnosis. They lived apart."

The feds all looked at each other, and one of them said, "Heavy duty."

"Did Barber kill Green?" Novatny asked.

"Barber or one of his group," Jake said. "I don't know that for sure, but that's what I suspect."

"Jesus Christ."

One of the functionaries, looking like he couldn't wait to get to a telephone, said, "And the vice president is going to re-sign?"

"Yup," Jake said. "He's toast."

After a moment of silence, the sober,

middle-aged presidential counselor said, "Given his home state, more like a grilled-cheese sandwich."

When Jake got back home, a little after three o'clock, the place smelled wonderful, though meat-free. Madison was still cooking, barefoot in jeans, wearing one of his T-shirts, crunching on a stick of celery. She stood on her tiptoes to kiss him, asked, "All done?"

He thought, *What a gorgeous woman this is,* and said, "Everything we're going to do, unless there's a grand jury — and I'm sure there will be. But that's probably not going to happen until after the election. You Republicans don't want to talk about what Lincoln did, we Democrats don't want to make the Landers mess any bigger than it is . . . so it'll be a while."

"I still don't want to go to prison," she said.

"Don't worry about it. You could get hit by a car before then."

"God, you're such a comfort."

"Mmm . . ." He looked at the potful of chili. "Think we could stick a pork chop in there?"

They ate early. As they were eating, Fox

flashed a newsbreak: "Sources at the White House are telling Fox News today that there is speculation the vice president will resign. We repeat: Vice President Landers may be resigning his office. Sources say he has been accused of corruption going back to his administration in Wisconsin . . ."

"In my day, when I was on TV, you generally didn't let your nipples show through your blouse," Madison said.

"Poor girl's excited," Jake said. "She can't help herself."

"I think we should go into seclusion," Madison said. "The New York apartment — we could leave a phone number for Novatny."

"If we did that, we could walk over to the Met, down to MoMA."

"Museum of Natural History."

"Spend a lot of time in the bathtub," he said.

"Down on Madison Avenue. I could use a new hat."

"Hide out until midnight," Jake said. "Catch the red-eye out of National."

"Good idea."

A minute later, he said, "Sooner or later, I'll go down to talk to Arlo. We need an understanding."

"Is he going to be vice president?"

"No. As I understand it, the front-runner is the senator from Texas."

"Hmm. Our first female VP," Madison said. "It's gonna be tough to get you fuckin' Democrats out of there, if all the girls are voting for you."

"That was the thought," Jake said.

The vice president announced his resignation at seven o'clock, his weeping wife, in a pale orange dress, seated behind him. Landers was a large man, pink and fleshy, with thick political hair going white.

"If these absurd and tendentious charges came at any other moment, I would fight them from office, as the president has urged me to do. But they are being made, as Lincoln Bowe was perfectly aware when he began this conspiracy, at the one moment when I could not afford to fight them from office — at the beginning of a long and difficult reelection campaign.

"Bowe and his criminal gang have succeeded to an extent: I am going. But they attacked me not because they wanted to damage a mere vice president. They attacked me as part of a greater game, to damage our party, our president, and indeed the aspirations of the American people, as reflected by this presidency. I won't allow that to happen. I will fight with all my might, but I will not allow the best American president since John F. Kennedy to be handicapped during a campaign of such great importance to the American people."

The speech was widely ridiculed in the papers and the television talk shows the next day, as was his wife in her orange dress, and his daughter, who was overweight, and who was filmed eating a caramel-and-pecan bun at a bakery near her apartment in Cambridge.

The bodies of Darrell Goodman and George Brenner sat in the SUV for four days, until somebody got curious about the fact that the truck hadn't been moved. When the somebody got close enough, he noticed a "peculiar odor" and called the cops.

Arlo Goodman blamed the gangs, and vowed to free up more funds for gang-suppression efforts.

The FBI announced a massive investigation under the direction of a special prosecutor, the federal district attorney from Atlanta, Georgia.

"You remember when I begged you to appoint him," Danzig said to the president. They were in the president's private office, drinking a wonderful single-malt Scotch that the president had extorted from the distiller, using the British prime minister's office as the pry-bar.

"I remember that. I was reluctant. There was some question about his integrity . . ."

"There was no question at all," Danzig said. "He's crookeder than Landers, and I've got the sonofabitch's testicles locked in my desk drawer. That 'independent counsel' theory can kiss my ass."

Jake and Madison hid out in New York for two weeks, talking only to Danzig and Novatny. Then Jake called Arlo Goodman from a pay phone, and flew out to Richmond on a Wednesday afternoon. Goodman walked out of the governor's mansion at six o'clock, the sun sliding down in the sky, told his bodyguard to take a break, and met Jake at the corner.

They walked along for twenty yards without speaking, looking at the day: a good day in Richmond, summer heat coming on, but not there yet; flowers in the gardens next to the sidewalk. Two men walking, one with a limp and a cane, the other with a bad hand half curled in front of him.

Goodman opened. "That was a cold thing with Darrell."

"I didn't invite him out there."

Goodman grunted. "Don't bullshit me, Jake. You had him on a string and you pulled."

Jake said, "I wouldn't have done it, if it weren't for Wisconsin."

Goodman looked at him. "Wisconsin? You don't think . . ."

"I do think. I can prove it," Jake said. "And I think I can prove you knew about it. Enough to thoroughly fuck you. Maybe, with the right jury, get you sent away for first-degree murder."

Goodman thought it over. Then, "Gimme a hint."

"Did they do an autopsy on Darrell?"

"Of course."

"Then they would have found some scratches on his arms, already partly healed. Wouldn't have been a big deal, given the rest of the damage. The thing was, the scratches were put there by the secretary out in Madison. The FBI took skin and blood off her fingernails. They don't know who it belongs to; don't know where to look."

"Darrell was cremated," Goodman said.

"Yeah, but you weren't," Jake said. "You share most of Darrell's gene load. If they did a test on you, they'd know that the skin didn't belong to you, but that it did belong to your brother. And I've rounded up a few pieces of paper. Cell-phone calls, state airplane records . . . they don't make it a sure thing, but they would cause you some trouble."

"The dumb shit," Goodman said. They walked along. "You can believe me or not, but I didn't want those people in Madison to get hurt. Wasn't any point in it. We wanted the package, but if we didn't get it, knowing that you had it was almost as good."

Jake nodded. "You could have pushed it out there, the way you did on Howard Barber and Lincoln Bowe."

Goodman smiled, not a happy smile, but resignation. "Yup. But that fuckin' Darrell . . ." He sighed. "If you mess with me, Jake, they'll probably find the Madison Bowe surveillance tapes in Darrell's safe-deposit box. They'd pretty much establish that she knew about the Landers package, and that she's been lying about it."

"We know about the tapes, of course," Jake said. "We'd hate to see them get out.

Also, Madison has some . . . ethical . . . concerns about the investigation into Darrell's death. We'd hate to see some poor broken-ass Mexican hauled up on murder charges, just so you can clear it."

"Won't happen. I got my dumbest guys running that investigation." A few more steps. "So we're dealing?"

"Mmm. We think everything is fine as it is now. We've got a good vice-presidential nominee, you're the respected governor of the great Commonwealth of Virginia, Madison is recovering nicely from her husband's death. Why stir the pot?"

"That was exactly my thought," Goodman said. "There's no reason at all — no reason to stir up anything."

"What're you going to do next year?" Jake asked. "When you leave office?"

"I don't know. Go fishing. Go on television. But I'm a pretty damn good public executive, Jake. I like the work and people like me. Would've been a good vice president . . ." He sighed. "Well. I'll find something. Maybe the president will have something for me. A year from now, all this noise will be ancient history."

They didn't shake hands; Arlo just peeled off as they walked back toward the mansion, said, "If you ever need anything,

I'd hesitate to ask me for it."

"I will," Jake said. "Hesitate." And on the way back to his car, thought about Goodman hoping for a job offer from the president. *Over my dead body* . . .

Danzig said to Jake, about the national convention, "There's a big goddamn hang-up on the electrical work. We've got three different unions and two city councilmen going at it tooth and nail, and we need somebody to go talk some serious shit with them. Figure out who to talk to, how to get it done. The media's already screaming about their booths, they can't plan their setups until they can configure their booths . . ."

"I've been spending some time in New York," Jake said. "I've got a couple of guys I can call there. Probably a matter of money more than anything."

As Jake stood up to leave, Danzig asked, "You figure out what you want?"

"I want peace and quiet," Jake said. "However I can get it. However Madison and I can get it."

"I believe that can be had," Danzig said. "I have a relationship with the special prosecutor, although you don't know that. What else?"

"That's a lot. But there's this girl who used to work for Arlo Goodman, as an intern. She'd like to move up to the White House. She's smart, she'll take anything. No big deal, though."

"Tits and ass?"

"Excellent."

"Give me her name — we'll find something," Danzig said.

"Thanks. I'll get going on New York. What's the timeline there?"

"Gotta be done by yesterday," Danzig said. As Jake got to the door, he asked, "Is this gonna be a full-time thing? You and Madison Bowe?"

"We're pretty tight. I don't know — it could work out." Jake hesitated, then asked, "Is Goodman gonna get behind us for the election? I know he wanted the vice presidency."

"The president's talking to him next week," Danzig said. "We're worried about what happened down in Norfolk, with his brother. Unregistered machine guns, camouflage suits, it looked like an assassination went bad. Now all this stuff is coming out about interrogation techniques, and the Watchmen. I don't know . . ."

"I've been talking to people," Jake said, and thought, *Just take a second to fuck*

Goodman for good. "There's a lot of stuff that's going to surface when Goodman's out of office, when he's out of power down there. There are literally going to be bodies coming up. Death-squad stuff. I thought you guys should know about it. I leave the decision up to you; this is the only place I talk about it."

One of Carl V. Schmidt's neighbors called an FBI man who'd left him a card. "Agent Lane? This is Jimmy Jones down by Carl Schmidt's house, you asked me to call you if I saw anything going on down there? Yeah? Well, Carl just got back. What? Yeah. He's standing right here. He's a little pissed . . ."

Carl V. Schmidt took the phone: "Hey. What've you guys been doing in my house? The place is wrecked. What the hell is going on here?"

After an active phone call, Schmidt agreed to wait at his house for an FBI man to get there for an interview. When Schmidt hung up, the neighbor asked, "Where'n the hell you been, Carl? Where'd you get that tan?"

The president said to Arlo Goodman, in the Oval Office, "How the heck have you been, Arlo? Man, has this been a month, or what?"

"This has been a month and a half, Mr. President," Goodman said, as they sat down. Goodman crossed his legs. "The Lincoln Bowe thing . . . who would have thought?"

"The man was crazy," the president said. "Maybe the medication . . . or maybe he was just nuts."

"That's my theory," Goodman said.

The president allowed the slightest frown to glide across his face: "I was shocked to hear about your brother. How's that investigation going?"

Goodman shook his head. "It's going nowhere. Darrell was off on his own. I may have screwed up, letting him run too free, but he solved a lot of problems down there. Now . . . might be time to tighten the reins on the Watchmen."

The president nodded. "They seem a little too . . . what? Executive? A little too military?"

"It bothers me," Goodman confessed. "I think there are still uses for the organization, but more as a goodwill brotherhood. Remove any idea that there might be police functions."

"Excellent," the president said, rapping

the top of his desk with his knuckles. "Listen, I'm almost embarrassed to ask, but how heavily can we lean on you for the campaign? You must be tired, you have your own problems. I suspect you might have liked the vice presidency . . ."

"You did exactly the right thing, there, Mr. President." Goodman was embarrassed; he could feel himself brownnosing. "She absolutely guarantees that you'll carry Texas — and she'll be a good vice president, to boot. As for me, I'll do whatever you want. Work as hard as you want me to, or go as easy. Actually, I think this campaign is gonna be fun. We're gonna kick ass and take names."

The president said, "We're counting on you, Arlo. And it could be tough. Now let me ask you one other thing . . ." He glanced at his watch. "What do you think of Ham Peterson?"

Ham Peterson was the former governor of Nevada and head of Homeland Security. The calculator in Goodman's head began to churn. "He's a good guy, but he's had some problems . . ."

"He steps on his own dick every time he turns around," the president said. "I'll tell you, Arlo, we won't fire anybody right after the election. Leaves a bad taste. But

Ham should retire back to the ski slopes. Why don't you bone up on Homeland Security? I'll have Bill Danzig send you some materials . . ."

A half hour later, the president was talking to Danzig, and said, "Send that Homeland stuff over to Arlo."

"He bit?"

"Like a ten-pound bass," the president said. "He'll bust his ass during the election, finish out his term, and then . . . he'll just go away."

"He's not going to like that," Danzig said.

"We have an old farm saying in Indiana that covers the situation," the president said. "Fuck him."

Jake sat on top of the horse, one knee curled up over the flat saddle. Madison sat one horse over. Jake said, "I feel like an asshole. These pants, these boots . . ." He was wearing knee-length riding boots and jodhpurs.

"You look terrific," Madison said. "You'd look even more terrific if you'd get rid of that ridiculous cowboy hat."

"That won't happen," Jake said, touching the hat. "My grandfather gave me this hat. He wore it on the Old Chisholm Trail."

"Jake, you bought it last week in New York," Madison said. "At a gay boutique in SoHo. I was with you."

"Oh, yeah." Good hat, though.

"Eventually, if I can teach you to jump, you're going to land on your head and kill yourself because you're not wearing a helmet," Madison said.

"Maybe I could rent some stall space from you," Jake said. "Put in a couple of decent quarter horses. Get a real saddle."

Across the fence, a dozen head of black angus drifted along, grazing down the spring grass, like inkblots on green baize. Cows liked to watch people; Jake had, on occasion, wondered if they were plotting something.

Madison asked, "How're we doing?"

Jake thought for a moment, then said, "We're doing better than expected."

"Expected by who?"

"By us," he said.

"You trust me yet?" She asked it in a light voice, but she was serious.

He bobbed his head. "I do. It's not like I figured something out. I trust you in my gut. I trust you like I trusted my guys in Afghanistan."

More angus drifted by, chewing.

"I've fallen in love with you," Madison said. "I didn't expect to, but I couldn't help it."

He couldn't think of anything to say, so he said, "Jeez."

She said, "If I'm going to have kids, it'll have to be soon. I'm getting on in years."

"I'd like a few kids," Jake said. "I'd be good at being somebody's old man."

"We oughta start working on it, then."

"Fine with me. As long as I can keep my hat." He touched the horse with his heels, moving down the fence line.

She called after him, "So we have a basis for negotiation."

"Yup." He turned in the saddle to look back at her and caught a quick flash of teeth. "Made you smile," he said.